Slippin'

By Michael Merrett
www.thefog.com

*To my mom Elizabeth
for her love and inspiration*

Contents

Chapter One- Chasing a dream
Chapter Two- Fort Knox debacle
Chapter Three- Going Home
Chapter Four- Picking up the pieces
Chapter Five- To drive or not to drive
Chapter Six- Meeting with Dr. Berson
Chapter Seven- Jeopardy on the job
Chapter Eight- So many losses
Chapter Nine- Hitting rock bottom
Chapter Ten- The age of computers
Chapter Eleven- CNA
Chapter Twelve- Returning to Drum Corps
Chapter Thirteen- The vending program
Chapter Fourteen- Increasing discontent
Chapter Fifteen- Ferguson
Chapter Sixteen- Time to say goodbye
Chapter Seventeen-One last ditch effort
Chapter Eighteen- Realizations

Forward

**"There are hermit souls that live withdrawn
in the place of their self-content;
There are souls like stars that dwell apart
in a fellowless firmament."**
-Sam Walter Foss

    Fear of the unknown is one of the oldest and most primal of human trepidations. It is a sensation everyone experiences at one point or another but to those among us who are visually impaired, the feeling can be increased tenfold. No one truly knows what the future will bring but after being given a chilling prognosis by a renowned member of the medical community in 1980, the uncertainty of my future took on gargantuan proportions.
    After a fair amount of research, I discovered that there have been very few attempts to document the experience of dealing with vision related difficulties. As long as humans continue to lack sufficient telepathic abilities that would allow us to probe each other's minds, I strongly feel that such documentations are relevant and necessary. Particularly to those who may be dealing with such a condition or to anyone who may be involved with someone struggling with failing vision. Therefore, I have attempted to offer such a first hand account on the pages that follow.
    Sharing our experiences can help us better understand one another and can enhance the learning experience as a whole. I cannot imagine anyone for example, who was not deeply touched while reading the account of Helen Keller's life. Her story was later adapted for the big screen. Her personal challenges inspired millions and spawned charitable organizations all over the world.

Reading personal accounts written by others can indeed be compelling. I can say with a reasonable degree of certainty that I will never attempt to climb Mt. Everest. After finishing two particular books on the subject. (Jon Krakauer's "Into Thin Air" and Anatoli Boukreev's "The Climb") I feel that I gained a keen insight into how it felt for these climbers who chose to undertake such a formidable challenge.

Few of us, my self included until recently, really knows how it feels to walk in the shoes of someone who is dealing with a handicap. There are countless others who struggle daily with a crippling illness or disease. The undertaking of this book was for the simple purpose of giving the reader a first hand glimpse into the lives of my brothers and I who were chosen by the natural order of selection to be born with defective genes and were forced to contend with the never-ending challenges that result from vision loss.

There were moments that were comical, and others that were downright agonizing but they are recounted here not to evoke sympathy or pity. Everyone has crosses to bear in life. This is by no means an attempt to suggest that the plight of my brothers and I was in any way shape or form more difficult than any one else's. It is merely a humble attempt to share our experiences with the following hope. The next time you observe someone trying to navigate their way along the streets and sidewalks of your neighborhood by slowly groping along or with a plastic cane extended in front of them, you will have a better idea of what that person is experiencing. You may even learn a thing or two as to how to approach them should you choose to do so.

There are thousands of blind people who live alone and in total darkness in this world. Personally, I cannot imagine anything more tragic in scope and magnitude.

The research I have conducted has given me a greater appreciation for the plight of those who, by no fault of their own are destined to live their life as a member of the handicapped community. The history of treatment towards this group has not been a rosy one but fortunately, conditions have improved immensely. We can only hope that they will continue to do so as we mature as a species.

I was hoping to complete this project in time for my father to be able to appreciate it. That hope ended last week when, while recuperating from yet another bout with pneumonia, my mom must have seen him suffering and came to take him away where they could be together again in everlasting love.

Remarkably, neither his faculties nor his vision ever failed him right up until the final moment of his life. I thank the Lord for that because he was as decent a human being as ever walked this Earth. We will miss this humble giant of a man and his departure has left a huge void in our lives.

As you read further, open your eyes and guard against making the same mistake I did. Never take your vision for granted again.

Thank you, and may the road you travel through life be manageable and as pleasant as fate will allow.

Chapter One – Chasing a dream

There is definitely something to be said for the innocence and naivety of youth. We are so hopelessly oblivious as children are we not? Conflicts that were occurring around the globe while I was still a child seemed so distant they might as well have been taking place in a galaxy far, far away because I was too preoccupied with just being a kid. That was so long ago and the world of my childhood seems so remote, like a veritable alien landscape now that I have reached adulthood. Life as a grownup can be so convoluted that there are moments when I pinch myself and wonder if I was ever really a child at all. I occasionally ask, did that really happen or was it just some strange, magical dream? I remember vaguely that war, poverty and strife seemed a million miles away. In my adolescent mind, genes were something I slid my legs into when I wanted to go out and play. The world was our playground and even though I was forced to wear thick glasses that kept falling off my nose at the most inopportune moments, there always seemed to be a friend around to help me find them and bring my world back into focus. If problems did arise that we kids could not handle, moms and dads would always be there to take care of everything. I was oblivious to whatever potential dilemmas the future might have in store for us. I remained completely unaware of the gathering gloom that would soon swirl around me. If I had to do it all over again, I would have gone the route of Peter Pan in a heartbeat and simply refused to grow up.

The history books recount the 1950's and 1960's as being somewhat turbulent decades. I suppose I should consider myself fortunate indeed to have come through them relatively unscathed being a nearsighted lad and all. There were a few exceptions, like that day the older kids in our neighborhood were having difficulty finding an activity to amuse themselves. A few of the more inventive geniuses (who I seriously doubt went on to become members of the

Mensa Society) came up with the brilliant idea of perching themselves on top of the garage in our back yard... with a bunch of rocks. While their accomplices below lured unsuspecting younger kids into the garage, the older kids on top would wait for them to walk back out and they would drop their projectiles trying to bonk them on the head. This brilliant scheme probably started out as innocent fun but whoever was assigned the job of collecting the rocks must have been one sadistic son of a bitch. They were not little pebbles like any halfway-sane person would employ and were instead the size of a fist.

Fortunately, the older kids who assumed the duties of dropping the rocks all suffered from "terrible aim syndrome" but as luck would have it, they did manage to hit one unsuspecting fool...and that was me.

It was a glancing blow, but it did draw blood and once everyone saw red they all panicked and the game quickly ceased. I was patched up by my mom and escaped with little more than a slight dent on the hood. While it could be my imagination, I can still feel it to this day depending on the amount of alcohol I consume on a given occasion.

Getting hit on the head by falling rocks aside, childhood was still such a joyous affair. Frolicking in the snow, endless days at the beach, toys on Christmas morning...ah the memories are almost too much to endure. Before I could say "I want a Genie just like Barbara Eden when I grow up" however, it all came to a crashing conclusion. I found myself at an age where it was too late to worry about going off to fight in Vietnam since that conflict had already ended, and I was too old to remember what Howdy Doody looked like. The gut-wrenching assassinations of the '60's, the civil rights upheaval and Gilligan's Island had all come to an end by the time the seventies rolled around. By 1978, even the memory of "Tricky Dickey" and Watergate was fading from memory as the nation seemed to slip into a coma, totally numb after twenty years of stressing about the cold war, nuclear

8

proliferation, and who shot JR. As the reign of King Reagan loomed on the horizon, I found myself a disillusioned 24-year-old member of the "baby boomer" generation and I still was not sure how I wanted to make my mark on the world. Every year however, I faithfully returned to the optometrist where I received my annual prescription upgrade, which meant even thicker glasses. I just thought it was all part of the natural order of things. They say ignorance is bliss, but I soon learned that bliss can also revert to pain. If left to its own devices, ignorance can turn on you like a rabid Tasmanian Devil and bite you square on the ass if one is not careful. Of this, I am certain.

After college, I found myself working for a bank accounting department and while I cannot remember exactly how I ended up there, I do vividly recall being bored out of my tree. I found working with numbers about as appealing as being hit by fallen rocks and I was going nowhere in that position fast. Even worse, getting up for work everyday was beginning to feel like Chinese water torture. The first few drops seem ridiculously easy to tolerate but it isn't long before you find yourself begging like a whimpering child for your tormentors to make it stop. Not that I have ever had first hand experience with such matters but I have been told on more than one occasion that I possess an incredibly over-active imagination.

They say when all else fails, "follow your dreams", and having dreams is what makes life tolerable. I had finished my schooling like a good doobie but choosing the right career path to follow still eluded me. It was time to stop bobbing for apples, so out of sheer desperation, or maybe just for the hell of it, I reverted back to my deepest, darkest desire that had been burning within me since my grammar school days. No, I am not talking about becoming an astronaut. Neil Armstrong had already set his big fat foot on the moon so all of our dreams of becoming astronauts went right out the porthole on that eventful day in 1969. If we cannot be the first, we are not going at all right gang? Nobody ever remembers the astronaut who came in second. Of course even if I wanted to pursue this popular childhood infatuation, it was a tad late in the game for me at that point. No one in their right mind just walks in to NASA Headquarters at the age of 24 with absolutely no previous experience and asks to fly the space shuttle. For that would be utter lunar-cy.

In the spring of 1978, when a golden opportunity presented itself, I jumped at it like King Midas on a pile of nuggets. I had always wanted to be a journalist, perhaps a sports writer like Oscar Madison only cleaner, but I had become sidetracked and never thought my writing skills were up to snuff. There is always the possibility that after reading this, you may find yourself arriving at the same conclusion, but that is a risk I am willing to assume, for I have become a true master at laughing in the face of adversity.

I had bounced around from job to job like an over-inflated ping pong ball, a proverbial rolling stone that gathered no moss, and no position to that point had offered me what I was really looking for which was, in a word, creativity. I learned from a good friend of mine that the military offered careers in many areas so I did some research and learned that in the post Vietnam, no-more-draft U.S. Army, they were actively seeking quality personnel for their new all-volunteer army and sure enough, they offered opportunities in journalism which delighted my sense of curiosity to no end. Hopefully, the phrase "seeking quality individuals" was open to interpretation in my case. After careful deliberation, I shrewdly surmised that the military might represent a viable vehicle I could utilize to bring my life long dream to fruition. I was totally naïve and like most people my age I was hopelessly wandering through life not knowing why the hell I was even put on this Earth and in my small mind, I had nothing to lose. At that point in my existence, I was willing to try just about anything.

If only I had been aware that a time bomb was ticking deep within my genetic makeup that was just waiting for the moment to explode, perhaps I could have prepared for the days ahead with a clearer sense of resolve, but alas, there is that naivety of youth again always getting in the way.

Off I went on yet another woefully under-researched and misguided journey. The U. S. Army recruiter's office was located at the Commonwealth Armory in Boston so like Destiny's demented child, I headed over there one Monday morning in March of 1978. As I entered the huge, aging, dilapidated building through a small doorway on the street side, I was greeted by two middle-aged men in army fatigues sitting behind two old wooden desks. The room looked and smelled as musty as the basement of a 100-year-old house. It was dark and dank and seemed to be the kind of structure that could benefit greatly from someone dropping a 2000-pound bomb on it.

"Hi there," said the bushy-haired soldier with glasses. He strongly reminded me of that barber on Andy of Mayberry with his unkempt mustache and the empty stare in his eyes.

"Can we help you?" he asked.

I was a bit nervous but not unusually so.

"I understand this is the place to sign up for the Guards, is that correct?" I asked almost innocently.

The other soldier stood up and extended his hand. "This is the place all right!" he said with enthusiasm.

I shook his hand firmly but apprehensively, as he seemed a bit disingenuous. He sounded phony too.

"I'm Sergeant Thomas and this is Corporal Rivers. What did you have in mind?"

"I am interested in journalism in particular, but I understand you have to pass some sort of tests or something?" I asked, looking around the drab, dingy room. It compelled me to think to myself, "If this place was a bowl of fruit, it would be rotten and covered with mold."

"That's right, and we can give you the necessary tests right here right now if you are serious about this," said Sergeant Thomas.

"Oh, I'm serious all right" I responded. Both of these men had been wearing shit-eating grins since the moment I walked through the door and I suddenly felt like I was being hustled by two used car salesmen rather than dealing with soldiers.

"Why don't you come right over here, uh, what did you say your name wuz?" asked the corporal.

"Mike Merrett" I answered.

"Well Mike, why don't you sit down right here and we can get the written test for you and see how you do."

I took a seat at a dusty desk against the right-hand wall of the dusty office and inhaled a big lungful of dusty air. I really wasn't expecting to be sitting down to an in-depth written exam five minutes after I walked in but this seemed to be the procedure so who was I to question the United States Army. I began to sense that the two men seemed unusually excited that someone had actually come to visit them for the morning. "Maybe they didn't get many visitors and they're just lonely," I thought to myself.

"Now," said Sergeant Thomas, "you have one hour to complete the five part test. This is a standard issue test the army gives to determine what the applicant is qualified for and the results will tell us what fields you are eligible to pursue. Just as an example, if the applicant fails to score sufficiently high enough, he may have no other option but to enter as an infantryman. Do you get my drift?"

"Perfectly sarge," I answered, somewhat surprised at how comfortable I was at addressing someone as "sarge" for the first time in my life.

"Have you had any high school?" he asked.

"Are you serious?" I answered incredulously.

"Well," he said uneasily, "you'd be surprised at some of the people we get in here with this all-volunteer army. How about college?"

"Yeah, I've been to college," I answered. I was not about to tell them how much college, where I was an incorrigible under-achiever.

"Great, great!" he gushed. "Well, here is a pencil, just answer the questions to the best of your abilities and we will check back with you in one hour. Are you ready to begin?"

"Ready as I'll ever be," I said.

"Ok, begin please," ordered the Sergeant and he walked back to his desk.

I opened the booklet and looked over the first page of questions not knowing what to expect. Any concerns I had however, were quickly put to rest as I realized this was a test that anyone with an IQ of 70 could pass. An entrance exam to Harvard this was not.

I finished in 40 minutes and announced this to Sergeant Thomas and he came over with that big wide grin of his and said, "Already? You sure now, you still have 20 minutes to look it over if you need the time."

"No, I'm all set. I'm comfortable with that," I said, handing him the booklet and pencil.

"O-K," he said with a puzzled look on his face and he turned to Corporal Rivers and asked for the answers to grade the test.

The two of them looked over the booklet together. After five minutes of "Hmmm," and "Wow!" and an assortment of other indiscernible observations on their part, I interrupted them out of impatience.

"So what do you think, do I qualify for journalism school or what?" They may have perceived my entire demeanor since first walking through the door as one of impertinence and borderline disrespect but hey, I'm a civilian. We're supposed to act like that around military personnel aren't we?

The big smile was back on Sergeant Thomas's face. "Hell yes boy, you could be a brain surgeon with these test scores."

"I should have remembered to bring my hip boots," I thought to myself, "the bullshit is starting to get awful deep around here."

They shook my hand with glee and had me sign a few documents. Then they called some Captain from an adjoining office to come in and as it turned out, he was the actual recruiter. These two yahoos were just screeners.

"How do you do Mr. Merrett" said Captain Williams, shaking my hand.

"I'm fine thank you. So what comes next?" I asked. I cannot exactly say why but these men just did not impress me at all. This was definitely not what I expected to see upon my introduction to the United States Military, reputed to be the finest military in all the world. I had just aced a test written for third graders, I was being rushed through the initiation process as if they were afraid that if I thought about it too long, I might change my mind. All of which had exactly that result as I began seriously second-guessing myself. I genuinely did want to pursue a career in journalism though, so I tried to restrain my apprehension and not pre-judge them too harshly. In a nutshell, I could pay Boston University tens of thousands of dollars to obtain a degree or, I could have the government pay me while I pursued this life-long dream. It seemed like a no-brainer, but then most of my brilliant ideas that ended as total disasters in life started out under similar pretenses.

"Well, we'll sign you up for the next scheduled physical which takes place in another part of this building," said the captain, "and then we'll make final arrangements to induct you into the Army National Guard."

"Do you know when that might be?" I asked. I was out of work since I had closed the door on my accounting career, so the sooner the better if I was actually going to go through with this.

"Sergeant," said the Captain, turning to Thomas, "Could you check the schedule and see when the next day of physical exams are being conducted?"

Thomas picked up a binder and opened it. "Well, Mr. Merrett, it would appear you don't have long to wait. They are being performed this coming Friday."

The captain turned back towards me. "Great, then we'll see you back here Friday morning at 9. Be prepared to be drug tested and perform all the other necessary requirements associated with physical exams. Until then, congratulations and we look forward to seeing you."

I said my goodbye's to the three men and headed out to my car to return to my apartment. My increasing sense of apprehension continued to grow as I pondered what had just transpired. This was no walk in the park, no casual jaunt through a department store leisurely picking out a comfortable new pair of slacks. This was a major league life-altering decision, the kind of fork in the road that does not come along very often in one's existence. Had I thought this through clearly enough, I kept asking myself? I was all of a sudden drowning in self-doubt and uncertainty. It reminded me of another time in my life I was drowning in something. That was an occasion when one of my friends had thrown me from a raft at Bella Vista Beach in Salem, New Hampshire after I had consumed far too many cans of Schlitz beer. As I recall, the sensation of being under water and gasping for air was not all that pleasant.

Friday morning came rather quickly and as I returned to the armory, which was still in need of a good cleaning, I soon discovered that I was not the only one being given a physical that day. There were probably 50 men being tested and there was a complete staff of military personnel conducting the exams. I knew I would have no problem with any aspects of the tests EXCEPT for the eye exam.

I bravely signed in and took my place in line. First, I was given the color blindness test, which involved looking at the pages of a small book containing various color schemes and I had to pick out a number that was hidden in each group of colored dots. I, of course am color blind as many human males are and there was no way I could find the damn numbers, except on certain pages towards the back of the book (I think it was labeled "section for dorks".) The dots on those pages were so pronounced the numbers practically jumped off the page and assaulted my optical nerve. The man in fatigues sitting behind the desk conducting the test, most likely operating from the standpoint that the recruiters had a quota to meet, picked up on my dismay. He took his pen and began to draw the number right on the page.

"You can't see that" he said wryly, drawing the number 6 with his pen?

"Oh sure, now I see it. 6!" I felt a bit silly but hey, if they did not have a problem with my inability to differentiate between various colors, why should I? I was not completely colorblind. I only had difficulties with minute differences like navy blue and black, or dark brown and dark green. Under proper lighting situations, I was generally OK with colors. After I guessed at a few more movements of his pen, he said, "Ok, you pass. Go into the next room and see the sergeant."

I marched dutifully into the next room proud as a peacock, got in line behind two other applicants, and realized I had come to that part of the exam that was causing me the most anxiety since I awoke that morning. The dreaded wall chart. I was wearing my glasses but I still had trouble reading these damned things.

When it was my turn to step up, I took my place at the line and looked over at the chart, which was about ten feet across the room.

"Read line number 3 please" said a rather large-around-the-middle uniformed man behind the counter to my left.

I strained and stared, and tried my hardest but there was no way I could read the third line down. My heart rate quickened and I began to perspire slightly. I glanced around the room nervously looking for a suitable means of escape.

"Hey, the chart's over there" he said impatiently. "Can you read line 3?"

"That's a big negatory there guy" I said in a low voice. There were people in line behind me and my face was flushed with embarrassment, which I did not want them to notice.

He walked over to the wall chart and pointed to the second line down.

"How about this line, can you read this line?" he asked, slightly annoyed.

Well pardon me; I thought to myself that I forced you to have to move that hulking body of yours the ten feet from behind the counter over to the wall chart. It was probably the most exercise he had gotten all day.

I could read some of the letters on the second line. "C-R-F-D" I said.

He pointed at the big "E" at the top of the chart. "Can you see the big E?" he asked pointing right at it.

With a prompt like that, what was I going to say, no? In actuality I could see the E clear as a bell, although, why every eye chart has a big E at the top is beyond me because everyone knows it's always there. You would think they would change the letter occasionally to keep people honest.

Therefore, I went along for the ride. "Oh yeah, I can read the E" I said meekly.

"Alrighty then, pass. Next!" He walked back behind the counter to his extra large coffee and box of donuts, never giving me a second look.

I proceeded through the rest of the physical without incident. When all was said and done, my recruiter friend, Captain Williams was there greeting and congratulating those who made it through, which just happened to be everybody. What a coincidence, I thought to myself. Aren't we a healthy group of specimens?

"Well Mr. Merrett," gushed the Captain when he noticed me. "Congratulations. You passed the physical. It's off to Fort Knox for you mister and time to start your new career."

I shook his hand and said "Thanks" with reserved enthusiasm. The eye test had really bothered me but I just wrote it off thinking that perhaps they did not require perfect 20/20 vision from applicants who were planning on taking up Journalism. It is not as if I had requested sniper school right? They are the United States Army so they must know what they are doing. I was so naïve.

"We'll have a swearing in ceremony Monday morning at which time we'll give you your travel documents and all the paperwork you'll need once you arrive at the airport in Louisville. We'll see you back here Monday morning."

He turned to congratulate another applicant so I walked out of the armory and over to my car in an almost zombie-like state.

It had all happened so fast it was almost dizzying. I gripped the steering wheel in an effort to steady myself. There I was pondering the potentially portentous reality that my next stop would be Fort Knox, Kentucky. Reputed to be the armor capital of the world, at that precise moment in time it was also a huge somewhat frightening unknown. I could only hope that this particular paradox did not turn out to resemble in any way the jaws of a great white shark, figuratively speaking of course. I mean, everybody knows there are no great white sharks in Kentucky. Are there?

I had already quit my job, which constituted no great loss. I would have to give up my apartment, which I didn't mind leaving to that nasty little cockroach I had caught having a party in my dishwasher the previous night. I would have to sell my car but the hardest part of all would be saying goodbye to my girlfriend Dyan, whom I had been dating for about 2 years and loved dearly. I would be heading off to boot camp for a duration of six long months. What was I thinking! I had never even flown in an airplane before. My inaugural flight would be by my lonesome, leaving every aspect of stability behind to jet off to parts unknown and overwhelming uncertainty. This all added up to one great big emotional quagmire to say the least, if not less. As I started the ignition and threw the shifter into drive, at least half the bones in my body struggled to carry me back inside the building to tear up my test results. That however, would be totally undignified. One of the most valuable lessons I have learned in life thus far is that they can take away your car, your house, and your money but they can never take away your dignity and honor.

Dyan and I had met 6 years earlier when I was 18 and both of us were marching members of the Immaculate Conception Reveries Drum and Bugle Corps from Revere, Massachusetts. We did not actually start dating until four years into our friendship. While we were close companions since the moment we met, our relationship became much more than that once we decided that mere casual friendship just wasn't enough. It happened during a long steamy bus ride to Pennsylvania. The corps was a bit short on funds so we were forced to ride on one of those orange school bus's that were not equipped with modern conveniences like air conditioning, reclining seats or rest rooms. It was over 90 degrees during the entire route from Revere to PA. The skies occasionally opened up with torrential downpours forcing us to choose between keeping the windows closed or drown in the deluge. We all needed comforting during that bus ride I can tell you.

She remains to this day one of those "top 10 people in my life" who left an indelible mark on my heart and soul that will remain with me forever. She was a beautiful girl with strawberry blond hair, blue eyes and an endearing smile that could light up a room. It was not going to be easy saying goodbye to her for six months and to make that even more difficult; she had thrown a going away party for me that Saturday night at her house. Many of my friends who I had marched with in drum corps showed up for which I was eternally grateful. There was so much going through my mind but her love and their friendship really moved me beyond words.

I kept telling myself it would only be for 6 months. If we meant that much to each other, our relationship would endure the test of time. At the young age of 24, this was without question the most difficult adventure I had ever embarked upon. All my life up to that point, I had been surrounded by 12 brothers and sisters, a loving mother and father, and too many close friends to count. For the first time in my life, I would be completely alone, cut off from the support group that I was so accustomed to having around me at all times.

Sunday afternoon, I enjoyed a wonderful meal of lasagna and garlic bread prepared especially for me by my mom and dad. It gave me a chance to say goodbye to them and enjoy the company of some of my brothers and sisters who were tremendously supportive as well.

With a heavy heart, I boarded an American Airlines 727 jet the following Monday morning and headed for Louisville, Kentucky. It was April 7th, one week after my 24th birthday. As I sat in the front row of the plane waiting for it to taxi out to the runway, my heart was pounding in my chest like a 26-inch bass drum. It took every ounce of courage I had to stay on that plane. I was a bit ashamed that I had not even left Boston yet and I missed everyone already.

The flight was uneventful other than a slight movement where the outer wall of the plane to my right met the inner panel in front of me. I was sitting in the very first row and found that to be just a bit unnerving especially as a first time flyer. It was rather slight and probably normal while the plane was in flight so I decided not to make a fuss unless the outer wall actually broke loose from the plane entirely. If that happened I would really raise hell I can tell you. I did not see any gremlins ripping up sections of the wing either so that was a good thing, but that flight still seemed like the longest 3 hours of my life.

I landed in Kentucky around noon. I exited the plane and headed for the meeting place inside the terminal where I was instructed to go when given my reporting papers back at the Commonwealth Armory. Once I arrived there, I noticed there were about six other men seated in the waiting area. I checked in at the counter where a nicely dressed man and an attractive woman were standing and looking ferociously bored with life in general.

"Good morning" she said pleasantly. "Or should I say good afternoon. I lost track of the time. Can I help you?"

"I'm supposed to report here for a bus to Fort Knox," I said apprehensively. My conscience kept screaming to me "Go back you fool!"

I handed her my papers.

"Oh, from Boston huh?" she said with an inviting smile. "I could tell right away. That accent is unmistakable."

No, please don't say it I thought to myself. It was no use though as her male co-worker chimed in "*Park* the *car* at *Harvard yard*." He followed it up with a silly-ass grin.

Does everyone on this planet utter that line every time they meet someone from Boston, I pondered?

"Actually I don't even own a car, I sold it," I answered dryly. "But if I did have one, I wouldn't park it there. It's too far to walk to my house."

They both just stared at me blankly for a moment. They had no idea what to think at that point and were obviously unaccustomed to my world-class rapier wit.

"Well, the bus should be here in about fifteen minutes," said the nice woman. "Have a seat over there with those other misfits and we'll let you know when it gets here."

"Thank you ma'am" I said with the utmost sincerity.

I turned to find a seat and looked over the motley looking group of recruits sitting before me. They all appeared to be primates but I could not be absolutely certain as to what degree. One big blonde-haired individual had a box of Twinkies on his lap and was totally immersed in his cream-filled spongy delights. Another was trying to be discreet about picking his nose but we all know that eventually, nose-pickers get caught. A thin man with clothes that looked like they had not seen a washing machine since the last lunar eclipse had his head back and was snoring away. Judging by what I saw, coupled with my experience at Commonwealth Armory, I found it difficult to believe that this all-volunteer army was bearing fruit. If you asked me, we would have trouble fending off an invasion of marauding field mice based on what I had seen so far.

I noticed an African American man sitting by himself reading a paperback off to my left. He looked like the only one who could read out of this bunch so I headed for the chair next to him hoping he could provide me with some stimulating conversation to take my mind off where I was and where I was going. Besides, he was wearing thick glasses just like me. Hey, we're twins!

"Hey, how's it going" I said extending my hand.

He was a little unsure of me at first but he shook my hand anyways, not wanting to appear rude most likely.

"Hey, nice to meet you, Victor Church" he said.

"Mike Merrett. Been waiting long?" I asked.

He shifted in his chair as I sat down next to him. "Not that long. My flight got in around 11 so I've been here for about an hour. Good thing I brought something to read. It is taking my mind off how nervous I am."

Honesty and humility. I like that, I thought to myself.

"I know what you mean. We must be out of our minds huh?"

"Where are you from" he asked.

"Everett, just outside of Boston."

"I'm from Baltimore," he answered.

"Hey, Orioles country, good team, how are they expected to do this year?"

"Fairly well I guess but no one is going to beat the Yankees. Ever since Steinbrenner bought the team he has been spending big bucks and loading that team up. They've got Reggie Jackson now. They have the best pitcher in the league in Ron Guidry. They're stacked."

"Yeah, I know. That's why I'm a Yankee fan," I said smugly.

"I thought you said you were from Boston?" he asked with amusement.

"I did but I've been a Yankee fan all my life. My dad was a Yankee fan so, like-father like-son."

The woman at the desk interrupted us.

"Gentlemen, the bus is a few minutes early so you can all head out that door to your left and get on board. Good luck to all of you."

A tentative chorus of "thank-you's" came from the group as we all grabbed our bags and headed out the door. As we got to the bus, a relatively new Peter Pan tour model, I could see that there were people already on board and seating would be tight but at least we were going in style. I turned to Vic and said, "Do you mind sharing a seat?"

"No problem" he said.

We both grabbed the third double-seat on the left and after a few moments, we were on our way to Fort Knox. There was no turning back now and my adrenalin was really beginning to kick into high gear.

"You know the only reason I signed up was so I could find a way on to the base and steal some of that gold," I said to Vic.

Fort Knox, for those of you who may not know, is where the United States keeps its gold reserves, billions of dollars worth. It was the setting for the James Bond film "Goldfinger" in the 1960's.

He just smiled. "Yeah right, good luck!"

We pulled onto the base after an unusually quiet 25 minute drive and I was immediately impressed with how vast the place appeared to be. There were barracks spread out in all directions but they were all painted in depressingly drab colors. It gave the place a very pale look as light greens, browns, tans, and grays all blended together to form a truly uncharacteristic landscape that was both uninviting and unappealing even to my less-than-perfect eyes. Hopefully, my experience here was going to be a lot more colorful than this, I thought to myself but I just could not shake the nagging sense of foreboding that was still tugging at my subconscious mind. At that moment, I would have sold my very soul for a crystal ball that actually worked worth a damn.

Chapter Two - Fort Knox Debacle

The bus pulled down the main street, then took a left and rolled to a halt in a small parking lot. The sign outside said "admitting area" so I shrewdly surmised this must be the building where they admit people. Momma didn't raise no dummy.

"Let the games begin" I said to Vic, noting by his silence for the past ten minutes that he was every bit as nervous as I was. I had been second-guessing myself all morning.

A drill sergeant, complete with squared off jaw and wide-brimmed hat, walked onto the bus and greeted all of us.

"Alright ladies, I want everyone to fall off this bus and head right into the building in front of you, then have a seat. Let's move!" he shouted.

"Wow, it's just like in the movies," I said to Vic, trying desperately to inject a little humor into the situation.

We piled off the bus, and I was immediately struck by how chilly it was. It was about 50 degrees and the morning dew was still hanging in the air. I had done a little research as to weather conditions this time of year in Kentucky and I expected it to be a little warmer.

We filed into the one level wooden structure and entered a large room with several rows of metal folding chairs neatly lined up from front to back. The place smelled like a men's locker room though. Vic and I sat down in the fourth row and I was tempted to jump up and yell "Ok, how many of you guys forgot to shower this morning?" but I was a tad concerned about what kind of first impression that might make. When everyone was seated, another sergeant walked to the front of the room to address the group.

"Welcome to Fort Knox people" he said in a booming voice. "We're going to get you situated today, let you get acquainted with your barracks and drill sergeants. Then tomorrow we start in earnest with getting you through your physicals, issuing equipment and processing you through. We have some simple rules here in the early going. Keep your mouths shut when you are supposed to and do what you are told without delay. Now that's simple enough isn't it?"

Nobody answered. It must have been a rhetorical question, I thought to myself.

Then it dawned on me. "Did he just say something about a physical?" I said to Vic in a hushed voice, but the room must have had special material on the walls or something because my voice apparently carried.

"Did you say something boy?" the drill sergeant asked in a very annoyed tone.

Everyone turned to look at me and all of a sudden, I felt like I had carrots growing out of my ears.

"Nothing important sergeant" I answered. I do not know why exactly but while I may have been nervous; all of this didn't overly intimidate me which somewhat surprised me. Maybe my eleven years of discipline while marching in bands and drum corps was helping me adjust more quickly than I thought I would.

"Then shut your pie-hole when I'm talking, you got it?" he said sternly.

"Yes, drill sergeant, my apologies." I smiled ever so slightly. I cannot say why but the nervousness was melting away and I was beginning to accept the fact that the worst was over. "I'm here;" I thought, "I have completed the most difficult part of this adventure." The three-hour flight and the bus ride had been filled with a myriad of terrible unknowns. Now that I could see the place and had met the parties involved, my anxiety levels began melting away like a scoop of "Steve's" Ice Cream on a torpid July afternoon.

Except for this talk about another physical. That announcement kept reverberating inside my mind like a possessed racquetball.

As I looked around the room at the 40-50 other recruits, I tried to size up the situation in my mind. At 6 feet and 185 pounds, I certainly wasn't the smallest recruit in the group. Intellectually I felt I could match up against most if not all in the class so I was starting to feel a bit more at ease and a tad more confident. Even the experience of being the first one to be lambasted by a drill sergeant did not faze me as much as I thought it would.

"As I was saying," he continued, "we're going to leave here, take you to your barracks and get you settled in. Are there any questions?"

There was a pause for a moment and I half expected someone to raise their hand and ask, "When do we eat?" but no one apparently had the guts.

"Ok then, Corporal Davis will take it from here. Just follow him and we'll get you checked in. Welcome to the United States Army people. Do not disappoint us!"

We all filed out of the building and I immediately noticed that the nice comfortable Peter Pan bus that delivered us to camp had since departed. In its place stood a dreaded yellow school bus. It immediately brought back memories of my drum corps days when we traveled the countryside in these sweatboxes on our way to parades and competitions. "No more riding in comfort from here on in," I thought to myself. "Our asses belong to Uncle Sam now."

We all filed onto the bus and as we pulled down the street to head for the barracks, Vic and I were seated near the back. I heard the sound of a loud engine pulling up behind us. I turned around and found myself staring right down the barrel of an M-60 Tank that was cruising right behind the bus. I was a real tank freak as a child and used to build model kits as a hobby. It represents an activity that has gone the way of the hoola-hoop and today's kids would rather let the computer do all the imagining for them.

"Wow!" I thought to myself, "An M-60! My first day at Knox and I'm 20 feet away from the real deal." It was an impressive sight and everyone turned to check it out. I could only imagine what it must be like to be in actual combat and have one of these juggernauts rolling to attack your position. Fifty tons of deadly steel thundering towards you with every one of its guns blazing. I would not want to find myself in that situation.

I could recognize many tanks by sight, having built miniature versions of them during my youth. The German Tiger, US Sherman, Russian T-34, the British Churchill represented some of my previous plastic works of art. I was looking forward to seeing a few of our countries' current arsenal while I was here. Fort Knox was called the "armor capital of the world" because it was the largest tank training facility on the planet. It supposedly had more tanks on site than anywhere else in the world.

As we continued down the street, the M-60 hooked a right so I was able to see it from a side angle as well.

"Awesome tank huh?" I said to Vic. "50 tons, 105 millimeter main gun, crew of 4, two 50 caliber machine guns and a top speed of 30 miles per hour."

"You making this up as you go?" asked Vic with a smile.

"You really can sling the bullshit," said a rather large recruit in front of me with dark hair and a huge "Jimmy Durante-like" nose.

"That I can, that I can," I said, not really wanting to engage in a confrontation on my very first day, but I could not let it go completely.

"Do you even know what kind of tank that was?" I asked him.

"Yeah, the metal kind" he answered with a grin.

Genius, pure genius I thought to myself. This guy is depriving a village somewhere of an idiot.

The bus pulled in front of another wooden structure that turned out to be our assigned barracks. As we exited the large vehicle, two drill sergeants were waiting there to greet us but to my surprise, the gung-ho, in your face shouting and screaming I had seen in the movies was not in evidence here. I was so disappointed. Oh, they were telling us to hop-to and step lively but it was more low-key than I expected. It was 1978; we weren't at war with anyone so

28

maybe they figured it was all right to ratchet the discipline down a notch or two?

As we walked into the barracks, I looked around and it was exactly as I pictured it in my mind. A large room with polished hard wood floors and lines of double bunk beds on both sides near the windows. There was an office and bedroom near the entrance, which I presumed was the drill sergeants' sleeping quarters and the rest room, or latrine was at the far end of the building.

"Just stake out a bunk for now," said a tall, thin drill sergeant with wire-rimmed glasses who greeted us as we entered. "Stow your gear and prepare to assemble at the foot of your bunks next to your foot lockers. You've got five minutes."

Vic grabbed a bunk on the other side of the room with a few other African American recruits, which was cool with me. Hell, I just met the man a few hours earlier and I was not offended, so I grabbed the bottom bunk of a bed at the far end of the room, and threw my bag in the footlocker assigned to it. There was not much in my bag to begin with. I expected the army would issue all the uniforms I would need, so I merely packed some toiletries and a couple of paperbacks along with some undies, a few pairs of socks, two pairs of jeans and a few shirts, and that was pretty much it.

A short man with blonde hair and a mustache stowed his stuff and claimed the bunk above me.

"You don't snore do you?" he asked.

"Well, I stayed awake all night one night to see if I snored and I didn't" I answered.

He gave me a puzzled look and I could immediately tell he did not quite know what to make of my 3-Stooges reference, which was fine by me. Psychologically, when first melding into a social group, it is advantageous to send subtle signals that imply, in no uncertain terms that you are not soft or a pushover. When you first integrate into a group setting like this, it is a good idea to establish yourself early in the game so that your peers know exactly where you stand. This was the initial period where everyone in that room would be feeling each other out to see who the potential leaders were, and who the followers would be. I have never been much of a follower and had no intention of becoming one now so it seemed like a good time to start playing the "jockeying for position" game and assert myself every chance I could.

"Bill Johnson" he said extending his hand.

"Mike Merrett. Where are you from Bill?" I asked as I looked around the room.

"New Jersey, Elizabethtown, how about you?"

"Boston, as in Massachusetts. I thought it would be a little warmer for this time of year but I guess not. I bet it is really cold when they roust us in the morning. There's just nothing like waking up and heading out into the cold pre-dawn air for a day at boot camp huh?"

"Well, screw that," he said with a chuckle. "I'm definitely not a morning person."

The drill sergeant returned and took up a position at the far end of the room near the entrance.

"OK people, fall in at the foot of your bunks," he ordered.

We all formed two straight lines on each side of the room.

"My name is Drill Sergeant Cronin; I will be your drill sergeant during your processing-in for the next 3 days. Then you will head over to another section of the base where you will begin what we refer to as the "boot camp" or basic training portion of your indoctrination into the army."

He was an impressive looking figure with his army fatigues, wide brimmed drill sergeant's cap and military boots, but the tone of his voice was not all that forceful. He was not trying to intimidate anyone, I could tell. His voice had a firm but sensitive quality that, at least to me, conveyed the impression that he was an understanding type of guy who was there to help us with the difficult transition from civilian life to military duty. Judging by the looks on

30

the faces of some of the people in that room, they needed all the comforting they could get.

I immediately liked this drill sergeant.

"In a few moments I want everyone to fall in out on the street. We're going to march over to the mess hall, grab some chow, and then we'll get outfitted with some military gear before we head back here for further instructions."

He began pacing the floor in the open area between the two lines of men.

"Before we go, I am only going to tell you this once. These barracks are to be kept clean. I will personally instruct you later on tonight just how to keep these barracks pristine and I will personally inspect them every morning. Believe me people if you fail in this responsibility, you will grow to not like me very much. Because I do not take kindly to people who choose not to follow my orders. Is that clear?"

We all answered, "Yes sir!"

"Wow," I thought to myself, "I'm in the military for real now."

"Drill sergeant will do, ladies, I'm not an officer."

"Yes drill sergeant!" we shouted even louder. Now everyone was getting into it.

"Ok, fall out in the street and let's get this show on the road."

We filed out onto the street and lined up in rows of five. Then Sergeant Cronin led us in a casual march over to the mess hall. It was obvious that most of these men had little to no marching experience but for me it was second nature. I could have done it in my sleep and I knew my drum corps background would come in handy in many ways during my initial training period.

We arrived at the mess hall in a matter of minutes and to my delight; we were the first recruits to arrive. There is nothing better than being powerful hungry and discovering that your group was first in line for eats.

The mess hall was housed in a building much larger than our barracks. There were rows upon rows of tables and the serving area was just to the right as we first came through the double doors. As I filed in, I grabbed a tray and prepared to gorge myself. I had not eaten since early that morning, ignoring that paltry "meal" they served on the plane, which consisted of a container of yogurt (Yech!), a midget apple, and a bite sized granola bar. A mouse could not subsist on what they serve you on airplanes nowadays.

When I soon discovered it was all you could eat, I was really starting to dig the military life. I waded through the line with the rest of my group stopping at every station to have something deposited on my tray by the assortment of cooks working behind the counter. By the time I was through, I must have had 4 or 5 pounds of turkey, mashed potatoes, carrots, string beans, stuffing, rolls and cranberry sauce piled up on my plate, and dessert was still to come. "They must be trying to soften us up in preparation for the extreme hardships ahead". I thought to myself. "There is no way the menu could possibly be this good at every meal."

I plopped myself down at the first seat I came to. At this point, I did not care who I sat with. It was the chow hall, and there was no need to be on guard here. The only thing anyone would have their mind on in this place was impressing others with how much food they could consume, and I must admit, for a chow hall, the food wasn't all that bad. I made a mental note to show a bit more self-control from that day on however. If I ate like that 3 times a day I would look akin to Jabba the Hut in no time. There were some really big recruits in that chow hall and I strongly suspected some of them were going to have a tough time getting through the initial weigh-in never mind basic training.

Afterwards I just wanted to take a nap, but that was not about to happen. They marched us over to the supply building and we went through the clothing line picking up our army fatigues, belts, boots, jackets, hats, socks, and bootstraps. It was quality stuff too. The fatigue jacket was especially nice. It fit like a glove, was warm as toast and had pockets everywhere. So far I had been given all the free food I could eat and all the free clothes I would need. How bad can this be?

A rather portly and well-stuffed recruit stood next to me as we were donning our gear.

"Hey, this must be where you keep your hand grenades huh?" he asked, looking in the upper pockets of his fatigue jacket.

"Yeah, or maybe they are for hiding extra sandwiches for between-meal snacks," said another recruit who overheard him. I really felt bad for the first guy. He was destined to take some serious abuse in the days ahead. I had heard that the military could be a very inhospitable place to those who suffer from obesity.

The rest of the mid-afternoon was spent with Sergeant Cronin showing us around the area, then we marched back to the barracks and were introduced to various responsibilities, such as how we should properly wear our uniforms, areas of the barracks that needed to be cleaned every night and how the inspections would be conducted. After everyone chipped in and thoroughly policed our barracks per Sergeant Cronin's instructions, we then had an hour or so before dinner. The supper hour chow was equally as scrumptious as lunch and after devouring some Salisbury steaks, more mashed potatoes, vegetables and desserts, I again made a mental note that in the future I would show more restraint when visiting the chow hall. We returned to the barracks and had a few hours of reading and getting acquainted time before lights out and our first nights sleep under the love and care of Uncle Sam. The day was over like a blur.

I lay back in my bunk and tried to absorb all of the day's events. It was without question one of the most nerve-wracking in my entire lifetime up to that point. It is not very often that one gets to experience his first day in the United States Military so I really was not sure what to make of it all. There I was, sleeping in a large room surrounded by total strangers. I wondered long and hard if any of them may have been sexual deviates and whether it might be a good idea to set up some sort of defense perimeter around my bunk to alert me in the event of an intruder. My mind swooned in an attempt to assimilate everything that was transpiring.

I tried desperately to keep my thoughts off the fact that I missed everyone at home dearly. Also, that statement the sergeant made earlier kept haunting me. "Did he say something about another physical? Does that mean another eye exam?" It took some time but I eventually fell into a troubled slumber.

The next morning at 4:30 sharp, we suited up in our fatigues, which really made my bunk-mate Bill very happy. Then we passed inspection with flying colors. As far as I was concerned, that was no big deal since it involved little more than making sure the barrels were all emptied properly, the latrine was spotless and the bunk areas and footlockers were clean and orderly. We had a decent group of recruits, many of whom may have been custodial and janitorial workers before they made the bold decision to embark upon new careers because they really seemed like they knew what they were doing. Our counterparts in the next barracks over however, did not fare quite so well. It was now 5 o'clock in the morning and we were already dressed, inspected, and standing out in the dark street with the cold air chilling our bones when we found ourselves waiting for those misfits to finish up. We couldn't go to the chow hall without them since we shared the same drill sergeant. It became painfully clear that they had failed miserably in their responsibilities when a full sized trash can came hurtling out the front door of the barracks. All we could hear from inside was the sound of the drill sergeant's booming voice cursing out the recruits. Damn, I thought to myself, how could they possibly screw up something as basic as keeping the place clean? They had only occupied the building for less than 24 hours.

We finally headed over to the mess hall and were greeted by the inviting aroma of coffee brewing. The enticing smell of scrambled eggs, bacon and home fries titillated my senses and we all dove in with glee. I once again made a mental note that in the future I would show more restraint in the chow hall. This time I really meant it though.

By the time we finished, the sun had finally come up, and we were scheduled to head to the medical facility for physicals. I could not quite understand the purpose of this, as I had just undergone a full physical back in Boston, which I had passed with flying colors; except of course for the vision test. I just assumed they passed me because they could clearly see by my paperwork that I was scheduled for journalism school. Maybe this field did not require the candidate to possess 20/20 vision.

However, my silent objections were irrelevant. We were going to be tested again so I told myself I might as well suck it up and prepare for it as best I could.

We marched over to the base hospital and were admitted in groups of 10. The first stop was the blood tests. I was pretty fortunate when it came to that particular phase of the physical, as I am not squeamish at the sight of blood as long as it is mine and not someone else's. Nor does it bother me to have someone inject me with a needle. Some recruits did have trouble with this however, and I saw two men pass out in the ten minutes I was in there. That is not sufficient grounds for a general discharge however.

How about flunking the eye test, I thought to myself?

As we were led into the next room I could see doctors seated against the far wall behind machines that looked like little television sets. There were lines of recruits waiting to sit in front of them, and all of a sudden as I moved a little closer, I was panic-stricken. There would be no flunky wall charts here, no one was going to point and guide me through this time. These were the types of testing machines used by the Registry of Motor Vehicles back home, where you had to look into the machine and read the letters across.

There was no way in hell I was going to be able to see those letters. I already knew this because I had taken this test for my driver's license and failed every time. Only with a letter from my physician was I able to continue driving.

As I drew closer to the machine, my pulse began to race. My mind filled with dread and despair. I started talking to God. "No, you're not going to do this to me, not now," I implored Him. "I've come all this way God, don't put me through this again!" I frantically eyed the exits, maybe I could make a run for it but it would be one hell of a long walk home. Maybe this man behind the machine would turn out to be a nice man like the one back in Boston. He will help me.

Sure he will, answered my conscience, and maybe if you leave a tooth under your pillow tonight the tooth fairy will leave you a friggin' quarter!

It was the longest line in which I had ever waited. My imagination ran amuck as visions of an old film danced in my head depicting the poor unfortunate souls who had been forced to endure the Bataan Death March during World War II.

When it was finally my turn to sit down at the machine, I took a seat and stared inside. My heart felt like it was threatening to explode in my chest. All I could see was a collective blur of bright light and rows of imperceptible dots. My goose was cooked and I do not mean al-dente.

"Read the second line down" the white haired man behind the machine ordered.

Second line? I could not see any line. I could not clearly make out one single letter anywhere in front of me. I might as well have been staring at a page of hieroglyphics. I did not know what to do. I could hardly speak. Maybe I should just do the honorable thing and tell him the truth, I thought. Maybe they would respect me more in the morning. Perhaps they will bring out a wall chart and give me special dispensation. Not! This was the Army you idiot, my conscience retorted. Do you really think they give a rat's ass about you? So I did the next closest honorable thing. I tried to lie.

Maybe he was not paying attention, I thought, so I gave it my best shot.

"C-R-P-....uh, T....uh, Q" I stammered. Then I waited breathlessly.

"That's what you see on the second line?" he asked, obviously not falling for it. "I said the second line please," he repeated.

"Oooooh, the second line" I said. "I thought you said the third line." I was sweating big time now as I bravely tried to fudge it again.

"B-G....uh...Q...uh...L" I stammered. Again, I held my breath and waited.

The guy just looked at me. "Are you making this up as you go or what?"

"Why do you ask?" I answered innocently. I was angry and frustrated as hell now and totally unwilling to accept what I feared was about to happen. This was the crossroad of my indoctrination process. Everything hinged on what transpired in the next few seconds.

"Can you read the second line or not?" he asked impatiently.

"Well, you don't have to get huffy about it. I'm doing the best I can" I shot back. "Have you no patience?"

I was not even sure if this person had a military rank, but maybe I could appeal to his compassionate side, assuming he had one, but it was hopeless.

"Patience has nothing to do with it" he retorted. "Either you can read the letters or not. Now can you or can't you read line number two?"

So much for his compassionate side.

I sat back in the chair, took a deep breath and exhaled to release my hostility.

"I can't read the second line." I said despondently. The man looked back at me completely puzzled.

"Can you read any of the lines?" he asked, apparently not willing to give up on me.

37

"No" I answered, "I can't."

He paused for a moment. I think for a split second he empathized with what I was feeling, the utter torrent of emotions that were swirling through my entire being.

Empathy or not however, there was nothing he could do. He was not going to pass me and I suddenly came to the realization that once you reached this point, things were handled a bit differently than back in Boston. They apparently were not concerned with anyone's field of expertise or written tests we had passed to get here. There were no quotas to be filled. This was pass or fail based on uncompromising military specifications, and I had just failed.

"Didn't they give you an eye test before you came down here?" he asked.

"Sure, they asked me to read the big 'E' on a wall chart and I did. I know I don't have 20/20 vision but I assumed I had sufficient visual acuity to be admitted to the army's school of journalism. Hey, what do I know? You people are running this show, not me."

He stamped a piece of paper and said softly, "Sorry Michael. Take this to that lieutenant at that desk behind me."

I took the sheet of paper and got up from the table, which took every ounce of strength I had. My limbs felt like cement. I did not want to go over to that desk. I did not want to see the damned lieutenant, because I knew what he would say. They did not know me, they were not my friends, and they did not owe me anything. To these examiners, if I could not pass the physical that every single recruit was required to pass using the same exact guidelines that applied to everyone, I was not getting in…period.

It was time to find out exactly what that meant for me. My intellect could absorb what was going down, but my emotions would simply not allow me to accept it. I had to hear it from someone in authority, so I walked up to the lieutenant at the desk and handed him the sheet of paper.

"Good morning" he said in a stern voice. He looked at the paper for a moment. "Well, Mr. Merrett, this means that unfortunately we will not be able to let you go on to basic training. I know that is not what you want to hear but that is the reality of the situation. Did they give you an eye exam before you were sent down here?" he asked with a tinge of understanding.

"Yes they did, but it merely involved reading a wall chart, not these high-tech machines", I answered, staring down at the paper that sealed my fate.

"Well, I am very sorry but they should have evaluated you better and you would not have had to come all this way. It will take us a few weeks to process your paper work before we can send you back home. Again I am sorry." He stamped the form again and the sound of the stamp hitting the paper was like the recoil from a .357 Magnum in my ears.

My hands made two fists and I rested them on the counter trying to control my rage.

"What do you mean it will take a few weeks for you to process my paperwork? What do you expect me to do until then? And you think I'm just going to accept this without a fight?" I spoke in a caustic but hushed voice. I was embarrassed enough as it was and I did not want the entire room to know what was transpiring.

"I confess I might be a little bit naïve as to how the U.S. Army conducts itself" I continued "but I know how honorable people are supposed to conduct themselves. Do not sit there and tell me what your fellow soldiers should have done in Boston. What does that do for me? I quit my job, sold my car, and moved out of my apartment to come all the way down here. I was led to believe by your people that my visual acuity was functioning at a sufficient level to warrant admission into your army. I sacrificed all that just to have you tell me I am going right back home again! What kind of treatment is this from your own government? Do not preach to me about what members of your army should have said or should have done. Aren't you people connected at some level? Someone had an obligation to tell me from the get go that I needed 20/20 vision to be accepted. What kind of chicken-shit garbage is this?"

"You are absolutely right; someone had that obligation in Boston," he answered in a controlled tone. "And I am sorry they failed in their duties. However, there is nothing I can do for you on this end. If I were you I would take it up with them when you return to Boston."

"And a fat lot of good that is going to do me isn't it?" I snarled. "Let me ask you something lieutenant. Can you spell snow job? And now you just want to give me the brush-off, is that it?"

I slowly began to realize I was wasting my time arguing with this man so I snatched the letter from him and turned to walk out. All around the room recruits were still being tested and as I looked up, I could see that there were three of them waiting in line behind me to talk to the good lieutenant. They looked every bit as dejected as I felt. I took a deep breath, then exhaled and just stood there for a moment trying to compose myself. Then I turned back towards the lieutenant.

"Just one last question mister" I said quietly, purposely ignoring his rank in what was probably a lame show of disrespect. I leaned over the counter towards him and asked, "Could you tell me where I could purchase some live hand grenades on base?"

He looked at me incredulously. "Look, I said I am sorry, what else do you want me to do?"

"Oh, my friend" I seethed. "You do *not* want to hear my answer to that question!"

I walked out the door, slamming it behind me and headed back to my bunk. I never felt so humiliated in my entire life. I entered the barracks mad enough to beat my recruiter like a farm animal if I had him in front of me, then I saw someone out of the corner of my eye. He was lying in his bunk halfway across the room. I started walking towards my bunk in utter embarrassment, not wanting to talk to anyone when I realized… it was Victor Church.

I walked over and sat down in the bunk next to his.

"I'm almost afraid to ask," I said, "but are you here for the same reason I am?"

He opened his eyes and I could tell he was a proud man and like me, would not allow himself to cry.

"Flunked the eye test too huh?" he asked in a broken voice.

"Oh, I was flawless Vic," I said bitterly. "I could not make out one god-damned letter in that machine, and I have just been told to hang around for a few weeks until they are good and ready to send me home. It just doesn't get any better than this, huh? Royally shafted by our own government!"

"I just can't believe I went through all this and came all this way just to be told I am being turned right around and going right home again" he said somberly. "I always knew my vision wasn't perfect, maybe 20/40 to 20/60. That machine is for people with 20/20 eyesight. If you are anything less, I guess they do not accept you. How am I going to face my friends and family?"

Jesus! I never even thought about that as a Nova-sized light illuminated in my head. I had been so preoccupied with anger and indignation it never even crossed my mind how I would face those I left behind. Dyan had just thrown a going away party for me three days earlier and now I had to go back and face them in total disgrace.

Vic and I were moved that afternoon to another barracks where failed recruits were housed while waiting to be sent home. We would receive no basic training, no honorable discharge, and no military benefits of any kind. The army was saying in no uncertain terms, "Just go home. You are not sufficiently physically fit for Uncle Sam."

Our new barracks was known as F-troop by its' inhabitants, and I soon learned the reasons why. It was a holding tank for all the recruits who had flunked the physical and were not welcome by the army, and at that moment, the place was filled to capacity. Bad backs, bad knees, poor vision, mentally challenged, these were just some of the ailments represented in this unfortunate group. Hanging out with this unhappy lot would just add insult to injury I thought to myself as I dumped my stuff in a foot locker and prepared to sit and wait for the army to complete my discharge paperwork.

As good fortune would have it though, they turned out to be a good group of men with one or two exceptions. Vic and I became very close friends during those three long weeks in limbo. They were unpleasant weeks to be sure; the army was not going to let us off easy. They still shaved our heads, and they made us perform mindless grunt details every day to keep us busy. Really fun stuff like scraping nasty layers upon layers of paint from kitchen cooking equipment and keeping the grounds meticulously clean. All of this did nothing more than add to the utter humiliation so after one week of this nonsense, I figured out a way to take advantage of my situation. I learned that there were dental services available to all recruits while stationed at the base. My wisdom teeth had really been bothering me and had grown in crooked, which was causing painful cold sores to form at the back of my mouth. I informed my immediate superior that I wouldn't be picking up trash one morning and headed off for an appointment with the base orthodontist.

After my first visit during which one of the base dentists removed the two teeth on the right side, I returned to the barracks to recuperate. I was still feeling groggy from the massive amounts of Novocain I requested. (I absolutely abhor pain). As I walked towards my bunk, there was a squat little man sitting on the bunk beneath mine. As I approached him, he was just staring blankly out the window.

"Hey, how's it going?" I asked suspiciously. He just continued to stare out the window.

"OK, I guess," he answered meekly.

"Are you…new here? I don't think I've seen you before," I probed further. I cannot exactly say why but something about him told me he was not quite right in the head and he was positioned right under the bunk where I slept. A tiny voice inside me kept sounding the red alert signal. "Danger, Will Robinson!"

"Yeah," he muttered. "I just got here." He still had not looked up and his gaze never left whatever it was outside the window that he found so fascinating. I tried to surmise what could possibly be that mesmerizing on a military base. There was nothing but an empty street with cumulus clouds overhead. I could only assume that this was the first time in his life he had actually had the chance to focus on, then truly appreciate the awe-inspiring wonder of cloud formations.

"You...like clouds do ya?" I asked. A fellow F-Troop resident who I had gotten to know walked over and grabbed my arm, pulling me a few feet away.

"He's a Section 8," he whispered. "You know, fruit-loop, mental defective, and just think, he's decided to take the bunk right under yours." His face formed a huge shit-eating grin.

"Friggin wonderful!" I fumed. "This just gets better and better. He hasn't killed anybody or anything like that, has he?"

"Not that I know of," he said amusingly and just walked away.

I walked back over to him and he still had not moved an inch. He did not appear to be agitated and seemed harmless enough.

"Are you alright my friend?" I asked. I did feel bad for the poor guy as he looked completely lost. "I know it's rough being treated like this by your own government but everyone in this room is in the same position you are. We're here for you if you need us OK?"

He still showed no reaction and was really starting to give me the heeby-jeeby's. My Spider sense kept tingling so I thought it best to try and convince him to sleep elsewhere out of total futility.

"Hey guy, not for nothing but the sun is really strong on this side of the room, it's so much cooler on the other side," I cajoled.

"I like the sun," he muttered like someone in a trance.

"But the bunks over there are so much nicer. These bunks are old and they creak and they are infested with nasty spiders and bugs."

There was no response. He just sat there and while I was not completely unsympathetic of the fact that he had probably just been rejected like the rest of us and was feeling mighty low, he looked like the mother of all unstable individuals and it unnerved me big time.

I looked around the room but there were no other bunks to be had, every damn one was occupied. I did not sleep a wink for the next two nights and while he did not make any threatening moves, I did hear some rather ungodly sounds and remarks bellowing forth from his direction. I made up my mind that if he was not gone by the third night, I would sleep in the latrine if I had to. God must have heard my plea because on the third day, I returned from my appointment to find his bunk empty. I can only hope that he found relief from his ordeal because I am sure it was every bit as unpleasant as mine. For the rest of the day I just went around singing "All and all it's just a…nother brick in the wall."

I milked the dentist thing for a week, which got me out of the degrading duties they had us performing and while I felt a little guilty, I decided it was every man for himself at that point. Vic understood completely. He remarked to me that he wished he had been having problems with his teeth and he applauded my attempts to beat the army at their own game as this dental work would have cost me a pretty penny back home.

I also became quite the malcontent. I wrote letters to whomever I could up the chain of command but it was to no avail. I was going home, plain and simple, but for that entire 3-week period after I was officially rejected, I responded in kind by doing everything in my power to reject everything that was the U.S. Army. Whenever we were out in public, we were expected to salute officers. I did not care if General George Patton walked by, the chances of which of course were slim to none since he is in fact deceased. I absolutely refused to salute anybody. I was stopped on a few occasions by assorted lieutenants and captains and asked why I had not saluted. To which I responded, "Well sir it's like this. The army will not accept me because they say my eyesight is insufficient. I made many sacrifices to come down here and now they tell me I have to hang around this dump until they are good and ready to return me home, so if my vision is not up to the army's specifications, it sure as hell isn't sufficient to recognize you as an officer. Have a nice day."

What were they going to do, throw me in the brig? In my deranged mind I wasn't even officially a member of the military. They probably did not appreciate my being insubordinate but I really did not give a damn, and they apparently had nothing to gain by pushing the matter.

On another occasion, Vic and I were standing in a small line of recruits waiting to enter the movie theatre. We were wearing our fatigues, as we were still required to do, when this man in civilian clothes standing about 10 feet away ordered Vic to take his hands out of his pockets. I took one look at this scrawny little sprout and said loud enough for him to hear, "Don't listen to him Vic. You don't have to do what he tells you." The man came charging over to me, pulling out his ID in mid-stride and waved it in front of my face. He was a sergeant.

"What was that boy?" he shouted.

He really was not a very intimidating fellow but he sure was pissed I can tell you. I just embarrassed him in front of his friend who was standing next to him not to mention the nearby group of recruits who were all trying to suppress laughter. I was still fuming over this whole debacle and had not completely powered down my hostility levels yet.

"Did you just call me boy?" I answered, putting my hands in my pockets. I thought the blood vessels in his head were going to explode. I have always had this amazing sixth sense about me that I could tell during most confrontations with others when my health was actually at risk and when it was not. I felt fairly comfortable that this guy was just going to blow off steam in an effort to save face and was little more than a control freak.

"YES I called you boy and didn't anyone teach you how to act when you are addressed by a higher rank!" He was shaking with rage at this point and I knew that if I did not defuse the situation, this could only end in a lengthy, totally non-productive shouting match. I decided to play stupid and let him off easy.

"Nope, nobody has taught me shit!" I answered in the most mockish southern drawl I could muster. "As a matter of fact, they won't even let me into this here army. We are all members of F-Troop. You know, rejected during physicals?"

I had nothing against this man, and I am not a troublemaker by nature as anyone who knows me can attest, but we were just standing around waiting to go watch a movie. There were no majors or generals around and there was no reason for him to go off on Vic for something as insignificant as having his hands in his pockets. His tone was so condescending and hell, we were not even officially in the army. We were members of F-Troop Godamit, and nobody was going to talk to us like that.

"Well you better show some respect, you hear me!" he shouted as he took one-step closer.

"Loud and clear Sarge," I answered in a conciliatory tone. It was time to back down. I had nothing to gain by goading him any further.

"And take your goddamned hands out of your pockets!" he screamed even louder. He was so close by now that a tiny barrage of spittle struck my face, and like most people, I find it moderately intolerable to be spit upon.

Through all my acts of rebellion during that truly interminable three-week waiting period it was never my intent to grossly disrespect anyone. It was just my way of voicing disagreement with how the Army had handled itself during the entire affair. My beef was with my recruiter more than it was with the men stationed at Fort Knox, but everyone, and I mean everyone, has their breaking point. This guy was pushing me closer and closer towards that edge. I slowly drew my hands out of my pockets as my facial expression tightened into the most menacing look I could manage, which, to most people, probably is not really very menacing at all.

I weighed my options. I could sucker punch him and most likely end up in the brig. I could refuse to obey at which point he might lose it and sucker punch me, which would probably really hurt. So instead, I decided to do the honorable thing, and spit back.

"SSSSSuffering SSSSSuckotash SSSSSarge, you don't have to fly off the handle," I slurred. "SSSSorry if I SSSShowed any disreSSSSpect!"

He paused for a moment, then took a big step back and wiped his face. I had gotten him really good too. He was still fuming but I do not think he really knew what to do at that point since I had just apologized in front of everyone. Sloppy as it may have been, it was still an apology.

We just stood there eyeing each other for a few moments with everyone else just looking on intently. Vic was poised to help in the event both the sarge and his traveling companion tried to jump me. The sergeant's friend, like me, knew nothing was to be gained from a physical confrontation so he grabbed the sarge by the arm and pulled him away.

"Come on sarge, let it go," he said as he separated us even further. The sarge stumbled off cursing under his breath as he went.

"Puck you too," I muttered.

"You keep this belligerent shit up Mikey and you'll be lucky to get off this base alive," said Vic with a smile.

I knew I was way out of line but this 3-week waiting nonsense was really getting to me. The army had kicked our ass and now they were rubbing salt into the wound. There was no way I was going to let that little pissant add to the barrage of bullshit being hurled our way. The day I let anyone give me crap because I have my hands in my pockets is the day pigs fly, but Vic was right. If I did not begin to accept my fate, start powering down my anger and let the healing process begin, I was going to end up getting into serious trouble. I was like a ticking time bomb, and fortunately, that altercation with Sergeant Spittle proved to be my final act of outward defiance against Uncle Sam. From that point on, I made a concerted, conscious effort to chill out, and find a yoga class on base to help stop the daily tirades. The other resolution I had made earlier to show restraint in the mess hall however, went right out the window as soon as that swine lieutenant stamped that rejection letter.

Frig them, I thought. If they are going to give me the shaft, I am going to eat them out of house and home for the rest of my stay here. I am going to set records for personal consumption, those sons of bitches! I'll just go to Jenny Craig when I get home, or is that just for women? Hey, I like women.

We eventually did get in to see the movie, which was "Saturday Night Fever." How appropriate, a story about a man just about my age who was unhappy with where he was at that point in his life.

On the final day of our incarceration, we were allowed to buy whatever items of our uniform we wanted to take home and I opted for the trench coat and boots. I should have gone with the fatigue jacket but they wanted too much money for it. They checked our bags before we boarded the bus for the airport and wouldn't you know it?

They confiscated my dummy hand grenade that I had purchased at the BX for a souvenir. I asked the sergeant conducting the search why they sold them at the BX if we were not allowed to have them? They had a large wooden bin full of them and I thought it would be a cool memento of my tumultuous stay at Fort Knox. They were completely harmless and of no threat to anyone.

He just shrugged his shoulders and replied, "I dunno why they sell 'em."

"Well then give me back the $20 I paid for it," I demanded.

"I'm not giving you $20," he answered belligerently.

One last kick in the teeth, I thought to myself. They just had to get in one last parting shot. Then it dawned on me. I was no longer their property. We had already been processed out of the army. I was officially a civilian once again.

"Well," I said in utter defeat and frustration. "I can't tell you how much I have enjoyed my stay here. I want you to know that I will never forget you and this place. Oh, by the way. Do me a favor will you? Take that hand grenade and shove it as far up your ass as you possibly can."

Then I grabbed my duffle bag and I headed out for the bus and the journey home.

There was a song by the group Steely Dan, that permeated the airwaves during that spring of 1978, and it became my theme song and would remain in my head for years to come every time I thought back on my Fort Knox experience. It was called, "Deacon Blues."

I learned to work the saxophone
I play just what I feel
Drink scotch whiskey all night long
And die behind the wheel
They got a name for the winners in the world
I want a name when I lose
They call Alabama the Crimson Tide

Call me Deacon Blues

    I did not know it at the time but Fort Knox was just the opening salvo. The time bomb hiding within my genes was starting to go off and for the first time in my life, my increasing nearsightedness prevented me from pursuing a course of action that really meant a great deal to me. The anger, frustration, and bitterness from that experience would linger for a long, long time to come and I remained in a relative state of confusion as to what had caused this terrible fiasco to occur. The answers however, would not come easy.

Chapter Three- Happy Cause I'm Going home

     My older brother Richard picked me up at the airport when I arrived back in Boston on April 28th. As I opened the door and got into the car, I braced myself for his reaction to seeing me with no hair. I was not pretty. Of course some would say even with a full head of hair I was anything but. The physical ordeal of my military experience may have been over, but I would now have to contend with the emotional trauma, which would linger for many months to come. It was, frankly, the most humiliating experience of my entire life, and my lack of sufficient visual acuity was completely to blame. It has been said that everything in life happens for a reason, but whatever the reasoning was for this fiasco was completely beyond my level of comprehension.

     "Nice hair cut" he said as soon as I closed the door behind me.

     "Just don't call me egg-head. And I won't take too kindly to cue-ball either" I snapped.

     "How about plain ol' baldy?" he answered. "I don't envy you having to walk around looking like that."

     "I'll deal with it," I muttered. What else could I do?

     As he drove home, I conveyed to him the details of my experience after which he informed me that he had noticed his vision was deteriorating at an alarming rate as well. Neither of us had a clue as to the reasons why. How could we know? It was happening without the slightest sensation of physical stimulus or pain of any kind. To add insult to injury, when we discussed it further with our four other brothers later that week, we realized that five of us were no longer merely dealing with minute levels of nearsightedness. All but the youngest were beginning to experience severe difficulties to one degree or another with rudimentary functions of day-to-day living. In addition, we were beyond the point where any corrective lens could improve our vision to anywhere near 20/20. It was all one big unsolved riddle and we remained hopelessly oblivious to whatever was causing it. We were painfully aware however that something just was not right here.

We were not completely unmoved in regards to our regressing eye conditions growing up but vision loss acts like a sneak thief in the night. The actual degree of visual acuity lost from day to day is almost negligible but by the end of a 12-18 month period, we are left staring at an object trying to figure out what it is and asking ourselves, "What the hell just happened?"

I still vividly remember my personal introduction to the world of high myopia (nearsightedness). I was 8 years old and returning home from a school play. As I walked along the edge of the sidewalk with some classmates, I turned to glance across the street to my left when I walked head first into a metal street sign. Clanged it real good too I can tell you. The ensuing laughter from fellow classmates was so thunderous I could even hear it above the shrill ringing in my ears. That was the day I also learned the definition of the term "peripheral vision" and how vital it is to human navigation systems…not to mention avoiding street signs.

My brothers and I grew up as children of the fifties and sixties, before society found any need for "Amber Alert" systems to track disappearing kids. Before video games, computers and terrorists flying jets into skyscrapers. Back when kids cried when it was time to come in from the great big outdoors, when a stick and a ball were all we needed to keep us entertained for hours on end. Before metal detectors in schools, back when guns in the classroom were as alien to us as "My Favorite Martian" and "Lost in Space." People in our neighborhood never used to lock their doors at night, a completely unthinkable notion in today's whimsical world of diversity and out-of-control immigration policies. The world was our playground and it was a safe playground at that. Today they are fraught with danger so kids choose instead to stay indoors where the play area rarely extends beyond the edges of a television or computer screen.

We had our entire lives in front of us, but for the Merrett boys, our childhood joys began to evaporate into teenage uncertainty. My older brothers Bert and Richard both began wearing high-prescription lenses at a very young age. As a result, they also experienced many of the traumatic side effects that are associated with wearing spectacles that were rather unkindly referred to as "coke-bottle" glasses. The innocence of youth can be severely impacted in the life of a young child who for any number of reasons looks different from "the established norm." To most children, survival means blending in with the group and being "one of the gang." Most kids will do anything it takes to avoid becoming the target of teasing from their peers. When you are walking around with Mr. Magoo glasses as we did, it is difficult to achieve true stealth mode. If only youngsters were more sensitive to how terribly it hurts to be called names, but then we were all children once and guilty of such transgressions to one degree or another. Wisdom comes only with age. Through experience, we can only hope that greater numbers of us learn the invaluable lesson that cruelty is wrong, and that compassion is our greatest attribute.

Regrettably, by the time many youngsters learn such valuable lessons, the damage is already done. Some of those who are ostracized from group play simply because they are different for whatever reason grow up emotionally scarred and the effects can last an entire lifetime.

My oldest brother Bert was declared legally blind by his optometrist in 1978. A distinction defined as having less than 20/200 vision in the best eye with correction, or having a severely impaired field of vision (tunnel vision.) He had been dealing with the types of roadblocks vision loss constantly places in our path for his entire life. Nearsightedness negatively affected every aspect of our schooling and athletic endeavors during our younger years. None of us could see the blackboard clearly but like most shy adolescents, we knew that to admit it left you open to ridicule so at times we would play dumb in an attempt to just blend in and remain unnoticed. It was certainly not the most courageous approach, I am now willing to admit. I often wonder how differently things might have turned out and to what degree our lives and confidence levels might have been enhanced if we could have just seen the damn ball and read the blackboard more clearly.

As Bert grew older, it began to affect him occupationally as well. As an auxiliary police officer in the nearby city of Chelsea during the 1970's, he applied for entrance to the State Police Academy. He intended to become a full-fledged police officer, but he was denied entrance because of his poor vision. He made the difficult decision in 1980 to explore an employment opportunity offered by the federal government known as the Randolph-Sheppard Program. It offered legally and totally blind residents of each state the opportunity to manage their own small business such as a snack bar or coffee shop. He was married by then and had a family to feed so he decided to give it a try out of pure necessity, not out of choice.

My next oldest brother Richard had noticed his vision was getting progressively worse as well. After attending the Woburn Trade Center and obtaining a certificate in electronics, he was forced to change direction when his acuity diminished sharply. As a result, he could no longer perform the detailed, visually demanding nature of working with electronic circuitry. He then attended Bentley College of Business where he achieved a certificate in bookkeeping. When he was unable to secure employment in this competitive field, he settled on a position with the state of Massachusetts as a corrections officer. I questioned him regarding the problems that could arise with the safety issues involved in such a volatile environment. His duties would require him to interact with murderers and rapists on a daily basis. Knowing that his vision may over time become inadequate for such an occupation did not deter him however. He discovered that the eye test they administered did not require him to have perfect 20/20 vision and regardless of the risk, he needed the work.

My two younger brothers David and John began wearing glasses in their early teens but sadly, they were not as adept at handling the teasing and the frequent unkind remarks hurled at them by insensitive classmates and neighborhood kids. While Bert and Richard developed gruff demeanors and fought back, David and John were far more passive and as a result, took an emotional beating. This severely damaged their confidence levels and self-esteem over time.

Stephen, the youngest of the Merrett boys, has had his difficulties as well but to a far lesser degree. He has worn glasses most of his life but of the six boys, his vision has remained at a relatively high degree of efficiency, which is peculiar indeed for the following reason. Bert, Richard, David, and I were all born while our family resided in Crown Point, Indiana. John was born after we moved to Massachusetts in 1956, but my mom became pregnant with him while still living in the Hoosier State. Only Stephen was the result of a pregnancy that began in Massachusetts, prompting all of us to ponder whether there was something in the water in Crown Point, or perhaps our visual deficiencies were in some other manner environmentally influenced.

My mom Elizabeth, or Betty as my dad affectionately called her, was a truly amazing woman. A nurse by trade, she was one of the most well read and knowledgeable people I ever knew. The more aware she became of the difficulties her sons were having, the more of an emotional toll it took on her as well. She never gave up in her attempts to find some answers to this baffling riddle. After bringing 13 children into the world, she took the bold step at the age of 43 to re-enter college. She obtained her Bachelors Degree in Nursing and through her contacts in the medical community, she was determined to find a doctor who could help us unravel the mysteries of this strange condition her sons were contending with.

My dad, Berton, a proud veteran of World War II, was a manual laborer most of his life. He lost his mom two weeks after he was born in 1920 as the result of complications during childbirth. He was raised by his grandparents after his father abandoned him, apparently unable to deal with the emotional loss of his wife. My dad is the most honest, decent, and hard working man I have ever known. Both he and my mom are representative of what I often refer to as "the finest generation America has to offer." Their age group survived the great depression, World War II, the Korean War, and the Cold War. If any age group can be referred to as the "salt of the earth" in this great nation of ours, it is our proud elders.

My brothers and I have seven sisters, Patricia, Linda, Jeanne, Mary Therese (or Terry), Rosemarie, Anne, and Laureen, none of whom ever experienced any vision problems which baffled us even further. They all inherited my mom and dad's great qualities and three, Linda, Rose and Terry, went on to become nurses as well.

We have always been a very close-knit family and while there has never been a dull moment, as would be the case in any household where you have 13 children growing up under one roof, we remain supportive of one another to this day. The credit all goes to mom and dad. They created a home environment that still lives vividly in my memories. Home was our sanctuary, it was warm and inviting and never lacking in love and friendship. No matter how bad things would occasionally become in the outside world, no matter how badly our day had been at school, we could always go home and there would be someone there to comfort us and keep us from harm.

We slept four to a room and our family cornered the market on bunk beds, but as a result, we learned some important lessons in life like sharing, sacrifice and getting along with others. Mom and dad always felt that a strong sense of Christian spirituality was an essential element to a child's upbringing and it continues to remain a binding, cohesive force in our family to this day.

Each of the boys, myself included experienced damage to our self-esteem having to deal with severe nearsightedness but in many ways we were still fortunate indeed. I often wonder if we would have survived as well as we did if not for all of those wonderful qualities my parents exhibited. If there is a more effective therapy than parental love when dealing with a degenerative condition during adolescence, I have not discovered it yet.

We all desperately wanted answers to what it was that was beginning to gnaw at our eyesight but for the time being, I needed to get my life back in order. That was first and foremost in my mind so I temporarily shelved my dream of becoming a journalist. I felt relatively certain that the literary gods had sent me a message by way of this incredible Army fiasco that perhaps it just was not meant to be.

Seeing my family again proved to be the best medicine available, and I knew that re-connecting with my friends and most of all Dyan would fortify my re-acclamation to post-Fort Knox life even further. I was still a little apprehensive considering I had nothing to show for my short-lived career in the military but a shaved head and a "general" discharge. That meant no benefits, no pension, no nothing but I had to move on.

I was still seething when I got home but if anyone could help me feel better, it was Dyan.

I borrowed Richard's car that night having sold mine four weeks earlier like an idiot, and drove to Dyan's house in Revere. I rang the bell; she came to the door and without a word gave me the world's biggest hug. It felt so good to have her back in my arms again and it made much of the pain that I had been feeling melt into nothingness.

"Are you OK?" she said thoughtfully. She had such beautiful eyes and at that moment, they were filled with genuine concern.

"I'll live," I said "and thanks for not goofing on me about my hair, or lack thereof."

"I didn't get to that part yet," she said with a smile. "One thing at a time huh?"

We spent the next few hours just talking and comforting each other in her room while listening to the album "Hearts" by the group America. Some of the most peaceful moments of my life were spent listening to that album while holding Dyan in my arms. The combination of her warm embrace and their enchanting sounds just had a way of chasing all the world's problems away, even if just for a little while.

We talked at length about how I should proceed and I asked her how she was doing in school. She was finishing her second year at Bridgewater State College and she said she was planning to attend graduate school in Chicago. We both knew it would test our relationship and that we would not see much of each other after she left but that was still two years away. For the present, I just wanted to enjoy each moment with her and forget about barracks and army bullshit.

The following day I went apartment hunting and job searching. My younger brother John was still living at home and agreed to go in on an apartment with me so after a search of the local newspaper ads, we found a third floor flat that satisfied our logistical and economic needs. After coming to terms with the owner on the rent, we moved in the following week with the understanding that he would pick up a slightly larger portion of the rent until I found some serious gainful employment. I love my brother John but as personal habits go, we were like the "Odd Couple." He was Oscar and I was Felix. I am an organizational freak; I have to have things neat and orderly whereas John treated the apartment with an attitude of "wherever it drops, so shall it lay." That eventually created a little stress, but it was nothing compared to the weekly ordeal of carrying groceries up three flights of stairs. I made a mental note to NEVER RENT A THIRD FLOOR APARTMENT

AGAIN! For the time being at least, I was no longer sponging off mom and dad and I was able to pick up a cheap used car to boot.

    I was collecting a small amount through unemployment but times would be tough for a while so I took a security guard job to tide me over. I would venture to bet that there are very few males in this country who have not worked as either a security guard or gas station attendant at one point or another in their lives. This position did not involve firearms of course, probably because the owners of the agency took one good look at my thick glasses and quickly thought better of issuing me any side-arms. My duties simply required me to sit around on the night shift making sure no one stole any scrap metal from the roof of the old Sullivan Square train station, which was being torn down in the neighboring city of Charlestown. Usually I just slept through the night listening to the radio in my car and made sure I was wide-awake and looking chipper by the time the workers began to show up around 7AM. I failed to do this one morning when the foreman found me snoring away in the front seat of my car. Fortunately, he let it slide that one time but it was not long before I would get bagged once too often. Staying awake all night on the "graveyard shift" was a monumental chore I soon discovered, especially when your job duties involved little more than staring at an empty building for eight long hours. I became re-acquainted with a dreaded word I had not experienced since my accounting day's known as monotony. Suddenly, working with numbers did not seem all that tedious.

    My emotional well-being was still shaky though and I could not just let the army kick me in the ass without attempting to do something about it. I contacted my district Congressman Ed Markey and lodged a complaint with his office about the way the Army had handled the whole affair. This was before I was old enough to understand that most congressmen are generally as useless as tits on a bull. They are only concerned with their own self-interests and getting re-elected, unless of course the issue just happened to involve very large numbers of registered voters. It also helps your case immeasurably if you are a major financial contributor to their campaign fund. I was still relatively young and naïve and had no idea this would be a complete waste of time and energy.

One of his staff members named Peter called me in to his office a few days later and took down all the details and then I waited patiently for results. Six months later, I was still calling, and in a nutshell, they had done nothing, they were not going to do anything, and I quickly discovered that Ed Markey is one of the U.S. reps most responsible for the following adage. If pro is the opposite of con then what is the opposite of PRO-gress? You guessed it…CON-gress.

I did discover through my own research that one year later the scandal broke on a national level. It involved recruiters who were fudging physicals in order to meet their quotas but the investigation was the result of a Pentagon initiative and not the result of anything Markey had done. It was costing the government enormous sums of money to fly recruits back and forth when they should never have been approved in the first place. I was just glad the practice was discovered and remedied so that others would not have to suffer through the kind of ordeal Victor and I were forced to endure.

I never spoke with or saw Victor again after we parted company at Fort Knox. I suspect that like me, he just wanted to put the whole traumatic episode as far behind him as he could. I think of him from time to time though and I will always be grateful to him for helping me survive those horrendous three weeks while waiting to be sent home.

Chapter Four- Picking up the pieces

There was one other place I could go in my world besides home where no one ever called me four eyes. That was within the proud and dignified realm of the drum corps community. By re-immersing myself in the activity that I loved more than any other, I was convinced I could help the healing process immensely.

I began my involvement in the marching music activity in 1965 when I joined the Immaculate Conception parish band in Everett, Massachusetts. I had my heart set on playing trumpet because while everyone else was listening to the Beatles during the 1960's, I was hopelessly hooked on Herb Alpert and the Tijuana Brass. Herb was, at that time, the most famous trumpet player in all the land. To my utter chagrin, there were no openings in that section so the band director asked me how I felt about playing drums.

"How hard is it?" I asked him, not the least bit enthused about the idea.

"It's no harder than any other instrument," he answered. "You learn to play rudiments and various rhythms."

"What's a rudiment?" I asked dumbly. Hey, I was only 12 years old.

"Why don't you just go over there and sit with the drum line and they'll show you everything you need to know, alright?" he instructed, pushing me gently towards the percussion section.

"Sure," I thought. "Dump me off on the friggin' drum line." I was very young and I had no clue what I was getting into. I was only there because a few of my neighborhood friends had talked me into joining in the first place. As I walked towards the drum section and eyed this huge blonde-haired kid licking his chops and giving me the evil eye from behind a large bass drum, I felt like I was being fed to the lions.

To my utter relief, the entire section embraced my addition and they turned out to be a great group of kids.

Little did I know that such a seemingly insignificant moment in time would have incredibly long lasting and far-reaching repercussions, pardon the pun.

I worked my way up to snare drum after just one year of perfecting my technique with the sticks as a tenor drummer. I learned relatively early in the game that if this was the military, snare drummers would be the generals and colonels of the drum line so I was convince from the get go…that was the position for me. Roll over Napoleon. You too Beethoven.

Seven wonderful years later, I graduated high school in 1972 and felt that at the age of 18, it was time for something a bit more serious. I left marching band to join the IC Reveries Drum and Bugle Corps in the neighboring city of Revere. It was a decision that I would never regret.

Drum corps is far more intense than marching band and it offered everything an inquisitive young person like myself could possibly ask for. It provided me with great friends, great adventures, extensive travel, and the excitement of open competition. As youth activities go, this truly had it all. I still believe to this day that it represents the finest youth activity known to man.

The experience of marching in an upper echelon drum and bugle corps is not all that different from touring with a rock band. We traveled the country in buses playing before thousands of fans and collectively had the time of our lives. The most notable difference was that we never got rich or became individually famous but then, fame and fortune isn't everything, although I wouldn't mind trying it out for just a little while.

Marching opened up so many doors for me. It was during my latter years with the parish band that I met my first love, Diane Sarabia. She was color guard captain at the time and we both attended Pope John XXIII high school together. We dated during my entire senior year and she accompanied me to my senior prom, which was held at Anthony's Pier Four in Boston. As fate would have it, this was the very same night that Bobby Orr and the Big Bad

Boston Bruins were kicking the crap out of Brad Park and the New York Rangers to win the Stanley Cup in game six of the finals.

It was an eventful night in other ways as well. When the prom was over Diane and I exited through a side door, where there was a ramp leading down to the parking lot but it did not have any railing and it was very dark. In one moment, she was talking to me and in the next, she was turning around asking our good friends Danny Diamond and Sue Talbot as to my whereabouts. She must have thought I had vanished into thin air, not realizing that I had fallen right off the outer edge of the ramp.

I could only thank God that the ramp was not over the water as Pier 4 is located right on Boston harbor. It was only about a four-foot drop to the asphalt below and I escaped with little more than a few scrapes and scratches, not to mention a severely bruised ego. Danny could not stop laughing, after he knew I was physically all right of course. All of the prom attendees exited through the same door that night but only one nearsighted fool walked off the ramp. Just lucky I guess, and I hadn't even been drinking.

Diane was part of the reason I went to the Reveries in the fall of 1972. I was still in love with her but she had gone off to join the 27th Lancers drum and bugle corps also from Revere. She thought I was too possessive which I was. The Lancers were far and away the better of the two corps and were ranked in the top five nationally at that time. Diane and I had split up and she began dating a horn player in the Lancers so it would have been very uncomfortable for me to join 27th and have to endure seeing them together every night. Given the right set of circumstances, I can be a very sore loser so I did the noble thing instead. I joined the Reveries who were a little younger and a tad smaller in numbers. I later discovered that through a bizarre sequence of events, they were formerly the Lancers' junior corps. Life, you see, can be wondrous and bizarre all at the same time.

This is drum corps history folks so listen up. In those oh-so-turbulent 1960's, the Immaculate Conception Parish of Revere sponsored a senior and junior corps. The Senior IC Reveries had competed at a contest in Elizabeth, New Jersey in 1966. At the conclusion of the preliminary part of the afternoon show, they finished in thirteenth place. To each and every member of that corps, that was a big-time bummer because only the top 12 made the finals and could compete for the championship later that night. After a quick look at the score sheet, they felt they were cheated out of a place in the finals because of a small technicality.

That did not sit well with the corps director and some of the parents, so that night, the Reveries marched onto the field after telling the gate keepers they were St. Kevins drum corps who had made the finals. Most of the corps during that period wore cadet-style uniforms and it wasn't always easy discerning one from another. They then proceeded to boldly pull off the first and only sit-down strike in the activity's history. After a one half hour stand off, the show coordinators allowed them to perform but they did not receive a score and were not a factor in the shows' final outcome.

The pastor back at the Immaculate parish in Revere became so incensed when he learned about the brazen act that he disbanded the corps leaving only the junior unit as a parish-sponsored entity.

Senior Reveries corps manager George Bonfiglio asked all the members if they wanted to stay together as an independent unit with a new name with his financial backing and on that fateful day, the legendary 27th Lancers were born. In a truly bizarre twist, the senior and junior corps went from being of the same family to competitors over night. They chose uniforms to match their name, which were fashioned from the poem "Charge of the Light Brigade" by Alfred Lord Tennyson. It consisted of British khaki jacket and pants with aussie-style hats and on some occasions the drum line even wore kilts, the sissy faggots. Some observers thought it was really cool but it left them open to some serious barbs from other competitors including me. It was all in good fun and done with the utmost respect but it still didn't make them any less sissy faggots.

Contrast that uniform against the nautical 'swabby' outfits sported by the Reveries. Wide-rimmed black sailor hats, black jackets, red and white striped shirts and white bell-bottomed pants fashioned after those worn circa 1812 aboard the USS Constitution. Difficult as it was for me to swallow, theirs made them appear much older and far bigger and it further drove home the point that the Lancers were the more impressive corps.

The junior Reveries did eventually grow up however. Between 1967 and 1973 they matured to the point where they were beginning to make some respectable headway locally. It was not long before the lofty Lancers started looking over their shoulders at their former junior corps. That is right about the time that I decided to join the fray. I vowed to do everything in my power to assist the corps and raise them to a level where they could eventually kick their former senior corps' collective asses. It was also a noble attempt to prove to Diane that she had chosen the wrong guy! No one will ever accuse *me* of being petty.

The Reveries were never successful in accomplishing that objective however, although we did come close at the World Open in 1974 when we caught the Lancers at one of their lowest points in the organizations' history. 1974 was the only year that 27th failed to finish in the top 12 at the Drum Corps International Championships, which were held at the end of each competition season. While the World Open was merely a regional championship, we lost to them by a mere six points.

I eventually got over the pain of losing Diane and by virtue of my membership in the Reveries; I met my second love whose name was, just by coincidence, Dyan also but she spelled it differently. Life was good again.

My somewhat less than illustrious 11-year marching career came to a sad end when I "aged out" in 1976 due to

Drum Corps International (DCI) rules that prohibited members from marching beyond their 22nd birthday. It was in fact a youth activity so what could I do other than accept the inevitable. Even the great Mickey Mantle had to hang up his glove at some point in his career. The Mick and I had a lot in common too. We both had the same initials, I was born in Indiana and I am reasonably sure the Mick visited Indiana at some point in his career, we…both had the same initials. Oh well, I'm sure I will come up with some other examples later on.

    In all seriousness, retiring from drum corps was not easy. The last corps I marched with was the North Star of the North Shore of Massachusetts, an organization that resulted from the merger of the Reveries, the Blue Angels of Danvers, and the Cardinals from Beverly. All three of these corps had grown weary of losing to 27th year after year and as their individual numbers diminished, they felt the only way to beat them would be to join forces. Two years after I aged out, North Star finally ended the Lancers 8 year reign as number one drum corps in the entire New England region. It was a very satisfying moment in time for former members of the junior Reveries like myself. We used to practice side by side with the Lancers for years behind the North Gate Shopping Plaza in Revere and I still believe that living in their shadow made us a better corps. We hated the Lancers, but we loved them at the same time. There was something very special about our relationship, and about the drum corps activity as a whole. Being part of it proved to be one of the most influential components of my entire life. It represented one endeavor which vision loss simply could not take away from me. Not yet at least.

    After I became too old to march, I decided to continue my association with the activity, so I began teaching as a part time occupation in 1976 when I was hired by the Ambassadors Drum and Bugle Corps in nearby Malden. I was a member of the Malden staff when I embarked upon that ill-fated adventure to Fort Knox. My good friend Tom Shaheen, a fellow snare drummer while I was with the Reveries who was like a brother to me, was nice enough to take over the reigns while I was away getting bushwhacked by the army. When I returned from that mauling, I had no trouble picking up where I left off with my instructional duties.

By the end of the 1978 summer season, which proved to be a very successful one for the Ambassadors as we won the Eastern Mass. Class B Championships, I still found myself working part time and in need of serious employment. I also continued to wrestle with the urge to go back to the Commonwealth Armory and pummel my recruiter to within an inch of his life. It was lucky for him that last impulse was fading however. The anger management classes I had signed up for were really beginning to show results.

The Malden instructional staff was sitting around at a meeting with corps manager Tom Chopelas one night in late November and during the course of the conversation, I just happened to mention that I was still in need of full time work. Tom and I had become more than mere business acquaintances since I began teaching in the Malden organization and we had become relatively close friends. He had children in the corps and was dedicated to doing whatever it took to keep the corps afloat and financially healthy.

Tom looked at me and said, "I didn't know you needed a full-time job."

"Well, I don't like to go around broadcasting it but it's been pretty rough since I left Baybank," I replied. "There aren't a lot of jobs out there."

"Have you put together a resume?" he asked.

"Sure, why?"

"I work for Kemper Insurance as my full time job. You guys probably think being director of this corps is all I do and I know this probably comes as a shock but I actually have a full time occupation as well," he kidded. "I know Kemper is looking for people so let me see what I can do."

"Hey, I appreciate it Tom. That's very kind of you," I replied, although I am a true skeptic at heart and didn't really expect anything to come of it. I was in a rut that was just about the size of the Grand Canyon.

The following Monday morning Tom called me and instructed me to go over to the Kemper Insurance office in Arlington to fill out an application. He instructed me to speak with the manager who's name was Tom Thompson. I asked him if everyone at Kemper was named Tom, then I thanked him and followed his directives. Little did I know that I would end up interviewing that very same day for an appraiser position? Now that's what I call service!

Tom Thompson, who I later discovered kept a picture of himself and college buddy/actor Burt Reynolds on his desk, struck me initially as a rather gruff type of individual but I needed a job badly. I chose to interpret his demeanor as nothing more than his personal choice of management style, then I tried to finagle my way through the interview to the very best of my abilities. I can perform pretty well under pressure and even though I knew absolutely nothing about the insurance claims racket, I managed to make a reasonably good impression with my communication skills and general demeanor. Translation-I slung the bullshit really good.

Apparently, it was not quite good enough though. I waited patiently by the phone for 4 days, going through 4 boxes of Cheezits in the process when at the end of the week, Mr. Thompson finally called. He regretfully informed me that although I had performed well during the interview, they had given the job to another candidate by the name of Neil Deacon. I did not know Neil but I immediately wished upon him that he receive a visit from the "Zanti Misfits."

For anyone who is not familiar with the 1960's "Outer Limits" television series, the "Zanti Misfits" episode involved a space ship that landed in the Arizona desert filled with large ants with human-like heads. It turned out that the ship was a prison ship and the ants it held prisoners were convicts from the planet Zanti. They eventually escaped and attacked an American Army outpost where they were summarily dispatched with chairs, pistols and whatever else the soldiers could find to squash them with. The ants were only about 8-10 inches in length and one frightened soldier actually lobbed a hand grenade at one of them. Talk about excessive use of force.

The scene where the ants attacked was actually quite comical, but right after they first escaped from their little spaceship, there was this unfortunate guy wandering through the desert who ended up being their first victim. As he lay there on the ground with the ants crawling all over him, he screamed in agony begging the army people who were listening in by remote radio to come and save him. As a kid, it seemed pretty scary but now looking back, I cannot understand why the poor sap did not just get up and run instead of laying there like a complete wimp offering no resistance. Contrary to what the incredibly hot looking Seven of Nine proclaims on the recent TV series Star Trek Voyager, resistance is *not always* futile.

What is the relevance to all of this, you ask? My goodness, some people just want everything. The relevance is merely this. When some people do not get their way in life they oftentimes curse and throw really juvenile temper tantrums. Some even resort to smashing things, then frantically try and glue them back together again in utter regret. My approach? I just hurl imaginary curses that they receive a visit from the Zanti Misfits. I am a diehard sci-fi fan and it works for me. Then again, some have actually had the audacity to call into question *my* mental stability, but I dismiss such observations as nothing more than petty jealousy.

I hung up the phone and began to question whether I would ever pull out of the troubling funk that possessed me. The Army ordeal had really shaken my psyche, and my self-esteem had sunk so low it was out there in the North Atlantic looking for the Titanic in a deep-sea submersible. Now, in hindsight, what I should have done was find out where Bill Gates was hanging out at the time and buddied up with him, but hey…who knew?

I was 24 years old and going back to college was an option I may have to seriously consider, I thought, although it would be difficult with the limited financial resources I had at my disposal.

To my surprise, the following Monday morning Thompson called again. He said they had another opening for an adjuster's position and asked me if I was still available.

"I'm at a bit of a loss here Mr. Thompson, I thought you hired Neil into that position?" I asked.

"No, no, that was an appraiser position," he answered.

Appraiser, adjuster, what the hell is the difference I thought to myself. You say tomato, I say tom*a*to. I had no clue.

"The adjuster's position is an office position," he continued. "If you are interested the job is yours. I have already interviewed you once and there is no need for a second. When can you start?"

"You tell me when and I'm there," I answered, trying to contain my excitement.

"How about tomorrow morning at 10 o'clock," he said. "We can introduce you to your supervisor and get you acclimated to the position."

"Ten o'clock it is. And Mr. Thompson…" I added, "Thank you very much." Hey, I thought to myself, maybe he's not so gruff after all.

"You're welcome, but you can thank Mr. Chopelas too. He spoke very highly of you."

I hung up the phone and wanted to do a cartwheel but I did not know how. An adjuster's position, I was not really sure what adjusters did, other than adjust something, but I did not care. It was a job and I would just have to learn how to adjust. More importantly, this was a real job, not some security guard position keeping an eye on the rats and the copper at some abandoned train station, meaning no disrespect to all those security guards out there mind you.

As it turned out, Tom Chopelas was very instrumental in my being given the chance to interview and I owed him a tremendous debt of gratitude. Because the position offered me an opportunity to establish a new career and the salary was twice as much as I was earning earlier that year in Baybank's accounting department. I would soon learn the full nature of what adjusters actually did and I discovered that the position had every element I was looking for. The job involved investigating automobile claims, then evaluating the damages and/or injuries, negotiating settlements and finally disposing of the claims amicably. I would later discover that the word amicably is a very subjective term in this position. Everyone knows that claim adjusters make every attempt to settle cases in favor of the company because that is what they are paid to do.

I also learned that appraisers merely went out to body shops or other locations and wrote up the physical damage to cars, then turned their "appraisals" in to the adjuster. As it turns out, it is the adjuster who "assigns" or orders the appraiser to go look at a car once an accident report is received, which implies a subservient relationship of sorts where the adjuster is the master. Take that Neal!

I am so demented.

Not only was the position of adjuster a technical/professional position which gave my confidence and self-esteem a much needed boost (hell, it was in the gutter so it had no place to go but up) but it provided the kind of financial security that I had never known before. Within 8 months of being totally humiliated by the Army, I was fully employed in a position I could take tremendous pride in, and I was the head percussion instructor for one of the areas up and coming drum corps. I had a decent automobile under my butt again in the form of a 1976 Buick Skylark hatchback, no dents even, and I was still involved in my relationship with Dyan who was there for me at every turn. We were knocking on the calendar door, ready to usher in a new year and life could not have been better.

For the time being at least it appeared as though my eyesight was not changing all that much and had maintained some level of stability. I was still driving, reading normal sized text with just my prescription glasses, and I could fudge my way through most daily tasks without too much difficulty. I was maintaining my independence, which as we all know is a very precious commodity indeed. While it was taking increasing amounts of energy and imagination to overcome the minute daily challenges nearsightedness was creating, my condition was manageable.

I began my career at Kemper the day after Christmas in 1978. I spent the previous day as I always did on Christmas, with my family and at night, I held Dyan in my arms on the couch in my apartment listening to Christmas carols and thanking God for not forsaking me. I was nervous as hell about starting the job the next morning, but it was a good nervous and that year was truly a Christmas to remember.

Kemper's Arlington office was a short twenty-minute drive in the morning and the route wound its way past scenic Mystic Lake in nearby Medford. It was a very pleasant drive and a rather nice way to begin each day. My mom and dad used to take my twelve siblings and I to this beach when we were kids. Not all at once of course. They just did not make station wagons big enough to hold that many people at the same time and a bus was simply too impractical as it would never fit in the driveway.

During my tenure at Kemper's Arlington office there was many a morning when I would be cruising along on a warm summerday and have all I could do to resist pulling off the road to enjoy nature at its finest. I would hear the birds chirping, I would look over and see the trees and flowers blooming and the inviting allure of the cool pristine water and I would just sigh. I would ask myself, what would Henry David Thoreau do? Would he go to work or would he play hooky? Sometimes when I snapped out of yet another daydream, I would look up and realize I was in the oncoming lane so I would swerve back into my own lane as the car behind me honked its horn frantically.

First things first however. As I walked into the office the first day, I had no idea what to expect. It was a large, wide-open office on the second floor of a two-story building located on Massachusetts Avenue. As I walked through the front door, all of the employees were in full view. The clerical staff was on the left side of the room and the claims staff on the right, probably 20-25 desks in all I estimated.

It felt great to be coming to work for a Fortune 500 company where I could establish myself in a position that actually sounded like it had a lot to offer. Every claim would be different and offer unique challenges; as compared to the tedious repetition I experienced working with numbers at the bank.

A tall very cute brunette greeted me at the front counter.

"Can I help you?" she asked very business-like.

"Yes, hi, my name is Mike Merrett and I'm starting work today. Is Mr. Thompson in?" I asked nervously.

"Oh!" she said, her face lighting up, "You're the new guy! Hi, I'm Maryanne."

God, I hate being called that, but her smile more than made up for it.

"Yeah, I'm the new guy. Nice to meet you," I replied. "Is Mr. Thompson in?" I asked again. I wanted to get this introductory stuff out of the way as quickly as possible. Everyone has been in this position at one time or another, and no one looks forward to his or her first day on the job. While being carted around and introduced to everyone, I felt like an alien, and did not have a clue as to what to expect. Meeting a group of total strangers and then trying to remember their names ten minutes later can be daunting for me on a good day, so I wanted to become a part of the team as quickly as I could.

Maryanne led me to Mr. Thompson's office who greeted me with a terse smile and a firm handshake. I resigned myself to the fact that Tom was definitely what I would call a no-nonsense kind of guy and I was perfectly OK with that.

Then Tom took me into an adjacent office where he introduced me to my immediate supervisor, a tall, thin man sporting a goatee by the name of Brent Twyon. Brent and I hit it off splendidly. During the early weeks while I was becoming acquainted with the position, he was patient, supportive, and was a tremendous help to me. I was extremely grateful too because I am reasonably sure that I drove him nuts on more than one occasion. The rest of the Arlington staff was nothing less than awesome as well. I could not have asked for a better group of co-workers.

Claims handling however, was a fairly difficult position I would soon discover. There was a great deal to learn, taxing my diminutive little brain to its limits. There are 13 parts to the Massachusetts Auto policy and I had to learn them inside out. The policy represented a contract between the company and the insured and adjusters had to know what they were talking about when dealing with not only our own customers, but agents and attorneys as well.

It was also necessary to have a fundamental understanding of automobiles and their many intricate parts. I had to complete a two-week intensive course on property damage at Kemper's salvage yard in Braintree where we learned all the different parts of an auto and how they are repaired and serviced. I scored an 89 on the final exam so I was pleased with that result. I was also the first one in the class to finish and head out the door to beat the traffic on Boston's dreaded Southeast Expressway. During the entire test, all I could think about was getting the jump on that bumper-to-bumper traffic so I could get home at a reasonable hour. Heck, it was Friday afternoon and the weekend was here. Never let it be said that I have any problems keeping my priorities in order.

Then of course, there was the necessity to develop an expertise in evaluating liability. It was the adjuster's job to determine who was at fault for the accident, after a thorough investigation. The adjuster acted as judge and jury, period. I soon discovered two very peculiar and intriguing characteristics about Massachusetts motorists. People rarely tell the whole truth when giving their version of what happened, and no one likes being told they are at fault. I know that is probably difficult to believe but it is true just the same and if you have ever been involved in an accident, you know exactly what I am talking about. Because being deemed at fault means getting whacked with a surcharge. The number one rule of thumb in Massachusetts seemed to be, when faced with the threat of having to pay a surcharge, bend the truth to try and avoid it.

The saving grace was, that type of work really interested me and I do not ever remember waking up on any given morning and dreading going to work. I almost felt guilty that I was actually enjoying my job.

Earlier during that fall of 1978, Tom Chopelas had called a meeting of staff members and parents to discuss the possibility of merging the Ambassadors with another Class B drum corps from Arlington, Mass. called the Heightsmen. After much debate during which every single member of the staff and every parent spoke against the merge feeling we did not need it, Tom announced that indeed we would merge. Because whatever Tom wanted, Tom got. Tom had contracted a severe case of what we called in those days, "DCI Fever", an uncontrollable desire to manage a corps that finished in DCI's Elite "Top Twelve" at the Nationals, and it was during the 1970's that corps began to merge at an alarming rate. This new phenomenon would become one of the biggest contributing factors to the activities overall demise in the years that followed. While the merger initially created a more competitive unit, it was still one corps where there was previously two.

The merge increased our size to near full membership (128 was the limit a corps could field by DCI Rules) and we were forced to move up to Open Class which meant we would be competing against the top corps in the country… The Concord Blue Devils, the Santa Clara Vanguard, and Madison Scouts to name a few….the mere thought of which sent shivers up my spine. This new corps was christened with the name The Royal Marquis. While we had enormous potential and raw talent, the two staffs and management teams that were melded into one fought incessantly over creative differences that involved everything from show programming and design to finances and logistics. The merge collapsed by the end of the 1979 summer season and both corps went their separate ways. Arlington survived but Malden lost all its' remaining members to other corps, most of who went to the 27th Lancers and North Star. It had an immediate impact as the large influx of new members lifted 27th to a second place finish at the DCI Finals in 1980. It would be the closest the Lancers would ever come to winning it all.

That summer of 1979 was not a total loss, however. During our 3 week tour up and down the East Coast, the members of the staff who did manage to get along found the time to enjoy ourselves. We spent a day in Washington DC checking out the sites in the 95-degree heat, then we stopped off to see the Chatanooga Choo-Choo in Tennessee. Three members in particular, brass instructor Kevin Mactaggert, drill instructor Mike Kelly and I even got our pictures put up on the walls in a number of restaurants in various cities. The photos were accompanied by the caption "Do not admit under any circumstances".

Kevin usually started the messy fracas. We would order dessert and he would get something with whipped cream and once it arrived, he would look at it strangely, then hold it up to me or Mike Kelly and say, "This smells funny, does it smell alright to you?"

Then, when I would lean over to smell it he would smash it in my face and a really nasty food fight would ensue. We did not take our cue from that memorable scene in the movie "Animal House" mind you, and it was never on that scale. Oh no, we were much more covert and it usually stayed within the boundaries of our booth, but it wasn't long before the female staff members refused to sit with us and I felt sorry for the person who had to bus our table after we paid them a visit.

The Marquis experience proved an invaluable one as it gave me my first opportunity to write an Open Class percussion show, which also inspired me to study for my judging cards that year. Through much hard work and help from a dear friend by the name of Paul Bush who had previously marched with the Boston Crusaders and was himself a judge, I successfully navigated my way through a rigorous testing process and became a card-carrying member of the Mass. Judges Association. The position helped my marketability immensely and opened up a world of teaching opportunities as well. For the present, I thought, things were looking up both in my part time position with drum corps and my full time position as an adjuster.

I performed well enough at Kemper that when a workers' compensation field adjuster's position became available in the fall of 1979, branch manager Tom Thompson offered the position to me and I decided to accept it as it was a complete no-brainer. It came with a raise, a brand new company car and it meant 2 days a week in the office and 3 days on the road. It was a dream job and I was the envy of the other adjusters in the office.

It involved investigating industrial accidents and at that time, Kemper was doing a rather robust workers comp business in Massachusetts.

My new supervisor was Jim Russell, a very nice person but everyone in the office thought he was a little loopy. I just considered him eccentric but he was a unique individual with his argyle socks and the odd way he would shake hands every time I walked in or out of his office. We got along well and for the first few months, I settled into the job rather comfortably.

    Professionally, everything was falling into place. My insurance career and my judging and teaching careers were all in full bloom. Personally, however, all was not well in the garden. A storm began to form around my brothers and I as our visual conditions continued to worsen. Both Bert and Richard were starting to show real signs of having major difficulties with the logistics of day-to-day living and it was beginning to affect their dispositions as well. I became acutely aware that they smiled less and I could actually sense the joy of living ebbing from their outlooks on life. I had no idea how to assist them in their struggles. There were no pills they could pop to make it all better again.

    My enriching four-year relationship with Dyan came to an end by 1980. She had already been away at college in Chicago for more than a full year and like most long distance relationships, ours did not survive the enormous amount of time spent away from one another. She had met a fellow student who was pursuing a similar career path as hers and she was soon engaged to be married. Wouldn't you know it? His name was Michael also. What a coincidence I thought to myself as I contemplated placing a call to the Zanti Misfits, but I loved her too much to do anything but let her go. All I could do was gather up all the many precious moments we had spent together and lock them away in that secret vault of memories we all hold in our hearts. I wished her the very best, sucked it up like any level-headed mature individual would do, then I placed an emergency call to the suicide watch hot line. It was many months before the vision of her smiling face would fade from memory as I lay in bed nights trying to forget her. It is said that "it is better to have loved and lost than to never have loved at all." I'm sure to some that is quite poetic, but it is a small consolation to anyone with a broken heart.

Chapter Five- To Drive or Not to Drive

    Tom Chopelas and his lovely wife Linda started another drum corps the following year after the Marquis debacle and they called this one the Diplomats. First, the Ambassadors, I thought to myself, now the Diplomats. Makes sense. What's next, the Chambermaids?

    Despite the troubles we had experienced the previous summer, they invited the Malden staff back to work with the corps. I took over the reigns of head percussion instructor, with former 27th Lancers soprano player Don Mactaggert and former Beverly Cardinal alumnus Ron Genest returning as brass and marching and maneuvering arrangers respectively. The three of us had been working together for 3 years and the problems that arose the previous summer did not involve us. They were mostly confined to differences Don had experienced with Arlington's brass staff.

    The Diplomats did well their first year out winning the Class C championships in both CYO (Catholic Youth Organization) and Eastern Massachusetts circuits, which, was a great feeling, and I was receiving more judging assignments as well. I am not one to take life for granted and I considered myself very fortunate at that moment in time.

    However, how long can a good thing last? "Life is like the seasons, first comes winter, then the spring" as the song goes and catastrophe can be waiting around the next curve in the road.

    I was driving through Malden square one sunny afternoon on my way to an activity check on an insured who was supposed to be out on workers comp with a bad back but was rumored to be remodeling his house. I came up on a signal light and as I went to take a left turn, all of a sudden a car appeared out of nowhere coming in the opposite direction right towards me. I jammed on my brakes as he continued to proceed but another split second slower on the brakes could have resulted in a head on collision. I would lay strong odds that he went straight home to change his underwear.

As an auto adjuster the previous year I had taken numerous recorded statements from both insured's and claimants alike. I had learned that anytime a driver claimed that the other car had "come out of nowhere" it usually meant that they just had not looked in the direction the car had come from. Because if you think about it, common sense would tell you that unless your accident was with Harry Houdini as the other operator, cars do not just appear all of a sudden out of thin air.

In my case however, this car *had* come out of nowhere. A blind spot that had previously been indistinguishable due to its small size had increased in my left eye, which was my dominant eye. It was now beginning to affect my field of vision. It was as if a grey cloud was hovering just above center and anything that entered it simply disappeared. I had always had a blind spot on my right eye but now my good eye was being adversely affected as well.

I had been a licensed operator for the past eight years and for the first time, the thought of not being able to drive entered my mind. The repercussions of this, if it did in fact come to pass, would send a tidal wave of chaos throughout my entire life and would adversely affect everything I was involved in.

I pulled up in front of the insured's house and threw the car into park. My mind was still reeling but I had a job to do. I had always been locked into a mindset of denial to some degree so I began to pray that this latest regression would only be temporary.

Just as I looked towards the insured's house, a man was coming down the front stairs carrying a huge wooden door. I got out of the car and approached him, still a bit shaken from the near miss.

"Mr. Davis?" I asked, now just ten feet away from him.

He put down the door and looked at me with distrust. "Yes, what can I do for you?"

"Mike Merrett from Kemper Insurance, how are you today?" I asked and I thought he was going to have a stroke right then and there.

"Oh….uh….good…..uh…." the poor man did not know what to do or say. I had caught him red-handed. Bad back indeed.

"It's Ok Mr. Davis, relax. I'm just out here making sure you are receiving your benefits." That was the premise we used to do activity checks on people who we suspected were milking their worker's comp benefits. Companies that we insured would notify us if they heard through the grapevine that an employee was doing something improper. We also took a closer look if we received a doctor's report that stated the claimant showed no signs of being disabled and could return to work.

"I was keeping myself busy," he said nervously as he wiped the perspiration from his forehead. "Gets awful boring being out of work. You have to find something to do with your time." He was stammering now and I really did not want to upset him.

"Hey, like I said, I'm just checking up with your payments. If you are not having any problems with your checks, then have a nice day sir."

I left the poor man gasping for words and got back in my car to write up a report. He scurried back in the house and probably headed straight for the bathroom to change his shorts too. Twice in one day I thought, I am on a roll!

I did not get bent out of shape at this kind of thing. In the seventies and eighties, the Massachusetts worker's compensation laws were in serious need of a major league overhaul. The system was being exploited from all sides. Claimants, doctors and especially lawyers all had their hands in the pie and insurance companies were getting their asses handed to them. The best we could do in that situation was request a hearing before the Industrial Accident Board and they were so backed up they would not even review the case for up to nine months, so Mr. Davis could milk his situation for that long without the company being able to do a thing about it.

    Kemper insured a mattress company in Chelsea and word had spread throughout the Hispanic community that they hired predominantly Latino workers. Once the employees discovered how lenient the worker's comp laws were in this state, they quickly found ways to exploit them. They would even send word back home to relatives in Puerto Rico who would then come here and join the fray. It was quite a scam. After one week on the job, they would purposely injure themselves by driving a metal spring through their hand or something of that nature. It was always non-life threatening, then they would go see Saul Kraft, attorney at law and he would take it from there. Saul and I were on a first name basis and I was a frequent visitor to his office where I would take statements from his injured clients. All of them stated they could not speak English of course so Saul employed an interpreter. We constantly warned the mattress factory to screen their employees more thoroughly but they did not seem to care. They could exploit these people and they were not going to change their hiring habits just because we suggested they do so. I can only imagine how much they paid for premiums as a result of all the abuse.

    I managed to deal with the blind spot, which had appeared just above center by trying to look indirectly at objects. This seemed to work temporarily but as time went on that year, I noticed I was having ever-greater difficulty reading street signs and the numbers on houses. It eventually became so difficult that the stress was simply too much to bear. I went into Jim Russell's office one Monday morning and closed the door behind me.

    "Jim," I said softly, "I've got a problem."

    "I know, I know, everybody in the office complains about my argyle socks. Do they really bother you that much?" he asked with the utmost sincerity.

I was speechless for a moment. "Jim, it's not about your socks!"

"Oh good, what is it then?" he asked attentively.

"I am having problems getting the job done. I can't read street signs anymore or the numbers on the houses and it is taking me longer and longer to finish assignments. I used to love to read maps and navigate my way from point A to point B. It was like solving a crossword puzzle or finishing a jigsaw puzzle and I always prided myself on my map-reading skills but that is beginning to become more and more difficult as well."

"I suspected there was a problem," he responded. "I wasn't going to say anything until you brought it up but I am glad you did."

He was very understanding about the whole thing, as was Tom Thompson. For the first time I was about to discover just how solid a company Kemper was when it came to dealing with employee issues such as mine. Tom set up a transfer for me to the Malden office, which was 2 minutes from my apartment, and I returned to the position of office rep in the auto unit.

Giving up the company car and coming in off the road was a tough pill to swallow though and for the second time, vision loss put me in a humiliating position.

Like riding a bike, I settled back into my old position without too much difficulty. The people I worked with in the Malden office were every bit as high quality as those I worked with in Arlington, but I would soon miss my old friends very much. I had become very close with many of the appraisers and members of the secretarial staff and it was hard to say goodbye. Kemper was a high-class company and it prided itself on a well-trained, highly professional staff.

The Arlington crew threw a going away party for me at the Victoria's Station Restaurant in Cambridge on the Friday night that was to be my final day. I was the last to arrive as it was a complete surprise and as is often my custom, I made a grand entrance. It was really dark in there and after Brent Twyon guided me to my seat, I sat down and started talking to Maryanne, the office receptionist who was seated to my right. We had become very close and I was contemplating asking her for a date but she had just started dating one of the office appraisers who was also a good friend of mine. I would never do something so scurrilous to a buddy like Peter, especially when he was twice my size.

As I turned to speak with fellow adjuster Scott Johnson who was seated directly to my left, I failed to see the full pitcher of Miller Lite beer the waitress had set down right between us. As I turned, my elbow sent it hurtling right into Scott's lap. I had not been there for five minutes and already I had made a total ass of myself. I never even saw the damned thing as it got lost in the blind spot. Scott's lovely wife Nancy was seated next to him and fortunately the two of them took it really well. The rest of the evening went off without any further embarrassing displays and as we parted company, I knew I would come to miss them very much. Billy Shakespeare was right, "Parting is such sweet sorrow."

My mom remained diligent in her efforts to unravel the puzzle as to why her sons were having such enormous difficulties with their eyesight. Through her medical contacts, she learned about a doctor in Boston who was working on an eye disease that sounded like it had all the symptoms we were dealing with. So we each made an appointment to be evaluated by his office in November of 1980.

Sometimes I look back upon the experience and think that maybe I should have let sleeping dogs lie. That November day is still a vivid memory. It was cold and overcast outside as we spent the entire day in the examining room of Dr. Elliot Berson, one of the most prominent physicians in his field at the Massachusetts Eye and Ear Infirmary in Boston. The Mass Eye and Ear, like many of the medical facilities in Bean town, is a world-class hospital. At the very least, we could only hope that we had started our search for answers in the right place.

They could not examine all of the six boys at once so my older brother Richard and I were the first to be evaluated. My mom, Rich, and I underwent 8 hours of grueling tests, the likes of which we had never been exposed to before . By the time it was over, I was so groggy they could have told me I was not of this Earth and really from planet X and I would have believed them if they would just *let me go home*!

The testing was not something I would look forward to repeating very often and we were paying him for administering these high levels of discomfort. He was not paying us but I reiterate here and now for the record that I am not a masochist. Shortly after our arrival, an assistant to Dr. Berson put drops in our eyes in order to dilate our pupils. She explained that this gave the doctors better ability with which to see to the back of our eyes, which of course is where the retina is located.

For the rest of the day we remained completely in the dark as they had put patches over our eyes. We could not read therefore and I had no idea what to expect so I did not bring a radio.

The only time the patches were removed was during the actual testing. Because there were probably 10 or 11 people being evaluated that day, it was a long, excruciating process.

The procedures had different objectives. One was for testing the patient's ability to discern colors, another tested fields and peripheral vision, and my personal favorite was the eletro-retinagram. For that one, I was led into a completely dark room where my patches were removed and I was seated in front of a large machine. Then an assistant inserted hard contact lenses into each eye that had wires attached to them that were fed to another device nearby. I was asked to stare into this machine for what seemed like an eternity as a strobe light was flashed at me with varying frequencies. I was supposed to sit there motionless just staring at this incredibly bright flashing light with my eyes dilated. To add insult to injury, I was constantly being reminded by the technician that I should "try not to blink" while the machine was registering the results of my eye's reaction.

It only took about five minutes when my head began throbbing, my eyes were watering and I just wanted to rip those things out of my head and run as fast as I could to the nearest exit. At one point my mind swooned with crazy ideas that this would make a terrific torture device somewhere in the world. I almost found myself blurting out, "I'll talk, I'll talk!"

That was the final test of the ordeal, thank God. All in all the day of testing at Berson's office proved to be an exhausting experience and I do not recommend it if you are the least bit squeamish.

We kept reminding ourselves however, that while unpleasant, it was also necessary. Hopefully, the tremendous discomfort we endured would all be worth something in the end.

Outside the hospital it was dark and dreary while I sat there pondering weak and weary. Daylight savings time had set in and as much as I loved autumn, one thing I did not like about the Fall was that the daylight hours grew shorter and it was dark by 4:30PM. It wreaks havoc with our biological clocks not to mention the difficulties it created for people like Rich and I who were beginning to experience night blindness.

After we had completed all the tests, there was nothing left to do but sit and wait. The nurse suggested we go and grab something to eat in the cafeteria on the seventh floor, as it would be about an hour before we would have the chance to sit with the head honcho himself and review the test results together. Up to that point, I had never even seen Dr. Berson so he remained a total enigma.

The three of us now patch less navigated our way down the hall to the elevator banks, nearly walking into walls as we went. We occasionally had to grope with our hands to avoid objects and were still groggy from the lingering effects of not only the tests but also the drops. Our pupils would remain dilated for another 24 hours. I had never had this done before so I was oblivious to its side effects. As many of you may already be aware, once your pupils are dilated, your eyes become incredibly sensitive to light. Like most hospitals, this one had fluorescent lighting and the glare from them was so bright I was getting dizzy. I must have looked like a drunken sailor walking those hallways.

My mom seemed to be recovering a bit more quickly from the drops than Rich or I and she was the only one of us who had the sense to bring sunglasses with her. She was fortunately able to navigate her way around the cafeteria far better than we could.

"Do you both want coffee?" She asked us, observing us fumbling around trying to figure out what everything was.

"Sure, that sounds great," I said. "I could use some caffeine right about now." She looked very subdued and I could tell she was not enjoying any of this but these are the sacrifices loving parents make for the benefit of their children. She was determined to find anything or anyone who could help her sons.

As we approached the check out line with our trays, mom glanced at what we had grabbed and noticed no one had picked up any milk for the coffee.

"Wait here, we forgot a carton of milk," she said.

"I have milk right here," said Rich.

"Unless you like orange juice in your coffee, you better put that back," she chuckled.

"Yeah, and that wasn't sugar you put in your coffee, it was grated cheese. You trying to invent a new latte?" I asked.

"Jesus Christ!" he said in total frustration.

"Don't worry, I have two cups," I said. "I didn't want to mention it until you sat down so you wouldn't feel embarrassed."

We enjoyed our coffee and sandwiches in relative silence. Rich and I were still feeling a bit groggy and downright lethargic. Our silence was the result of wondering whether our deepest fears would be realized. We knew something was going on with our eyes, something very serious, but up until now, it was a complete unknown so we just dismissed it away hoping for a better tomorrow. Something told us that today we might finally learn the truth. With truth can come clarity and definition, which can often be a very scary thing. Truth cannot be ignored and dismissed away like the unknown can. I looked up and stared at the clock as the minutes continued to wind on.

Chapter Six- Meeting with Dr. Berson

When we returned to the waiting room, we were the only patients left. Mom and Rich were led in to meet with Dr. Berson first and when they came out, they just had blank looks on their faces so I had no idea what they had learned. When it was my turn to go in, an assistant led me to the consultation room, where I was introduced to Dr. Berson himself.

He was a stout man, perhaps 30 to 35 years old with dark hair and a warm smile.

"Good evening Mr. Merrett" he said pleasantly, "it is nice to meet you and I am sorry for the long day you had to endure but I assure you these tests are quite necessary. Won't you sit down?"

As I sat there in the leather chair, I was relieved that the ordeal was almost over. This was the final phase of the day when we would hopefully discover what the doctors had learned. Mom and Rich had already met with him and it was merely explained to us by an assistant that the doctor preferred to meet separately with his patients upon their first visit. So I wondered why mom and Rich were seen together but I was too tired to ask.

I noticed that there were three other doctors sitting around the brightly lit room. I was seated in the patient's chair directly across from them. The swiveling mechanical device that allowed the doctors to examine a patient's eyes was located to my left. Doctor Berson was sitting to my right. He and the other three doctors, two males and one female were all wearing white lab coats. Berson proceeded to converse with them and it was apparent that he was the teacher and they were here more in the role of students.

They continued talking amongst themselves for quite a while when all of a sudden through my delirious haze, I began to feel like a parakeet in a cage. I was being completely ignored and I was not sure if I should start 'tweeting' to get some attention or merely remain sedate.

They were not speaking very loudly, just talking among themselves when I could have sworn I heard someone say, "There is a good chance he will be blind by age 40."

At that point, I perked right up. "Uh, excuse me?" I said loudly enough for all to hear. My patience was wearing a bit thin at that point. I had been there all day undergoing a battery of tests that in my estimation were designed more to further their research than to benefit me. I had no problem mind you with lending my time and my eyes for such a noble purpose, but now I was sitting in this chair feeling like a lab specimen and someone had just uttered a very distasteful word.

"Look, no disrespect Dr. Berson," I said with a slight hint of frustration, "but could you kindly direct your comments at me? I've been here since O-dark-thirty this morning and I feel like I just went 10 rounds with Joe Frazier. We came here for some answers and so far, I have none. Now I don't think it would be asking too much for you to clue me in on the discussion?"

Dr. Berson was in fact a very compassionate man, I would soon discover. Most doctors treat you like just another slab of beef and to some degree, I guess I can't blame them. It would be totally impractical not to mention psychologically devastating for them to become emotionally involved with every patient they treated.

Dr. Berson turned in his chair away from the three associates and addressed me personally.

"I am sorry Mr. Merrett, we are not ignoring you intentionally," he said in a reassuring voice. "We have a certain schedule to the day's regimen and perhaps we come across as evasive and indifferent but we usually discuss the results of the tests amongst ourselves for learning purposes, then we go over the findings with the patient."

"Well, I didn't mean to interrupt but it has been a long day for me, my mom and brother. We came here as much for our own peace of mind as we did to assist in your research by volunteering as patients and I have not learned anything after (I looked at my watch) a total of 9 and a half hours now. Would you be so kind as to tell me what we are dealing with here? If you were sitting in my place right now and you overheard someone say that you would be blind by age 40, you would be a bit alarmed too wouldn't you?"

"Yes I would," he answered. "And while that is not a certainty, I must tell you that in most cases we have seen of people at your age with similar test results, there is a strong likelihood you could lose a good deal of your vision by the age of 40. That goes for both you and your brother Richard. These test results indicate that by current standards, you are both already at the legally blind stage, which means, by law; I am required to register you with the Mass. Commission for the Blind, which will make you eligible for services. Do you know the definition of legal blindness, and what it means?"

"Yes," I answered somberly, "I know what it means."

Hearing it again just made my head feel worse. I was tired and the glare from the overhead lights was blinding me and gave the room a surreal look. My brain felt like silly putty and now this. My mind was swooning with apprehension, confusion, and anxiety.

"So what is causing it?" I asked as calmly as I could.

"The condition, disease, however you wish to refer to it is called Retinitis Pigmentosa or RP for short. It is a degenerative disease of the retina, sex linked in nature which is why only your brothers are affected by it and not your seven sisters."

That paradox had come up on more than one occasion during family discussions.

"Your mom carries the gene," he continued, "even though she is not affected by the condition. That is how the disease runs. If you were to have children and they were female they would be carriers and their sons would be affected." He handed me a chart, which showed the progression of the condition from generation to generation.

"We have been studying this disease for about ten years now as it is a relatively new field of study," he said. "In other words, it has probably been around for a long time but only recently have we been able to pinpoint what it is exactly and how it works. Unfortunately, our research has not yet proven successful in the way of a treatment or cure."

He put his hand on my forearm. "Look, I know this does not come as pleasant news but we have an extensive laboratory here at this hospital working solely on this disease and with luck and hard work, we may come up with a treatment someday. But I am not going to give you false hopes because we have nothing to offer right now."

I was completely naïve to exactly what caused the condition, and as it turns out they did not seem to know either, other than to write it off as hereditary, but for the moment, I was only concerned with making it go away, so I began asking off-the-wall questions like any plebe would do in my shoes.

"What about transplants or laser surgery"? I asked, feeling a bit out of my league.

He turned slightly in his chair looking a bit inpatient but to his credit, he stayed with me on this one.

"Most people do not realize it but eye transplants only involve the front half of the eye. They are mostly used in such cases as industrial accidents where the cornea is damaged or burned and the front half can be replaced. Unfortunately, the retina, where RP is centered, is attached to the optical nerve, which sends signals directly to the brain for processing into images. The retina is located in the back of the eye and is made up of light receptors we call rods and cones. In patients who have RP, these light receptors slowly over time lose their ability to function letting less and less light through to the optical nerve. It is the last frontier of medical eye research and we just do not have the technology to deal with it yet. Laser surgery is not an option as it is not designed to correct something like this."

He picked up another chart and showed it to me. It was a layout of the human eye and all of its parts.

The other three doctors waited patiently in their seats across the room and that was OK with me, I thought to myself. I have been patient all day, and besides they are on the clock. They are being paid for this.

He was doing his best to explain this in layman's terms for which I was grateful. I had a basic understanding of the way the human eye functioned and the various parts that make up the eye but I am sure there was much more involved here that would have been beyond me if he wanted to speak in detailed medical terminology.

"Now the other problem you and your brothers have is Macular Degeneration which, in your case, is related to the RP. That is what is causing those blind spots you have just above center. While there are various forms of Macular Degeneration, such as wet age-related, and dry, yours is a direct result of the RP. In essence you have a dual problem. Your retina is the source of the failing rods and cones and the blind spots are going to get larger over time."

"And the good news is?" I asked, trying to inject a bit of levity into the discussion.

"The good news is….you can go home," he answered with a warm smile.

I sat back in my chair and sighed. I was wiped out and could not even come up with any more stupid questions at that point. It was all too much to absorb after such a long day. I had learned more in the past fifteen minutes of speaking with him than I had in all the years leading up to this eventful moment. I had been seeing ophthalmologists for years for updated prescriptions but this was the first time I had actually learned that there was an accursed disease at work in our family.

"Well, I guess that's it then," I said with utter resignation, but I could not leave just yet. "There is nothing anyone can do so what do you recommend as a course of action? I mean is there anything we can do to slow the regression? I don't know. Eat more carrots? You never see rabbits wearing glasses." Nobody laughed.

He could sense the utter frustration I was experiencing and I think it genuinely bothered him that there was nothing they could offer in the way of treatment.

"For now, I think it would be best if you and your brothers would come in to see us at least on an annual basis and let us update your condition. I can assure you if we do come up with anything in the way of a treatment or if we have any news, we will contact you immediately. But, I am sorry to say, that is all we can offer you at this time."

I looked into his eyes and I actually felt bad for him. He made quite an impression on me that night and I could sense that he actually cared and felt empathy for the people he was seeing on a daily basis who were dealing with the devastating effects of vision loss. I sensed that it really bothered him that there was absolutely nothing he could do to ease their suffering.

My mom and brother Richard were waiting out in the seating room and one of the three doctors escorted them into the room where we huddled together for a brief final wrap up with the four doctors.

I looked into my mother's eyes and I could see what the news had done to her. I could only imagine what she must have felt when informed that she was carrying a gene that was causing her sons to go blind. My heart ached for her but I was not really sure what I could say or do that would ease her pain.

Dr. Berson offered up more words of encouragement and we expressed our gratitude and headed for the elevator. Rich just stood there looking despondent and we waited in stunned silence until the elevator arrived.

When we reached the ground floor and walked through the lobby to head for a taxi, I took mom by the arm and said quietly, "Don't worry huh? Trust me, we will deal with this. Think of the bright side. It is going to be a while before it gets really serious. And besides, doctors have been known to be wrong on occasion."

She smiled but there was nothing anyone could have said or done that was going to relieve the guilt she would endure for the rest of her days.

We were the first three members of the family to be evaluated by Dr. Berson but in the weeks that followed, the entire immediate family of 13 siblings and my father paid him a visit and underwent the series of tests. Three of my other four brothers were all diagnosed with the symptoms, Bert, David, and John. My youngest brother Stephen was the only boy who was not showing any symptoms at all, which left the doctors at a bit of a loss as to why this was occurring. Ironically, our dad had the eyes of a hawk, and my seven sisters all had perfect vision.

I suppose on some level we should consider our family fortunate indeed that RP works indiscriminately, afflicting some and sparing others. We took great comfort in knowing that at the very least, our sisters and their children would probably never have to deal with this unwelcome guest that had come into our lives, but to my four brothers and I, Dr. Berson had opened up one hell of a can of worms.

That night I lay in bed feeling psychologically like I had been hit with a wrecking ball. My mind became mired in a seemingly inescapable bog of confusion, anger, and uncertainty. My brothers and I always knew that there was more involved here than normal nearsightedness and we had been dealing with poor vision for as far back as we could remember, but we had never heard a doctor, especially someone of Dr. Berson's reputation; use the word "blindness" in our diagnosis. Not only did he direct it at me, but it meant I might possibly have to watch helplessly as four of my five brothers lost the use of their eyes as well.

I reacted as anyone would, by asking the compelling questions: Why us? What did we do to deserve this? Could they be wrong, and was it really a certainty or just their opinion? How much time did we have before the lights went out completely? How would we all deal with it as the condition regressed?

The psychology of vision loss is a strange one indeed. I began to feel tremendous anger deep down inside me but it was not directed at anyone in particular. How could it be? It certainly wasn't my mother's fault that she was carrying the gene which caused this, and displaying anger against the creator is fruitless and from what I hear, most unwise, but the anger was real, it was tangible, and if not dealt with, it could become an all-consuming cancer.

For the first time in my life, I began to experience real fear. The thought of becoming blind in an oftentimes-unkind world was unnerving to say the least. Up until then the condition had felt like some unseen force had its hand on a dimmer switch and was slowly, and mercilessly turning down the lights in my world, but the thought of everything going completely dark was simply beyond my willingness to accept. I had always felt confident that I could take care of myself under most circumstances, but if the worst-case scenario did come to pass, how would I take care of my family in the event that I became married some time in the future?

Then there was guilt; nagging self-loathing kind of guilt. My mind started to play tricks with my conscience. When we were adolescents, one of the most common forms of punishment was, at least in our household, having something taken away from us for a period of time when we misbehaved. Over time vision loss was beginning to take many things away from me, permanently. It was threatening my ability to drive a car, my mobility, the ability to read, and for that matter, it was beginning to negatively impact upon every aspect of my life. I could not help feeling as though I was being punished for something and I did not know why? As a result, I feared that diminishing self-esteem might become a growing concern.

As a life-long Catholic and a recipient of 12 years of parochial school education, I can personally attest that one need look no further than the Bible itself for a historical connection between sin and being handicapped. One passage refers to an incident where Christ leaned down to heal a cripple by uttering the words, "Your sins are forgiven you." The implication that he was crippled because of his sinful acts is inescapable.

Of the five human senses, roughly 90 percent of what we assimilate from the world around us is absorbed through the human eye. It is the sense we depend upon more than all the others combined. Without the use of the greatest tool God gave us for clarifying my world around me, I had no doubt that my life could become a veritable living hell in the not too distant future.

Even the Internal Revenue Service recognized the unique difficulties vision loss creates when they established a special tax exemption solely for people who are legally and totally blind. Who would have thought that the IRS would actually do something nice for anybody indicating that there is still hope for the world?

As I lay there on my bed staring at the ceiling, I just wanted to cry, but crying doesn't solve anything and merely squanders our precious bodily fluids, so, as I often did, I internalized it all. I raged inside my mind and turned my anger towards the doctors, refusing to accept their prognosis. They cannot be sure and they seemed to know so little about this disease. I simply refused to believe what they had told me and I went into a complete and utter state of emotional denial.

My brain however was still hanging on by a thread, so I tried to prod my limited intellect into action. I attempted to formulate how this might affect my future and I forced my mind to try to deal with this rationally. It was too early to start learning Braille, the mere thought of which caused me to shudder. I began by attempting to solve the riddle as to how this came to pass. I was desperate for answers, anything that would help me understand what brought this doomsday scenario upon us.

Fortunately for us and at the risk of sounding boastful, my mom and dad raised 13 genuinely likable children. Our parents instilled in us some good old fashioned Christian values such as sacrifice, caring, responsibility, and compassion for others. We are not perfect, but we try to adhere to their teachings. We are still to this day a very close-knit family, and while we may not have produced any Albert Einstein's, Leonardo Davinci's or Mozart's, none of us have ever seen a day in custody or jail. Each of us has worked hard all our lives, many have raised families of their own and through it all we have made every attempt we could to be positive, contributing members of our communities and never embarrass our family name. We have also been blessed with many truly great friends who have enriched our lives immeasurably.

The boys however, had one very bad habit growing up. We all sat too close to the television set as toddlers. Dr. Berson claimed Retinitis Pigmentosa is hereditary in nature. There are many diseases that lay claim to being genetic in origin, but my skeptic side told me that it was easy for doctors to write off all these so-called hereditary conditions as gene-related because it leaves the patient in a position where he/she has no recourse. You cannot sue your deceased ancestors. I wanted to know how it got into my genes in the first place. There has to be a reason. Everyone on this planet, barring any tragic birth defects of course, is born with two eyes, two ears, a nose, a mouth, etc. All of which are hereditary characteristics of our species, but everyone is not born with Retinitis Pigmentosa so how were we, like hundreds of thousands of people around the world unfortunate enough to contract it?

  I delved further for answers realizing full well, that Hercule Poirot was in absolutely no danger of losing his job. Since the turn of the century when electricity became so prevalent that it now literally surrounds us 24 hours a day, cancer rates among humans have skyrocketed. Could this be the result of the electro-magnetic fields we have created? EMF's are part of our everyday lives but scientists and doctors alike remain relatively uncertain as to their long-term effects on living things. Are EMF's causing assorted diseases in millions of people? Should I switch off the light next to my bed and light a candle?

  Likewise, in the early days of color television, it is common knowledge that these sets emitted low levels of radiation. Could they have caused the damage to our eyes? Some might say "then why isn't everyone going blind?" To which I respond, why isn't everyone allergic to tomatoes or strawberries? Why do some people who lay out in the sun contract skin cancer while others with the same amount of exposure do not? Our individual body chemistries are quite unique and it could be that some are more sensitive than others to such external forces. Can you imagine the impact on the economy if word got out that watching television or sitting too close to your computer screen may over an extended period of time cause severe eye damage just as staring at the sun can severely damage the human retina? Could the television industry be conspiring to keep this information from us, just as the tobacco industry tried for years to hide the facts from the public regarding the harmful effects of nicotine?

  The television is the greatest control device ever devised by man. It tries to tell us what to think, what to buy, and where to go and while it could have served as the greatest educational tool we humans have ever invented, we have instead allowed it to become a babbling idiot box with the sole purpose of selling us more crap. All of which has absolutely nothing to do with the subject of vision loss but I simply could not resist an opportunity to comment on my utter disdain for the Hollywood ilk. So to get back on track, I am left to ponder whether sitting too close to the television set was the cause of our affliction.

My puny little mind delved further. Are these hereditary illnesses simply the result of our ancestors fooling around with one another? The ancient Romans, for example, who routinely engaged in incestuous relationships, were completely unaware that having sex with their siblings was not a very prudent activity to engage in. Could they be the cause, those filthy animals?

Serious eye research is still a relatively new field of endeavor. Not until the last fifty years or so has the technology existed to closely examine it in detail, which is why there are so many new conditions that, prior to 1950 were completely unheard of. The existence and causes of RP, Glaucoma, and Macular Degeneration to name a few were complete unknowns until recently.

Additionally, aging and modern technology are placing new demands on the human eye which never existed before. Not only are people living longer which means our eyes have to work decades beyond those of our ancestors, but they are also being expected to do more visually demanding functions. We spend hours and hours each day in front of computer and television screens often causing many people to experience severe eyestrain. I have always felt that staring at a little square electronic box all day as an occupation is both unnatural and unhealthy. These are just two devices we have created in the new high-tech environment that doctors and scientists remain unsure as to their long-term effects on our senses. Add cell phones, x-rays and microwaves to the mix and the issue becomes even more complex.

There simply was no easy answer, I concluded humbly. I only knew that I detested hearing the word blindness in relation to our future and it infuriated me that there was not a damn thing I could do about it. Going back to med school to find my own cure was out of the question since I was never there in the first place, and no matter how much I shook my fists at the heavens above, I needed to consider how to approach the days ahead sensibly and prepare for the worst. Then I thought, how would my brothers handle it? Like typical males, we rarely discussed our emotions amongst ourselves and especially not with others. Instead, we buried our feelings deep within us and like stoking a furnace, they would eventually threaten to consume us. We were afraid that talking about our dilemma would portray us as whiners and we did not want to be perceived as wallowing in self-pity.

We came from a large post-war family. While none of us developed the kind of self-esteem you might see from children in today's families where one or two offspring is the norm, our parents instilled in us the kind of indomitable survival skills that more than anything else, would enable us to deal with this new predicament. For that, we love them dearly and are eternally grateful. They constantly put aside their own material needs in favor of the needs of their children. My dad never cared what kind of car sat out in the driveway as long as it was a station wagon big enough to haul around his kids. BMW's and Mercedes were complete unknowns and totally irrelevant. We were not wealthy and were just barely middle class but there are some things in life that money can't buy. The two commodities that were never in short supply in our household were parental love and guidance.

As I lay there slowly losing consciousness, a steady rain began to fall. I had always loved the sound of falling rain and it had the most relaxing and tranquil effect as it lulled me to sleep. For a moment, I felt as if St. Michael himself was sending me a signal that everything was going to be all right. I pulled the covers tight up around my shoulders, and resigned myself to the fact that energy levels in my brain cells were pretty much depleted. There was absolutely nothing I could say or do that would reverse the day's events, so I drifted off to sleep, thankful to have that roof over my head and a loving family not far away.

I returned to work the following day and while I couldn't be absolutely sure, I think that my fellow adjusters sensed I was acting a bit differently than I had been prior to my visit with Dr. Berson. They knew nothing regarding the circumstances surrounding my time off the previous day. My eyes were still a bit dilated, and the glare from the office lights was causing me to squint slightly. I must have looked dizzy or hung-over but they respected my confidentiality and kept their curiosity to themselves. The only way my intellect could deal with all of this was to immerse myself in work because there was really nothing any of us could do to alter this new dilemma we were handed.

My mom was a bit more tenacious though, and for many months following our visit to Dr. Berson, she attempted to conduct as much research and ask as many questions as she possibly could. It would be to no avail but I think it made her feel better that she was making some attempt to find any kind of relief. Guilt became her demon but love and compassion would remain her greatest weapon in her never-ending struggle to undo what her genetic makeup had created.

Chapter Seven- Jeopardy on the job

During the next two years, the Diplomats drum and bugle corps stormed through Class B in 1981 and '82, winning championships in each of those seasons. My judging career was blossoming as well although my failing vision was beginning to have a negative impact. I tried to limit myself to "field" judging which put me up close to the drum lines rather than judging "general effect" which required that I sit in the press box at the top of the stadium. I could have tried binoculars but not only was I too embarrassed, they probably would not have solved the problem. There were times when the corps members would be spread across the entire length of the football field and there were no binoculars on the market that offered an adequate visual field that would stretch that far. Besides, I felt reasonably certain that more than a few instructors "wouldst protest rather vehemently" upon discovering that one of the individuals judging their hard work was legally blind. I tried to conceal my limitations and any visual aides I attempted to use such as binoculars would be a dead giveaway. I was indeed fortunate that my hearing skills were still sharp and my verbal communication skills were as charming as ever, giving me the ability to clearly absorb the quality of music and then competently articulate and explain how I arrived at the scores I assigned to each performance.

My visibility and moderately stupendous reputation as a judge eventually led to teaching offers from a number of sources. I accepted part time positions with drum lines from Somerville high school band, North Reading high school band and later in 1984, even the Old Orchard Beach marching "Seagull" band from Maine came calling. I spent some time working with North Star as well which by 1979 had established itself as a DCI finalist and featured one of the most innovative marching percussion ensembles on the continent. The head percussion instructor for North Star at that time was Dave Vose. Dave also taught at the Berklee School of music in Boston as his full time profession. He and his staff had done a marvelous job with the line and in 1979, North Star drummers finished second to the highly prestigious Santa Clara Vanguard.

At the peak of my teaching career, I found myself with as many judging assignments as I could handle. At the same time I served as head percussion instructor for four separate units, not to mention an assistant with a top 12

DCI corps. I had never enjoyed that kind of personal satisfaction and success at any previous time in my life. While it may not have been a utopian existence, it sure did feel good while it lasted. Slowly over time, I was learning a valuable lesson in life and that was, enjoy the treasures we have and never take them for granted. One never knows when fate might rip them away from us in the blink of an eye.

      One morning in the spring of 1982, after a weekend of experiencing increasing difficulties in seeing things that had previously not been a problem, I went to work, sat at my desk, opened my first file and was struck by a feeling of utter dread. I could not read the words on the page without severe straining and struggling. The blind spots had gotten bigger. I began to perspire and a tidal wave of anxiety rushed through me like an emotional tsunami.

      I had been forced to make constant adjustments over the past few years, more so than at any previous time in my life and it seemed as if the regression was accelerating again. I had cut down on my driving to "only when absolutely necessary", like the 2 minutes back and forth from work, but this was simply too much for me to bear. I feared that my job was in jeopardy now and this accursed disease was threatening to put me out of work. I sat back in my chair and found myself muttering "Time to assume the position." I knew I had to get out of there. I was not prepared for that kind of humiliation so before the manager and my other co-workers arrived, I bravely bolted to my car feeling absolutely numb and just wanting to be alone. I was at a total loss as to what else to do. The cupboard in my brain that normally provided answers and where all of my accrued intelligence was stored seemed to be bare, as if someone had forgotten to go shopping.

      There was very little traffic on the route I took back and forth to work everyday. It involved side streets mostly and I knew the route like the back of my hand. I always kept my speed down and was extra careful in every way.

When I arrived home, I made a cup of coffee, sat at the kitchen table and just let my mind wander.

For the first 28 years of my existence vision loss had been a mere nuisance. It was always there requiring thicker glasses or more recently, stronger contact lenses every year, but for the most part I was able to deal with it. The dam was always in danger of breaking but I had been able to stay one stride ahead of the ever-impending flood. Even while dating Dyan, she had been nice enough to overlook my coke-bottle lenses, as I did not start wearing contacts until 1979. I enjoyed a rewarding marching career for 11 years and now was a successful instructor and judge. I had lettered in high school football, enjoyed playing street hockey and virtually every other sport during my youth. I had been able to hold vision loss at bay and make the necessary adjustments to prevent it from completely bringing down my house of cards that I had been so carefully building over the years.

Since the Fort Knox ordeal however, that was all beginning to change. Now it was affecting my employment status and threatening my ability to drive a car. After my visit to Dr. Berson in 1980 when I discovered the name of this accursed disease, his words kept reverberating in my mind like thunder claps. "There is a good chance you could be blind by age 40," he had told me.

I did not want to believe him, even though it was shortly before seeing him that I was forced to come in off the road at Kemper. Now, I was at the point where I might have to give up driving and worse yet, I could no longer perform the requirements of my job at a sufficient rate that would prevent putting an added burden on my fellow adjusters. They would have to pick up the slack from my inability to handle a full workload and this was only 2 years after seeing Berson. I was beginning to realize that I had better be prepared for the worst because his prognostication, dire as it sounded, was beginning to ring true. As he was required to do by law, he had registered my brothers and I with the Mass. Commission for the Blind.

Ron Paris, the Malden office manager, called me later that morning to ask why I was not at work. I almost broke down telling him what had happened and I informed him I had intended to call him but I just had not built up the courage. He genuinely sounded concerned and asked that I keep him informed of the situation. I felt terrible, as I knew the nature of the claims department all too well. When an adjuster was out for any reason, insured's, claimants, and attorneys were not very sympathetic. When they called for a status on their claim or were prepared to settle, they did not want to hear and would not accept that the adjuster was not available. The other adjusters would have to cover for that person on top of handling their own backlogs, which were usually overwhelming to begin with. I envisioned every one of them cursing me out as my imagination became consumed by guilt and paranoia.

My heart could not have sunk any further. I went in, lay down on the couch, and put on some Moody Blues as I needed some serious meditation time. The "Moody's" had that special ability to wash away anxiety with their enchanting melodies. I was totally confused as to what to do and prayed that somewhere, something existed that would allow me to function in my job. I was becoming more of a pessimist with each passing day however. I had always considered myself a fairly capable individual, able to deal with most problems I faced and if I couldn't, I usually was successful knowing where to look to find the necessary resources. This, however, was completely beyond me. How do I stop my eyes from failing? The best doctors in the world could not find an answer to our dilemma and they had intelligence. What could I possibly come up with? Somehow, it just did not seem fair, but I have lived long enough to learn that no one ever said life was always going to be fair.

Reluctant or not, it was time to contact the Commission for the Blind. This was way out of my league and it was time to accept the fact that simple ordinary tasks like picking up the morning newspaper and checking out the sports section was now beyond my ability. I needed high-tech visual aids and hopefully, the Commission could provide them.

This was a huge step for me. Contacting a state agency that dealt with the handicapped felt alien and just seemed so foreign considering where I had been all of my life, which was amongst the world of the "non-handicapped."

I received a return call from the agency that afternoon and was informed that a Mr. Richard Leland was the vocational rehabilitation counselor for my area so I scheduled an appointment with the receptionist to meet with him the following morning.

Richard showed up at my apartment the following day and struck me as a genuine, helpful individual so I explained the situation and after he took some background information, he suggested I meet with Bob Mcgilvary who was the agency's low vision technician. I thanked Richard for his quick response to my request and the following Thursday, I met with Bob early in the morning at my office in Malden. Bob was a short, bushy haired man of about 35-40 years of age with a soft-spoken, almost dry demeanor but I would grow to become very fond of him in a very short time. He brought with him a CCTV (closed circuit television) which I had never seen before but was quite intrigued with. We met very early as I was not emotionally ready to deal with the embarrassment of my situation and I did not want other adjusters around when Bob was conducting his evaluation. Stubborn pride and shameless vanity I admit, but my attitude towards such things is one I have developed over long, sometimes arduous years of hard work, devotion to my core values, and experience. When faced with a crisis, always take the path of least resistance.

Bob set up the CCTV on my desk and found an outlet where he could plug it in. I was immediately struck by the way Bob conducted himself. I was very impressed by his kindness and I genuinely felt that here was a person who was prepared to do anything it took to help me solve my dilemma.

The CCTV is nothing more than a television without a tuner so it is not designed to receive TV transmissions. It had a magnifier attached to the underside of the casing with a camera that magnified any image placed on the tray beneath it and projected it up onto the 13-inch display screen above.

It had several control switches that allowed me to adjust the magnification level, the contrast, and I could switch the text from black-on-white to white-on-black. That was an important feature as I was beginning to discover that contrast was becoming a crucial determining factor in my ability to clarify my world around me.

The device definitely helped the situation by making the words appear larger on the screen, but it was not going to make the blind spots go away and the machine did have its limitations.

As I sat there with Bob who was doing everything he could to make this work, I felt embarrassed and depressed. Sure, I could read my files better, but was this machine going to allow me to function at the same level I worked at before? Even with magnification, it was still difficult to read with any acceptable degree of ease. I was an experienced adjuster and as such, I was expected to handle a certain sized workload and process claims at a sufficient speed. If I could not do that, other adjusters would have to pick up the slack. I simply could not accept that. It just was not in my nature to make life more difficult for those around me when they could hire a fully sighted person to replace me. Guilt is one emotion I have never been able to handle very well and at that precise moment, I was drowning in it.

"What do you think?" said Bob, as I sat there staring blankly at the screen.

I grabbed the police report I had taken out of one of my files and moved it around the tray under the CCTV. I could read the text with less difficulty, but because of the smaller field due to the high magnification, it would take me longer to scan for whatever information I needed. There was simply no way around it. The pace at which I was going to be able to perform the requirements of the job would be significantly diminished, and that, at least in my mind, was completely unacceptable. I was making this judgment without really knowing what would be acceptable to my employer of course. Kemper had always been great to me and in fact, the possibility probably existed that they would accept almost anything I could produce. I really did not know, but I knew what I was willing to accept, and anything less than 100% was simply out of the question.

"I don't know Bob, I just don't know," I said dejectedly. "I will never be able to work at my usual pace. I don't think you understand the nature of the claims business. It is a fast paced, volume oriented, business and if you can't produce, you don't belong in this chair. I'm just not sure what the company is willing to accept if my claim handling speed is reduced significantly. I can't expect others to pick up the slack. It's just not fair and they will resent me for it over time. I just know they will."

"Well, that is something I can't help you with because you are right; I don't know what they'll accept," replied Bob.

"Look, why don't you do this. Throw this thing in your car, and can you deliver it to my apartment? I only live five minutes from here. Maybe if I can familiarize myself with it under more private conditions than this office permits, I can become more comfortable with it and perhaps over time my speed will increase. Is that OK?"

"Whatever you think is best. I don't make command decisions when it comes to what your company is going to allow you to do, I'm just the messenger," he said with a smile.

"Well, let me worry about Kemper," I answered. "I'll deal with them and let them know the results of our little experiment."

So Bob packed it up before any of my office mates arrived, then followed me home and dropped it off at my apartment.

"Call me if you need me and let me know what you decide to do," he said. "And by the way, do you always drive that slowly?"

"I probably shouldn't be driving at all," I answered. "Oh, I almost forgot. What does one of these things cost?"

"Right now they run about $2,700.00, and the state is willing to provide them for employment purposes, but in this case they may ask Kemper to pick up the tab, which I don't think they would have any problem with. They've invested over 3 years in you so I doubt they want to lose you as an employee."

We parted company and I thanked him greatly for his efforts. I could tell immediately that Bob was a real asset to the agency.

As I closed the door behind him, the emptiness of my four-room apartment engulfed me completely. I never felt so all alone, the silence was deafening and I was too proud to call family or friends for help. They had their own problems and did not need to be burdened with mine.

No, I was determined not to discuss this with anyone. This was my problem, and it was my responsibility to deal with it.

I had a huge personal decision to make. I was standing at that threshold where one crosses the line from being considered what society refers to as "normal" and enters the world of the "handicapped." Psychologically, it scared the hell out of me.

My anxiety was well founded I would soon discover. At first, the world of the handicapped was a complete unknown to me, one filled with uncertainty and apprehension so for the next few days I immersed myself in researching this intriguing domain. I went to the public library and desperately searched for evidence of historical attitudes towards the handicapped, striving to reach Edgar Allen Poe-like levels of legerdemain and understanding in the area of good and evil's battle for control of the human spirit. I took anything I found home with me to practice using the CCTV. My findings greatly disturbed me.

The history of the human race and its' attitudes towards those with handicaps is not an uplifting one. African-Americans, Jews, and the American Indian to name a few, are all groups that have lay claim to being the most victimized in human history, and while all of these claims have some validity, none have suffered more abuse than the handicapped as far as my findings concluded.

As far back as ancient Greece, circa 500 BC in the legendary city of Sparta for instance, they demonstrated some unsettling examples of how handicapped citizens were treated in the ancient world. This was a period in history I had always been fascinated with, seeing that much of present day "Western Civilization" can be traced back to Greek influences. Historical Icons like Socrates and Plato called this nation their home. The inhabitants of Sparta, one of many Greek "city-states" were known as some of the fiercest warriors in history. I had fantasized as a boy what it must have been like to be there at the pass at Thermopylae. King Leonidas and his 300 Spartans fought gallantly to hold off the invasion of King Xerxes' much larger Persian army. They had fought and died to the last man in a valiant attempt to give the other Greek city-states more time to shore up their defenses.

Then I also learned how the Spartans used to take deformed and handicapped children to a "place of rejection" as it was called, a deep ravine where the poor souls, completely ostracized by their own families and deemed useless by society, were cast down on the rocks to die. I admired the Spartans for their courage and tenacity in battle, their disciplined way of life and their undying devotion to their traditions and their ancestors, but this attribute tainted their image in my eyes. I was forced to tweak my perceptions of the Spartans ever so slightly so that now my view is, "the 300 Spartans got what they deserved, the bastards!"

During medieval Europe, people with mental retardation were thought to be possessed by evil spirits and were routinely tortured in misguided attempts to exorcise their demons. What utter barbarity!

For centuries, Christianity, my own religion, has espoused a belief in a connection between Satan and being disabled. Parallels were drawn between the afflicted individual's own sins or the sins of his ancestors and the consequences of having to endure his/her particular malady. In other words, if you were born blind, you or your ancestors must have done something sinful so you deserved it.

More recently, we had Hitler's "final solution", an attempt to exterminate the Jews who he viewed as inferior, but many people remain unaware to this day of the much less publicized fact that Hitler's henchman began eliminating handicapped and disabled people before turning their hatred towards the Jews.

During those same decades of the 1930's and 1940's, countries in Scandinavia were heavily engaged in "selective breeding", attempts to purify their populations and breed away deformities and abnormalities. The term for it is eugenics. They wanted to rid their societies of handicapped people altogether. These efforts were government-sponsored mind you and that was a mere 60 years ago.

You should not need any help here drawing your own conclusions. For centuries, the message has been clear and simple. If you are handicapped, society does not want you, and does not want to have to deal with you.

Since the dawn of recorded history, people with handicaps have been treated as inferior, even sub-human in some cultures, and in many cases, they were ostracized as unwanted drains on society. The ancient Nomad tribes had a history of leaving their disabled fellow tribesman behind to die when they packed up and migrated from place to place. Gee thanks Attila. These prejudices are deeply ingrained in the human psyche and it was not until the

1800's that more enlightened members of various countries began to attempt to deal with them as people in need of help. Asylums were the solution some luminaries concocted to medically assist and house the mentally ill and terribly handicapped and while they were no doubt very well intentioned, the end results were downright horrifying in some cases. Many of these asylums were poorly staffed and inadequately supervised. In far too many instances, patients were abused far worse than they would have been if left in the care of their families.

It was not until the past century that the greatest strides have been made, a period in which the emphasis was shifted away from the disabled being viewed as a "welfare" issue and more as a "civil rights" issue.

This is precisely why I consider myself very fortunate indeed to have been born in the United States in this century. There is no other nation on Earth that demonstrates more compassion towards people with disabilities than right here in the U. S. of A. There are still many places on this planet where disabled people are being treated horribly. If this were the year 546 AD for example, I would probably find myself relegated to wandering the streets in tattered rags, holding a cup in my hand and begging for my very existence. Survival rates for people with disabilities over the centuries have not been very encouraging.

The more I researched, the more apprehensive I became about the future that lay ahead. I had grown quite comfortable in the world of the "sighted" and was filled with dread at the thought of having to leave it behind. This is not meant to give the mistaken impression that my personal views towards people with handicaps is in any way shape or form consistent with the above findings. To the contrary. My siblings and I were raised by two very compassionate and caring Christian parents who taught us that showing respect for others and displaying compassion towards our fellow humans, regardless of their circumstances, was essential to a healthy existence. I had always found most people I encountered, particularly my close friends to be caring, compassionate and kindhearted human beings.

My anxiety was more the result of knowing in my heart that while humanity as a whole has made great strides in its' attitudes and treatment of the disabled over the centuries, much still needs to be done, and given the choice, I do not know anyone who would choose being handicapped over not being handicapped. Not that I had such a choice any longer.

I had two paths waiting before me. Path number one led back to Kemper, where I could fight this, work with the CCTV, try to keep up and struggle to produce at a level where the impact on my co-workers would be as little as possible. I could endure the daily scrutiny of being viewed as "different" from everyone else in the office and try to deal with the tremendous stress that would undoubtedly ensue from this course of action. Kemper had apparently never been faced with anything like this and to my knowledge did not employ any legally or totally blind people as adjusters in Massachusetts. Dealing with this situation would be a first for them as much as it was for me.

The aforementioned path was a noble one, but it was the most difficult choice by far. Path number two led to the murky previously unexplored region known as disability. I had long-term disability coverage and would have absolutely no difficulty being approved for benefits, especially with a world-renowned doctor on my side who possessed the kinds of credentials Dr. Berson did. Harvard Medical School, Mass. Eye and Ear Infirmary, they do not come any more prestigious than that. There would be no one to stare at me with my CCTV, no stress trying to keep up and constantly worrying about what others were thinking if it turned out I was not pulling my weight. It was the seemingly safe, easy way out. Stay home in the privacy and seclusion of my apartment where I could deal with going blind on my terms.

Like a true coward, I took the easy way out. I was emotionally devastated and at the lowest point in my life, even lower than when I had been rejected at Fort Knox. I called Kemper's human resources department and informed the company nurse that the CCTV would not be sufficient. I told her there was nothing currently available that would allow me to do a job that was as "reading intensive" as claims handling was, and the nature of my disease meant that my vision would continue to regress. I added that there simply was no treatment and no cure, all of which was true to one degree or another.

By the following week, the disability claim had been submitted, Dr. Berson had filed the necessary reports outlining the results of his tests along with the prognosis involved, and I found myself sitting at home wallowing in self pity. I was now not only handicapped, but officially classified "disabled" as well. Vision loss and all its devastation had reached full force now and had delivered a knockout punch that I never even saw coming. At least at Fort Knox I was prohibited from pursuing a course of action before I became too deeply involved. This time, I had been an adjuster for 3 years and had established myself in a very promising career. That is what made it so much more painful to accept. This encounter had left me gasping for air. Moreover, something told me this hereditary demon was not through with me yet.

My brothers were not faring any better than I was. We were all becoming punch drunk from having to adjust to the month-to-month changes occurring in our visual acuity. I found myself becoming retrospective and introspective at the same time. It seems as though it is during moments of great adversity that we tend to reflect back on our lives in a desperate search for answers. Unfortunately, the older we get the more complex the riddle becomes. Where had the years gone? How had it come to this? It seemed like only yesterday that my brothers and I were absorbed in youthful play and floating through a world of wondrous childhood adventures. How could so much innocence and promise morph into a situation where we felt our selves being dragged into a room that we did not want to enter? In my mind, I envisioned it as a dark, lonely room with no exits. The uncertainty of it all was suffocating and I felt ashamed that I had no idea where to turn.

Chapter Eight- So Many Losses

Open any history book at any library and browse through its pages. You will most likely see some very great names of those who have accomplished great deeds. Napoleon, Caesar, Alexander, George Washington, and Teddy Roosevelt to name just a few. These men never met one another but they all had one very important human characteristic in common and that was confidence. Confidence and self-esteem are absolutely essential to a successful and fulfilling life, of that I am certain. These great figures in history would never have accomplished their collective memorable deeds without a healthy supply of this precious commodity at their disposal.

My confidence was just as important to me as it was to any of the aforementioned icons of human history, and at that moment my strength levels were beginning to show so many holes I was starting to feel like a piece of finely aged Swiss cheese.

I was still teaching and judging marching bands and drum corps at that time, and I was able to keep my "disability" status a secret from most of my peers. If it had not been for drum corps to fall back on and occupy my mind, I might have lost my sanity completely.

Many of the competitions I was hired to judge along with the Diplomat performances I was required to attend took place in cities that were many miles away. My ability to operate an automobile was now being severely compromised. Pedestrians and small animals everywhere were circulating petitions to have me removed from the roadways permanently. If fire hydrants, trees, and chain link fences could speak, they would have joined the conspiracy as well. The voice of reason inside my head that was once a mere whisper had now reached thunderous levels and I could not ignore it any longer. I had another extremely thorny and life changing decision to make, and it would be far and away the most difficult one of all.

If I continued driving, I risked injury to other life forms and inanimate objects alike. I could try to limit my driving to daylight hours only since my night vision was deteriorating badly but I was only fooling myself. It would be terribly irresponsible of me to wait for the inevitable tragedy to occur to decide that it was time to give up the keys. I knew this would be even more gut wrenching than losing my job. In a mobile society such as ours where cars are an integral part of our daily lives, not being able to drive any longer was going to wreak havoc upon my social life. Our cars empower us, and they make a pronounced statement about whom we are. They give us the ability to go wherever we want to go, whenever we want to go there, and to the male members of society, cars are downright vital, even more so than they are to members of the female gender in my humble opinion. In the fun-loving world of dating, there are few things more humiliating and difficult to overcome than asking a woman for a date, then following it up with, "Oh, by the way, I don't drive and don't have a car. Can you pick me up around 8?" At that point the voluptuous woman you have been adoring from a distance trying to muster the courage to invite to dinner pushes the jettison button. Before you know it, you find yourself spiraling down the proverbial garbage chute that leads to the dreaded purgatory of rejected suitors. You are done. You are in the archives of hopeless wannabes.

I loved driving and I really liked my car, and above all, I cherished my independence. It gave me the ability to hop in my car and go anywhere any time day or night. My conscience kept telling me I had to do the right thing here though, the choice was inescapable. Therefore, I listened to the voice of reason screaming inside my head and as soon as I took what I thought was the honorable path and made the decision to relinquish the keys, I became acutely aware that every other commercial flashing before me on the boob tube was a car commercial. I began to detest them more and more with every passing day. It was as though vision loss was taunting me from inside the television set with chorus after chorus of "See the pretty car? Ha! Ha! You can't have one!" Thank God for remote controls. I cannot get to the "change channel" button fast enough. It is a never-ending battle between my TV and me because car advertisements are downright ubiquitous nowadays.

It was nothing short of agonizing but I sold my 1980 red Chevy Monza that I owned at the time to a friend. While I was still trying to endure the trauma of being pushed out of the "non-handicapped" world into the realm of the "handicapped", now I was also going to have to contend with being banished from the world of "motorists" and relegated to that so-often-victimized domain of the lowly "pedestrian."

There is something truly primal about the relationship between auto-drivers and streetwalkers. Since the dawn of recorded human history, the strong among us have victimized the weak. It is an indisputable fact. There is nothing ancient about it. There are some misguided souls among us, who actually believe that today's earthly inhabitants have evolved beyond these primitive instincts. They are in serious need of correction.

Therefore, I submit that as recently as 60 years ago the Germans were exterminating the Jews because they saw themselves as superior. At the same time on the other side of the world, the Japanese were raping and pillaging the Chinese for the same reason. What does all this have to do with driving a car? It demonstrates how most humans react when put in an advantageous position over another human. More often than not, we will exploit it, and the average driver with 2-3,000 pounds of cold-hard steel under their butt is not going to let some puny pedestrian get the better of him in most cases.

After just a short time of existing in this strange new world and navigating my way around the streets of my home city on foot, I was left with the philosophical impression that everyone should have the opportunity to experience being a pedestrian at least once. Might I be so bold as to suggest that the next time it rains, leave your keys at home and walk to your next destination. It might give you a greater appreciation for what pedestrians go through. Sometimes it seems, motorists conduct themselves as if they receive bonus points for every near miss with a defenseless pedestrian who is just trying to cross the street. You would think they received super bonus points for speeding through puddles and drenching unsuspecting streetwalkers.

As further proof of the divide that exists between the two groups, all one need do is examine pop culture. During the 1990's, some sadistic software engineer came up with a video game called "Carmageddon" where the player controls his own virtual automobile. The object of the game is to drive around town purposely running over and otherwise obliterating pedestrians for which the player receives points. You must admit, it just does not get any more primal than that, and it sold millions of copies, which simply reinforces my contention that we remain a very primitive species.

Driving is really about freedom and independence. Vision loss I soon discovered, forces us to give up our independence and we often find ourselves totally relying on others to get around. I soon found myself at parties, in parking lots after contests and sitting through some God-awful movies merely because I had now lost the ability to leave at my choosing. I would now go home when the person who was nice enough to drive me there was ready to leave, and while I was eternally grateful to all the wonderful people in my life who were so forthcoming with offers of help, I would nonetheless begin to resent my inability to drive and come and go as I pleased. Like rust on the quarter panel of a 1981 Datsun, it began to eat away at me with ever-increasing intensity.

Cars are also a status symbol in today's society. A good friend of mine purchased a red Porsche and was immediately overwhelmed with the increasing amount of attention he received from female admirers. It is no myth. Without a car, we are like a cowboy without a horse, like a sheik without a camel, like a sailor without a ship, like a hermit crab without his shell. Woof, enough already.

One by one, the driving status of my brothers and I began toppling like dominoes. My brother Bert had given up the keys years earlier but he was fortunate in the fact that he had his wife Barbara to cart him around. It was every bit as difficult for him as it is for anyone to give up the keys forever but he was managing. Richard was stubbornly holding on and in his defense, it is not easy to make that final decision as to when is the right time to hang it up, but he unfortunately paid the price. A deer jumped out in front of his car while he was on his way to work at Norfolk Prison in Walpole where he was a corrections officer and in the ensuing collision between Nissan and Bambi, Bambi lost big time. That incident troubled him greatly for a long time and eventually, in 1986, he knew it was time to retire from his position behind the wheel. Even though he too was married by that time and had his wife Judy to assume the driving responsibilities, I noticed that his depression level increased dramatically.

John discovered it was time to find an alternate means of transportation when he was driving home from work at the Ritz Carlton one night. As he approached a tunnel entrance on Route 99 leading from Charlestown to Everett, he failed to see a manned police car, which was parked sideways blocking the entrance to the tunnel. In John's defense, he insists the car had no flashing lights on but it didn't matter. John broadsided him knocking the startled officer unconscious. He eventually came to, and was fortunate to escape serious injury. John on the other hand received a hefty citation and had to appear in court.

David, like me, did not wait for such jarring occurrences to decide it might be a good idea to relieve the world of one more dangerous driver. Seemingly, in the wink of an eye, only Stephen was left as the one among us able to commandeer an automobile. We were beginning to feel like a bunch of hapless invalids. My mind remained mired in a depressive whirlpool of unanswerable questions.

Things were not supposed to turn out this way, I kept thinking to myself. This was not the way life was supposed to be and we must have done something terribly awful to cause the good Lord to become so miffed at us.

     I was not prepared for the isolation that would accompany my decision to quit driving. The transition was sobering to say the least and I could not bring myself to talk to anyone about it. If not for public transportation, I do not know what I would have done at the time because that was the only means of getting around that I could utilize. I absolutely loathed having to ask for help and I would do anything to avoid it. I detested feeling like a burden to others. Public transportation is greatly limited, and I slowly began to realize that giving up driving would affect me in more ways than I could possibly have imagined in the early going. It even dictated where I could live. I became completely dependant on buses, the subway, taxis, and any city or area that did not offer these services was simply no longer a viable option. This meant I might have to remain a city dweller for the rest of my days, which would not have been a problem in the seventies when the vast majority of my closest friends and family lived within five to ten miles of me. When the eighties arrived, I became acutely aware of the incredibly vast demographic changes that were occurring within the greater Boston area. One by one, my siblings and friends began moving further away from the inner cities, mostly to southern Maine and New Hampshire, which offered more desirable rural settings. The inability to drive a car would now have a major impact on my ability to go and visit them. I loved my family and friends but they were now moving beyond my reach.

     Nothing highlighted the transition from being able to drive my own personal car with all its comforts, privacy and climate control settings, than taking the subway on a hot and steamy July day. I found myself in the midst of other commuters packed like sardines into a dirty non air-conditioned train. My nose precariously poised just inches away from some of the worst smelling armpits on the planet. There is simply no experience on Earth that can match the euphoric bliss that one derives from wafting in the joy of humanity on a packed subway car.

There was no escaping the harsh reality of the situation. Unless the medical community came up with a miracle cure, life as I had known it and grown quite fond of would simply never be the same again. My cruisin' days were over.

Kemper was incredibly supportive and sympathetic in the early months of my disability, but after a year, they stopped calling and must have assumed I was on a permanent siesta. I was getting too comfortable relaxing at home, partying and teaching at night and getting a nice check in the mail every month. In addition, I was approved for Social Security Disability Income from the government, so I was making almost as much money not working, as I used to take home when I was putting in 40 hours a week. All of which was weakening my resolve and motivation to get off disability.

Over time, it began to take its toll however. It wasn't long before I realized that this was not a healthy existence. As human beings, we always seem to be at our best when we are challenged and faced with obstacles to overcome. While dealing with vision loss may have been more than everyday adversity, and in my estimation more like a full-fledged shit-storm, I was not satisfied with how I was conducting myself at all. Shame and guilt were starting to gnaw at me like hungry wolves with really big teeth.

By the grace of God, there were some bright spots from which I could draw strength. The Diplomats enjoyed their most successful season to date in the summer of 1983 finishing second in Division 2 at the DCI Nationals in Miami. Of course, if I ever run into the genius whose idea it was to hold the Nationals in Southern Florida I intend to pummel him severely. It was nearly 100 degrees in the shade and the humidity levels were downright unbearable and caused one to perspire rather profusely I can tell you.

We also swept through our local Eastern Mass. Circuit schedule undefeated and had actually won the US Open prelims in Toledo, Ohio before coming in second to a very good drum corps by the name of Florida Wave in the Finals. Our entire corps was on an emotional high all summer.

Relations between corps manager Tom Chopelas and the staff were headed straight for the crapper as the season progressed however. Tom wanted to have more say in the show programming which he had no experience in whatsoever. That is what he was paying the staff to do. We felt his job was to manage the corps, raise the money we needed through the operation of various fundraisers like the weekly corps bingos and then get us to where we were supposed to be. Nevertheless, personalities clashed and tempers continued to boil over all summer long. Prior to the Eastern Mass. finals at the end of the season, rumors began circulating throughout the local drum corps community that he intended to fire the entire staff. It was not long before the rumors reached the impressionable ears of the marching members. They were noticeably upset and responded with a very touching gesture. They took the field at Dilboy Stadium in Somerville for the last performance of the year and came through with their most spirited effort of the season. They dedicated the performance to the outgoing staff members and it was a very moving display of affection and appreciation. My mom was in the stands for that one and I was thrilled that she was able to witness a performance by one of the units I had worked with. The emotional level of the corps brought tears to her eyes.

The season ended and pink slips were issued but during the 4-week break period before the corps would regroup and begin working on the following years' program, I was informed by Tom that the percussion staff could stay on. Apparently, he had second thoughts about our part in the rampant bickering of the previous season. He apparently decided that either we were indispensable and it would be a mistake to let us go or, there was just no one else available. For whatever reason, after discussing it with my capable assistant staff members Tyrone Parker, Art Fabrizio, Kevin Macdonald, and Dave Surface, I informed Tom that we would stay with the corps.

    I quickly discovered however that it just was not the same. I felt like a traitor to the other head instructors who were fired, drill instructor Ron Genest, brass instructor Don Mactaggert, and Doloris Zappala who worked with the color guard. It did not feel the same anymore and I felt like there was a dark cloud hanging over me so I made the difficult decision that I would resign. I would only do so however under the condition that my number one assistant Tyrone Parker would be allowed to take over the reigns. Ty was a former snare drummer with the 27th Lancers and was not only an accomplished player but he was a talented instructor as well. Tom Chopelas agreed and at the year-end banquet in October, the former staff was there and I could at least look them in the eye with a clear conscience. I am not sure why but it just felt like the right thing to do. Ronnie, Donnie and I had taught together for 6 years and loyalty has to count for something. Between marching, teaching and judging, I had been heavily involved in the activity that I loved so deeply for 18 straight years. While I knew I would miss it terribly, maybe now was as good a time as any to take a breather. The previous summer had turned out to be a grueling one indeed. The corps had spent three practice-filled weeks on tour and it was exhausting to say the least. Of all the jobs I have had throughout my lifetime, teaching drum corps, while one of the most rewarding, was also the most taxing. Coupled with the emotional strains of navigating my way through the increasing obstacle course vision loss was laying out in front of me, I was completely drained emotionally and needed to somehow re-charge my batteries.

    It may not have been the most judicious time to make such a decision. The number of active drum corps in Massachusetts was shrinking rapidly due to decreasing membership and financial demands that forced many corps to go under. If I did attempt to make a comeback however, there was always the high school band scene. I continued judging sparingly in an effort to stay connected at least minimally in the event I wanted to return to teaching.

Oh, how fleeting that connection turned out to be. In November of 1983, I was judging a high school band show in Lowell, Massachusetts. I was assigned to adjudicate General Effect that night because the other percussion judge only had his field-judging card so someone had botched their hiring assignment. I had not judged General Effect for some time at my own request. I knew it would lead to difficulties eventually because I was now relegated to relying on my sense of hearing and not my sense of sight. The art of judging within the marching musical activity involves evaluating the quality of the sounds you hear but much of it has visual applications as well. While I could still function at a reasonable degree when at ground level, which allowed me to be within ten to twenty feet of the percussion section at all times, judging General Effect meant I would be up in the press box and more than 100 feet from the bands. That spelled trouble.

As the contest progressed through about 21 bands in four different classes, I felt reasonably comfortable in my performance and with the numbers I had assigned to each band. However, I was still a bit uneasy. Lowell stadium is one of the larger stadiums in Massachusetts and the GE box was pretty high, so I experienced some difficulties visually zeroing in on where the drum line was much of the time. It was a night show and the stadium lights were grossly inadequate, or so it seemed to me. I was forced to rely solely on my sense of hearing. I could not even tell what color uniforms each of the bands were wearing. In the final analysis, this would not represent an insurmountable problem because the score sheet placed more emphasis on musicality and brass to percussion coordination than it did on visual content.

After the competition concluded and the scores were announced, there was usually a "critique" session, which was an opportunity for band instructors to talk with the judges. We would go over the scores and band directors could pick our brains for any help we could give them to improve their unit's performance for the next contest.

    As the critique began winding down, my dear friend Michael Goff who was an instructor for one of the bands competing that night and a fellow marching member of the Reveries years earlier, walked up beside me as I was conversing with the drum instructor from Gloucester High School. I shook the man's hand and told him what a great job he had done and to keep up the good work. I had given them the highest score in their class. I turned towards Michael. "Is it time to exit stage left or what?" I asked. "Do you believe they want us to judge 21 friggin' bands and then hang around for a critique too? My appendages are killing me."

    "Let's git the hell outahere," he said, every bit as anxious as I was to blow this clambake. The show had lasted over five hours, most of which I spent flapping my gums and my jaw muscles had just about had it.

    Unfortunately, the band Gods were not through with me just yet.

    "Excuse me," came a voice from over my shoulder, and it was not a happy one.

    Mikey and I turned around and I fully expected a beef. As in all contests, there were winners and losers. Mostly losers since there can be only one winner per division and oftentimes, the also-rans were not happy about their positions. In this case, it was the drum instructor from Hull High School. I had given them the second highest score in their class behind Gloucester.

    I was exhausted but this instructor deserved just as much of my time as anyone else so I grudgingly decided to engage him. In the words of the late great Hunter Thompson, "After all, we are professionals."

    "What can I do for you?" I asked.

He took up a position about two feet in front of me and I could tell he wasn't smiling so I braced myself for a confrontation.

"I just wanted to ask you a few questions here," he said, his tone softening. He handed me the score sheet that I had written up in the box with the breakdown of the various captions that make up the bands total general effect score, such as co-ordination between brass and percussion, staging, musicianship, etc.

"Hull, huh?" I said looking over the sheet to refresh my memory. First of all, he probably thought it a bit weird that of all the judges, I was the only one using a heavy black magic marker instead of a pen. I had to or I would not be able to see what I was writing. Using any visual aides during judging assignments was not only impractical, but would be a dead giveaway that anyone who had to use such devices had no business being up in the GE box to begin with. By continuing to judge, my intent was not to deceive anyone. I was merely trying to desperately hold on to something I had worked very hard to achieve and loved to do.

After several grueling hours of judging 21 bands, no single performance stuck out in my mind at that point and everything was just a blur, but after a brief moment, I did remember them slightly. They were respectable but there was no way they deserved to beat Gloucester so I was not sure what his beef was. I had them above four other bands so it was not as if they came in last, and I was only one of seven judges whose numbers all contributed to his band's final placement.

Michael was right next to me and stood by patiently out of respect for both the instructor and myself. Michael was a marching and maneuvering instructor so this conversation would only be of minimal interest to him anyway.

"I don't have a problem with your number," the man from Hull began in a non-provocative tone. Well, I

127

thought to myself, at least we are on the same page here. That is a good start to any meaningful relationship.

"But I listened to your entire judging tape and you never once mentioned the visuals we do during our show. I know Gloucester has a better drum line than we do but I think we deserve some credit for being more visual than they are. Other judges have given us credit for that."

I looked into his eyes and felt like the biggest jackass on the planet. He really looked hurt and yet, he was being totally respectful towards me when he had every right to tear into me like a ravenous grizzly bear devouring a succulent slab of salmon.

I was speechless for a moment, which I could only hope he did not perceive as aloofness. I did not see any visuals. I never even thought to look for any visuals. These were high school bands, not drum corps. High school bands were minor league stuff and intricate stick visuals were still light years away for these people, or so I thought. I was obviously in error.

I had to gather my thoughts quickly. I was the judge damn it and I did not want to sound like a witless fool in front of this man. However, I could not fool Michael. He heard the entire exchange and knew I was in trouble, and like a true friend, he tried to come to my defense.

"Well, if you don't mind me adding my two cents worth," he interjected, "some judges place more emphasis on musicality and some on the visual aspects. Isn't that right Mikey?"

I looked at him and back at the man who was still standing there expecting and deserving an explanation. I was not going to bullshit anyone. I had been expecting this moment to come and had been wrestling with it long enough.

"Thanks Mikey, I appreciate the support," I said putting my hand on his shoulder. "But this man deserves the truth. The truth is I have perfect hearing and my hearing told me that Gloucester deserved a higher score than Hull did. No amount of visual content is going to change that because it won't be enough to overcome the difference between the two units in musicality. Musicianship garners more points under the present scoring system than visuals do. However, my vision is failing and the reason I did not comment on the visuals you were doing in regards to sticking and special effects was due to the fact that I did not see them well enough, plain and simple. The other percussion judge who was assigned to work today does not have his General Effect card so I was forced up to the GE box from down on the field where I am more comfortable. I apologize for that and I would encourage you to continue enhancing the visual aspect of your performance. You should also spend equal if not more time on improving the musicianship of the players if you want to take it up a notch and have any hope of catching bands like Gloucester. Best of luck to you and please convey my best wishes to your kids. Tell them I did enjoy their performance." I shook the man's hand and turned to walk away.

I detected by his expression that he appreciated my candor and maybe even felt sorry to have brought it up in the first place. As I turned to Mike or Miguel as we used to refer to one another affectionately, I could tell that he really did not know how to react. He knew I was struggling with my feelings, and in my mind, I had started to grow numb to the never-ending obstacles vision loss was constantly placing in my path. It seemed like every day something else that I used to enjoy doing was being ripped away from me. This was just another precious commodity that was being stolen away by this despicable unseen abomination.

"I am done Miguel. That is it; you have just witnessed the end of my judging career. That man just pointed out the obvious. I have no business being up there anymore."

"Come on Miguel, maybe you could confine yourself to field judging only, that way you are up close and personal with the players," he said encouragingly.

"No Miguel. No matter where I am positioned there are going to be things that I am going to miss because of these damn blind spots and it could spell the difference between winning and losing to two drum lines that may be in a tight battle, and my vision just keeps getting worse and worse. I have to suck it up and admit it to myself that it is time to hang it up out of fairness to these kids. Can you imagine the uproar if any one of these band directors found out one of the judges was legally blind? There would be hell to pay."

It was a long ride home that night and Miguel tried his best to cheer me up with some vintage tunes from the rock group "Chicago" in the tape player and a cold Miller Lite. He and I had grown very close over the years and had shared many memorable experiences during our marching days and that ride home reminded me that I was very blessed indeed to have friends like him.

It was not just a band contest that ended that night. It seemed like everything had come full circle. Vision loss had won the contest and had taken it all. In the span of just two years, it had robbed me of my insurance career, my judging career, and the keys to my car, which controlled my very independence. The thread I had been desperately holding onto that was my life up to that point had slipped from my fingers. I had lost the battle and when I got home that night, there was not an album in my entire collection that was going to offer any solace. I didn't even turn on the lights in my apartment. I just sat there in total darkness, trembling at the thought of what would come next. How much more can my hidden enemy take, how many more losses would have to be endured?

Chapter Nine - Hitting rock bottom and starting to dig

The walls had come tumbling down and for two long years, I wallowed in limbo. Staying at home on disability was bringing me to new depths of depression that I had never experienced before. My self-respect hit rock bottom and the old adage "idle hands are the devils' workshop" began to take on new meaning.

Cocaine use in the early 1980's had swept the country and I was not spared from this epidemic. It started in Hollywood, where most of our nation's ills seem to originate, and it swept across the nation, eventually invading every walk of life including high profile institutions as Wall Street and Washington, DC. It did not matter what your social standing was, whether you were a lawyer, doctor, stockbroker, or janitor, millions fell victim to the temptation offered up by the Colombian drug cartels. Collectively, our entire nation fell victim to its' lurid lure. By 1984, I was a social cocaine user but fortunately did not become so addicted that it controlled my life. I was a "weekend partyer" and chased the dragon only when in the company of others who used it socially as well. My apartment was known as party central and on any given Friday or Saturday night there would be anywhere from 10-20 people hanging out and having a good time while grooving to the sounds of Steely Dan, the Eagles, and Tom Waits. They were all full time workers, most in professions and careers of their own and not deadbeats by any means. In fact, I was the only one not working at the time and it bothered me to no end. The others were no different from millions of other Americans just trying to unwind after another long week of toil and strife at the office.

Snorting "coke" made me feel better temporarily. For a short time, it masked the world of chaos that vision loss was creating in my life. I knew it was not good for me, but I am a human being, and no one will ever accuse us of being the most intelligent life forms in the galaxy. We smoke cigarettes and pot, we drink alcohol, we take all kinds of prescription and non-prescription drugs, we bungee jump, we hang glide. Some are even brash enough to try and climb Mount Everest just so they can say they did it, ignoring the fact that it has already been done a hundred times before. All of which makes us who we are. We all think we are immortal so we ignore the risks.

By the July 4th weekend of 1985 however, I found myself recovering from two days of partying. I spent Sunday night on the couch with abdominal pains that were most likely caused by whatever was used to "cut" the cocaine I had been snorting for the past two nights. That is the scary thing about illegal drugs and the biggest reason why people with any intelligence at all should refrain from using them. Not only are they just plain unhealthy but they are extremely dangerous as well, because you can never really trust where they came from or what harmful elements they may contain.

I got up off the couch that Monday morning, walked into the bathroom feeling like an SOS pad was working its way through my entire system, and I looked at my reflection in the mirror. I did not like what I saw.

I wasn't working, I wasn't teaching, I wasn't judging, I could not drive anymore and was spending too much time confined to that four-room apartment and I was going absolutely nowhere. Although they did not say it, I knew I was losing the respect of my friends, my family and the one that hurt most of all, my mom. Out of 13 children, I was the one she had the highest expectations for and I felt like I was failing her miserably. She never actually came right out and said it, but I knew she was deeply disappointed in me.

As I looked in the mirror at the tired, forlorn look on my face, I muttered, "You have got to get your shit together!" It was as if an alarm went off inside my head as I stood there, hunched over in pain, staring at the worthless human being I had become. I was appalled at the reflection that was staring back at me and there was no way in hell I was going to let this go on any further because if it did, there was only one way it could end. Celtics' draft choice Lenny Bias regretfully found that out a few years later when he died after an evening of partying with the white powder. I was utterly disgusted with myself. I was at the lowest point of my entire life and it was now or never. The road I was on only led to one place and that was final tragedy.

I kept telling myself, you are better than this. "Fight goddamit!" my conscience screamed in my mind, "Look at what you are doing to yourself!" If ever I had an epiphany in my life, it was at that very moment. Something snapped, the forces of good inside me found new strength and somehow vanquished the demons that had taken control of my life. This was the turning point and I felt as though God was throwing me a life preserver and if I did not grab it then, I would not get a second chance.

I decided then and there that I would never do so much as a granular of any narcotic substance again and that I was not going to allow vision loss to ruin the rest of my life. It was time to dig deep, and draw on every ounce of strength I could find and pull myself out of this terrible abyss I had fallen into. This was *my* problem and *my* responsibility, and it was high time to grab a hold of whatever self-respect and dignity I had left and open up a can of major league whoop ass!

I made a pot of coffee, gathered every once of courage I had and picked up the telephone to call Kemper's main office in Quincy, Mass. My hands were trembling slightly from nerves and the residual garbage running through my system. I made a mental note that if cocaine king Pablo Escobar and I ever crossed paths, he was a dead man. The Zanti Misfits were too good for the likes of him.

A receptionist answered at the other end, "Good morning, Kemper Insurance."

"Yes…ah… John Mooney please," I answered. John was the head man for Kemper's New England region and was someone I had met a few times during my three and a half years with the company so I hoped he would remember me. I must have been off my rocker asking for the top dog. He was equivalent to the vice president of the company and people did not usually just pick up the phone and ask for him unless you were someone else on his level.

"Can I tell him who is calling?" she asked.

"It's Mike Merrett," I answered with as much conviction as I could muster. I used to feel at least a small degree of pride when introducing myself to others but that seemed so many moons ago.

"Thank you, one moment please," and she put me on hold. My heart was pounding in my chest and I almost hung up the phone. He will never pick up. He is John Mooney for Christ's sake. What was I thinking? I should have asked for human resources or someone in a lesser position. How completely arrogant to think that a man in his position would give a damn about me. I had been on disability for over 2 years, but something inside me kept telling me that if I was going to do this, talk to someone in authority. One thing I knew John would not do if he did pick up the phone was give me a run around.

I heard someone pick up at the other end.

"This is John Mooney," he said and I recognized the voice right away.

I took a deep breath. "Hello John, this is Mike Merrett," I said, trying to contain my nervousness. I could hardly hold the phone to my ear. "I'm not sure if you remember me or not…" I stammered.

"Don't be silly Mike, of course I remember you," he said cheerfully. "How are you doing?"

I breathed a huge sigh of relief. His tone was one of understanding and genuine concern. Now I remembered why it was Mr. Mooney that I called of all the previous co-workers I had known with the company. I remembered him as being a man of class and substance.

"I could be doing better John," I began with a tad more emphasis. "It was very difficult for me to leave my position with the company. I enjoyed working for Kemper very much and considered them an outstanding group of

134

people. I only left because I was afraid I would not be able to pull my weight. But I never gave myself a chance to find that out. I was just wondering if there were any claims positions available as I would like to try and come back to work?" I felt like I was groveling but I did not care. It was time to swallow what little pride I had left and get off my duff before it was too late. I was desperate and even though I did not have much hope that this phone call would bear any fruit, I had to at least make the attempt.

"Sure, why don't you come on in and we'll see what we can do," he said, almost as if we were talking about little more than having lunch together.

In my mind though, it did not quite register. That was too easy, I thought. I had become so accustomed to everything in life being such an ordeal lately I was unwilling to accept the possibility that something good might be happening for a change. I felt completely undeserving and was riddled with depression, guilt and shame.

"Really?" I responded. "I wasn't sure if it was alright to call you and I didn't want to impose but I really miss working." I was blabbering now and unnecessarily. He had already offered me the opportunity but my conscience was still racked with anxiety.

"It's no problem Mike, really. You had a good reputation when you were here and it is the least we can do to try to help you get back with us. When you come in just see Melissa in human resources and she'll discuss our options."

It was just a phone call, but it felt as though Apollo himself had just lifted an enormous weight from my shoulders. The Quincy office was accessible by public transportation so the travel gods were smiling on me as well.

"Thanks John," I said. "You don't know how much I appreciate this."

"No need to thank me Mike. We'll see you soon," and he hung up.

135

On some level it slowly hit me that while I was busy digging a huge hole and beating myself up over not handling my condition very well, there were actually people out there who thought more highly of me than I thought of myself at that moment in time.

My head was tingling as I drank my coffee but it tasted better than it had in many months. My spirit was soaring at the thought of putting an end to this painful purgatory I had imprisoned myself in for the past few years. I thanked God above because that phone call probably saved my life. I never touched a narcotic again and I was back to work sitting behind a desk with my CCTV in the Quincy claims office 2 weeks later.

There were monumental residual benefits that followed. I would soon overcome my fears of what others would say and what others would think. Speaking with Melissa, the nurse in human resources helped me to understand that I had it all wrong. I was always fearful that my fellow adjusters would resent me if I could not function as fast as they could but she opened my eyes to the fact that they are imperfect people too, but good people nonetheless.

"How do you know they aren't looking at you and thanking God that it isn't happening to them?" she told me during our first encounter. "Everyone has difficulties to deal with in life. We have people with this company who have all kinds of problems. We have women who have to break from their jobs for maternity leave, some of our employees have required assistance dealing with alcohol abuse. You are not alone Mike, you need to understand that. This is a big company and we deal with all kinds of issues. Don't put all this pressure on yourself that you are going to let us down. The company can handle a visually impaired employee working for us, trust me."

Her words of encouragement proved invaluable. Because she helped me realize that the eyes of the entire company would not be on me. When I finally arrived for work that first day, I was nervous as hell, I was wearing odd colored socks and did not know it, and I had no idea what to expect but the building did not collapse and everyone did not stand around gawking at me. Even the sight of Bob Mcgilvary setting up a CCTV on my desk only aroused mild curiosity. Melissa was right. The other employees had their own concerns in their lives and with their jobs and were far too preoccupied to be worrying about what I was doing. They were strangers at first but soon became good friends and I quickly came to realize that even though they could read and process claims faster than I could, I could operate at a sufficient rate that the company was perfectly willing to accept. The phobia I had created in my mind had no basis in fact as it turned out and I learned for the first time in my life that we can sometimes become our own worst enemy. I was the one who had placed the imaginary Sword of Damocles over my head, not the company and only I could make it go away.

The euphoria I felt was almost too much for words. My first phone call was to my mom and I could sense the relief she felt after being increasingly concerned about my state of mind the past few years. It did my heart good to put her fears at rest. With 13 children and the strain of knowing her five sons may lose their sight someday, I did not want to exacerbate her suffering in any way. No mother should have to endure watching one son deal with vision loss never mind five.

For the first time in many months the dark clouds hovering above me had given way to some much-needed sunshine. Returning to the ranks of the living had many residual effects. During my 18 years of marching, teaching and judging within the drum corps activity, I was a bit of a "black sheep" in my family. I had so many social contacts and events to attend I was rarely home and saw my family mostly at holidays and special events. By 1985, I was no longer involved with drum corps so I was able to spend more time with my family. It was time to make up for all those precious moments lost, so I took full advantage of the situation.

Later that summer I took my mom and dad to Disneyworld for their first time and they absolutely loved the Magic Land of Mickey and Minnie et al. We stayed in Kissimmee with Anne and Al Graves who were dear friends of my mom. This was a blessing on another level as well because it gave my mom and Anne a chance to spend some quality time together as Anne suddenly died of cancer a few years later. She was a fabulous human being and went out of her way to make our visit as comfortable and enjoyable as she could for which I will never forget her.

In September of 1986, my sister Linda and I took mom and dad to Ireland for nine days. My mom absolutely loved Ireland and everything about it. She was a bit of an aficionado when it came to Irish folklore, music and literature and was a big fan of the author James Joyce. We visited the Blarney Stone, which I would NOT kiss under any circumstances. (Too many germs.) We visited Bunratty Castle and shopped in the stores in downtown Dublin. Ireland had an enchanting, down-home feel to it that had a genuine lasting effect on all of us. My personal high point on the trip was staring out over the Atlantic Ocean from the very top of the Cliffs of Moore. That view was quite impressive as was the sight of the sun setting on Galway bay. Galway was the last leg of the tour before we headed home and we were all treated to a full course dinner in one of its historical castles. All in all, the Emerald Isle was a difficult place to say goodbye to.

I also began to take the time to become more involved in how my brothers were contending with vision loss. Collectively, we rarely discussed it amongst ourselves. We were all in denial and found it too painful at times to sit down and openly express how it was devouring us inside.

Bert was still working in the vending program, which was governed by the Mass. Commission for the Blind. He was the vendor of record at the Sears location in Peabody, Mass. Most of the locations were in state and federal government buildings and Sears was the last of the "private sector" locations the state was involved with at that time. It was a small cafeteria and Bert took to it very well as it gave him the opportunity to be his own boss. The Commission may have administered the program, but once a vendor took over a location, he was pretty much the manager and acting owner of the business.

Richard was still employed as a correctional officer at Norfolk Prison in Walpole, a medium security facility that also had a small maximum-security section. Norfolk shared its back yard with Walpole prison, which was the largest facility in the state. He excelled in his position and was appointed a member of the prison's "tactical team" which was the unit called upon to respond to the most serious situations. However, his vision was deteriorating as well and walking amongst murderers and rapists without the ability to clearly see what was coming at him at all times was beginning to wear on his nerves and he knew he would not be able to keep his condition hidden from his superiors for long.

David was forced to give up his occupation as a truck driver and he and his wife Jane soon found themselves with two children, David Jr. and Sarah. He journeyed from job to job trying to stay one-step ahead of his failing vision but eventually he was forced to settle into the vending program as well.

John managed to remain in his career at the Ritz Carlton as he now relied on public transportation to get around. He married as well, and was enjoying life with his wife Angela. He was fortunate enough to take advantage of his financial situation and traveled extensively. They visited China, Rome, Greece, and Morocco just to name a few locations. I was glad for the two of them that they availed themselves of the opportunity to travel and see the world because he had no idea that unlike his four brothers who were dealing with just one disease, he would have a far more devastating condition to contend with in the not too distant future.

Stephen, the youngest of the Merrett boys was following a path very similar to mine, working many jobs when he was younger until he finally found the right fit. Now in his twenties, he still showed no signs of degenerative vision loss but that did not mean that in time, it would not pay him an unwanted visit. None of us had any way of knowing what the future would bring. He eventually worked his way into the cable and satellite communications industry and before long, he was managing an office for Williams Corporation, a fortune 500 company that specialized in communications. He once told me that it was our mom's teachings that had sustained him through the years. He fondly remembered her encouraging us that not only was learning fun, but the learning process never ends. No matter how old we become and no matter how much we think we know, there is still so much more to learn. There are always new areas of the human experience waiting to be explored. All of her children tried to absorb her wisdom and philosophy, which proved beneficial in so many ways. It was one of the greatest gifts she gave us. Instilling in us the desire to explore our world and to always keep an open mind.

For the most part, my brothers and I were all in the early stages of serious visual deterioration so we each dealt with it as best we could, doing everything possible to minimize the negative effects on our lives. However, RP is not something we could hold at bay for very long. Eventually, we feared it would reach a point where, like a storm waiting far out to sea, it would finally make landfall and if we were not prepared, the destruction it could cause might be devastating.

Together, we each made a commitment to be more open in the future and to meet and discuss ways in which we could help one another to deal with our ever-changing situations. Remaining in total denial, we all agreed, would accomplish nothing.

Along with reconnecting with my family, it was my close friends who sustained me during those troubled times. It is amazing how a little thing like working again can rejuvenate a person. During all those months of wasting away in my self-made state of limbo, my friends never bailed on me. Now I was like a kid in a candy shop and I just wanted to get out and absorb the whole world around me. I wanted to get involved in whatever they were doing.

It was all tied to one of the reactions I felt when I first learned my prognosis. I wanted to do and see as many things as I could while I could still navigate with some degree of safety. Unfortunately, I had been wallowing in self-pity and had lacked the ambition to act on that impulse. Returning to work helped cure me of this melancholy malaise. Now, I wanted to drink it all in like a man who had been wandering through the desert searching for that mythical oasis in an effort to quench his insatiable thirst. With the help of my friends, I took up skiing, white water rafting and even mountain climbing. My good friend Jumbo and I decided we would take a stab at New Hampshire's Mount Washington. It was something we had both talked about doing for years so on a clear, sunny, early October day, we began climbing the Amonoosock Trail which started out at the Cog Railway Station. The trail wound its way up to a rest area where there was an old log cabin called the "hut above the clouds", then the trail turned sharply to the north to the summit where there is a weather station, small gift shop, and a restaurant.

The Cog Railway is one of those old style locomotives that runs on coal. It provides its riders a picturesque view as it ascends slowly from the station to the top of the mountain. We had planned to take the train for the return once we reached the summit because I did not trust my eyes to climb back down again. Anyone who has ever climbed rocks can tell you climbing up is much easier than trying to find your footing climbing down.

Even with my failing visual acuity, the scenery was still absolutely breath taking as we traversed our way up towards the hut. The foliage was almost at peak and the various ravines and gorges we encountered presented a landscape that was truly humbling in its beauty and splendor. There were some tricky areas where my diminished vision prohibited me from climbing without some assistance from Jumbo. He would point out what lay immediately ahead but I could still see well enough to appreciate the panoramic view. It was so breathtaking it caused me to pause and reflect on how much of natures' awesome brilliance we shamefully take for granted in our daily lives.

We had begun our ascent around 10 AM and Mt. Washington can be climbed in a day. We stopped for a brief lunch of canned raviolis once we arrived at the hut, then we continued on and reached the top of the tree line shortly thereafter. That is the point where everything turns to rock. The mid-afternoon sun soon gave way to clouds and snow flurries. Mt. Washington features some of the worst weather conditions on the planet and as we progressed, we came across signs warning climbers to head back down if the weather looked ominous. There were at least six crosses along the way marking those who had not heeded the warning signs and had died on the mountain.

For me personally, turning around was simply not an option. I did not care what the weather was doing because climbing up the last 1000 feet seemed eminently more desirable than climbing back down the 3000 feet I had just completed. Mt. Washington is the highest peak in the Northeast United States at 6,223 feet but once we arrived at the Cog Railway station, we were already at an elevation of 1000-2000 feet.

As we struggled up the last 500 feet, the snow began falling more heavily and it was difficult to see more than ten to twenty feet in front of us. Jumbo did all the navigating at that point and even he was having some difficulty finding the yellow arrows that marked the trail to the top. My legs felt like cement by then and I had to stop every twenty feet or so to take a breather. I was ashamed to admit it but he was in better shape than I was.

As the autumn sun began to set and the snow began to accumulate, the mountain began to take on an eerie, desolate aura about it. The images of all those crosses we had passed along the way began to appear in my mind and for a moment, I felt as though we had stepped onto another planet. It was deathly silent, and it was like no place I had ever been before. However, it was not fear I was experiencing. I never felt like we were in any danger to speak of. After all, this was New Hampshire, not the Himalayas. If anything, it was more a feeling of exhilaration that I was standing on a patch of earth that probably had not been tread upon by many other people. In contrast to the crowded subways and office buildings I was accustomed to dealing with, I could only imagine what it must have been like for some of the great explorers like Lewis and Clark and Marco Polo. They ventured forth to parts unknown not knowing what to expect or whom they would meet. I bet they too felt as though they had the whole world all to themselves. It was a sensation that I will never forget.

As the sun disappeared over the horizon though, it felt as if it took the last ounces of my strength with it. Jumbo was about ten feet ahead of me and just when I thought I could not take another step, he turned and shouted down at me, "We're at the top! I can see the weather station!"

"Hallelujah brother!" I shouted up to him. As we stepped up onto the summit and looked out, we were exhausted, exhilarated and mildly disappointed at the same time. It took us a tad longer than we thought it would to reach the top and the sun had set. On a clear day, you can see for a hundred miles from up there and the view is reported to be spectacular.

Unfortunately, due to its well-known reputation for intense and erratic weather conditions, the top of Mt. Washington only sees the sun an average of once every six days. Even if the sun had not already set, we probably would not have been able to appreciate the view all that much. The summit was completely clouded over and it was snowing lightly. It did not put a damper on our feeling of accomplishment entirely though, so we walked around the large open area that was roughly a hundred yards across. We noticed that the exterior walls of the small weather station and restaurant were severely weather-beaten which was understandable. I had read somewhere that a wind was recorded up there on one occasion at 277 miles per hour. We made note of where the train was sitting for its descent down the mountain. Then, after checking out what little view there was from all sides, we entered the restaurant to grab some chow before heading back down. We both ordered some clam chowder and as we sat at a table, we gave each other a high five and prepared to enjoy a well-deserved victory snack.

Neither of us had bothered to check the schedule for the Cog Railway of course. As I prepared to devour my clam chowder, I heard a voice over the loudspeaker.

"Last train leaving in two minutes, this will be the last train down the mountain leaving in two minutes!"

"Oh shit!" we exclaimed, almost in perfect unison…which shouldn't surprise anyone since we were both in fact, rudimental snare drummers.

It was 4:30 PM and the sun had already set. Climbing down was completely out of the question in nasty weather and total darkness, and there were no sleeping quarters that we knew of, so we slammed covers on our bowls of chowder and ran out the door. We just barely made the train as it began its slow, arduous descent down the mountain.

Climbing Mt. Washington was the experience of a lifetime but I was beginning to grow increasingly aware that I was slipping into a realm I had previously been totally unfamiliar with. Every one of my friends was sighted, and things were happening that made me feel, for lack of a better word, detached from them. As Jumbo and I climbed, he would occasionally point out something he observed like a raccoon or chipmunk scurrying off to our right or left. The only problem being unless it was less than 10 feet away, I simply could not see it.

Three other friends joined Jumbo and I the next day back at our campsite. Chris Langlois, Tom Buckley and Mike Kelly were fellow instructors during my many years with the Malden organization. Tom and Chris had marched with the Ambassadors when we merged to form the Royal Marquis in 1979. When the corps split, they joined up with the Lancers and marched for two very successful campaigns. 27th finished second in 1980 and fourth in 1981 at the DCI Finals and the corps was also honored with an invite to do a performance at the 1980 Olympics in Lake Placid, New York. They were there for the U.S. hockey teams' historic 'Miracle" upset of the Russians.

We were camped at a state camping ground not far from the Bretton Woods Ski area and Mt. Washington. Most people do not go camping in New Hampshire's White Mountains in October because the temperatures usually start falling into the single digits at night but that was exactly why we chose that time of year. We could enjoy ourselves, be as loud as we wanted and not have to worry about who was around to complain of our presence.

One night the temperature dropped to 13 degrees so we built a roaring but well-contained fire and broke open a bottle of tequila. We were well aware that drinking alcohol thins the blood and was the worst thing we could do under frigid conditions but as I am so fond of saying, no one will ever accuse we humans of being the brightest lights in the cosmos.

Chris had brought along his battery-powered television set to catch Larry Bird and the Celtics playing the LA Lakers in an early season game. Jumbo, Tommy, Chris and I were sitting around the fire watching and listening to the contest. Mikey Kelly was resting in his van with an upset stomach, hopefully not brought on by my culinary art skills that were on display that night. I had prepared a dinner of steak tips cooked on the grille, canned corn and rice pilaf. I didn't think it had turned out that bad but then, it had always been my assessment that while God was punishing me by taking away my eyesight, he compensated for it by blessing me with a cast iron stomach. Mikey on the other hand had a very sensitive tummy.

As we sat there drinking some Miller Lites and sipping tequila, I heard a rustling of branches in the woods off to our left. The camp area was wide open but almost completely surrounded by trees and our tent was about twenty feet behind us. It was pitch dark beyond the glow of the fire and I could not see a thing.

"Did you hear that?" I asked.

"Hear what?" Chris replied.

"I heard it too," Jumbo added.

"Maybe it was Jason," chuckled Chris.

"Turn down the TV Chris," ordered Tommy.

Jumbo and I contemplated retrieving our Ruger .22 caliber rifles that we used for target shooting. One might think it unwise for a legally blind person to be firing a weapon, even a small caliber one such as a .22. We both employed the utmost safety in our handling and discharging of the weapons however. We both had four power scopes mounted on them but I still could not hit the broad side of a barn. I always made sure I was at least pointed in the opposite direction of anything that even remotely resembled a homo sapient. At that wooded campground during that time of year, we were reasonably sure that there was not another soul around for miles other than the five of us.

A loud crack resonated from the woods directly behind us. It sounded like something had just snapped a tree in half.

"What the hell was that!" exclaimed Tommy in a hushed tone as we all jumped to our feet.

I grabbed the lantern style flashlight I had kept at my feet. I could not go anywhere at night without it and as I shined it around the site, I relied on them to let me know if they saw anything.

"It sounded like it came from behind the tent," whispered Chris. We were all on red alert now and you could cut the tension with a knife. Whatever it was, it sounded very large and very close.

As I continued to scan, I shined the beam of the flashlight towards the tent.

"Oh shit!" whispered Jumbo.

"Hey, it's Bullwinkle!" said Tommy excitedly.

"Mikey, hold it right there. Don't move," Chris said.

"What is it?" I said impatiently. I couldn't see anything.

"Don't look now," Jumbo whispered, "but there is a full-antlered bull moose standing about twenty feet in front of us and he's right next to the tent."

I could not see a blasted thing. This might be the only opportunity I would ever get to see a full grown, real live moose in the wild and I was missing out completely.

"He's friggin' huge!" exclaimed Chris. "What should we do?"

"Should you guys get your guns?" asked Tommy.

"We can't shoot something that size with a .22. It will only tickle him and might make him mad," said Jumbo.

"He's just standing there," said Tommy, "your flashlight is probably blinding him."

"I can't even see him godamit," I said angrily. "What if we get closer. You know, reassure him that we mean him no harm?"

"Hey good idea Mikey," said Chris, "why don't you go over there and tickle him under his chin and see what he does?"

Then the huge beast let out a loud snort and stomped his hoof on the ground in a possible act of aggression.

"Then again, I know what we should do," said Chris.

"Yeah me too. Run!" Tommy yelled.

All four of us bolted for Mikey's van like little kids running from an imaginary boogieman. We flung open the doors and jumped inside, then we slammed the doors behind us, rudely awakening a slumbering Mike Kelly.

"What the hell is going on?" he shouted.

"There's a giant moose out there!" shrieked Chris. "It had flames coming out of its' nostrils and antlers as big as a tree!"

"It was so dark, I never even saw it," I said remorsefully.

"How could you miss something that big?" kidded Tommy.

"Don't worry Mikey," said Chris, "You didn't miss anything. He was even uglier than you are."

We all started laughing and as we sat there for the next half hour waiting for it to meander back into the woods, Mike Kelly read a chapter from a wilderness book he had brought with him that contained an entire section on the North American moose. It turns out that this time of year was mating season and any creature caught in a male moose's territory risked being set upon and stomped to pieces. We were probably in more danger than we even realized.

I had far more pressing issues gnawing at my brain however. While they fretted over the moose, I was trying to come to terms with the fact that I was starting to feel like an outsider. There have been many times in my life that I have thanked the Lord I was not born totally blind. At least I had been blessed with what is commonly referred to as functional vision. I can still get around without the use of a cane but cannot see things around me with a high degree of clarity. With increasing regularity, I found myself in situations where an occurrence would take place that everyone else would see clearly except for me. I was therefore prohibited from participating in any post-event discussion. Someone would do something funny causing those around them to laugh or some type of commotion would draw people's attention to it and each time there was a connection made. As my vision continued to diminish, I was beginning to feel more and more out of the loop and a childhood fear was beginning to resurface. No one wants to be involved in a social setting and feel like they are an outsider, a non-participant and unattached from the group. I found myself becoming more subdued and helplessly remote.

Another disturbing trend pertained to my motor skills. I had always prided myself on my athletic abilities. As a teen, I succeeded at high school football, and was adept at street hockey where I enjoyed a reputation as being one of the best defenseman in my neighborhood. I marched as a snare drummer in an Open Class drum corps, a position that most members with any ambition aspired to become but few achieved. Due to my failing ability to see, I was beginning to slow in my movements as every step became hampered by increased caution and uncertainty. I was now seen as prodding and almost clumsy while engaging in activities such as skiing. Unlike my fellow skiers, I could not see moguls in front of me so I wiped out with far greater frequency than my friends did. My intense competitive nature was beginning to take a beating. I was never the very best at anything, but I was always in the running and could always make a good showing of myself no matter what it was that I was doing. Whether it was playing pool, ping-pong, pinball, air hockey, softball or basketball, I could participate without embarrassing myself. I loved athletic endeavors but one by one in the days that followed, the recreational activities I so enjoyed would begin to fall by the wayside and disappear from my life. Slowly, over time, I would begin to find myself more in the role of spectator instead of participant, and I despised the very thought of it. It greatly increased the feeling of isolation that frightened me to my very core.

When I returned home from that camping trip, I dealt with a myriad of self-conflicting emotions. On the one hand I kept telling myself I had no right to complain about anything. There were people in this world who were far worse off than I was. Once again I kept reminding myself how fortunate my brothers and I were that our condition was not accompanied by the slightest degree of physical pain. But that is what made it so difficult to accept. Illnesses and disease aren't supposed to be painless. That's demented. Our eyes felt perfectly fine. So why didn't they work perfectly fine?

Chapter Ten- The age of computers

    While things had been looking up at work, it was not long before turbulent waters began rocking the boat once again. In 1987, Kemper decided to switch from a paper-based claims system to a computer based system. The technology age was about to gobble us up and unfortunately, accommodating my situation was not going to be easy.

    In March of that year, we began undergoing training for the new computer system, which was to be implemented 4 weeks later. However, by the time Friday afternoon rolled around prior to the weekend when the transition was to take place, we still had not been able to find magnification software that would work with Kemper's incoming computers. I was sitting there at 3:30, knowing that come first thing Monday morning every other adjuster in that office would switch over to the new system while I would be left sitting there twiddling my thumbs. I would be completely unable to perform any of the aspects of processing claims. My pride would not allow me to show up for work and just sit there waiting for the computer tech people at Kemper to resolve the problem. They were well-intentioned people and I was not ungrateful for their efforts, but they were not the one who would have to suffer the humiliation come Monday morning.

    How does that expression go? When the going gets tough, the tough get going. That's not always true though. Sometimes they panic. Out of complete frustration, I decided to walk. I wrote a letter to my supervisor Dottie Loring, who was a top-notch individual and one of the most supportive and understanding people I had ever worked with. I wrote her that I just could not deal with the humiliation that would certainly come with showing up to work on Monday morning and not being able to participate with the office-wide transition as a member of the group. Again, I would find myself on the outside looking in. It was just another shameful moment of weakness and I was fully aware of it, but I simply cannot stand humiliation, even when it is unintentional and unavoidable.

My brother Richard and I had purchased a two family home together earlier that year in the city of Everett. That weekend I sat in my first floor apartment and I cursed the fates with a new level of ferocious ferocity. I was getting tired of the constant adjustments that were necessary every time something changed in my life. I yearned for some stability and for all the vision loss related issues to leave me alone, but no matter how much I ranted and raved, I found myself on disability once again.

God must have heard my prayers this time though because it only lasted for a month. To my utter relief, we received the magnification software program we had been waiting for called "Vista". A special circuit board was installed in my computer that was compatible with Kemper's operating system.

When the day came for my nerve-wracking return to work, I expected every other adjuster in the office to form a lynch mob and string me up by my tie. That wretched demon known as overwhelming guilt was rearing its' ugly head again, reminding me that any time an adjuster is absent it creates further hardship on others who have to pick up the slack. Claims cannot just sit there on hold and I had left a backlog of about 120 files when I walked out a month earlier. I was ashamed, embarrassed, and wracked with regret, all of which were emotions I was growing totally disgusted with.

I walked in as quietly as I could and sat down at my old cubicle. After I performed a quick review of how to use the "Vista" program with Kemper technician Kevin Wells, I tried to bury myself in my work. I prayed that any indignation that the other adjusters probably felt towards me would fade over time.

However, when all the adjusters had arrived at work, Beth Anderson, the hottest looking female in the office came over and tapped me on the shoulder.

I turned around and looked up into her gorgeous blue eyes and thought to myself, well, if I am going to be called on the carpet by my fellow adjusters at least my punishment was going to be administered by someone who would make it a little easier to endure.

"Can you come with me please?" she said with a warm smile.

"Why Beth?" I asked tentatively. "If you are miffed at me for ducking out last month I don't blame you one bit so just let me have it here and we can get on with our lives. I know I screwed up."

"I'm not miffed at you," she said, genuinely surprised, "what makes you think that?"

"Well then," I stammered uncomfortably, "where are we going?" I always liked Beth, she was an absolute sweetheart and Kemper did not operate a torture chamber that I was aware of so how bad could this be? Take your punishment like a man, I said to myself. I had let my co-workers down and I should have handled this new crisis far better than I did. I deserved a good ass kicking or at the very least, a rousing public reprimand.

She took my hand and now I knew I was in deep trouble. "Just come with me," she said leading me into the lunchroom.

I walked through the door and the entire claims office was sitting around the long rectangular table in the center of the room. There was a huge cake surrounded by paper plates and plastic forks so I relaxed my guard for a moment. There wasn't an offensive weapon in sight, just that cake. I knew it wasn't my birthday so I surmised with utter relief that this probably wasn't even about me.

"Whose birthday is it?" I whispered to Beth, relieved that she apparently was not mad at me after all.

"It isn't anyone's birthday silly," she said loud enough for everyone to hear. "The cake is for you. We wanted to welcome you back to work."

I looked around the room at Bert Kelly the branch manager, Dottie and Bob the supervisors and all the secretaries and adjusters, then I looked back at Beth and just stared into her spellbinding eyes and her smiling face and I almost broke down and cried.

"You're kidding me right?" I said. "You guys should be angry as hell with me and instead you're giving me a cake? It's the exploding kind right?" I was very embarrassed and felt completely undeserving of this.

That was just the kind of people they were though. You simply could not ask for a better group of co-workers and I was just blown away by the whole affair. We all had some cake and coffee, talked for a few minutes and everyone just acted like nothing had happened. Not one single person complained or displayed any animosity towards me whatsoever. I had caused them to take on extra work, not too mention the enormous levels of aggravation that probably went with it. Yet, they showed no hostility of any kind. I will never forget their overwhelming display of compassion and understanding. We could not hang around for very long as it was Monday morning in an automobile claims office. The phones were already ringing off the hook with angry claimants anxious to raise hell so I went back to my desk and thanked God for small miracles. "That is one classy group of people," I thought to myself as I breathed the biggest sigh of relief the world had ever heard. Once again, the phobia I had created in my mind turned out to be completely groundless, so I tried to think of a way to show my gratitude.

Kemper Insurance was the first company in New England to establish a Special Investigative Unit, or SIU. Their primary purpose was to investigate fraud and questionable claims, thus the nickname "fraud-squad." Ron Large headed up the unit and they worked right upstairs from us on the second floor. I had been handling stolen auto claims off and on for about 8 years and had referred more than a few cases up to Ron and his boys. I actually found these types of claims a bit more interesting than your typical "fender-benders."

Dottie Loring overheard me say something to that effect one day and asked me if I would like to handle more of these types of claims. I still felt a bit inadequate because I knew the more my vision deteriorated, the slower my claim handling speed would become. So when she made this suggestion, I gave her the red light to pile on the stolen car claims. I knew this would make me very popular in the office since most adjusters despise these claims as they are usually the most contentious, and they would have preferred to handle any other type. When the announcement was made at a weekly staff meeting that I would be handling almost exclusively stolen auto claims, I sensed a big smile on the face of the other five adjusters sitting around the table.

"I don't care what they say about you Merrett, you're alright in my book" kidded my good friend Peter Carloni who was sitting directly across from me.

Beth was sitting next to him. "Gee thanks Mike!" she said with that irresistible smile. Maybe this would get me a date with her, I thought to myself. Fat chance. I found out she was engaged to some guy already. I didn't know anything about him but I detested him purely out of principle. I made a mental note to call Zanti and give the Misfits his address.

It wasn't long before I began handling the dreaded theft claims that no one else wanted to deal with. At that time, Massachusetts was considered the theft capital of the world. For some reason, we experienced a much higher rate of stolen cars, which kept people in my profession very well employed. I strongly suspected that the greatest contributing factor may have been that Massachusetts drivers paid higher premiums than almost anywhere on the planet, except maybe Baghdad.

Anytime an insured had difficulty selling his car outright, rather than continue to pay high insurance premiums on the vehicle, they more often than not hired someone to torch it or drive it into salty ocean water at the nearest beach. There are so many ways to get rid of a vehicle and we in the insurance industry fully suspected that 80-90 percent of stolen car claims were fraudulent. The tough part was trying to prove it. That was my job.

So I worked very closely with the SIU unit in the days ahead. Once I conducted my investigation and felt I had sufficient evidence to prove that there was involvement by the insured, I would refer the claim upstairs. They would then look at it and decide whether it warranted their involvement.

It was a tough job because you dealt with the seediest elements of the insurance company's customer base. Some of them were real pieces of work to say the least. The ultimate claim for me personally was when a first report came in where the vehicle was a late-model Cadillac and the insured's last name was Italian. As soon as I saw that combination, I knew I was in for a battle. I am not suggesting that Italians are more involved in fraudulent claim activity than any other nationality. It is just that whenever a claim involved this pairing, more often than not the insured felt that the vehicle was worth five times what my research said it was worth. Try telling an insured you are prepared to offer him $3,000 for his vehicle, which conveniently disappeared from the face of the Earth when he responds by shouting back at you that it was worth at least $15,000. That's when the fun begins and I had to call upon every ounce of negotiating skill and tact I could muster in an attempt to explain to the insured why the figure I was offering was fair and equitable. During the transmission of this message, of course, he proceeds to threaten my life and hits me with my favorite punch line of all time, "I'm gonna get an lawyer!" To which my standard response was, "Please do. I'm sure he will be a lot easier to deal with than you are."

When you work as an adjuster long enough and you know your craft and the Mass. auto claims policy inside out, attorneys do not scare you. Like any profession, there are attorneys that are easy to deal with, and attorneys who make you wonder how the hell they ever passed the bar.

There was an overabundance of shady lawyers licensed to fleece in Massachusetts at that time.

That is why by the year 1988, 3 insurance companies had already pulled out of Massachusetts, deeming it an unprofitable environment in which to conduct business. Unlike other states, Massachusetts insurance premiums are set by the Insurance Commissioner who is appointed by the Governor. There is no competition, companies cannot set their own rates and they charge what they are told to charge.

We began hearing rumors that Kemper, a national company, was thinking about following suit. They had already pulled out of Rhode Island, one of the most corrupt areas in the country and a hotspot for organized crime. It had become so bad down there that Kemper appraisers were refusing to visit certain repair shops fearing for their lives.

I was already having enough trouble just trying to stay in my job and I did not need to hear that my employer might be leaving the state. Kemper devised a scheme with a different slant to it however. Unlike Allstate before them who had just packed up and left without a fight, Kemper did not want to jeopardize its other profitable lines of business, which they would lose if they stopped writing auto insurance. The state had a strict rule that if a company stopped writing auto coverage, it had to stop writing everything. It was a punishment of sorts but if you think about it, it was necessary as a safety valve to prevent more and more companies from pulling out of the state. That would eventually create utter chaos with consumers, who would be left in a position where they would be unable to find coverage. The legislature could have approached it differently and addressed the reasons that made it unprofitable for companies to do business in Massachusetts, but then, they are politicians. It is easier to punish the companies than it is to address the source of the problem.

Kemper proposed to create an entirely new entity in its place that would take over its automobile business, while allowing them to continue to write homeowners and workers compensation policies. They would fund this new company, which would be known as Arbella, for 3 years at which time it would have to sink or swim on its own.

Then, John Mooney went out and hired former Massachusetts Attorney General Frank Belloti to lobby the legislature to OK the deal.

We adjusters on the other hand, started to become edgy. We were told that we would receive a bonus of an amount to be named later if we hung around until the transition and we would then become employees of Arbella. There was a great deal of uncertainty in many people's minds and some adjusters began jumping ship.

I was working for an annual salary of $26,500 at the time. I was one of the lower paid adjusters in the office because I had missed salary increases due to my two periods of disability so I reluctantly began to look elsewhere as well. I thought the world of Kemper but things were getting a bit crazy and something told me it might not be wise to wait around for the hammer to fall. The first place I looked was across the parking lot at the company sitting right next door to us, CNA Insurance.

A few other Kemper adjusters from our subrogation department had already been hired there and I had more experience than both of them combined. However, Kemper had offered me a security blanket of sorts for years. I had never gone job hunting as a "handicapped" individual. This would be a totally new experience and I had no idea what to expect, but I really wasn't sold on this Arbella thing. What would happen if the company failed? Where would I go? Staying where I was might be risky. So many questions, so few answers which left my mind pondering the never-ending question... stability, wherefore art thou?

I put together a resume, called up CNA's personnel office and was invited in for an interview without hesitation. I informed them of my visual status and the fact that I was using a visual aid but it didn't seem to deter them in their desire to talk to me. That greatly eased my sense of insecurity somewhat, so I prepared to head on over for a little pow-wow the following day. Look at the bright side; I thought to myself. I won't even have to learn a new route to work. Brilliant!

I did not know all that much about CNA Insurance other than the fact that they occupied the building right next to Kemper on Newport Avenue in Quincy. I had previously developed friendships with the two adjusters who had already left Kemper so I had given them a call prior to contacting CNA's human resources department.

Both Bill Barry and Marla Gaines spoke well of the company during conversations I had with them and they said they would be happy to put in a good word for me if I decided to make a move in that direction, which was very kind of them. When I learned how much they were earning, I was even more intrigued. I was fully aware that this was a risky move on my part knowing that Kemper had been so supportive of me during the entire time I was in their employ. They had never failed to assist me with any vision-related work issues I encountered, but everyone was a little nervous about them pulling out of the state. Frank Bellotti was a very influential public figure and was lobbying hard on their behalf. We were reasonably sure that the Mass. State Legislature was going to allow Kemper to stop writing auto insurance if it was willing to establish a new company in its place.

It was September of 1988 and apparently, my friend Bill Barry had already told David Weisman in CNA's human resources department that I was a very capable adjuster. As a matter of fact, he told him I was the best adjuster in the Quincy office, which I never asked him to do. I later discovered he was just setting me up so that I would be obligated to buy him a slew of lunches in the event I was hired. Everybody has an angle.

I had never been in this position before. Apparently, Kemper had a reputation throughout the industry of having some of the best-trained adjustors in the business. That made its employees very attractive to other competitors. I was not aware of that at the time and I soon found myself in a position where, if I really wanted to, I could have marketed myself to the highest bidder. While we're not talking about a situation paralleling that of Roger Clemens, it still felt good to know that I could go into this interview in a position of strength. There was a good chance that the company was already interested and maybe even willing to make an offer before I walked through the door.

The next morning, I walked into the CNA building which, like Kemper next door, was a relatively new four-story structure but it differed from Kemper in one major characteristic. Whoever the architect was who designed the building for Kemper apparently was more interested in aesthetics than he was with efficient use of space. As you walked into 150 Newport Avenue where Kemper called home, there was a reception desk where guests were greeted but as you walked past it you found yourself in a huge open atrium that stretched from the first floor right up to the roof. The offices were built around the atrium so that you could stand on all four sides of it and look down into the lush green vegetation from any floor. It was a very nice effect, resembling a big hollowed out square block of cement but the atrium took up so much of the buildings' available interior workspace, Kemper outgrew the building within the first year it opened.

CNA had no such beauty to offer its workforce and while it was a relatively attractive building, I would soon miss that atrium very much. I walked into the HR office and was warmly greeted by Mr. Weisman. We spoke casually for a few moments, then he handed me an application and took my resume.

"I know you brought your resume with you," he said, "but the company still requires an application be filled out. I hope you don't mind and you can sit right here and just let me know when you are finished."

"No problem, I'll be happy to," I said, when I was really thinking, "What a major league pain in the ass these applications are." All it does is ask for the exact same information already covered quite nicely on my resume. I deplore redundancy in life, unless of course, it has to do with things like having sex or eating a hot fudge sundae with strawberry ice cream topped with fresh made whipped cream and mixed nuts. Then it is OK.

Mr. Weisman seemed like a nice enough man though, so I sat down and filled out the 2-page application, which was annoyingly tedious until I reached the final question. It was of particular interest. It read "Salary requested.

Hmmmmm. I sat pensively for a moment. I was currently earning $26,500 and for 1988, that was a decent salary, even for a hobo like me. Therefore, I had to put down something higher than that. It did not make sense to give up a nine-year relationship with Kemper unless it was for a higher salary, regardless of the uncertainty of the company's future hanging over my head. I could put down $500,000 but then I thought, what if they have no sense of humor? So I wrote $28,000, but then I thought about it a moment longer and remembered that Bill had already told them I was the best adjuster in the office and I was a bit underpaid with Kemper due to my 2 periods on disability which CNA knew nothing about. I crossed it out and wrote $30,000. That represented a $3,500 increase over what I was currently earning and would bring me back in line with other adjusters with the same number of years experience that I had. I had absolutely nothing to lose. Besides, I was never able to show any self-control in buffet lines so why show any here, I thought. Go for the gusto.

The interview went well, but was shorter than I expected and I thought to myself, are they just interviewing me because two of their employees spoke well of me? I explained to them the circumstances regarding my visual limitations and gave them a brief overview of my current responsibilities, including my specialization in stolen auto claims. I did not leave there with the utmost confidence however. It just seemed as though they should have asked more questions, dug deeper into who I was and whether or not I was the right person for the job. I really could not put my finger on it but it just seemed as though the evaluation process had been too superficial. Even when I informed them that I required visual aids, which I had in my possession, it did not seem to cause a stir.

It felt even more strange walking out of the building, across the parking lot back to Kemper, hoping no one had seen me. I did not want Kemper to know that I was looking elsewhere.

That afternoon Mr. Weisman called me at my desk.

"Hi Michael, it's Mr. Weisman, can you talk?" he asked.

"Sure, no problem," I said softly. I looked around to see if anyone was within earshot, which was totally ridiculous. Everyone knows the last guy anyone would hire to perform surveillance work is a legally blind guy. "What can I do for you? Did I forget something?" I wondered momentarily if I had forgotten to give them a piece of information on the application necessary to complete the process or something.

"No, no, nothing like that," he said. "We have everything we need and we just wanted to make you an offer as we are very interested in having you come to work here at CNA. We would like to offer you $32,000 to start with full benefits. I can give you all the applicable benefits information when you come in. So why don't you think about it and if you could get back to me as soon as possible, I would appreciate it."

$32,000? I had only asked for $30,000. I could only assume that I made a better impression on them than I first surmised. They were offering me $5,500 more than I was currently making, a 20 percent increase which I just could not refuse.

"I don't have to think about it Mr. Weisman. I accept your offer and I'll be by as soon as you would like to finalize the process."

"Great, great, good to have you on board, and if you know anyone else over there who is interested in talking to us please let me know."

"I'll do that," I said softly "and thank you."

Apparently, word was out that Kemper adjusters were jumping ship and the other local companies were circling like vultures. However, I was only concerned with my situation at that point. I did not know the degree to which my vision would continue to deteriorate and I had to earn as much as possible while I could still function in my current position. Plus, I simply could not say no to a 20 percent increase. Even if it meant saying goodbye to a company I thought the world of, a company which had stood by me every step of the way, and a place where I had made so many great associations and friendships. While I might have felt a tinge of guilt, I would never have taken this action if not for the fact that Kemper had announced they were calling it quits in Massachusetts.

I went home that day feeling more positive about myself than I had in a long time. CNA had not switched their claims system over to computers yet and that meant returning to a paper-based system. That would be no problem as I would just bring my CCTV with me and the issue would be solved. For once, a transition would be a piece of cake, preferably chocolate mousse with whipped cream.

By the end of the week, I had given my notice and it did not sit too well with branch manager Bert Kelly. I think Kemper as a whole was taking it hard that so many of their adjusters were bailing out. Kemper had a lot of time and resources invested in training us and they did not like seeing the fruits of their labor benefiting their competitors. I would have stayed and taken a chance with the new company they were establishing if they were willing to match the salary offered by CNA, but Mr. Kelly had not

163

offered to do that. Furthermore, Beth was engaged, so there was really no reason to stick around anyway.

All kidding aside, I knew full well that there was a good chance that I might end up regretting the move at some point in the future. Everyone craves some degree of job stability and as a newly deputized member of the handicapped community, I craved it even more so. My euphoria at the prospect that I would be earning more money was counteracted by my overwhelming sense of prevailing apprehension. Once again my future became uncertain. That as we all know can be very unpleasant at times.

Chapter Eleven- CNA

I had become quite fond of the people in Kemper's Quincy office and as I suspected, I never realized how much I would miss them until I started my new job. The adjustment to my new position proved more difficult than I had expected. Kemper was one of the most efficiently run claims departments in the industry and that made the adjusters lives so much easier. They made every reasonable effort to streamline the claims handling process, which led to more timely settlements and indirectly minimized stress levels on their employees.

CNA's claims department was, for lack of a better word, a circus. There are two more commonly used words I could employ that would be even more appropriate…it's called a cluster fuck! (Did I just risk losing my G- rating?) I quickly discovered why they were so anxious to hire Kemper's adjusters. Maybe they were hoping that if they could bring enough of them over here, we might bring sanity to their madness. Their claims handling procedures were archaic, annoyingly cumbersome, and heavily laden with paperwork such as forms upon forms for record keeping purposes. I quickly discovered that the adjusters working there spent more time complaining about the drudgery than they did actually investigating and settling claims.

They were not a happy bunch and to top things off, I had a female supervisor by the name of Sue Shacman who apparently felt threatened by someone with my experience coming on board and she made my life a living hell. At Kemper, my settlement authority was $10,000, meaning I could settle any claim up to that amount without prior approval by anyone. They were so paranoid at CNA, the adjusters had a maximum settlement authority of $1,000 and everything had to be approved by your supervisor and your manager, which ground the entire process to a crawl. Within one month, I was home sick for Kemper big time.

The only saving grace was that the adjusters were unified in their contempt for the way the claims department functioned, so I just jumped on board that chuck wagon and went along for the ride. Because there was nothing any of us could do about it. The powers-that-be in the company apparently did not care about the opinions of those working under this outdated system. They had been doing things that way for years and were reluctant to change, even if everyone who had to work within the system knew it was archaic and were totally miserable.

That was the fall of 1988 and while I was having some difficulty settling in with my new employer's half-assed way of doing things, it proved to be a time when changes began happening so fast in my life it was downright dizzying.

I had spotted an ad in the local Everett newspaper that the publisher was looking for contributors to his weekly tabloid. I had forgotten about pursuing anything having to do with journalism since the Fort Knox disaster ten years earlier. After being hired at CNA my confidence was running higher so I decided to rekindle the flame of a dream that had been long since extinguished. Besides, I had always adhered to the time-honored belief that positive healthy diversions are a good thing. I contacted publisher Nick Deangelo, told him a little about myself and offered to submit some material at no charge. He seemed amicable to the idea, especially when he learned it would not cost him anything, so I began submitting weekly sports shorts covering the two local high schools, Everett High and my Alma Marta Pope John. The Everett News was a far cry from the Boston Globe or the Washington Post but it still turned out to be a lot of fun. The high school athletes loved it because prior to my arrival on the scene they weren't getting any press coverage at all. While it did not completely satisfy my life long desire to become a big time sports writer, it certainly proved sufficiently rewarding enough in so many other ways to justify the effort.

Over time, covering local small town sports did get a bit dull though so after a few months I asked Nick if I could have my own opinion/editorial column. For most of my life, I had been so pre-occupied with drum corps, dealing with vision loss and battling employment related issues that I had never paid all that much attention to politics, other than at the national level. I knew who the president was and in 1988, it was still Ronald Reagan although that would be his last year in office. I knew who the mayor of my city was, and I was not completely oblivious to events occurring around the globe. This would be a tad different however, transitioning from interviewing high school coach's after games to commenting on how the president was not directly responsible for the demise of the Soviet Union and bringing down the Berlin Wall. These were just two events for which Reagan received far too much credit. I was hungry for more meaningful topics to write about and hell, I wasn't being paid for this. I was doing it for pure satisfaction and recognition.

Surprisingly, Nick was warm to the idea so the first "As I see it" column rolled off the presses in December of that year. My picture appeared at the top of the column and despite the fact that I was not making big money as a result of it; I was at least to a limited degree, living my dream of being a journalist. In time, my column became rather popular in local circles and Nick eventually expanded his coverage territory into the nearby cities of Malden and Stoneham.

For the moment things didn't suck all that bad which is always worth toasting with a glass of cheap champagne. I was an adjuster full-time and newspaper columnist part-time, but something was still missing in my life. It had been five years since being involved romantically and I deeply missed having a significant other to engage in playful mischief. For the longest time I viewed myself as being completely unworthy of anyone. Being handicapped and having such an ominous, uncertain future hanging over my head was really taking its toll on my mojo

. I was absolutely terrified to ask a woman out to dinner when I was not able to pick her up in a respectable set of wheels. We're human males living in the 21st century. Some of us would rather be castrated than have our cars taken away from us.

It has often been said that love comes knocking when you least expect it. My brother Richard was still barely holding his own as a corrections officer at the time. He was now married with two daughters and he had put an ad in the local paper looking for weekend side jobs to earn extra money. Nothing that required a high degree of carpentry, electrical, or plumbing skills mind you. Hopefully the work wouldn't require a high level of visual acuity either. Just odds and ends type jobs, some refer to it as grunt work. One day when he received a call from an elderly woman who lived a few blocks away, he did some sheet rocking work for her in a hallway leading up to the third floor of her house.

He came home that Saturday afternoon and stopped in to my apartment to tell me that he had to go back and finish the job the following week. He added that it might be a good idea for me to accompany him. The elderly woman's name was Lucy, and her niece lived on the third floor with her three and a half year old son. She was divorced, and quite attractive according to Rich, so I decided to take him up on his job offer. My predatory instincts had not vanished completely.

The following Saturday I returned to the house with him and perhaps it would be more appropriate to describe it as 'returning to the scene of the crime." I took one look at the sheet-rocking job he had done and exclaimed, "Were you drinking last week? I mean, what are you using for tools, rocks?" Granted it was a tough place to sheetrock as the staircase wound up and around from the second floor to the third. He had cut little pieces and tried to make them all fit rather than doing big sections and it ended up looking like a badly smashed together jigsaw puzzle.

"Hey, I'm doing the best I can" he said.

"I hope Lucy has really bad eyesight too," I joked.

As we started working, I could hear that the niece was moving about upstairs, and I heard the TV on. I needed an excuse to go up and see her so I knocked on the door knowing that Notre Dame was playing football against their archrivals that afternoon, the Trojans of Southern California. I took my cue from my dad when it came to sports loyalties. He was the reason I was a fan of the New York Yankees and Notre Dame, as he had always been a life-long supporter of these proud organizations. Asking the niece if I could check the score would be a great way to break the ice. So suave, so debonair was I....and, so very desperate. I knocked on the door.

"Come in," she said, knowing it was one of the two hacks her aunt had hired to fix the hallway. It represented an act of terribly poor judgment, which she would soon discover.

I opened the door and there she was sitting in a white bathrobe trying to fix a calculator for her son who was sitting next to her. They both looked at me at the same time with wide eyes and I got the impression that maybe they did not get many visitors.

"Hello," I said as pleasantly as I could. "Sorry to bother you, but I heard the TV on, and I was wondering if you wouldn't mind checking the score of the Notre Dame game for me. They are playing Southern Cal today in a big rivalry game."

She was indeed a very attractive woman, 35-40 years old I guessed with shoulder length blonde hair, blue eyes and an athletic figure. She eyed me for a moment and then went back to examining the calculator.

"No problem. We're not watching anything in particular," she said in a totally disinterested humdrum tone. I obviously made quite an impression on her.

"We're trying to fix my calculator!" the little boy said excitedly. He, on the other hand seemed thrilled to see a new face but then, small minds are easily amused so don't get excited, my ego told me. She is the one you have to impress, focus your energy on her.

"Really," I said, "what's wrong with it?" What a stupid question. If they knew that, it would be fixed by now.

"I don't know," he said shrugging his shoulders.

I knelt down next to the two of them and asked if I could see it. She handed it to me and I could tell that she was completely frustrated with it. I didn't know jack about fixing calculators but I had to try and help the little guy so I acted like I knew what I was doing as I examined it carefully.

"Did you check the fanotony rods?" I asked him.

"What's a fanotony rod?" he asked.

"I don't know. I thought you knew," I kidded him. He just laughed.

"So what's your name?" I asked him as I checked the batteries and looked it over to see if it had been damaged in any way.

"Matthew," he said innocently. "What's yours?"

"My name is Michael and it's nice to meet you Matthew." His mom got up to change the channel on the TV.

'What channel is the game on?" she asked.

"I believe it is on four," I said, eyeing her figure as she leaned over to adjust the channel knob on the set. I thanked God once again that I was not totally blind and could still appreciate the enticing way she filled out that bathrobe.

"What's your name by the way," I said since she was not going to volunteer it on her own. I did not blame her for being a bit distrustful. She had a young son and an elderly aunt down stairs and she was doing the right thing by remaining on her guard. How could she know she was in the presence of someone as trustworthy and honorable as I was?

"Julie," she answered.

170

"Well, it's nice to meet you Julie," I answered. She really was a fine looking woman.

"I don't know Matt," I said, "I think this thing has seen better days. We may have to blast."

He had no idea what I was talking about but he just stared at me and smiled.

I looked around the apartment as Julie continued to scan for the game. It had three small rooms and was on the top floor of a one family house. The living space really was tight and while she kept the place clean and tidy, it couldn't mask the fact that the apartment was old, run down and judging by her expressions so far, not where she wanted to be at this point in her life.

My heart went out to the two of them. I was legally blind but here are two people who needed someone like me, I thought to myself. I was not rich, I was not famous, but I was the son of a mom and dad who taught their children that there is no greater joy that comes in life than that which is derived from helping others. I had been single for too long and feeling down about my prospects of becoming involved again. I have had three serious relationships in my life, each of which was memorable and rewarding in its own way, but now I was in a rut and felt that no woman would want anything to do with me because I was going blind. Well maybe, just maybe here was a situation where she might see my positives as outweighing the negatives. Either way, I decided to make my move.

"So, you look like you work out," I said.

She found the game and Notre Dame was up 10-3.

"I play racquetball at a club," she answered, sitting back down in the little chair next to Matt.

"Really, I play racquetball too." I was lying. I never played racquetball in my entire life. Desperate men say desperate things.

"Who's winning?" Matt interrupted.

"Looks like ND is up 10-3," I answered. "Do you like football?"

"I don't know," he answered, "I guess so."

171

I could hear Rich banging away down in the hallway. I could only imagine how it was going. He meant well but with his lack of visual acuity, this was definitely out of his league, and if he expected any help from me, he was in deep trouble. I am dangerous with a hammer in my hand. When it came to working in that type of environment, my friends nicknamed me "wrecking ball."

I focused my attention back on mom. "Would you be interested in playing some time?" I boldly asked. This was it. I threw my cards on the table. I had absolutely nothing to lose and everything to gain.

"Sure, but I have to warn you, I'm pretty good." She was looking at the TV and I could tell she was still apprehensive.

"Great, why don't you give me your number and I'll call you sometime," I said, trying to conceal my glee.

She delicately ripped a little piece of paper off the calculator and wrote down her telephone number. I did not know anything about her at that point but I did not care. She filled out that bathrobe pretty nicely and I hadn't been on a date since the last presidential election. At that point, as long as I could be reasonably sure she was not a relative of Squeaky Frome's, I was determined to re-enter the whacky whimsical world of sharing a dinner table with a member of the opposite sex.

She gave me the slip of paper and for the first time looked right into my eyes. They say the eyes are the gateway to the soul and I could see that this woman had been through some rough times. There was sadness there and the look of someone who had almost lost hope. I was very touched and was even more determined that this might be a good thing in the making.

"Thanks, I'll call you in a day or two and we'll get together." I turned to Matthew. "Well, Matt, sorry I couldn't fix your calculator but maybe Santa will bring you a new one in a few months. You take it easy huh? And remember always root for the Irish."

"Who are the Irish?" he asked innocently.

"Uh, the Irish are the Notre Dame Football team. That's what they call them, the Fighting Irish."

"Why do they call them that?" he asked.

"Well, it's a long story. I'll have to tell you sometime."

Kids, why do they have to be so damn inquisitive?

"Nice meeting you Julie," I said shaking her hand.

"You too," she said with a tentative smile. I walked down to where Rich was working and said, "Ok, I got what I wanted, now have fun huh?"

"Yeah right. Get your ass back here and help me finish this mess."

He was clearly running out of patience. I felt bad for him so I hung around and with my skill and determination, the final product was something right out of Mack and Meyer for hire. We both felt so badly for Aunt Lucy we only charged her for the materials. She never called him back for any additional work.

I called Julie two days later, not wanting to appear overanxious as I delicately delved into the dizzying dilemma of dating.

"Hello," she said cautiously.

"Hi Julie," I said cheerfully. "It is Mike from the other day. How are you?" I was a bit nervous but not overly unsure of myself. I was not on disability any more. No sir, I was in a professional position and a high-flying newspaper columnist just brimming with confidence.

"I'm doing OK," she said with the slightest hint of hostility. "You might say I'm doing a heck of a lot better than the job you and your brother did in the hallway."

Ouch!

"Hey, I never said I was a carpenter. I am an insurance guy, white collar all the way. Put a tool in my hand and I can do some serious damage."

"I can see that," she said, although I could tell she wasn't really all that upset.

"So, would you like to get together this weekend, say Saturday night?" I boldly asked.

"You mean to play right?" she answered.

"Play? Play what?" I said dumbly.

"Uh, racquetball remember?" she answered curtly.

"Actually, I thought we could do dinner first and that would give us a chance to discuss strategy and the nuances regarding our personal philosophical approaches to the game. Besides my racquet is being re-strung," I explained.

"Re-strung?" she responded dubiously. "Really? I have an extra racquet so that is no problem. So where do you play mostly?" Women. Always probing our defenses.

The jig was up and I had to come clean. I was only digging a deeper hole for myself.

"Well, now that you mention it, I haven't really played in a long time. I have been so busy playing ice hockey lately with a semi-pro team and I was just trying to finagle your phone number out of you so I could invite you to dinner. So, do you want to hit me now or later?"

"That's pretty hard to do over the phone but I'll make a note of it," she answered.

She didn't hang up on me so I figured that was a good sign at least.

"So what do you say, dinner at 7?" I held my breath for a moment. I really did miss spending a night out enjoying the type of companionship that only a member of the finer sex can provide. I had a slew of male friends but there wasn't a single one of them who had long blonde hair, blue eyes and a figure like she did I can tell you.

"Sure, why not. So what did you say you do for work?" She was still apprehensive but that's Ok I thought to myself.

"I'm an insurance adjuster for CNA Insurance and I write for the local newspaper part time. You haven't seen my column in the Everett News?" I asked proudly.

"No, but I'll check it out," she said.

174

I could hear Matt in the background making a fuss so I thought it best to end the call before she changed her mind. Kids just have that way about them. As soon as they see you talking on the phone they want your attention and they want it now.

"Listen, you have to go but I'll look forward to seeing you Saturday night. Have a good week in the meantime."

"Thanks, you too," and she hung up the phone.

I sat back for a moment thinking that too many good things were coming my way all of a sudden and I almost felt like fate was setting me up again. Richard and I owned our own home together, I was making good money at CNA with full benefits, and I was living out my fantasy as a newspaper columnist and to top it all off, a gorgeous woman with blonde hair and blue eyes had just accepted my invitation to dinner. Something was up I just knew it.

Now I had to figure out how I was going to pull off this date. I never told Julie that I was legally blind or that I didn't drive. That would be suicide. I had not driven in years even though my driver's license was still valid. I knew that if I had to, I felt reasonably sure that I could drive a short distance and if I kept my speed down, I could probably do it with an acceptable degree of safety. Then again, it could be a simple case of my being totally deranged.

Out of sheer desperation, I did something incredibly stupid. I went to see my good friend Tommy Upton who marched next to Jumbo, myself and our good friend Arthur Shannon when we were all snare drummers in the Reveries. Tom was now a car salesman at Smyly Buick in Malden. He gave me a great deal on a brand new Hyundai Sedan for $7,400.00. I was approved for a loan and I figured what the heck, there was nothing wrong with having a vehicle at my disposal. I could always sell it or give it to someone in the family if I had to at a later date. It was totally nuts but I could not bring myself to ask her to pick me up and risk losing her to a bad first impression. I must confess, just having a car at my disposal again, even if it just sat there on the street outside my front door made me feel more of a man than I had felt in many a moon.

I knew I was taking a huge risk. I had been fortunate in my life up to that point that I had only caused two fatalities that were direct results from my operation of a motor vehicle. Both had occurred several years earlier. The first victim was a small dog that had jumped in front of my car as I proceeded along Route 16 on my way to work while I was employed in Kemper's Arlington office. I saw him out of the corner of my eye but I was not able to jam on the brakes quickly enough as he sprinted from the sidewalk into the busy four lane thoroughfare. I grazed him with my right front bumper and sent him tumbling into the gutter. I was so devastated, I had gone home early from work that day, unable to handle my guilt-ridden conscience.

The second tragedy occurred in 1983 while I was driving to a judging assignment in Leominster, Mass. There were three other friends of mine with me who were judging that day also. As I proceeded down the wooded country road to the stadium at no more than 20-30 miles per hour, my friend Kathy Kerrins who was sitting in the back seat yelled, "Look out!" There was a person walking on the right hand side of the road in plain view so I said, "I see him, I see him."

However, she was not trying to alert me to the presence of a human being. From the left hand side of the road, a raccoon had darted out from the tree line, which I did not see. I did not actually hit him so much as he ran right under the car. As the vehicle lifted off the ground slightly, I sensed that he did not fare too well as a result of his close encounter with my Buick Skylark. I felt horrible as my three passengers justifiably razzed me unmercifully for the rest of the day.

The only other occurrence remains a mystery of nature. I once drove over something that remotely resembled a squirrel but it seemed to have too dense a molecular structure to be living tissue so it was either a rodent of some kind that worked out regularly or a rock that looked like a squirrel. I could not tell which. Then again, maybe it was an animal that had already been run over by a previous motorist in which case I could rightfully claim, "Hey, I didn't do it!" I wrote that one off as a close encounter of the blind kind. While I make light of these incidents, make no mistake about it. I love animals, and I was emotionally crushed over the above two incidents.

I try to deal with such things rationally, and when you think about it, blind people unknowingly extinguish the lives of many lower life forms. An assortment of bugs, small rodents and reptiles get squashed every day by people who are simply unable to see them in their path. Does that make us murderers or is it more likely just further proof that supports the theories of Charles Darwin? Survival of the fittest right? But alas, that is a debate for another day.

Driving a car was like riding a bike and it all came back to me with little difficulty. While my decision may have been totally irresponsible and bordered on gross negligence, I could not face the humiliation of revealing my situation to her at such an early stage.

I picked Julie up promptly at seven the following Saturday night at her house, which was only 2 blocks away. She looked gorgeous and appreciated the flowers I had picked up for her. Aunt Lucy watched over Matt while we were gone so we both headed out for the nice shiny new Hyundai parked in the driveway. I opened the door for her and she got in, tastefully revealing an incredible set of legs. I went around to the driver's side, let myself in and started it up. There was no turning back and it was either pursue that course which I knew was a bit deceptive, or reveal that I was legally blind and risk that it would all end right there before it had a chance to begin. The imagination can be our best friend, or in times like this, our worst enemy.

I put a "Swing out Sister" disk in the CD player and backed out of the driveway, then I headed up Argyle St. and out onto Broadway. The tunes helped relax me as I drove north towards the Italian restaurant I had chosen which was only about a mile up the road. It was straight all the way and the road was brightly illuminated. It was only a matter of time before she realized I was not super confident behind the wheel however. Out of the corner of my eye, I could tell she was looking at me awful funny.

"Can you…see …OK?" she asked nervously. Here it was our first date and I was making her even more skittish than she probably already was.

"Of course I can see OK," I answered, "Kinda."

I looked over at her and she just smiled. The jig was up. My $7,400 charade lasted all of two minutes.

"OK, so I am a bit nearsighted," I stammered. "But I'm really good at a lot of other stuff, except sheet-rocking of course."

"I'm glad you added that last part," she chuckled. "Just get me there in one piece OK? I don't want to wrinkle my dress."

Thank God she had a sense of humor, and thank God the road was so well lit. There were hardly any pedestrians out, traffic was light, and small animals were wise enough to keep their distance. At least, I do not remember feeling any unusual bumps along the way.

We made it to the restaurant in one piece, had a great meal and a really nice time after a brief uncomfortable moment when I informed her I had forgotten my glasses and could not read the menu so I needed her assistance. I did have a pair of glasses with a four-power monocular scope mounted in them that Bob Mcgilvary had introduced me to and I had been using for years. They were only affective in the best of lighting situations and most restaurants, like that one, were way to dark for them to be an option. Besides, my friends had given me the nickname "the Jeweler" because of the way they made me look whenever I wore them and I wasn't about to whip those out in front of Julie. It would have been a dead giveaway that I was probably not quite like anyone she had ever dated before. I was determined to break her in gently to my condition in the hope that she would not pre-judge and hit the jettison button. While I was succeeding rather nicely, she still insisted on driving home.

That was the very last time I drove anybody anywhere. I offered the car to my brother Richard and his wife Judy who, by coincidence just happened to need one at the time and all they had to do was take over the payments. I took the loss on the down payment but it was worth it. Because Julie and I hit it off splendidly and in no time, I fell deeply in love with her.

It was not easy at times and to her credit, she overlooked the additional duties my lack of visual acuity would place on her. I was still too self-conscious to use my telescope glasses in public so she would have to assist me with reading menus in restaurants. On some occasions when the restaurant was very dark as many of them are, she would have to guide me to our table. I'm reasonably sure that over time, having to do all the driving bothered her at least on some level, but she never complained. Eventually, my bruised ego adjusted to living in a male dominated world and having to be trucked around everywhere by my female companion.

My relationship with her son Matt, however, was a different story. He and Julie had lived alone for his entire life in a very small, closed-in apartment. Julie meant everything to him and as an only child, he had no siblings to bond with which might have eased his unshakable attachment to her. When I entered the picture, he felt, as any child would, that someone had come between them and in his frightened little mind, he feared losing his mom to me. No matter how hard I tried to reassure him that I was just mommy's friend and that I would never take her away from him, he remained on guard and at times would even push me away when I moved to kiss her goodbye for the night.

I learned a great deal during that first year about the dynamics of single moms who have one child and make the bold decision to begin dating again. I had developed an approach towards children that I had honed during many years of teaching music to kids ranging in age from seven to 21. It was simple but direct. I never berated them, called them names, or physically punished them in any way. I treated them with respect and demanded respect in return. I employed the technique of "positive reinforcement" at all times and demanded that my entire assistant staff abide by the same set of rules. However, in the never-ending battle of wills that exists between children and adults, I had one ultimate rule, and that rule was, "I don't negotiate!" When I told one of my students to do something, they were required to do it. I never said please, I never asked them because that is the biggest mistake parents make today…giving children an option. Once they know they can negotiate with you, you have lost the battle, period. While we are on the subject, that "time out" crap is just that: crap. Kids are not always going to like being disciplined and scolded by their parents, but that's life. Get over it. Setting limits for kids and consistently enforcing them is one of the greatest ways of demonstrating that we love and care about them. Though they may resent it on the surface, deep down inside they will understand our reasons as long as it is balanced with love and affection.

    This personal philosophy of mine became an issue whenever Matt would misbehave. I tried to be sympathetic and was fully aware of the fact that I was not his biological father, but regardless of whose child he was, I cannot sit idly by when a child misbehaves. When I would correct him, Julie, like so many single moms, would sometimes take offense to it. Her reaction, which was all too common among women in her position, conveyed a difficulty in controlling her natural instinct to protect him, which clashed with her duty to correct his bad behavior, and it got the better of her more often than not. Many times, she just could not recognize that I was chastising him for his own good.

    All of which contributed to occasional tension between us, but there was still enough of a loving bond building between us that 3 years later at the ripe middle age of 38, I asked her to marry me at the foot of the Don Orion Shrine in East Boston. The shrine is a 60 foot statue of the Madonna and my mom had taken us there as children when it was first being built. They had donation cans there that we took home and after canvassing the neighborhood asking friends and neighbors to donate, we returned the cans to help fund the completion of the project. So I always felt like I had played a small part in completing the shrine, which turned out to be a beautiful sculpture. It remains a very special place for me to this day.

  I would need her divine guidance in the coming days because Julie said yes. I thought my life was complicated before I got married! Little did I know that the fun was just beginning.

Chapter Twelve- Returning to Drum Corps

In the spring of 1989, Linda Chopelas called me and asked if I was interested in teaching a junior corps the Malden organization had just formed called East Coast Jazz. I had been away from the activity for 5 years but everything was clicking into over-drive with my personal life so I decided to take the position. I missed writing percussion arrangements and I asked one of my former students, Dennis Scott if he would like to be my assistant. Dennis, who was going to law school at the time, was a snare drummer in the 1983-84 Diplomats who finished in the top two positions in Division II for both of those years.

Life had turned completely upside down once again, only this time it was in a positive direction. I was the senior claims rep in my department, teaching a drum corps again, I had my own editorial column running in three weekly newspapers, I owned my own home, and I was involved in a serious relationship with a beautiful woman who actually accepted me vision loss and all. Airplane glue could not have gotten me any higher, although I was not about to test that statement. I had given that stuff up a long time ago.

My column had garnered me some recognition around town and the local school board had even reprinted one of my weekly entries in their monthly newsletter. It was a piece I had written in support of a strike the teachers were forced to initiate over a wage dispute. I will always contend that teachers and social services personnel are two of the most underpaid, un-appreciated groups in society.

Even though I had never been all that interested in politics, I made a bold decision that summer to run for the local common council. This might have been delusions of grandeur, and it may have been incontrovertible proof that I was totally out of control, but I was enjoying more self-fulfillment than I had ever known before. I had no way of knowing it at the time, but that precise moment in my life was as good as it was ever going to get. Like most humans do, I tried to exploit my good fortune. Because we never know what might come next, and like that old Schlitz Beer commercial says, "You only go around once in life, so you have to grab for all the gusto you can."

The City of Everett where I resided had one of the oldest forms of government in the country at that time. It was referred to as a Bi-Cameral form of government and it consisted of a two-body structure, one being the 7-member Board of Alderman and the other an 18-member Common Council. The mayor was the leading political authority and the city had a 7-member school committee. I used to joke about this in my column regularly that Everett had more politicians than Canada but no one seemed all that interested in modernizing and streamlining the system or making it more accountable. I courageously decided if you can't beat 'em, join 'em.

I threw my hat into the ring and then proceeded to order some signs and bumper stickers. I even went so far as to design them with a scientific approach in an effort to maximize their effectiveness. I researched the most aesthetically pleasing and easily discerned color combinations for the human eye to distinguish. It turned out that yellow letters on a black background were the easiest for the human eye to read so I ordered my signs and bumper stickers in those two colors. I then put together what I considered to be a fairly impressive flyer, which I distributed throughout my precinct thinking people would actually take the time to read it. I was so naïve. It is more likely that my flyer ended up being dumped on in kitty litter boxes all over the city. Nobody ever reads that stuff.

Rather than ask for help, I canvassed the neighborhood myself gathering signatures for my nomination papers during which time I discovered that every other house in the area had a nasty dog barking at the door. City hall only required 250 signatures to get your name on the ballot and that was relatively easy to accomplish.

I had an added advantage because I had the weight and influence of the Everett News behind me, not to mention the exposure it gave me. Julie and most of my friends and family were a bit skeptical and kept telling me politics was not the place for a nice guy like me. They felt I was too honest and would end up being totally corrupted.

As August approached, it was time to start ringing doorbells and campaigning. Newspaper ads and leaflets left on doorsteps were all well and good but there was no substitute for shaking hands and meeting voters face to face. This was one area of concern for me because as I met more and more people, I had difficulty recognizing them from a distance afterwards. I feared that if I failed to return a wave or an acknowledgement I would be perceived as an elitist snob. Voters would not know that I was legally blind. I was not sure if I should place an ad in the paper saying something to this effect: "Hi, my name is Mike Merrett and I am legally blind. If you happen to pass me on the street and wave and I do not respond, it is not because I do not like you…in most cases… or that I am a snob. I probably just did not see you. I beg forgiveness, and oh yeah, I am running for Common Council. Vote for me and I'll set you free!" Definitely not practical.

One of the most annoying aspects of losing my vision and not being able to do certain tasks that I was once able to do, was having to apologize for being legally blind. I am not sure why but I felt compelled to ask forgiveness for needing assistance on occasion even though it was not my fault that I could not see. Over time, I was really growing to detest having to constantly apologize for something that was completely beyond my control.

The fear of not recognizing people I had just spoken to the day before began to weigh on me, but I was determined to overcome it and ultimately persevere. I should have known however, that the fates, which had been so magnanimous to me that year, were merely taking a respite to sharpen their blades.

Because in August, CNA Insurance decided it was time to jump into the modern age and computerize their claims department. They were bringing in the newest state of the art computers, IBM PS2's, and the visual aid industry that always lagged six months behind the computer makers had nothing that would work with PS2's.

When the conversion took place, I sucked it up this time and did not walk. I was determined to fight through this, just another hand grenade thrown my way by the fates above for reasons I could not fathom. When the other adjusters were up and running and processing claims via the computers, I was transferred over to the subrogation department and relegated to performing clerical work while the company and the vocational rehabilitation people at the Commission tried to figure out what to do. After a short while however, I discovered there was nothing available at the time. The software did not exist which would allow me to perform the mechanics of my job. I was the senior claims rep in the office but it was time to bend over and assume the position once again.

"Thank you sir, may I have another!"

What invariably went through my mind as I repeatedly became embroiled in situations like this is my imagination began to run wild with insane thoughts of what the company might do next. The specter of long buried fears resurfaced like "what are my co-workers thinking" and "what does the future hold?" Suddenly the allure of going back on disability looked far more inviting than sitting there feeling utterly humiliated with a broken spirit and relegated to performing clerical work. I am not sure who it was who coined the phrase "the grass is always greener on the other side of the fence". Maybe it was Socrates, Aristotle, or some other person of great wisdom but at that precise moment in time, that phrase became an irresistible truism.

After a month of performing mundane, degrading clerical functions as the company wrestled with what to do with me, I simply could not take it any more. My strength of will caved in and I left the office one Friday afternoon and called Dr. Berson's office. I was throwing in the towel and on the following Monday I was home licking my wounds wondering when this maniacal roller coaster I was unwillingly riding for the last ten years was going to let me the hell off. The ups and downs were making me as dizzy as a seasick sailor.

The disruption at work had a ripple effect and the blow it delivered to my confidence carried over to my political aspirations as well. I stopped ringing doorbells and relied solely on my newspaper ads and literature drops. Unfortunately, my opponents were canvassing the precinct 2 or 3 times over and when election day arrived, despite the help of family and friends who stood by me all day at the polls, I lost the election finishing 4th out of 6 candidates.

After the results were announced election night, I crawled home, sat in my apartment with Julie, and tried to make the best of a disappointing situation. I have often wondered what "might have been" in my life had the events been different during that period of time. I knew full well I was as capable as anyone currently serving in Everett politics but the difference was in my confidence levels compared to theirs. There again was that essential element so vital to success and mine had failed me miserably when I needed it most.

Like a true sportsman, I was determined not to give the slightest impression that I was a sore loser. From that day on, the fact that I referred to Everett's bi-cameral form of government as the board of Oldermen and the Common Clowncil in my column should in no way be misconstrued as poor sportsmanship.

For the third time in ten years, I found myself staying at home on disability but this time I had a significant other to lessen the pain. Julie and I were engaged, I had a child in my life who would soon become my step-son and I had my writing and teaching to occupy some of my time. CNA was one screwed up claims department and I would not miss it one bit. I thanked God for having long-term disability coverage and Social Security Disability Income to fall back on.

I was in my mid thirties then and as I found myself enduring a third visit to the land of the disabled, I began to become aware that I was slowly withdrawing into myself as the result of my eye condition. In the ongoing struggle to hold onto things I enjoyed doing in my life, I was starting to lose ground. I gave up ice hockey because I was completely unable to follow the fast moving puck. Up until then I would just follow the direction of bodies and react to it but it was simply becoming too frustrating. They were just pick up games with friends and I had some serious explaining to do when Julie and Matt came to watch me play for the first time. "Semi-pro huh?" she laughed. "Right!"

Some talented young newcomers were beginning to show up to the games. I was growing tired of explaining my visual situation and I really think I was just getting in the way. One night I took a deflected puck just above my right eye, which sent me dazed and bleeding to the Lahey Clinic. I was wearing a helmet but no visor, which was ill advised I admit, but they tended to fog up which limited my ability to see even further. Still, a visor would have prevented the injury as I never even saw the puck coming. As I sat in the waiting room in full hockey gear with my friend Jumbo, who was also playing that night and nice enough to give me a lift to the hospital, I felt like a total idiot. Eleven stitches later, I took the doctors advice and hung up the skates for good.

Skiing fell by the wayside as did our annual white-water rafting trips. I no longer enjoyed going to professional sporting events because I had to hold up 20-power binoculars the entire game and it was just too difficult to follow the action.

The annual camping trips with some of my very best friends were just distant memories as well. Everyone was married, having kids and slowly drifting apart.

Depression was beginning to tighten its hold on my thought processes and I never realized what a powerful force it could be. However, I could not let it become my master. I was involved with someone now, and I had a child in my life who would come to depend on me. Surrender was not an option.

I tried to remain active and in 1990, I became involved in my first "big-time" political campaign. I was asked to help by attorney Tom Birmingham of Chelsea who had run for the State Senate the previous election but had lost to incumbent Fran Doris by just 2 percentage points. I had met Tom at an Everett News open house the previous year and he had made quite an impression on me. He was a genuinely compassionate, very intelligent individual and I immediately thought to myself, here is a man who has the tools to make a difference in politics. Harvard Law School, Rhodes Scholar, very impressive credentials indeed. I was more than happy to volunteer my services and besides, Tom had seen me in action at a candidate's night when I was running for office the previous year. He confided in me that he was more impressed with my speech than any of the others on display that night. Of course, the possibility exists that he privately said that to everyone else who spoke as well but I appreciated the compliment just the same. Genuine or not, I was always a firm believer that everyone should become involved in politics at some level. Apathetic, uninformed and disinterested voters lead to corruption in government. Or, as Plato once said, "The consequence to those who treat public affairs with apathy and indifference is to be ruled by evil men."

Politicians are human and prone to the same frailties we all are, and if left to their own devices with no one watching over them, they are more likely to abuse their positions. When it comes right down to it, we are a species of degenerates but to our credit, we continually strive to rise above it. I may be a hopeless cynic, but I have not yet given up all hope for humanity's future.

Tom won the election and by his second term, he was appointed chairperson of the powerful Ways and Means Committee by Senate President Bill Bulger. I was very involved with Tom's campaign the previous election and I do not ever remember seeing Bulger at any of the fund raising events. Then again, I am legally blind. It was only after I asked a few questions years later that I learned of the Birmingham – Bulger connection. They had been friends for years, their fathers were close friends as well and Bulger was lurking in the background the entire time, grooming Tom as his replacement for the Senate President's position when Billy eventually resigned in 1998. When Bulger moved on to become president at the University of Massachusetts, one of the first things he did was hire Tom's wife Selma to a high paying position with the University. I found all of this very intriguing considering Billy's association with his brother Whitey, the alleged kingpin of the Irish mafia in South Boston who remains a fugitive to this day and still sits at the top of the FBI's 10 Most Wanted list. All of which merely proved how incredibly naïve I could be when it came to big time politics. It did not change my opinion of Tom to any degree, and I still consider him to be a good man and a highly competent elected official.

      He was even nice enough to attend my wedding when Julie and I married in 1992. It was a splendid affair at the King's Grant Hotel in Danvers, Mass. and we followed it up with a honeymoon in sunny Orlando, Florida. We had originally planned a honeymoon in Kauai, Hawaii but changed our minds when I added up the final cost. We learned later that a Pacific hurricane had struck the island and devastated the hotel where we had booked our stay, and it happened the very week of our wedding so I took comfort in knowing that not all the gods had lined up against me. I managed to dodge that hurricane or Poseidon's trident which, judging by my luck of late, was probably aimed right at my ass.

It was at that time that my brother Bert approached me about the Randolph Sheppard Vending program. He had been working in the program for 12 years and I had never given it much thought but I was reasonably sure I was not going back to insurance. The constant disruptions due to the continual regression of my vision were just too much to endure. I would be out of work this time for 3 years and the vending program offered me the opportunity to be my own boss. At the time I wanted to put disability to an end once and for all and be working full time again so I was willing to listen to any suggestions hurled my way.

The state of denial I had been wallowing in came to a painful resolution when an incident involving Matt and I drove the point home with all the subtlety of an AC-DC concert. It convinced me with even greater finality that perhaps getting involved in some program for visually impaired people might be a good idea.

It was a Saturday afternoon and we were walking down Broadway to Everett Square together. I had a handful of mail, which I was taking to the post office. We had just passed Cottage St. and had almost reached the center of downtown when all of a sudden, a loud "CLANG!" rang out throughout the square. That sound of course, was the result of an impact between my forehead and an aluminum ladder that was set up in the middle of the sidewalk. It had to be aluminum right, I thought to myself. Why couldn't it have been made of wood, which would have at least muffled the sound so that not everyone within a square mile would hear it? The noise it made resonated throughout the square like Quasimodo ringing the bells of Notre Dame Cathedral. Everyone in the square stopped in their tracks, turned and gaped as the poor man holding on for dear life at the top of the ladder began shouting obscenities down at me. I was wearing sunglasses but I have a bad habit of looking down when I am out walking. I never even saw the damn thing because of the ever-increasing blind spots. Poor Matt did not know what to do and started picking up the mail, which was strewn all over the ground. He felt badly but it was not his fault. He did not realize that I would not see the ladder as it was certainly bright enough and the sun shone overhead. We scurried on our way after I made sure the ladder's occupant was OK. The lump that formed on my forehead was like something out of one of those old Saturday morning cartoons.

When I arrived home, I was really shaken. I had never been so embarrassed in all my life. This was even worse than when I fell off the ramp at my senior prom leaving the Pier 4 restaurant. Julie gave me an ice pack and tried in vain to make me feel better, but this was a new experience for me. Vision loss had never involved any physical pain to speak of, or at least not to this degree. I almost fractured my skull and knocked some poor guy off a ladder in the process. How would I have felt if the poor bastard had fallen? He was at least 15 feet in the air. My thoughts turned crazy for a moment. "What the hell was he doing blocking the sidewalk in the first place?! The son of a bitch, I should sue his ass!"

Then my rage turned on me. "You blind bastard! You are pathetic! You should have seen that ladder. What are you looking down for all the time?"

My head just kept throbbing and aching. After months upon months of plunging further and deeper into a well of depression, I hit rock bottom with a loud thud. Was it time to take that final excruciating step in this sadistic game the fates were playing with me? Was it time to swallow every ounce of what little pride I had left and learn to use a cane? I was losing the ability to at least publicly conceal the fact that I was legally blind. Refusing to surrender to the cane was my last act of defiance against the fates that had been trying to drag me into another world for years. I would not, under any circumstances let them take me there, I continued to assert in my mind. I'll strain with every ounce of strength and determination I have to stay in the world I had always lived in, the world of the non-handicapped.

However, the fates were wearing down my resistance. As I lay there in my living room stretched out on the couch, the ice pack on my head, I felt moisture running down my cheeks. Must be the ice pack, I thought to myself as I drifted off into a semi-conscious state of despair.

When I awoke, I headed down to the basement to release my rage. I had previously purchased a workout dummy called a "Slam Man" after watching a television infomercial a few months earlier. He was nothing more than a blue replica of a human male with a pedestal for legs and no arms. Apparently the manufactures wanted to be absolutely certain that he couldn't fight back. There were red lights on his chest and face to show where to jab during your work out regimen but I did not need any stinking lights that day. I put on the gloves and beat him within an inch of his artificial life. While I could not be absolutely sure, I was at least reasonably certain that his inner electronic mechanisms were sending out desperate signals to his creator to come and rescue him.

Afterwards, I still felt humiliated so I tried a somewhat more civilized approach. I sat down to write a poem in an attempt to make light of the incident. Some say it is good therapy. As a poet, I probably rank somewhere between hideous and just plain atrocious so read on at your own peril:

I walked into a ladder today,
It gashed my skull like a knife through clay
My mind did swoon, my brain was dazed,
I tried in vain to appear unfazed
But the man atop the swaying ladder
Was spewing foul unseemly chatter,
"You there below, you slovenly dolt!
Why give my ladder this jarring jolt?"
"I beg dear sir, forgive and be kind,
I am both clumsy and partially blind,
I'll show more care next time I pass"
"You'd best show care lest I kick your ass!"

"You'll kick my ass? Don't talk that way!"
"I'll come straight down, you'd best run away!"
"Ok, Ok, I seek not trouble,"
I turned to flee now seeing double.

 Either it was time for me to quit writing poetry while I was ahead, or call a shrink, I wasn't sure which.

Chapter Thirteen– The vending program

The following is a brief history regarding a program I knew absolutely nothing about prior to being registered with the Mass. Commission for the blind by Dr. Berson in 1980.

The Randolph Sheppard program was created by an act of Congress in 1936 and over 24,000 blind people have been employed in the program since its inception. West Virginia Representative Jennings Randolph and Senator Morris Sheppard of Texas sponsored the original legislation. They were two legislators who obviously wanted to do something substantial to assist those who are visually impaired in this country. They are both deceased now but anyone who has ever worked in this program owes them a tremendous debt of gratitude and should honor their memory.

The Act was amended in 1954 and again in 1974. The 1974 amendments greatly strengthened the provisions of the program and specifically included language that required the government to give "priority" rather than just "preference" to licensed blind persons whenever new concessions were constructed within government buildings. The program has annual gross sales of food and services in excess of $400 million and was once ranked among the fifty largest food service corporations in America.

The program was initially intended to assist veterans returning from World War One who suffered from blindness caused by chemical agents used extensively during that conflict. Members of congress were apparently moved upon seeing so many of these unfortunate souls standing around on street corners trying to sell pencils for a living so they created this program to offer them a better opportunity to support themselves.

Eventually, the program grew beyond its initial guidelines to its present day parameters, which includes any one who is registered as legally blind and a resident of this country. While the program is spelled out in the U.S.

Code making it a federally based piece of legislation, it is administered at the state level, so every state in the country has a vending program that is managed by a state agency. In Massachusetts, that agency is the Mass. Commission for the Blind.

What the act did in a nutshell was require the government to approach the vending program within the state where they were planning on constructing a new building, and offer them the rights to any concessions they had planned before they could put the locations out to bid for private sector companies. So let us say the IRS wanted to open a new office location somewhere in Massachusetts and they wished to have a snack bar or coffee shop on the premises. They could not just pick up the phone and call Dunkin Donuts or Starbucks without first offering it to the vending program.

In order to begin the process of becoming a vendor, an interested party contacts his vocational rehabilitation counselor who would then write up a referral to the vending program informing them of the client's interest in managing a vending facility. At that point, the director of the vending program would contact the blind individual and schedule him or her for an evaluation followed by training. The director of the program in 1992 was none other than Richard Leland who was my former counselor 10 years earlier when I first encountered vision related employment problems with Kemper Insurance.

I talked at length with my wife Julie about going to work in the program and at the time, she was employed as a legal secretary with the Hutchins and Wheeler law firm in Boston. I asked her to consider the possibility that if I was able to secure a stand, she might have to come and work with me since making toast is just about the extent of my culinary skills. Fortunately, she enjoyed the food business and was highly skilled in the kitchen. I, on the other hand, would soon discover that I absolutely loathed the food service industry.

I would be asking her to make a tremendous sacrifice and I would not have been upset if she had said no. She enjoyed a good salary with a full benefits package at the law firm. She would be giving all that up to come and work with me in a position that offered no benefits and a reasonable degree of financial uncertainty.

    I knew it would be a huge risk for me as well. It was not easy saying goodbye to my career as an insurance professional and I wrestled with that decision for many sleepless nights, but the previous ten years had simply been too chaotic. My vision was going to continue to deteriorate and claims handling was so unavoidably reading-intensive. I knew the day would come eventually that I would have to call it quits regardless of whatever visual aides came on the market.

    A gentleman by the name of Jack Lavelle was the field representative for the vending program at the time and he worked under Richard Leland. Jack visited me at my home in Everett one day and filled out some paperwork in order to get the process rolling. He asked me if I could begin training the following week. I told him by all means and before you could say "ham and cheese on rye, hold the mayo", he and I were in his car headed for a vending location at the MBTA headquarters building in Boston's Forest Hills section.

    There were approximately 45-50 locations in Massachusetts at that time and the program operated under a rigid seniority system. When a stand became available either due to it being a new facility or as a result of someone retiring from the program, the stand went out to bid amongst all the vendors. The bidding process did not involve money, and merely consisted of a letter of intent submitted by any vendor expressing interest in that location. On the day the bidding closed, the bids were opened and the person with the most seniority was awarded the location. He/she would then give up their existing stand, and that location would then go out for bid and the process would continue until the stands all had managers again. The program did allow for upward mobility into more profitable stands but because it was seniority based, advancement could be very slow going. If a stand went out for bid that no licensed vendor showed any interest in, it would then have to be offered to "any blind person" in the state. That is where I came in.

The program was not only for people who were totally blind, and as someone who had been declared "legally blind" I was eligible to become a vendor.

I was not even licensed yet and therefore had no seniority and no bidding power whatsoever so I did not have a snowballs chance in hell of being awarded one of the more lucrative facilities in the event one became available. Most of the vendors who occupied the five or ten best locations in the program never gave them up and more often than not, they quite literally died in them of old age. So again, the upward mobility aspect of this process tended to move very slowly.

Many of the vendors in the program were not totally blind and as such, they were not navigating their way around with a cane in front of them. Most of them were like me; legally blind people who could see well enough to perform this type of work, although in my case, bright sunlight was becoming a problem and going out at night was out of the question due to night blindness. The majority of the vendors could function adequately under most conditions in this state of being I call "no man's land". That murky, confusing, and frustrating purgatory that exists somewhere between the world of the sighted and the world of the totally blind.

I began training to become a vendor in early November of 1992, one month after Julie and I had tied the knot. Training was supposed to last for 12 weeks at which time you either passed the evaluation and were granted a license or, and this never happened to anyone that I know of, you failed and were sent directly to jail. Do not pass go, do not collect $200. The reason nobody failed I quickly realized was because all you needed to do to pass was walk and breathe at the same time. You did not even have to chew gum while you were doing it. The training program, at least in Massachusetts, left a great deal to be desired and I would later discover that other states take it far more seriously. As I would later ascertain with some degree of indignation, it was a direct reflection on the people running the program.

After one week of mopping floors, busing tables and peeling potatoes at the MBTA vending location, I called Jack and told him the work was too intellectually demanding and that I needed to give my brain a rest. I was doing OK the first few days but when I was told to peel hard-boiled eggs later that week that really put me over the top. I politely informed him to refrain from asking me to do any more training and to call me if there was a stand that nobody in the program wanted. He just laughed and said that would be fine. He knew my background at the time and had a hunch I would not survive 12 weeks of being used as little more than slave labor.

The training program they employed at that time basically consisted of Jack picking up the trainee and dumping him off for a week or two with various vendors who agreed to act as instructors. Neither party was compensated for their efforts. The end result was that the trainee was required to perform menial tasks with little to no applicable knowledge being exchanged and I found it to be a monumental waste of my time. The more I familiarized myself with the program the more I realized that very few vendors were qualified to teach their craft to others.

A few weeks later Jack called again and I learned that a stand had become available in Building 1600 at Hanscom Air Force Base in Bedford. I told him I would be more than happy to manage it. By not finishing my training, I would be penalized in the following manner. Licensed vendors who were awarded a location could not bid on another until they remained there for a period of 9 months. I presumed this rule was instituted to maintain some level of stability throughout the program. I would be prohibited from bidding out for twelve months. The additional three months did not bother me and as long as I would not be required to mop floors for someone else's leisure any longer, I accepted the terms. Once again, I was about to proceed down yet another occupational path which I knew relatively little about, but I was beginning to feel like life had become one great big maze and I was merely searching for a way out.

I visited the location the following week with Jack, who turned out to be a genuinely good person. I felt very badly for him over time because I sensed that he cared very much about maintaining a high level of standards within the program but was prohibited from doing so by the restrictions placed on him by his superiors, not to mention the heavy restraints of government bureaucracy.

The woman who had given up the stand at Hanscom claiming she was not making enough money was not there the day we visited the base and the shop was closed. Jack informed me that the absolute worst thing a vendor could do at these locations was close the doors for any period of time because customers are creatures of habit. If you turn them away they will find other places to frequent. All in all, it's just bad customer service. Jack had a key so we went inside the small room, which I discovered was L-shaped upon closer inspection.

The front counter area was only about ten feet across. There was a double door refrigerator, a single door refrigerator, and a four-foot high potato chip/snacks rack in front of the counter. On top of the counter was a cash register, a candy/gum rack and a counter top chip rack. Behind the counter was a five pot coffee brewer, a microwave, ice machine, under counter refrigerator and a creamer. To the right, wrapping around the corner was the kitchen area, which had a salad/sandwich bar, a stand up freezer, a refrigerator, a toaster, a microwave oven, and a meat slicer. According to Jack, this was pretty much standard equipment for a snack bar within the

Massachusetts program. There were no cafeteria setups in the state at that time, as Richard Leland didn't feel any of his vendors were qualified to run them. I learned months later that other states did have cafeterias in their programs so this was just a directorial decision on his part.

I looked closely at the equipment, which appeared to have some kind of alien growth thriving on its metal casings. Red Weed from H. G. Wells "War of the Worlds" probably looked like this I thought to myself. The place had a really funky smell to it as well.

"What was she cooking back here Jack, weasel stew?" I asked, holding my nose.

He just laughed. The entire facility was filthy, there was quite possibly every type of bacteria known to our world growing on the meat slicer and I was gripped by serious second thoughts about getting involved in the vending program.

"The National Center for Disease Control could have a field day with this place," I said in utter disgust. "Doesn't anyone inspect these locations? Look at this stuff. It looks like it hasn't been cleaned in months. It's so nasty even I can see it and I'm legally blind."

He just smiled. "We inspect each stand every six months," he said. "And the base inspectors are more strict than the ones who work for the state. I suspect the previous vendor is leaving because of problems she encountered with the base inspectors."

As I discovered later, the stands' shortcomings were not the result of the previous vendor being legally blind. I met her later that month when she returned to retrieve a personal item she had left behind. She could see even better than I could. It was more a case of pure laziness so my sympathy had its limits.

I think Jack was a little embarrassed during that first visit. I later discovered that it was his job to perform an audit/inspection twice a year. However, no one ever failed in the entire time he was there. The reason was that the standards they employed were set so low that anyone could pass them. The Commission felt that as long as customers were not ringing their phones off the hook with protests and complaints, they left the vendors alone. Short of an outbreak of food poisoning on a wide scale, they were allowed to conduct business as long as they sent in their weekly sales reports in a timely manner. The military inspectors, I soon found out, were brutally thorough however.

"You're going to pay for this Jack!" I said as we prepared to terminate our first visit. "I'll take the place but the agency will come in and clean it first right?"

"Yeah right, dream on," he answered and he was serious.

"Well, I can see why she wasn't making any money. Would you buy a sandwich in a place like this?" I asked.

Jack did not answer. He may have taken my remarks as a direct reflection on him and while I was pretty disgusted with what I saw, I didn't mean to hurt his feelings. Still, no one should be allowed to run an operation in that fashion. Where was this woman's self-respect, I thought to myself. I was not sure if the damage she had done to the stand's reputation would carry over and make it impossible to bring the customers back, but I was willing to try. I had grown bored of sitting at home and I was eager for a new adventure, even something as menial as this. The only positive to the situation was that I would at least be my own boss and in control of my own destiny. I could never do this kind of work if it meant being answerable to someone else. I remembered a quote from Milton's "Paradise Lost", which seemed at least somewhat appropriate. "It is better to rule in hell, than it is to serve in Heaven."

I tried not to be harsh with my criticisms of the program after that day at least for a while because I understood these vendors were visually impaired. When it comes to food safety issues though, there is no fooling around. I strongly felt that if a person's vision was so poor that they could not see the dirt and bacteria, then they needed to hire someone who could. The Randolph-Sheppard act does not prohibit blind managers from hiring fully sighted workers, and if that is what it took to maintain food safety standards, then that is what needed to be done.

The alternative is that an unsuspecting customer contracts some kind of food-borne illness. If you have ever found yourself in such a dire situation, you can personally attest that it is no trifling matter.

I walked out of there with some lingering and downright nauseating images floating through my mind and I never should have looked in the refrigerator. I never knew baloney could turn that color green before. Woof!

It took Julie and I two grueling eight-hour days to clean the entire establishment from top to bottom. While we were cleaning, people who worked in the building would walk by and noticed the remarkable transformation taking place. They could actually determine the color of the floor and counters. Building 1600 was in the middle of the base and the facility commander's office was right upstairs on the second floor. It was a 2-story building with over 200 employees but I could not seem to get a definitive answer from anyone as to the exact number of workers.

Getting to the base every day was going to be a real chore. Julie could not drive me, as Matt was still a mere seven years young and could not be left at home alone. The only way to get to Hanscom Air Force Base from Everett was to take the first bus out at 5:00 AM, which deposited me at Wellington Station in Medford. Then, I had to hop on an Orange Line train into downtown Boston, then switch to a Red Line train, which took me to Alewife Station in Cambridge. From there I had to board another bus for a 45-minute ride to the base. All in all the commute would take almost an hour and 45 minutes and would get me there at anywhere from 6:30 to 6:45, just in time to open at 7. It would require me to rise at 4:15 every morning and I had never had a previous job that demanded such a God-awful wake up time. My biological clock was in for a rude awakening and the ride home was just as lengthy so I would be spending over three and half hours a day riding trains and buses. That's almost twenty hours a week being cooped-up in closed-in vehicles with total strangers, some of whom absolutely refused to bathe on a regular basis. How inviting I thought, but I tenuously trudged on. What choice did I have? Vision loss was still cracking the whip like Yukon Jack trying to urge his sled dogs on to win the Iditarod, metaphorically speaking of course.

People seemed friendly enough when I opened the doors during Christmas week of 1992, and the initial response was good but business was very slow. I was working alone and Julie would come in around three in the afternoon to make sandwiches for the following day. She would wrap them in clear plastic and I would put them out for display while I just served coffee, tea, pastry products and ran the register. When I asked some of the customers where everybody was, they informed me that many of the military personnel went home for the holidays and they reassured me that there was no need to worry. After the first of the year, things would pick up. A woman by the name of Karen who worked upstairs for Cook travel voiced some much-needed encouragement. She told me that everyone was talking about how clean the place looked and how happy they were to have a new vendor take over who seemed to care about food safety. Personally, I could not understand the fuss. Running a dirty food establishment puts people's lives at risk. Other than clean, I said to myself, what other way is there to run such an establishment? This was not rocket science, I pondered, and your name doesn't have to be Oppenheimer to figure this one out.

After Christmas, I asked Julie if she wanted to make the move and begin her new career as the master chef of my coffee emporium. I knew if we were to make a successful go of this place we needed to have someone working the kitchen and making fresh-made sandwiches and specials. My dazzling charm and good looks were only going to take us so far and it just made sense to keep whatever income the place generated all in the family rather than having to hire someone from the outside. I would have to then provide them with workers comp coverage, health benefits, etc. which can be very expensive. She was growing tired of trucking into Boston every day via public transportation anyway. She always wanted to run her own kitchen so this was her opportunity to do it at a place where she could now drive to work and practically set her own hours. She made a huge sacrifice, for which I was eternally grateful, and once she came on board after everyone returned to work from their holiday breaks, we were soon doing six times the amount of business the previous vendor had done and we had only been there for one month. People started coming in by the herds and there were times when Julie and I almost could not keep up with the lunch rush.

In all my years, I have never seen anyone who could run a better operation than she could. She would have five orders going at once and every sandwich, soup, salad and special she prepared was delivered with a high degree of quality. The people in the building loved her food and we had that place cranking on all cylinders in no time.

I had difficulty understanding how anyone could have a problem running a place like this. It had a few basic elements that needed to be adhered to and that was pretty much it. Keep the place clean, keep it well stocked with snacks, sodas, etc., serve fresh coffee, good quality sandwiches and make sure everything was properly dated. Knowing a good deal about the FDA code (Food and Drug Administration) did not hurt either when the base inspectors came around, so I took it upon myself to study "the book" whenever I found some spare time.

It felt good to be back working even if it was not exactly what I wanted to be doing in my life at that point in time. I knew I was way over-qualified to engage in that type of occupation but the newness of it sustained me for several months. Like most jobs however, the novelty would eventually wear off in more ways than one. Visually, I was able to adapt the register and the front counter area to suit my needs. I was able to pour coffee without difficulty and for the most part, I was still able to function reasonably well. I had to hold dollar bills close to my face to determine what denomination the customer was handing me however. Very often this would generate strange looks or remarks from the customer such as "it's not counterfeit, don't worry," because many people just were not aware that I was legally blind or that this stand was part of the blind vending program. I would then have to defend my action with an explanation that left them feeling apologetic or uncomfortable. That just goes with the territory I thought to myself. I was not about to hang a "Commission for the Blind" sign for all to see as some vendors chose to do. In my mind, all that would do is announce loud and clear to that small percentage of dishonest customers that exist at every location: "Hey folks, if you feel inclined to steal something go right ahead 'cause I can't see for diddily squat." Theft is a major problem in every blind facility across the country and as troubling as it is to believe that anyone would steal from a blind person, it happens with alarming regularity.

There were four vending facilities on the base at that time and a man by the name of Mike Macdonald operated the biggest location, which was right across the street from us in headquarters building. Mike, who enjoyed a customer base of over 1,000 people in his building, was one of the more capable vendors in the program and indirectly, he played a part in the naming of my coffee shop. His place was called "Mike's" and therefore I could not very well call my place "Mike's" as it would have caused major confusion with both customers and our delivery people as well. Julie came up with the idea of calling our shop "Seagull's", which was a previous nickname of mine from my teaching days with the Old

Orchard Beach Marching Seagull Band, so "Seagull's" it was.

Mike and I became good friends but not until after he got over getting really angry with me one Monday morning. He showed up for work and was greeted by 'Seagull's Coffee' flyers taped to all the doors entering his building. Apparently, he had really angered a customer of his who's identity remains unknown. This phantom malcontent had visited our location and secretly took some of the flyers off my counter, then went back and taped them up in Mike's building to get back at him. It took me a couple of weeks to convince Mike that it was not my doing.

From that point on we were very supportive of one another. We treated each other in a manner that I always felt visually impaired vendors should treat one another…with mutual respect and cooperation for the benefit of everyone in the program. I only wished that all the other vendors shared this sentiment, because I would later discover, very few of them did.

By the end of the summer of 1993, we had just finished our first successful nine months at "Seagull's" and I was still writing and teaching. Everett News publisher Nick Deangelo had tried to expand his operation too quickly though in an attempt to increase circulation and soon found himself in financial difficulties. He filed for bankruptcy in 1994, the paper closed down operations and his sinking ship took my editorial column with it. I wasn't devastated by the events as I had been a columnist for five years and I had to admit, it was getting a little old. Plus, going to the base every day and being on my feet for 10 straight hours was kicking my butt and I had little energy left on the weekends for coming up with fresh new ideas for columns. During my years with the paper I had covered a wide range of interesting topics. From the Oliver North hearings, the Iran-Contra scandal and War in the Middle East to over-aggressive youth hockey parents. I even included one feature that was written at the request of many

Everett streetwalkers. In it, I admonished dog owners who refused to pick up after their pets leaving city sidewalks a veritable mine field of doggy depth charges. During my early days of covering sports, I had done interviews with Boston-area legends like Carl Yaztremski, Bobby Orr, and Brad Park. It was a great ride while it lasted, but I will be the first to admit, I was getting a bit stale.

I had dreams of writing a novel someday but I wasn't really sure when I would be able to find the time. I was approaching the big 4-0 and I began noticing that my energy levels were not quite what they used to be. After a week at Seagull's, I usually found myself laying on the couch on Friday night physically exhausted, mentally drained, and unable to function. We were making decent money but enjoying life less, and this was not a good combination.

Julie threw a surprise 40th birthday party for me at a local Chinese food restaurant that was located in downtown Everett right across the street from where I had almost knocked that poor guy off his ladder. The entire restaurant was filled with my closest friends and family and I was very touched and grateful for her gesture. However, after the euphoria of the party wore off, I was left with the lingering, depressing realization that age, as it does with all of us, was catching up with me.

Drum corps was a refreshing respite but to a lesser degree than it had been in years past. It offered some occasional relief from the tedium of working at the coffee shop and it represented the only real creative outlet I had left. You know what they say though. How long can a good thing last. Like everything else in my life for the previous 15 years, the fates always seemed to find a way to crash the party in their unique special way.

Following the 1993 season with East Coast Jazz, the staff had another falling out with director Tom Chopelas and sure enough, for the second time in 10 years, he gave most of the staff the boot. I was once again omitted from the "fired list" because I tried to steer clear of the all-too-frequent bickering that took place that summer. I had known Tom for almost 2 decades, thought the world of him, and was grateful for the many opportunities he had given me, but he could be one tough cookie to get along with sometimes. Trying to maintain a working relationship was starting to wear on me. It was his corps, and I was just an instructor so in the final analysis, he always got, and probably deserved to have the last word on just about everything.

Running my own business, small as it may have been, was really taking its toll. Additionally, my stepson Matt deserved more of my time and attention than he had been getting. So, after 28 years of being involved with the activity on one level or another it was probably a fitting time to say goodbye for good. I made the difficult decision to go into retirement again but teaching had become less enjoyable than it was in years past. It was the nineties now and video games and computers had begun to influence the minds and behavior of America's young people. Parents were using us as little more than a babysitting service, many of the kids were totally undisciplined and just didn't have anywhere near the level of enthusiasm and commitment for the activity that we had when we were their age. After 3 decades, maybe it was just time to say goodbye once and for all to the activity I had loved so much and which had given me so much in return.

I reversed direction and attempted to expose my stepson Matthew to as many activities as I possibly could. Under my careful guidance, he tried his hand at ice hockey, soccer, basketball and little league baseball, all at which he proved reasonably adept. I continued to attend drum corps shows every summer but the activity was changing so much, moving away from the military bearing and community-based roots to a more exclusive, less disciplined art form. The number of drum corps nationally had plummeted from over 400 in the 1970's to fewer than 75 in the 1990's. Joysticks were now replacing drumsticks.

The rigors of my commute were continuing to take a toll and I would often find myself falling asleep on the long ride home. I didn't drool but it was no less embarrassing I can tell you. This was a far cry from the 8:30-4 sitting-at-my-desk routine I was accustomed to at the insurance position. When you manage a vending facility, you are on your feet constantly and there is no such thing as lunch breaks. By Friday night, I was a zombie and I knew we had to move closer to the base if I was going to be able to keep this up for long. Therefore, in 1994, we moved to a new apartment in Lexington and my commute was shortened to a far more manageable 10-20 minutes.

This also meant that I would be transported to work in a very different fashion. Enter "The Ride." The Ride is a service offered by the Mass. Bay Transportation Authority (MBTA), a state agency, which operated all the train and bus routes in and around Boston and Eastern Mass. The Ride was established for elderly and handicapped people only and was expanded as a result of the Americans with Disabilities Act of 1990. It was a great service for those who depended upon it and could not access regular public transportation. The Ride vans and cars offered a door-to-door service and for the most part, they were generally on time. It was necessary for me to schedule my rides in advance and 99 percent of the time I was granted the times I requested.

While vision loss requires one to swallow his/her pride however, my appetite for such things has its limits.

I would encounter tremendous difficulties in the early stages of getting over the stigma of using this mode of transportation. I drove for 10 years of my life and I still missed it terribly. The ability to come and go as I pleased was something I cherished greatly. Now I would be relegated to depending on a handicapped van to cart me around and hoping that it was on time. Then, even if it was punctual, I prayed that there would not be too many stops along the way before I was dropped off at work where I had to open at 7 AM sharp. I soon discovered to my utter chagrin that a ten-minute ride across town could turn into a two-hour nightmare if too many other passengers were booked on the same van. On those occasions, no matter how much I complained, the stock reply from the dispatcher was always the same. "It's a shared service. There is nothing we can do about it."

For the most part the drivers were genuinely nice people and in the early days of my Ride experience, I encountered some very qualified individuals. I would later grow to become very fond of some of them and would even count them as good friends.

Then, there is the flip side of the Ride experience. Many times, I would get on the van and there would be a person in a wheelchair already on board. Sitting behind him might be an elderly man with an oxygen tank. I have the utmost respect for the elderly and nothing but admiration and compassion for the handicapped people who courageously head out to work everyday. When you come from the world of the non-handicapped however, there is a great adjustment to be made in regards to one's psyche when placed in this situation. I am not ashamed to admit that I was embarrassed to be dropped off at work in full view of my customers by a van for the handicapped. It was stubborn human pride and I was willing to accept that it was shallow on some level, but it still ate away at me with increasing ferocity. It was also depressing because I felt so badly for these people and could do nothing to help them. Further, I detested the feeling of helplessness I experienced having to be picked up and driven to work by anyone. I loathed the fact that I could not drive myself and that my independence had been stripped away from me.

The pedestrian existence can be very, very humbling at times. One morning when I got off the bus to walk to my coffee shop, a motorist stopped to let me cross and as I reached the other side of the street, I turned to wave in a gesture of thanks when I felt something slam me in the chest. It was a parking meter. A gray, very unyielding parking meter. My visual blind spots were gray too so I never even saw the damned thing.

    When I arrived home that night, I removed my shirt and the 25 cents indentation that was stamped into my chest had faded so I proceeded through my newfound ritual of pummeling Mr. Slam Man, then sitting down at my desk over a Corona with lime to immortalize the incident through the gift of poetry. I was becoming a very sick man.

Oh parking meter, so strong in might
I saw you not through that bright sunlight
As I hurried across the street that day
Never dreaming you'd suddenly be in my way
I waved to thank the car that stopped
Then wouldn't you know, I sure got popped
You really took my breath away
Just another collision, just another day

Move over Robert Frost.

Chapter Fourteen- Increasing discontent

By 1995, the fates had relieved me of my insurance career, my judging career, and I had left drum corps altogether. I was beginning to notice that not only was I losing my patience more easily than ever before, another emotion was starting to take control of my inner workings as well. I was beginning to get angry… very, very angry at all the things I was losing in my life and having to give up. I was getting sick and tired of the limitations vision loss was saddling me with, and on those rare occasions when I would come in contact with my other brothers, I could see that it was tearing them apart as well.

The more I learned about the vending program, the more frustrated I became with it as well. I was acutely aware that a combination of the anger over losing my vision along with the frustration at how poorly the program was being run was creating an unhealthy mixture of discontent in my mind. It was beginning to simmer like a nasty witches' brew with me as the main course.

Like most government programs, the Randolph Sheppard Act looks great in theory but it does not always hold up in practice. I learned that there were many factions who would like nothing better than to see the program abolished. Other special interest groups had designs on the program, such as the private sector companies who drooled over the prospect of getting their slimy little hands on some of the prime locations across the country. Then you have other agencies that represent those who are afflicted with other types of handicaps such as the hearing impaired. They do not have access to a program like this one. Are their claims justified, I asked myself? Perhaps, but a person who is visually impaired is at a much greater disadvantage than someone who is hearing impaired. That is an indisputable fact.

The envy and resentment vendors are sometimes subjected to can come from all sides. I have personally heard state employees remark on more than one occasion that "they wish someone had given them their own small business on a silver platter." To which I reply, "I'll tell you what. Give me your 20/20 vision, I'll give you my eye condition and you can have this place right now." As if I am supposed to feel privileged to have my own snack bar when I would give anything to A) not have to contend with going blind, B) leave the vending program behind and C) go back to my career and my pre-legally blind life.

Was it just me, I suddenly contemplated, or was the world around me becoming a less-compassionate place?

For the most part our customers at Hanscom were decent people and I made some very good friends there. We were still dealing with human beings, however, and military human beings at that. They sometimes viewed the vendors as being fortunate to have such "cushy" opportunities where we did not have to pay rent or utilities. As such, some of them would engage in activities that would adversely affect our daily sales. They failed to realize that the reason we were not required to pay rent was that if we were asked to do so, most of the vendors would throw the keys on the counter and go home. Most of the locations in the program were in out of the way, desolate places where no private entity in its' right mind would open a business. The idea that a Dunkin Donuts or Starbucks for example, would even consider opening a location in a building with 200 employees is ludicrous. Granted, there were a handful of stands in the program that did in fact show a respectable profit. They were far and few between however. For the most part, the majority of stands were not placed in what would be considered highly desirable, well-trafficked locations. Many of the current vendors were earning menial wages at best.

I became aware that some military employees were routinely visiting the base commissary and buying cases of soda at half the cost that I was required to pay by purchasing direct from Coca-Cola and Pepsi. As non-military personnel, the vendors were not allowed to shop there. Then they would sell sodas out of their offices for .50 where I had to charge .75 just to make a profit. This eventually escalated to include many other items like chips and snacks. There was already a number of office coffee clubs operating in our building that were established by employees who were probably fed up with drinking the inferior brand our predecessor had been serving up. It was an ongoing issue, which I had ignored for some time. Julie and I were doing reasonably well so I overlooked much of this activity, not wanting to upset the apple cart.

    Then one day I received a call from fellow vendor Cheryl Inman who was running a small concession in the Brown building, which was located near the Hartwell Avenue entrance to the base. She was in tears because the employees in her building were running yet another fundraiser and were selling tacos right outside the entrance to her snack bar. She had only sold one sandwich all day. This was just plain ignorance on someone's part and there is no other word for it. I could forgive this if the fundraiser was for some noble cause like cancer research or scholarships for needy students on base, but more often than not, they were held to raise money for their Christmas parties or some other nonsense. The perception these people had that we vendors were making all kinds of money and that it was perfectly acceptable to unfairly compete with us was totally misguided. In the first place, vendors worked long and hard and if everything fell into place, we could take home a "decent" weeks pay, and by decent I mean somewhere around the poverty level in this country. Generally speaking, when factored into the number of hours actually worked, a vendor in the program could expect to earn anywhere from 8-12 dollars an hour. Not a king's ransom by any means. When these employee fundraising activities occurred too frequently, our income could be drastically reduced. There are few things worse than coming to work at O-dark thirty, prepping for lunch, and then standing there with your thumb up your butt because some insensitive group of individuals is selling hot dogs right outside your door. It is disheartening and over time can destroy your desire to continue in this line of work which most of us were doing out of necessity to begin with, and certainly not out of choice. Not to mention the fact that these people were government employees and I doubt that any of this activity fell under the terms of their job descriptions. These were well-salaried employees with guaranteed paychecks, paid vacations and full benefits to boot. To us, our little vending operations were a matter of survival.

The United States military had used and abused me once before, so I was not about to let them do it to me again. I loved my country, and I liked my customers, but I did not love the military, necessary as they might be on some sadistic level. I was in a different position now. I was a handicapped individual. I was as yet oblivious to the fact that with that status came power, because no one wants to be perceived as being on the wrong side of a handicapped issue in this country. Politicians, military leaders, and public figures alike are more concerned with their public images than almost anything else, and they will do anything to keep their reputations from becoming tarnished. They would rather drink lead paint than be seen as having done anything that proved detrimental to a member of the handicapped community because that my friends is political dynamite. I could use this to my advantage and in this newly discovered, deranged state of mind I found myself operating with, that is exactly what I intended to do.

I proceeded to take action. I did not want to ostracize my customers or send the wrong message so I had to be diplomatic about it, but I decided to file a grievance with the Commission and force the agency to confront the Air Force. All four vendors on the base including Mike Macdonald applauded my action but none of us knew how it would affect customer relations. The bottom line was however, right is right and wrong is wrong and you have to stand up for your principles and self-dignity. Some of these "fly-boys" were in desperate need of a "dope slap" and I was just the guy to do it. Besides, if nothing else, it would give me a great outlet with which to vent my ever-increasing anger while giving "Slam Man" a much-needed rest.

Was this an attempt to seek real justice? Or, merely the actions of a man going slowly and imperceptibly out of his mind? I really could not tell which, but Edgar Allen Poe is my favorite author. What does that tell you?

Upon receiving my grievance, director Richard Leland contacted me and asked about the details of the problem. I could tell immediately that he wanted no part of this and the reason for that was, he rarely looked forward to getting involved in anything that would require him to put in some extra effort. I have learned from experience and observation that working for the government has a way of pounding you into a state of utter stagnation that I often refer to as "comfortably numb." It could be due to the slow pace at which the bureaucratic machinery churns but the full scope of the reasons have never become clear to me. I have heard that once a person remains a government employee for 10 years, they become "unemployable" in the private sector where as we all know, they expect results. While I am not attempting to disparage those who work in a government capacity, there is no doubt in my mind that their counterparts in the private sector are held to a slightly higher work standard.

When I laid out the nature of our dilemma to Richard, he suggested that he would set up a meeting with the base commander and address the issues. "What a brilliant idea," I thought to myself and I agreed wholeheartedly and wished him the best of luck, fearing that little would come of it. Diogenes was the Greek philosopher who founded the "cynic" movement of which I am a proud card-carrying member. He is still out there somewhere, carrying his little lantern and looking for that honest man in utter futility.

When the day of the meeting arrived, Rich showed up at my coffee shop just after 1PM and asked if I wanted to accompany him upstairs. I could tell by the shifty look in his eyes why he was asking. Rich was basically a decent person but unfortunately, he was a bit of a jellyfish and I could tell he was in no mood to take on the base commander 'mano y mano'. If I did not go with him, I feared this would end up being a mano-mental waste of time.

I asked Julie if she could handle things for a while and luckily, the lunch rush was over so Rich and I headed up to the second floor to confront the big cheese. As we walked down the hall to his office and past the little cheeses, some of whom were customers of mine, we received some strange looks but I was determined to see this through. The memory of Cheryl crying in my ear on the phone that day was all I needed for motivation. At that moment in time, the blind vendors needed a champion, and since there were none to be found, an angry deranged former insurance adjuster would have to do.

As we walked into the base commanders' office, an aide greeted us, then escorted us into the next room where we sat down at a long rectangular conference table. Colonel Adams came in and introduced himself to Richard. Then he took a seat directly across from me and opened the discussion. I did not feel comfortable because I was wearing my coffee shop attire of t-shirt, dungarees, and sneakers and here he was a full bird Colonel. He was probably thinking to himself, "Why is this dweeb wasting my time over a few cans of freaking soda pop?" I mustered every bit of confidence I had left and tried to imagine myself back in the claims office dealing one on one with claimants and attorneys. More than anything, I was operating from the position of strength in knowing that no matter how trivial he might think this situation was, the vendors were in the right and the Air Force was in the wrong. Period.

"So, what seems to be the problem gentlemen?" the Colonel asked smugly.

I looked at Richard to respond first out of respect for his position. He hesitated for a moment but then gathered his courage and proceeded to explain why we were there.

"Well Colonel, as you know the program has 4 locations at Hanscom and we have always had a good relationship with you people and appreciate everything you do for us," he started.

Good job Rich, very diplomatic I thought to myself.

"But Michael has filed a grievance with the agency on behalf of himself and the other vendors over unfair competition at the base and I am required to respond to grievances so that is why we are here today. I'm hoping we can come to some form of agreement that is amicable to both sides and we certainly aren't here to ruffle anyone's' feathers."

"Well, I wish you had come to me first instead of going over my head," the Colonel said looking at me and with a slight air of indignation. I had sent letters of protest to Congressman Markey and Senator Ted Kennedy's office hoping to recruit their help and support. Kennedy, for all his reputed shortcomings, has always been supportive of blind vendors in Massachusetts. There are five locations in the John F. Kennedy building in Boston where his office resides.

I shot right back at him. "I DID come to you first Colonel. Didn't you read the letters I have been sending you?" I was starting to feel a little impatient at this point. These two were both on my time. Julie was alone downstairs which was not easy for her so I wanted to wrap things up as quickly as I could. Besides, I didn't even like this smug, impudent, twit of a colonel. He looked too much like that lieutenant who had stamped an end to my stay at Fort Knox.

"Look Colonel, the bottom line is this," I retorted, "The vendors on this base show up to work everyday never even knowing if we are going to earn a days pay. We provide a valuable service to your people, we work very hard to provide that service to the best of our abilities and we do not need anyone cutting the legs out from under us with the kind of activities that go on all over this base. I do not have to remind you that buying items at the base Commissary and then reselling them for a profit out of offices is against your own Air Force regulations (I did my homework.) It is also prohibited in the Randolph-Sheppard regulations, which means in a nutshell that these people are in violation of the law. However, more than anything, it is unfair, it is wrong and it is hurting our ability to earn a living. We have rent to pay and children to feed just like you people do and if you're not going to do something about it, I'll go to the newspapers next."

    Both the Colonel and Richard were silent for a moment. I think it was at that point that they both realized just how infuriated I was over this whole affair. What they did not know was that I was not just upset about the unfair competition, I was furious with just about everything that was going on in my life, and I was like a human teakettle venting its steam.

    After a pause, the colonel spoke again. "Well, I really don't think that will be necessary Mr. Merrett. I will issue a base wide reminder to everyone as to the regulations and instruct them as to how they should conduct themselves in regards to the Randolph-Sheppard vendors. Will that satisfy you?"

    "Absolutely Colonel. But what happens if you issue this memorandum and it isn't worth the paper it's written on?" Oops. I just insinuated that his orders did not carry any weight on the base. "What I mean is, I find it hard to believe that employees do not already know they are not supposed to be doing this and that superior officers aren't just looking the other way. What assurances do I leave this office with that the Air Force will enforce the regulations?" I was being pushy now but I did not care. Memories of my Fort Knox experience were floating through my mind as I looked across the table at him, smug as a bug in a rug. As far as I was concerned, I was showing him more respect than he deserved. He knew this was wrong; he just did not give a damn.

"I will make sure that they are enforced," he said, "and if you still see this type of activity going on, I want you to bring it directly to my attention. Is that understood?"

"Loud and clear Colonel," I answered. "And rest assured I won't hesitate to do just that. One final thing. I don't want to leave you with the wrong impression. We have the utmost respect for the quality of the people we deal with here at Hanscom and I personally do not think that these actions are taken to purposely harm the vendors in any way. I just think it is a lack of understanding on the part of the few individuals who engage in this type of activity and it demonstrates a lack of sensitivity towards our position. If nothing else these people just need to be educated as to the effects this unfair competition has on some very hardworking people. Ignorance runs rampant in our world Colonel and perhaps, together, we can help stamp it out. So there is no disrespect intended and I hope none is perceived by you."

What a load of bullshit *that* was.

While it was not easy for me to say, there would be nothing to gain by making an enemy of the officer who was currently top dog on the base. I did not like him one bit, but no matter how we sliced it, we vendors were operating on their turf, and trying to maintain positive relations only made good sense, so I extended my hand as an act of conciliation. We shook hands and Richard and I headed downstairs but I had very little confidence that the Colonel was going to do all that much to rectify the problem. He really did not give a rat's behind about the vendors but he would have to issue the memorandum. If nothing else, it would send a clear message that the vendors were aware of what was going on, that we did not appreciate it, and that these activities were against regulations. On the surface, it would represent a moral victory for the vendors and give us the ability to point to the Colonel's orders, if and when we witnessed this activity in the future.

"So we'll see what happens," Richard said meekly as we arrived back at my coffee shop. He barely said anything in the Colonel's office but I never really expected him to. Then again, I really did not give him much of a chance to say anything come to think of it.

"Yeah, we'll see," I said. "But I really don't expect much to change. I want to see how strongly he words the memorandum first, and then we'll know if this meeting was worth my time."

"Then you don't know what you are going to do with the grievance? Do you want me to close it or what?" he asked.

That is really all he cared about at that juncture. The agency did not like grievances and Richard loathed them in particular because it made him look bad in the eyes of his superiors, so he wanted to resolve them as quickly as possible. Like I said, he was basically a decent person but he really wasn't all that concerned that some of the vendors were losing money to greedy Air Force personnel. Way down deep, Richard saw us as ungrateful malcontents who were fortunate to have such opportunities, and that was because for the most part, there were many vendors in the program who habitually did complain about everything. I did not want to contribute to that perception because there was some validity to it, but my gut told me there was just something that was not proper about this and I did not feel the least bit guilty about trying to do something to stop it.

"Don't cancel it yet Richard until I read the Colonel's memorandum. Then I'll let you know."

"I'll just wait to hear from you then," he said.

"I'll call you, I won't leave you hanging," I answered, and with that, we parted company and I went behind the counter to relieve Julie.

"Everything OK?" I asked.

"Everything is fine. How'd it go?" she asked. Even with something as simple as dungarees, a sweatshirt, and an apron, she always managed to look great. I did not know how lucky I was at the time but then we humans take so much for granted. As the song says, "You don't know what you've got 'til it's gone."

"He's going to issue a base wide reminder to everyone so only time will tell," I answered.

I called the other vendors and informed them of the outcome of our discussions. Everyone seemed satisfied but we all remained skeptical. Cynicism is a by-product of vision loss. It is increasingly difficult to maintain a positive outlook on life when some enigmatic eye condition is wreaking havoc on your world. I never bought into the "Life sucks, then you die" philosophy but it was beginning to burrow like a ravenous ground hog deep into the recesses of my cranium.

I received a copy of the Colonel's release two days later and it was worded even more strongly than I had hoped. The big question remaining was whether he did it merely to pacify us or was the Air Force really going to enforce what the letter spelled out? To our collective relief, none of us experienced any backlash from customers. In fact, many people felt badly that such things were taking place and causing financial hardships for the vendors. Like most places you go in life, the vast majority of the folks at Hanscom were good people with the usual smattering of idiots thrown in for comic relief.

Later that year a stand became available on the other side of the base that mildly piqued our curiosity. Julie and I were getting a bit stale at our present location, as it was very small and greatly limited the extent of what we could offer for a menu. After careful deliberation, I bid on the other location, as it was much larger and better equipped.

Since most vendors in the program were both unwilling to travel to the base, and fearful of the military health inspectors, no one else bid on the location. As a result, I won the bid and was notified that I could assume management of the location two weeks later. When we made the move to the new stand, which was located near one of the rear gates in the Phillips Lab building, our customers at Building 1600 were sorry to see us go. They had endured some bad vendors in the past but I told them not to worry. My older brother Bert would be my replacement. His location in Watertown was closing due to military cutbacks so he bid on my stand and appeared to be the high bidder. Bert knew what he was doing and would do at least as good a job as we had if not better.

Bert had already been working in the vending program for 12 years by the time I took the plunge and he was experiencing knee problems, backaches, kidney problems, all from being on his feet for hours on end. A troubling thought kept running through my mind, "Is that what I have to look forward to?" so I went out and bought a new pair of comfortable shoes. Brilliant!

Moving to Phillips Lab was a revelation. Most of the work that took place at Hanscom was of a high-tech nature and some of the best minds in the military operated out of this location. Hanscom had fallen on hard times however. The amount of activity taking place there was diminishing to the point where it was in danger of being closed. I noticed early on that many of the employees coming in to buy a coffee at Phillips Lab were complaining that they had no work to do, and to my further dismay, layoffs were taking place and the customer base was shrinking. We had no way of knowing this prior to the move.

Additionally, we were taking over from a vendor who had the type of facility and equipment at his disposal where he could have produced fresh-made items which is far more preferable to customers. Like some vendors though, he was, shall we say, lacking ambition and he chose instead to have pre-packaged sandwiches and salads delivered by a canteen outfit located in Medford.

The kitchen area had not been used in several months and was covered in dirt, dust, cigarette smoke and ash. Once again, we found ourselves facing a major clean-up operation before we could even begin doing business. I cursed the Commission for allowing a vendor to continue to operate in such a shoddy environment.

Once we were operational and making everything fresh, the customers responded like hungry wolves. There was a conference room right next door and we were benefiting from business generated by the meetings they held there as well. A female Colonel asked us to cater a meeting of 70 people one day. I agreed to do it for her and we enjoyed the best one-day sales total we had ever seen up to that point. I had to bring in my sister Pat who was not working at her job that day and I hired a part time woman from the base who helped as well. Her name was Hyun Ju, but everyone called her Rachel. A native-born Korean, she was the wife of a Lt. Colonel and was a very hard worker so that day we had four people trying to keep up with the orders.

Unfortunately, after 3 months, the Air Force had to go and spoil it. Some muttonhead got the idea that if they put in a coffee set up out back at the entrance to the conference room they could charge attendees $5.00 each for providing them with coffee and donuts. So much for Colonel Adams Memorandum. We could not see the setup from our coffee shop but a loyal customer had tipped me off as to its presence. I could understand such a move if we were doing an inadequate job or charging excessive prices but neither was the case. Someone just got greedy and wanted a piece of the action.

Even though Adams was the base commander, Phillips had its own colonel and he operated under a slightly different set of rules. Once I heard about the set up, I immediately filed a letter of protest with the base commander and the higher-ups at Phillips Lab, but no one did anything about it.

I had now been in the program for about 4 years and the drudgery and anger over being forced into this line of work due to vision loss was beginning to fester like a raging case of poison ivy. Business was falling off due to layoffs and the infernal coffee set up. To add insult to injury, we had to close for two days when a maintenance worker removed a trash bag full of soda cans that an employee had placed in our lobby. He released a cloud of fruit flies that infested our entire kitchen. I wondered why no one was buying any pastry that day until Julie showed up around 9:30 to prep for lunch. She noticed with utter dismay that all the pastry in the display case was covered with fruit fly's which I of course couldn't see. By then I was incensed, not to mention borderline homicidal.

    I met with a lawyer and had him file the necessary papers in United States District Court that would initiate a lawsuit against the Air Force. I was willing to represent myself but I needed a lawyer to correctly file the necessary documents so that the judge would not just throw out the case due to shoddy filing methods.

    The judge eventually threw it out anyway but not for that reason. The Randolph Sheppard act had a series of steps the vendor was required to follow prior to taking such an action. The cumbersome process involves filing an initial grievance, then going to administrative hearing, then arbitration, and finally to the Secretary of Human Services. I was so livid I tried to circumvent that process suspecting that it was probably established to make it next to impossible for a vendor to receive any restitution.

    I had just about had it at that point. Within the first few months at Phillips, the pipes under the sink had simply fallen off due to neglect. The dishwasher had quit on us, the 20-year-old grate that secured the location was falling apart. A freezer had bitten the dust because the previous vendor had never cleaned the compressor and I was ready to strangle someone at the Commission because of how poorly they ran the program. Rather than resort to physical violence, I decided instead to run for the State Committee of Blind Vendors thinking I could bring about some positive change. The Doobie Brothers wrote a song for just such an occasion. Perhaps you have heard it? It is called 'What a fool believes.'

What I did not recognize at the time was that the difficulties I was having with everyone around me were actually just manifestations of the whirlwind of emotions that were constantly intensifying in my mind. I was becoming more resentful with every passing day. I was so tired at the end of each shift I no longer had any energy to go down in the basement and beat the bejeezes out of Mr. Slam Man, so I had no way of releasing the growing stress. I knew this would eventually lead to problems and as usual, I was right.

The State Committee of blind vendors was a board of seven individuals who were elected by a vote of all the members. One could either be nominated by a fellow vendor or one could merely nominate his or herself. The Committee functioned purely in an advisory capacity per the Randolph-Shepard federal regulations. They lacked the authority to actually write policy but because the Mass. Commission for the Blind vending staff people were so indifferent towards the program in general, they bowed to the Committee's influence more often than not. I actually thought I could go in there and motivate the agency and other members of the Committee to institute stronger standards and guidelines for the program. I never would have guessed that at the age of 41, childhood naivety would still be around to cloud my judgment.

I managed to get elected largely on my reputation at the base, which gave me three votes right there. You only needed 10 or 15 votes to make the seven-member panel since there were nine people running for seven positions and there were only 50 vendors in the entire program. Half of them did not care enough about the State Committee to even cast a vote. Another well-intentioned vendor by the name of Ray Lewis ran for the first time as well and won a seat with me. Each vendor was allowed to vote for three candidates. Ray and I became very good friends and despite the fact that the other five members were vendors who had been on the Committee for several years, thereby representing the "status-quo", we both thought that if we approached it the right way, we could do some positive things for the program.

It was at our first annual vendors meeting that I realized the full extent of what I was up against. When I stood up and suggested that performance standards be considered along with seniority in regards to the bidding process, I was nearly lynched. One by one, the 20 or so vendors in the room stood up and to the best of their abilities, attempted to state their case as to why I was a despicable gutter-rat for even suggesting such a thing. The prevailing attitude seemed to be that all Ray and I were trying to do was circumvent the seniority system so that he and I could ascend through the ranks more quickly. Ray and I just looked at each other and shook our heads.

This was the first time I had met other members of the program en-masse. I quickly realized after listening to them speak that of the 50 vendors in the program at that time, only a very small handful had any education to speak of. Many of the others had been in the program all their lives and had no other work experience to draw upon. This was all they knew, and they resented two upstarts like us coming in and trying to tell them what to do even if what we were suggesting to them made perfect sense.

I was left to ponder the stark realization that the Randolph-Sheppard program was a novel idea initiated by two progressive minded legislators who were no doubt proceeding with the very best of intentions, but in practice, it had a myriad of glaring shortcomings. In Massachusetts, there were probably five to ten solid, highly trafficked locations, which offered the vendor a great opportunity to earn a respectable income if he/she was willing to work for it. Many of the other locations were stuck in basements or some desolate corner of a building where customers needed a road map just to find you. The vendor was relegated to working very hard and for long hours for what often constituted as menial wages.

Ray and I were only concerned with improving the standing of all the vendors and we were not talking about reinventing the wheel. We suggested little things like standardizing the way we all served coffee. Many vendors did not know or just did not care that a pot of coffee will begin to break down after 20-30 minutes if left on the heating element, resulting in coffee tasting burnt and bitter. I suggested that all vendors be required to use air pots, which kept the coffee fresh for up to 8 hours because they contained a thermos and had no heating element.

There was no standard way of doing anything in the program and everyone just did whatever they wanted. I could not make them understand that such an approach was fine if all the vendors were going to stay at their present locations for the rest of their careers. Unfortunately, when you have a program that involves upward mobility and vendors are allowed to constantly bid on better locations resulting in frequent movement throughout the program, we all had an obligation to one another to do things properly. By adhering to a set of sensible standards, we could better insure that we left a successful thriving business opportunity to the next person who succeeded us. Unfortunately, my attempts to get the point across were fruitless. I might as well have been talking to a room full of department store mannequins because many of them had closed their minds off to any new ideas before they even walked into the room.

Ray and I both left the committee after one year and resigned ourselves to the fact that, while a few of the vendors appreciated our efforts and agreed with what we were trying to do, we were not going to connect with the others who sadly represented a small-minded majority. We were left with an unhealthy environment that was totally counter-productive. On one side of the aisle sat the agency staff people who in some cases loathed the vendors, and on the other side sat the vendors who did not seem to have any problem with this long-standing adversarial relationship. To make matters worse, GSA (General Services

Administration), the government agency responsible for overseeing the awarding of new locations absolutely detested many of the vendors and the program as a whole. All of which added up to a major league cluster-fudge. We were left with vendors totally resistant to change who went around stabbing each other in the back, agency representatives who did not give a moth's behind about the people they were hired to assist and advocate for, and there were no new stands coming into the program. It was all so monumentally sophomoric but trying to initiate change would take far more convincing than Ray and I had time to commit. Judging by the level of hostility we encountered, we would be fighting a losing battle.

If nothing else, working in the vending program taught me a newfound respect for people who spend their lives toiling in the food service industry. I had only been working at it for 5 years and already I had varicose veins that made my legs look like they were preparing to lay down roots, my back ached constantly and psoriasis was making my skin look like something out of a low-budget science fiction movie. I had to repeatedly wash my hands while at the shop, as it just was not practical to wear gloves while handling food items, then trying to operate the register at the same time. Every night before I called it a day, I would go through a regimen of applying Bacetracin and band aids to the areas on my fingers that were cracking and bleeding. Julie once joked that I looked like a victim of mob retaliation.

I started to re-evaluate my decision to enter the program. It offered me no vacations, no sick days, no health benefits, no workers compensation coverage (being a sole proprietor), no pension plan and I detested the food business in general.

The novelty of running my own business had worn off completely, and business had dropped off so much that Julie took a job working as an assistant manager with Wendy's International. Working with your spouse is not a wise idea to begin with, I sadly discovered, and it had placed a strain on our relationship. I was now running the shop by myself and at times, I would just look out at the empty seats, feeling like I was the only person within a country mile. I would ask God what I had done to deserve this terrible fate. I had never felt so insignificant in all my years and I felt as though life was just passing me by. I was seeing less and less of my friends since entering the program and I missed them terribly. Many had moved away or were raising small children and none of us was active in the marching activity so the one strong bond that had always bound us together had now dissolved. I could not wallow in this lethargic state and I absolutely refused to fall any further into the rut that gripped me like a 30-foot anaconda. Whenever I reached points like this in my life, my underdeveloped intellect always told me take the bull by the horns and shake things up a bit. As the song goes, "Throw out your gold teeth and see how they roll. The answers they reveal, life is unreal."(Steely Dan)

    It was time to think about a new line of work. I had hoped that by the time I had reached my mid forties, I would have achieved some degree of stability in my career but I guess that just was not meant to be. Instead, I felt like the fates had me locked inside a laundry machine set on tumble-dry. I was hopelessly spinning around and around not able to find a way out, but by Green Lantern's light, I refused to stop searching for some relief. There had to be an oasis out there somewhere and I was determined to find it, embrace it and hold onto it for dear life.

Chapter Fifteen- Ferguson Industries

Once again, I was not alone in my abysmal abyss. My older brother Richard was experiencing his own collection of difficulties as an officer in the Massachusetts corrections system. In the early 1980's, the Mass. corrections officers throughout the state were being represented by AFSCME (American Federation of State and County Municipal Employees), a powerful national union with a very large membership.

The officers were growing increasingly dissatisfied with the representation they were receiving so a group of them, spearheaded by Rich and a few close friends decided to form a union of their own in an attempt to displace ASFCME. Taking on a nationally based powerful union is not only incredibly difficult, but in some previous situations in other states, it has also been proven dangerous as well. Officers who attempted to do exactly what Rich and his associates were doing were subjected to death threats, car bombings and other forms of intimidation. This particular group of Massachusetts officers was determined to fight for better representation however. Through determination, hard work, and perseverance; they were successful in convincing their fellow officers to vote in favor of forming the Massachusetts Corrections Officers Federated Union in 1989. Rich could have assumed the president's position but due to his failing vision and inability to drive, he decided to accept the role of treasurer instead. The president's position would have required him to be available to travel to the various correctional facilities throughout the state at a moments notice and Rich was becoming increasingly self-conscious because of his situation. He lived to regret his decision as the president's position would have presented him with many more opportunities. Once again, our hidden enemy dictated his actions and deterred him upon his path to success.

He served as treasurer for nine years, then, after losing a difficult election, he and his good friend Brian

Dawley formed their own consulting company. They proceeded to assist other corrections officers throughout the country in forming their own independent unions.

My younger brother John had lost his position as head bartender at the Ritz Carlton in Boston. Vision loss was affecting his ability to read labels on bottles and accurately mix drinks in the poorly lit bar areas. He had entered the vending program and was running the dog of all stands, which was the Department of Mental Retardation location in Danvers. The DMR saw its staff decimated when newly elected Governor Bill Weld decided to balance the state budget in 1990 by throwing people with mental illnesses into the streets and cutting the agency's staff in half. This left John with a skeleton crew of workers for a customer base. His snack bar had no air conditioning and in the summer months, the place turned into an absolute sweatbox. He rarely saw his daily sales exceed 50-75 dollars, which amounts to about 20-30 dollars net for an eight-hour shift. Illegal Immigrants won't work for that kind of wages. When he finally was able to bid out of the location, the agency wisely closed the DMR stand down, finally accepting the realization that it was impossible to earn a living with such a small customer base.

Few things are worse than showing up to work every day and trying to contend with the intolerable boredom that prevails under such conditions. Over time, it wears on you and not only destroys your morale, but it begins to eat away at your feeling of self-worth. I knew how John felt because I was beginning to feel that way at my location and I knew I had to do something before my self worth evaporated completely,

I had helped State Senator Tom Birmingham attain his seat in the Massachusetts Senate six years earlier and he went on to become Senate President. I had never asked him for anything and gave of my time for purely unselfish reasons. I honestly believed he was the kind of man who had all the tools to really make a difference on Beacon Hill. I was fully cognizant of the fact that I had no right to ask him for help of any kind and I still feel that becoming involved in the political process should not require the promise of favors in return.

  I had become soured however, on the realities of politics after helping with Tom's earlier runs for re-election. In 1992, I was appointed "precinct captain" for the Everett Armory location, which actually served as the voting center for two precincts in that city. As a result, it was necessary to have sign-holders and supporters stationed on both sides of the large entrance for the entire day. Single precinct locations only had one area for sign holders and required fewer volunteers. Fortunately, I have a large family and numerous good friends so there was a minimum of eight people holding signs for Tom during the entire 13-hour period that polls were open.

  At approximately 7:30 that night, I prepared to call it a day. I had been on my feet for twelve and a half straight hours, with only one break to show for it. I took 15 minutes around mid-day to grab a sandwich from a nearby sub shop. When the polls closed it was my responsibility to go inside the armory and listen for the workers to announce the voting results, then I would call them in to Birmingham's campaign headquarters so they would know more quickly how the election tallies were adding up.

  I was dog-tired, chilled to the bone from the cold November wind that had been blowing all day and I just wanted to go home and crawl under the covers. I made a decision to skip the post election party that was scheduled for the workers at 8:30 later that night.

  Then along came Mark Rotondo. Mark was a newly elected member of the Everett school committee and was employed at Buccieri's Market in Everett as a meat slicer. He looked like he had just stepped out of the shower, fresh as a daisy with his dress suit and red "power-tie". He walked right up to me and announced bold as brass, "Hi, how's it going? I'm here from the Birmingham campaign. They asked me to come over and get the numbers to call them in because no one was down here."

I looked behind me at my sister Laureen, her husband Al, and my nephew Michael who were holding large "Birmingham" signs and equally chilled to the bone, then I glared back at Mark. He had walked towards us from the other side of the armory and he could not have missed the four people holding signs on that side of the building as well.

"What is this, a joke?" I said. "There have been people here since 7 o'clock this morning. Who told you to come down here?"

"I don't remember the person's name but they just asked me to come down and take care of things," he answered.

I wanted to deck him right then and there because I knew he was lying through his teeth but I restrained my hostility. Birmingham himself had stopped by on two occasions that day and was fully aware of our presence.

"Look Mark. I don't know where you come off coming down here a half hour before the polls close and acting like you're taking over. Where have you been all day? Out slicing imported ham, I would guess. I have been right here all day and I will be damned if anyone is going to try and take credit for the hard work my friends and family put in today. So take a hike and leave the numbers to me."

"Hey, I'm just doing what I'm told," he answered defensively as he walked away.

"Yeah sure, and I'm the Easter Bunny," I retorted.

Sure enough, the opportunistic slug hung around but he kept his distance. When I went in to listen for the numbers after the polls closed, he slithered his way into the Armory and stood at the back wall where he thought we would not see him. When the numbers were announced, he made a beeline for the exit and no doubt headed for the nearest pay phone.

I would bet my bottom dollar that he attended the celebration party after contributing zilch to Tom's campaign effort. A close associate later informed me that Rotondo had worked at his store all day. In the chaos of the post election day party, he probably did everything he could to take credit for all kinds of efforts that he had nothing to do with.

He must have succeeded in snowing one of Tom's upper level campaign people, because the next time Birmingham ran for re-election, they called Rotondo to be precinct captain for the Armory. I heard through the grapevine that on that occasion, Birmingham's wife Selma stopped by the Armory on more than one occasion and there were no Birmingham supporters to be found anywhere. Justice is sweet.

It was beneath me to call and protest the incident but it was a stark reminder as to how the game of politics is played. I was not helping Tom with the hope of landing a job at the time as Mark Rotondo was probably doing. My motives were purely innocent and grossly naive. I should have attended the post-election party, blew my own horn, thus preventing anyone from robbing the true workers of the credit they deserved. So many people were involved in the day's events that it was difficult for the campaign coordinators to keep track of who did what.

That incident angered me greatly. My family and friends had stood by me in support of Tom and they all could not understand why I had not asked him for a job in return. It is an indication of how most people view the whacky world of politics. It seems that the general rule of thumb has always been; never help anyone without an assurance of favors beforehand, preferably in writing.

In my heart, I believe that Tom fulfilled his duties as public servant to the very best of his abilities during his tenure in office. I admired him for that, even though his task was made a tad easier in one huge respect. Tom was a Democrat, and in Massachusetts, the Democrats rule. There is no significant Republican presence to balance their authority, so they are able to tax, legislate and mandate to their hearts content. They remain virtually unchallenged as they carry out their predominantly liberal agenda with absolute impunity.

It was time now to put my principles aside, because here it was six years since Tom was elected and I was a desperate man indeed. I wanted out of that God-forsaken vending program and I did not care how I accomplished my objective. It was way past time to throw caution, ethics, and anything else I could get my hands on to the wind before I lost it completely.

One morning as I walked outside the building that housed my coffee shop, I looked around in utter disgust at the empty streets and sidewalks that were totally devoid of any human life forms, not to mention customers. I reflected on all the problems I had encountered since taking over that location and I thought up a great title for a country western song. "The fruit flies are back and I'd sell my dog for a truck load of Raid. " It frightened me for a moment that there was a slight chance that insanity was slowly but surely encroaching upon my state of consciousness, so I figured it was high time for yet another desperate act.

I placed a phone call to Tom's office and asked for my friend Leavritt Wing who had worked on the campaign and was employed as one of Tom's staff people. I asked him if Tom would vouch for me in an attempt to land a state position with the Commission. I had worked closely with a number of agency employees and found most of them to be great people. Bob Mcgilvary was a top-notch individual who would do anything for us when it came to visual aides. Kevin Smith was the equipment technician for the vending program and was a tremendous asset to the vendors. Any time we needed anything in the way of equipment, Kevin always did his best to accommodate us. Janet Hession was my vocational rehabilitation counselor and was an absolutely super person, always willing to assist in whatever way she could. She was compassionate, intelligent, and dedicated to her profession, and there were many others who I had gotten to know and respected a great deal. I came to the conclusion that if I was destined to lose my vision, what better place to be employed than the Commission. I would be in a position to help others and I would be back in a white-collar environment where I always felt the most comfortable.

It took a great deal of effort on the part of Birmingham's office but Commissioner Charlie Crawford agreed to open up a position of "Marketing Director" for the Commission's workshop located in Cambridge called Ferguson Industries. This manufacturing facility had been in operation since 1906 and it employed approximately 40 blind workers in a wide range of areas. They produced pens, linens, mops and brooms, and they performed a variety of sub-contracting work as well. I had never previously held a marketing position but I did have a fairly solid understanding of programs like Microsoft Publisher. I felt comfortable that I could produce reasonably good quality catalogs and brochures to suit their needs. I had spent the last five years perfecting the art of retail sales so I had that sufficiently covered. I fortunately possessed good communication skills from my many years toiling in the insurance industry so how difficult could it be to go out and promote the place, I thought to myself? I strenuously tried to stifle that little parrot in the back of my mind that kept chirping; "Polly want an ass-kicking? Polly want an ass-kicking?"

During the initial stages, Commissioner Crawford sounded sincere when he conveyed to both Birmingham's office and I that there was a genuine need for someone to provide marketing services for Ferguson. I therefore, went into this whole experience with confidence and a genuine desire to do honor to the position. Unfortunately, I was grossly naïve as to the way in which Ferguson operated and after talking to people who had worked there for many years, I learned many disturbing revelations.

When I informed Jack Lavelle that I was being sent to Ferguson, his face became grave. "You don't want to go there," he said with utter seriousness. "That place is a dumping ground. They only send staff people over there when they want to get rid of them. It's a miserable place to work."

I sensed a profound throbbing in my cranium so I made a mental note to get my blood pressure checked ASAP.

Crawford resented the salary I had requested, but I did not realize how little state employees were making at that time. I was accustomed to earning a respectable salary in the private sector and the wage compensation I asked for was in my opinion, very conservative by my standards. I never worked for the government, how was I supposed to know? To him, it was not all that much less than his six deputy commissioners were making at the time, which meant that, at least in my humble opinion after watching them closely over the next few years, most of them were grossly over-paid. He acquiesced and with cautious abandon, I left the vending program behind and prepared for yet another occupational adventure. In some respects I must confess, I was beginning to feel like "Major Tom", spinning hopelessly out of control in outer space and unable to grab hold of anything solid.

I tried to remain optimistic because I had a sneaking suspicion that Crawford was not being completely forthcoming with his motives. He knew very little about me and after our initial visit, I walked away sensing that he saw me as a lowly member of the vending program just trying to rock the boat. I have no idea where his air of superiority derived from. It was only later that I discovered that my resume was at the very least equal to his. He had little more than a high school education and no significant prior work experience to speak of.

In order to maintain some degree of emotional stability, I put such thoughts out of my mind since I was not interested in wasting any time worrying about Charlie Crawford. The only yard stick I have ever employed to measure a person is by the depth of their spirit. I never cared how intelligent, rich, or famous anyone might be. If he or she was a good, kind, well-intentioned human being, they were all right with me. As time would tell, Charlie was none of the latter.

I was not even deterred in the slightest when a reputable source at the Commission informed me later that the only reason he was appointed to the Commissioner's seat by Governor Mike Dukakis, was the fact that he was a drinking associate of Dukakis's wife Kitty. I call that somewhat dubious credentials. Unbeknownst to me, it was apparently common knowledge around the agency that the only qualification a candidate for the Commissioners' position needed was to be visually impaired. Charlie was blind and it always makes the residing governor look good in the eyes of the public to appoint someone who is visually impaired to head up the agency. It really did not matter how unqualified or incapable that individual might be.

The cold hard truth of the matter is the Commission for the Blind is a relatively insignificant agency in the minds of most state legislators. Compared to high profile agencies such as Massport (which runs Logan Airport) and the MBTA (which overseas public transportation throughout the state), most governors and legislators really do not spend all that much time worrying about how effectively the commissioner they appointed is functioning. As further proof, when was the last time you turned on the six o'clock news and the lead story was about the blind population? How many times have you picked up your morning newspaper and the main headline was about blind people? This segment of the population is rarely at the top of the priority list in the minds of politicians and the media.

The more I talked with employees of the agency, the more skeptical I became, but I was still determined to pursue the course with the best of intentions. There was no way I could have known that there were downright evil people who worked at the agency at the management level and that I was walking right into a hornets' nest, and these hornets made killer bees look like tiny gnats.

It all began with who was chosen to be my immediate supervisor. While Crawford agreed to create the position for me, he reserved the right to designate which of the 6-deputy commissioner's to whom I would be answerable. He chose the most contemptible one of the litter, Mike Dziokonski, who also just happened to be the deputy commissioner whose job it was to oversee the vending program. I had met him on more than one occasion and knew his reputation all too well. Once I got to know him better, my assessment did not change one iota. Mike Dziokonski remains to this day the most evil-minded human being I have ever encountered. When I first showed up to report to work for the Commission and had to meet face to face with him, I sat down in a chair in his office and tried desperately to show him all due respect and courtesy that I mistakenly thought he deserved. I gave every assertion that I intended to do everything I possibly could to help the people at Ferguson, Which, in truth, was all I genuinely wanted to do. I had no hidden agenda; I merely wanted to feel good again about what I was doing with my life. That would be the last time I would ever show him that kind of respect from that day on.

    I asked him what he thought of the vending program since he was in fact the person most responsible for its smooth operation. He was Richard Leland's boss but none of the vendors ever had anything to do with him. Dziokonski would never dirty his hands by being directly involved with the day-to-day operation of the program. He would never lower himself to actually go out and visit any of the locations to see if any of them needed any assistance.

    He proceeded to lambaste the program and portrayed the vendors as a bunch of whiney-ass, ungrateful, malcontents and as he spoke, I could actually feel the contempt he felt for them seething forth like an erupting volcano. He told me about various incidents involving vendors, like one occasion when a person was caught peeing into a cup at the back of his stand. Another incident involved a vendor who was preparing to close and refused to sell a carton of orange juice to a diabetic customer.

    "So in essence, you condemn all 50 or so vendors because of the actions of one or two?" I asked in disgust. He had such an odious demeanor it took every ounce of self-control I possessed to sit there and listen to him spew his foul venom.

"I'm not saying all vendors are bad, just most of them," he answered smugly.

My hands were turning white as I gripped the arms of the chair I was sitting in. Every muscle in my body wanted so badly to jump across the desk and beat this detestable wretch like an animal. Here he was the individual most responsible when it came to advocating for the vending program and it became crystal clear to me by his tone and choice of words that he loathed the vendors. He gave every impression that he resented that he was stuck in a position where he had to work with blind people in general.

It was my first day on the job and I was already beginning to feel like I had made a terrible mistake. I was not sure if I could lower myself to working for a person who I immediately despised. Prior to that day, I had only had minimal contact with him and had therefore not formed any kind of opinion about him one way or another.

I had heard others at the agency speak of him and they all seemed to have nothing positive to say, but I never rely on the opinions of others in such matters. I am well aware of our human propensity to gossip and perform character assassinations on one another over the slightest infractions. I like to form my own conclusions based on my own personal observations, and after talking with him one on one at length for the first time, I walked away with the troubling sensation that no one had ever made such a revolting first impression on me. It was so pronounced that I thought for a moment that by some remote chance, he was nervous to the point where he was acting out of character. Perhaps I was being too hasty in my assessment. Maybe I should give him the benefit of the doubt, I thought, and over time, perhaps some redeeming qualities would reveal themselves.

The more I interacted with him in the days that followed however, the more I realized that my initial assessment was, in fact, correct. This man had no redeeming qualities and I made it a point to have as little to do with him as I possibly could. My saving grace was that he worked at the Commission's main office in Boston while the vast majority of my time would be spent at Ferguson Industries in Cambridge. The more distance I could keep between us, the better the chance that I would be able to maintain my composure.

    I left his office with a troubled heart but I had to maintain my focus. Regardless of how I, or anyone else at the agency, felt about Dziokonski, it was still my intention to approach my new position just as I had approached every other position in my life. With personal pride and a strong desire to do the very best job that I could, an attitude that came directly from my family upbringing and my many years of being associated with drum corps.

    After boarding a Green line train, I headed over to Ferguson's building in Cambridge, passing the historic Boston Gardens along the way, which was being torn down at the time to make way for the new Fleet Center. I had enjoyed some great Bruins games there and I watched sadly as the wrecking ball took another chunk of memories with every swing, I was struck by the ominous feeling that my life was beginning to pass more quickly. I briefly reminisced about happier times when I was much younger. Time moves so slowly when we are children and the days seemed to have no end. Now, it almost seemed as if, in the blink of an eye, another decade had passed me by.

    I managed to find my way from Lechmere Station to the Ferguson building, which was just a few blocks away and as I walked through the front door, a receptionist greeted me. I introduced myself and asked to see Carol Caefer who was Ferguson's director at that time. I met with Carol and after a brief introduction; she gave me a tour of the facility. It was a large one-story building but Ferguson only occupied half of it. As I walked through the various departments, I watched the workers as closely as I could to see if they seemed the least bit content with what they were doing and to my surprise, they did not appear to be unhappy in the least. Everyone seemed to be working hard at the various workstations and the shop as a whole appeared to be running relatively smooth and orderly.

We headed back to her office afterwards and spoke at length about Ferguson's needs and as it turned out, we both had something in common. She had no use for Dziokonski any more than I did. It was nice to know we were on the same page on that subject. She then led me into the office I would be sharing with two other staff members, Jim Ralph and Tom Phillips. They had cleared a desk for me but all it had on it was a blotter. Dziokonski had known for weeks that I was going to be starting on this date and here I was with no computer with which to do the job. I sat there for about an hour gauging how to respond to this correctly, as there was nothing for me to do and nobody seemed that concerned about it because Jim and Tom did not seem to have all that much to do either.

As I sat there quizzing them both as to what Ferguson was all about, a sense of awkwardness overcame me. I had shown up for work that day in a three-piece suit and there I was sitting in a dirty, dusty, dingy office with two co-workers wearing Polo shirts and dungarees. I felt as out of place as a sumo wrestler at a weight watchers' convention. Jim and Tom both turned out to be truly terrific individuals. They proceeded to inform me as to how Ferguson operated and why neither one of them could understand why some buffoon at the Commission had gone out and hired a marketing person. I admired them for their candor, while internally I felt like the world's biggest idiot for taking the job.

Ferguson was like a subdivision of the Commission for the Blind, Jim told me, and as such, it was a government entity. As a result, it was forced to run as a government entity and could not function in the same manner a manufacturing facility would in the private sector. Because they operated on an annual fixed budget and the profits from the products they sold were returned to the state to offset the next years' budget. They were not allowed to keep any of it to re-invest in the facility.

"You're kidding me right?" I said, dumbfounded.

"Nope," he answered. "The state legislature gives us 1.7 million dollars a year as an operating budget and out of that money, retirees are given an annual pension which they are not required to pay into. Then staff salaries are deducted, rent and utilities are paid and the remaining money, roughly $300,000 is spent on raw materials for the various products that we make."

"So regardless of how successful I am in bringing in more business, you can only spend $300,000 on materials and when that is used up, we're done for the year. Am I reading you correctly?" I asked.

"Perfectly. There's very little room for growth here," answered Jim.

"Listen," I said, "you wouldn't happen to have a sharp object of some sort I could borrow just in case I get the sudden urge to slash my wrists?"

The two of them just laughed. The place was never set up to make a substantial profit and due to the fact that every time someone retired, more money would have to be funneled into the pension fund. That meant that Ferguson would eventually cease to exist because there would be no money to hire new workers unless the politicians increased their budget and that, according to Jim, was not about to happen any time soon. Ferguson was just another government welfare program for blind people that was poorly run by bureaucrats. In Jim's eyes, they really did not give a damn about the place or its workers when it came right down to it. The facility was established purely for political reasons, it was stagnating and the best marketing team in the world would not be able to change their plight.

In a nutshell, there was no room for growth, and no need for someone in my position. Well, April Friggin' Fools to me, I thought.

I wanted so badly to get out of the vending program and back into the white-collar world and I genuinely thought this was going to be a good opportunity to do positive things for some well-deserving people. I was blinded by pure ambition. Instead, I realized that Crawford was sending me over there to rot in a position that was unnecessary and filled with tedium and stagnation. I quickly realized that while the 38 blind workers out back in the manufacturing area were generally good, hard working people, this place was going nowhere and as a business, it merely existed for the sake of existing. It would never thrive and was never designed to thrive.

Even the administrative staff of 13 was bored out of their minds and they referred to the visually impaired workers as "the blind". Not blind workers or even blind people; merely 'the blind". The reference clearly insinuated an 'us and them' attitude that was tangible at every staff meeting I attended. It caused me to wonder if they had worked for the Department of Mental Retardation would they call the clients "the retarded"? I found it both insensitive and condescending but the workers, most of who had little to no education to speak of did not seem to object.

All of this made it a rather unfulfilling and depressing environment to work in but in the months that followed, I gave it my best college try. I redesigned catalogs and promotional brochures so that they looked more professional. I researched ways in which their limited raw materials money could be better spent on new, more profitable, lines of production. I also tried to encourage companies to take advantage of our low-cost sub-contracting services since it was the one area that did not cut into the raw materials budget and relied on little more than manpower.

Occasionally, I attended trade shows where I represented the company and distributed information to attendees. It was at one of these trade shows that I first encountered an embarrassing situation that was occurring with greater regularity in my life.

Billy Cataldo, the delivery man for Ferguson had given me a lift to a show that was being held at the Hines Auditorium in Boston one day and as we pulled up to the front door to drop off my supplies, there was a state police officer directing traffic. I got out of the truck, walked up to the officer, and asked, "Excuse me sir, is it all right if we park here for 5 minutes while we unload a few supplies?"

To which the female officer replied, her face beet red,"I am not a sir! I'm a woman!" If looks could kill I would be pushing up daisies for sure. I was having difficulty differentiating between the sexes and could not identify people who were more than a few feet away. Of course, if more women in this country would stop dressing like men, it might help! What ever happened to femininity anyway?

I decided to change my standard greeting and make it more gender-friendly, so instead of saying "Hello sir" or "Excuse me madam", I switched to "Greetings fellow human biped."

I knew that my efforts at Ferguson would only have a marginal impact under the circumstances. After several months, I began to sink into the same lethargic morass that seemed to grip everyone on the staff. It was as if the entire building was on a steady dose of valium.

Working with blind people for the very first time exposed me to some rather profound experiences though. One day after leaving work, I walked to the Green Line Station to catch a train home. As I arrived there and pushed my way through the turn style, I saw one of Ferguson's medical transcriptionists whose name was Pat, trying to get on the train which was sitting about ten feet in front of me. Pat was totally blind and used a cane, and I watched her repeatedly try lifting her leg to climb up onto the steps. She had no idea that she was about fifteen feet away from the door so she was just bouncing off the side of the train. She had lost her bearings and there were no passengers around to help her.

For a moment, I was stunned and simply could not move. It was the most pitiful thing I had ever seen. Pat was the nicest person you would ever want to meet and it just seemed so unbearably cruel that anyone should have to endure such hardship. The thought that this was what I possibly had to look forward to in my future momentarily left me paralyzed.

When I snapped to a moment later, I rushed over to identify myself, then I took her by the hand and together we boarded the train. Amazingly, she really did not seem badly fazed by the incident. She took it in stride as if it was just another bump in the road. I could not believe the courage this woman displayed and on some level, I felt ashamed that she appeared to be handling her emotional battle with blindness far better than I was and I was only partially impaired. The cross she bore in life was unquestionably heavier than mine and she carried hers with dignity and grace.

By 1998, I was ruing the day I had called Birmingham and asked for his help. My vision was deteriorating further and my siblings were faring no better. My brother Richard had suffered a detached retina causing him to totally lose sight in his left eye, which negatively impacted upon his occupational future. Additionally, working as a vendor was kicking the crap out of Bert as his knees and back continued to worsen.

All of us, most notably my mom, had kept our ears to the track for signs of relief from the medical community, but there was none to be had. The cavalry was not coming. We did hear of two Korean doctors who had invented a microscopic computer chip that they were implanting in the retinas of test patients and their efforts were actually showing positive results. We feared it would take years however, maybe even decades before the procedure was perfected and approved for wide-scale use.

I further surmised that all of the media hype surrounding advances in Nanotechnology was just that…hype. We would all be fertilizing the lawns of nearby cemeteries by the time any of those efforts bore fruit and could benefit patients in our position.

I cannot fully explain why, but I felt as though a terrible aura had begun to surround me. I began to feel the most ominous sense of foreboding and it was stronger than anything I had ever felt before. After reaching such a pinnacle of success, self-fulfillment, and happiness in 1988-89, everything had slowly but continually collapsed to the point where waves of anxiety greeted my every waking morn. I began to feel shell shocked as more and more catastrophic events occurred almost on a daily basis. Just when I thought things could not possibly get any worse, I was proven wrong once again. The fates unleashed their wrath with the power of mighty Thor's hammer.

My younger brother John was diagnosed with Multiple Sclerosis. I went to his house to visit him one day and as I waited in his kitchen, it took him almost ten minutes to drag himself the 30 feet or so that separated him from his bed and the kitchen table. He would not accept my help and stubbornly insisted on using his walker. As he finally made it to the table, he plopped himself down, exhausted and in tears.

"I don't want my kids to see me this way," he sobbed and the look on his face was that of a man straining with every fiber in his mind to understand what was happening inside him. Why had he been chosen to endure this crippling disease?

The anger inside me was reaching the boiling point. I began to question my faith in God. My Christian upbringing had always taught me that God was caring, compassionate and forgiving. He was a just God, that is what the Bible said. So why is he doing this to the people I cared most about? We were not perfect, we were not completely free of sin, but we were not Charles Manson or Adolph Hitler either. We had always tried to do the right thing and despite the usual human frailties we all give way to on occasion, we were basically decent, God-fearing people.

Everyone faces adversity over time; no one escapes from life's challenges completely. Someone once said that "God never gives you more than you can handle", but that statement was most likely never uttered by anyone dealing with a handicap, nor one of the countless individuals who have tried to commit suicide after giving up their fight with one of any number of human diseases. Bert, Richard, David, Stephen and I had only one condition to contend with and fortunately never hit such lowly depths that we would ever resort to inflicting pain upon ourselves. Heck, we did not have to. There were more than enough inanimate objects waiting in our paths on a daily basis that seemed more than willing to do that for us by refusing to get out of our way. John now had to contend with two demons. To add insult to injury, he had the additional burden of trying to raise four children, all under the age of 10. This was not self-pity. It was criminally unfair and nobody deserved that much anguish.

In my mind I kept screaming, "When is it all going to stop?" but it was utterly futile. It was unbearably frustrating being tormented by something we could not see and touch. Not being able to do anything to counteract the various diseases that were causing us so much torment was driving me insane.

Thankfully, mom and dad were both retired by then and after selling the house in Everett in which we had all grown up, they moved into an apartment and started spending their winters in Florida. I was happy and relieved that they were finally able to rest and enjoy their lives after years of working hard to raise 13 children. If anyone deserved a well-earned rest, they did. While they continued to assist us in any way they could, we constantly reassured them we were fine and strongly encouraged them to just enjoy their lives together. In retrospect, we were all very grateful that they heeded our pleas, because in 1998, we learned that mom had contracted colon cancer. During those months ahead, she dealt with it with as much courage and dignity as any woman could.

Right around that time, I stopped going to church. It just did not seem to matter anymore. Praying was not bringing any relief and I never really thought it would. God is not sitting attentively somewhere listening to the pleas of 6 billion human beings who all have trials and tribulations in life and constantly beseech Him to make their lives a little easier. It just does not work that way. In my mind and in my heart I still want to believe that God exists, but it would be unforgivably arrogant of me to think that He is going to personally come to my aid. I am no more worthy than anyone else. I braced myself as best I could as the sense of foreboding increased as time went on. I did not have to wait very long to find out why.

I made my bi-annual visit to Dr. Berson's office in April and after undergoing the daylong battery of tests, I was informed that indeed my vision had deteriorated since my last visit. As if I did not already know, so I made a conscious decision to see him less often. There was nothing they could do and somehow those tests just seemed to be a major league waste of time.

In the summer of that year, Julie endured her third miscarriage, and it took a huge emotional toll on both of us. The first two had happened early on and this was the first pregnancy that lasted long enough that during a routine ultrasound, I was actually able to see the fetus's heart beating. I was completely moved beyond words. Two weeks later, I found myself staring down at her recuperating in the hospital. As I stood there stroking her hair and repeatedly reassuring her that it was not her fault, they could have pulled the plug on my very existence right then and there and I don't really think I would have protested all that much. She just looked up at me with her tear-filled eyes and all she could say was, "Oh Mike…", and the sadness in her tone was overwhelming. I do not think there was ever a time that I loved her more than at that precise moment.

We were both crushed. The doctors told us it was a "chromosome" issue and that there was no reason we could not keep trying, but Julie was 47 by then and the risks would increase due to her age.

There was still much love between us, but we had not been getting along that well and my eroding emotional well-being was a primary culprit. I became angry with God above, shouting at Him in my mind, "Why are we not worthy to have children? What have we done that has offended You so? I am not perfect; I have made mistakes like anyone else, but I have never gone out of my way to purposely hurt anyone. Why Lord, why are we not worthy?" but I do not think God was really listening.

I had tried to be a good father to Matt but I do not think he ever fully accepted the fact that I was not going to take mommy away from him. I tried to get him involved in as many activities as I could to broaden his mind and help him build that all-important self-esteem but these attempts had their shortcomings. I was asked to help coach both his peewee hockey team and little league baseball team but had to decline the offers due to the fact that I simply could not see the puck or the ball. I was not going to embarrass myself in front of Matt. So I stood on the sidelines, stewing over the fact that once again, I was prohibited from doing something I desperately wanted to do.

This was self-pity, I readily admit, and I strained everyday of my life to resist from wallowing in it, but it is not as if I was standing around lamenting the fact that I did not own a Jaguar or win the lottery. I just wanted to help out with my stepsons little league baseball team, is that too much to ask Lord?

1998 was turning out to be that one year in my life that I wished I could just erase, or do over. In November, I learned that my Ferguson co-worker and friend Jim Ralph had contracted cancer of the kidneys. He had been complaining about backaches for almost a year and they had never bothered to check any further than his spine. In early November, Jim and I were walking together to the Green Line station when he told me he was going in for surgery the week before Thanksgiving. During the operation, the doctors found a huge tumor and removed it, hoping it would not metastasize. He went home four days later but complained about pain so he was re-admitted Thursday, Thanksgiving Day. I went up to see him in the hospital Friday night. He was breathing through a tube, incoherent and looked 20 years older than his age. He died over the weekend and I was left stunned and wondering what the hell had just happened. One day I was walking side by side with him to the train and almost in the wink of an eye, I was attending his funeral. I never saw anyone deteriorate so quickly and it was a stark example of just how rapidly cancer can snuff out a life. He was only 51 years old and the speed at which the cancer carried out its' deadly attack absolutely blew me away.

    I spent the night of Jim's funeral desperately trying to understand it all, and while I was completely unable to solve anything in the days that followed, it turned out to be a very brief respite from the carnage that was going on around me.

Chapter Sixteen- Time to say goodbye

Most people have no difficulty remembering that point in their lives when they stopped believing in Santa Claus. I, on the other hand have no recollection of that day whatsoever, so it must not have been all that traumatizing in my case. I do however; remember one Easter Sunday in particular when I awoke to find no Easter candy left behind by the Easter Bunny. I must have been thirteen or fourteen years old and as I washed up and prepared to head off to Sunday morning church services, my mind was awash with a myriad of conflicting emotions. I vividly recall being terribly sad as I wrestled with the difficult realization that my parents no longer saw me as a child. "I must be grown up now," I thought to myself and therefore I was too old for such childish pleasures. I am not sure why but I was terribly crushed.

I went to church, then walked home still feeling like this was the saddest day of my life. Candy was not the issue as it was nothing more than a symbol. I was lamenting the passing of my childhood. As I walked upstairs to my bedroom where I just wanted to lay down and cry, I noticed something on my pillow. As I moved closer, I discovered that it was one of those plastic tubes filled with candy with a sappy looking plastic bunny's head sticking out of the top. My mom had put it there while I was away at church. That tube of cavity causing sweets meant more to me than a winning lottery ticket at that precise moment in time. It signified in my mind that mom and dad still loved me and remembered me on Easter Sunday.

Isn't it strange how such a seemingly insignificant gesture can still live in my memories thirty years after it occurred.

Three short weeks later, that moment in time arrived that each of us dreads more than any other. Our mom succumbed to colon cancer 3 days before Christmas and in an instant, my world imploded, completely and with crushing finality.

She was our inspiration, our guiding light, she was the most influential person in my life, and her death left a void that could never be filled.

She used to read to us often as children and encouraged us to read everything we could get our hands on. She instilled in us a value system that stressed integrity, loyalty, compassion for others, and sacrifice, attributes that were strongly rooted in our Christian beliefs. She was loved and respected by so many and her loss utterly devastated our entire family.

She died Tuesday morning and because of Christmas, which came three days later, we were forced to delay the wake until the following Saturday. Christmas was always a very special time in our family but that one seemed interminable as we waited in grief and overwhelming sadness to say our final goodbyes.

I was elected by my brothers and sisters to give the eulogy, which I was not even sure I would be able to do. Christmas Eve morning I sat down and dug out some of my favorite poems she used to read with me. Two in particular helped shape my attitudes towards life and my world around me. They were, "Horatius" and "Let me live in a house by the side of the road and be a friend to man."

"Horatius" from "The Lays of Ancient Rome" by Macaulay, was a story of a Roman soldier who volunteered to protect a narrow path which would give his comrades enough time to hew down the bridge leading to their city in the face of an enormous invading army led by a traitor named Sextus, of which my favorite passage was:

"Then out spake brave Horatius
the captain of the gate,
"To every man upon this Earth
death cometh soon or late.
And how can man die better,
than facing fearful odds,

for the ashes of his fathers,
and the temples of his gods"

"And for the tender mother,
who dandled him to rest,
and for the wife who nurses,
his baby at her breast.
And for the holy maidens,
who feed the eternal flame,
to save them from false Sextus
that wrought the deed of shame."

"Hew down the bridge Sir Consul,
with all the speed ye may;
I, with two more to help me,
will hold the foe in play.
In yon straight path a thousand,
may well be stopped by three.
Now who will stand on either hand
and keep the bridge with me?"

Then out spake Spurius Lartius,
a Ramnian proud was he,
"Lo, I will stand at thy right hand
and keep the bridge with thee."

And out spake brave Herminius,
of Titian blood was he,
"I will abide on thy left side
and keep the bridge with thee."

"Horatius" quoth the Consul,
"As thou sayest, so let it be"
and straight against that great array
forth went the dauntless three.
For Romans, in Rome's quarrel,
spared neither land nor gold,

nor son, nor wife, nor limb, nor life,
in the brave days of old.

      Inspiring prose indeed, especially in the eyes of an idealistic small boy. Compassion for others was a virtue mom stressed as well and she used this next poem to highlight these qualities, and this verse, written by Sam Walter Foss, remains one of my favorites:

"There are hermit souls that live withdrawn
in the place of their self-content;
There are souls like stars that dwell apart
in a fellowless firmament.
There are pioneer souls that blaze their paths
where highways never ran,
but let me live by the side of the road
and be a friend to man.

Let me live in a house by the side of the road
where the race of men go by,
the men who are good and the men who are bad,
as good and as bad as I,
I would not sit in the scorner's seat
nor hurl the cynic's ban,
 Let me live in a house by the side of the road
and be a friend to man.

I see from my house by the side of the road
by the side of the highway of life,
the men who press with the ardor of hope
the men who are feint with the strife,
but I turn not away from their smiles and their tears
both part of an infinite plan,
Let me live in a house by the side of the road
and be a friend to man.

I know there are brook-gladdened meadows ahead,

and mountains of wearisome height;
that the road passes on through the long afternoon
and stretches away to the night,
but still I rejoice when the travelers rejoice
and weep with the strangers that moan,
nor live in my house by the side of the road
like a man who dwells alone.
Let me live in my house by the side of the road,
it's here the race of men go by,
They are good, they are bad, they are weak, they are strong,
wise, foolish-so am I,
Then why should I sit in the scorner's seat
or hurl the cynic's ban,
Let me live in my house by the side of the road,
and be a friend to man.

  I am not ashamed to admit that I went through half a box of Kleenex as I sat there preparing what I would say at her services. This poem was a stark example of her simple philosophy about life. Do not make judgments, and always remember that we humans are here to help one another, not to hurt one another. It was words such as these and her driving me on with unceasing encouragement that would lift me to whatever levels of success I might achieve.
  Monday morning finally arrived and I managed to hold myself together while addressing my family, relatives, and friends at St. Margaret's Church. Then we said our goodbyes to the most loving and supportive woman we would ever know.
  The last thing my mom had said to me two nights before she died was that the spark had gone out in me and that my spirit had been broken and she could not understand why. I knew that the guilt of having been the carrier of this accursed disease that was causing five of her six sons to lose their sight had worn heavily on her. Despite our efforts to ease her pain by never complaining or confiding in her as to how vision loss was turning our world upside down, she was still never the same after that

visit to Dr. Berson's office in 1980. I was devastated by her death but a tiny part of me was relieved that she would not suffer any more, not only from the cancer but also from the guilt.

I found myself totally adrift. I knew not where to turn anymore. A pall had been cast over my brothers and I and gradually I saw them all losing hope. I too felt all hope was lost. I just wanted to run away from it all. Two months later, feeling lost and not wanting to see anyone or do anything, I left Julie and Matt and found myself living on my own in a one-bedroom apartment on Revere Beach where I used to hang out as a teenager with my Reverie friends. It was not because I did not love her. I still do to this day and have continued to take care of her and Matt financially and assist them in any way I can. I was just miserable and felt totally beaten. I lost 20 pounds in just over three months due to stress and depression. I began to view the world in a totally different light. The anger and resentment that was continuing to well up inside me was skewing my view towards life and I began to realize that my mom was right. The spark was gone and my spirit was broken, and I was not sure I had the strength to rekindle it.

My apartment was on the top floor of a seven story red brick building and my balcony looked out onto Revere Beach boulevard. It provided a beautiful panoramic view of the Atlantic Ocean beyond. Visitors to my apartment used to comment on the view the minute they walked through the door. I, on the other hand, often walked out onto the balcony with them and I would just stand there in silence as they enjoyed the scenery. It was totally wasted on me. It might as well have been the Grand Canyon or the Hanging Gardens of Babylon because I could not see beyond the street below.

However, I would still sit out there, alone on most occasions and try to unravel all the emotions that were swirling around in my head. I had to at least try to come to grips with them, preferably without the artificial assistance of drugs or alcohol.

It was difficult sorting them out at times. It was as if the fates were toying with me because while most recent events were downright distressing, some were actually comical on some pathetic level. Walking into ladders, parking meters and street signs, while initially quite painful, gave me something to laugh about later when in the company of friends. Calling women of various ages sir, referring to men as Madame or miss, walking into ladies rooms mistaken for men's rooms in poorly lit restaurants all provided great fodder for conversations with family members at social events.

On one level, and at the risk of sounding too Carl Sagan-ish, I believe I was suffering from added psychological trauma caused by missing out on a crucial element essential to the natural progression of our species by being denied the ability to produce offspring. I always wanted to have children and I always believed that I would have made a good father. I never felt like I completely failed Matthew but it is not the same when the child is not your biological son. Matt had a "real" dad and though he was only involved in his life on a limited basis, it still caused confusion in his mind and was a constant distraction in our efforts to build any kind of lasting bond between us.

Matt was already five years old by the time Julie and I moved in together and if Sigmund Freud can be accepted as an expert on the subject to any degree, he claimed that a child's behavioral patterns and personality traits were almost fully developed by the age of five. It was therefore a little late for me to have any significant impact on the kind of person Matthew would grow up to be.

I was however, certain of one thing. There was only so much more I could take. Up until that point, I had never snapped physically and no matter how strong my emotional urges to act aggressively became, I was always able to control myself. I honestly was not sure how much longer I could continue to hold my pent up aggression at bay. The daily pounding I was inflicting on my "Slam Man" boxing dummy was no longer satisfying my insatiable thirst to retaliate for all the bad things that had been happening in my life.

In March, a month after I had left Julie, Ferguson was forced to close down operations because some dimwit deputy commissioner at the agency had let the lease expire in Cambridge before finding new quarters for them to relocate. After a few weeks of the entire work force having to stay at home without pay, they did manage to find temporary quarters in Malden at the old Caldor store location on Highland Avenue. The workers were relegated to filling a sub-contractors request of counting popsicle sticks and placing them in plastic bags of twelve because there was nothing else for them to do. It would be many months before the equipment would be in place that would allow them to resume full operations.

The staff people played cards, female staff workers did their nails or caught up on shopping and I refused to sit there and watch our delivery guy play solitaire on his computer all day while listening to punk rock. I was doing a slow burn because I knew that the workers found themselves in this very unpleasant situation for one simple reason. The totally inept, upper level management people at the Commission who were responsible for making decisions just did not care about the workers at Ferguson. I called Dziokonski and told him I would be working out of my apartment for a while rather than having to endure traveling to Malden every day and witnessing how their failure to do their jobs was affecting some truly good people. They deserved so much better and my heart went out to them. As far as I was concerned, the agencies inaction bordered on gross negligence and every one of those responsible should have been canned for dereliction of duty. I was not shy about vocalizing my sentiments to whoever cared to listen.

That of course did not sit well with Deezy, as I disdainfully referred to my so-called boss. During one of our blowouts over the phone at which point I asked him to come and meet me outside at the Malden location so that we could discuss things man to man, our relationship disintegrated to the point where I finally told him where to go. I was instructed by the incoming commissioner Dave Gavostas to answer to one of the other chronic underachievers they had employed as deputy commissioners, a man by the name of Bob Dowling.

In three years of working as a contractor with the state, I had submitted over one hundred pieces of correspondence to the Commission in the way of updated catalogs, marketing suggestions, brochures etc. and I had never received a single reply from Dziokonski to any of them. When I finally asked him one day why he never responded to anything I had sent him requesting his feedback, his reply was simply, "You get a check every week don't ya?"

Dowling instructed me to report to work at the Commissions' Boston office until Malden was up and running but when I showed up to work, he led me to a cubicle where there was a computer in pieces all over the desk and floor. He told me a tech would be along to set everything up but after 2 hours of waiting, I got the message and proceeded to set the computer up on my own, difficult as it was with my limited visual acuity. Unbeknownst to him, I am well versed in such matters. They were goading me into quitting since I was a contractor and they knew they had no grounds to fire me. My job performance was never in question.

I had been very vocal about the shameful way the lease had been handled. From where I stood, no one at the Commission seemed to give a damn about doing anything to remedy the situation . While I fully admit the place was established and continued to exist, at least on some levels, for purely political reasons, the workers did not deserve that kind of treatment. The higher ups at the agency were more concerned with finding their next car on the Internet than they were with accommodating a group of hard working, well-intentioned blind people who just wanted to have a place to come to work every day. Their unadulterated laziness and complete apathy absolutely nauseated me.

As I became more and more outspoken about the way it was being handled, I had already concluded that these seven individuals were merely frightened little men trying to protect their turf. I had no prior experience working with "political hacks" before and as I was an outsider, they resented the fact that someone was holding a mirror in front of them and forcing them to see themselves as they truly were. They were a disgraceful little band of fat-ass useless bureaucrats with no self-respect or sense of duty.

My private sector work ethic annoyed them. To my knowledge, the entire group of seven were "lifers." None of them had ever worked anywhere other than as politically appointed state workers so they were far more accustomed to the slow, grinding pace at which the government operates. When I was given an assignment, I always finished it in a timely manner. On many occasions, I turned in my work so quickly after being assigned it that Dziokonski and Dowling did not know how to react. To them, I was the horse that wanted to pull the cart faster than they wanted it to go, which in many cases seemed to be in perpetual neutral.

The truth of the matter was, it was not my fault some lazy son of a bitch was not doing his job, which directly resulted in everyone at Ferguson sitting around for what would turn out to be nine months counting Popsicle sticks. So after two weeks of sitting in Boston with absolutely no work to do and knowing it would be months before Ferguson would be functional again, if at all, I told Dowling and Dziokonski to go pound sand. I had far too much self-respect and pride to continue to lower myself by working for the likes of them. Mules had more personality than these two did, not to mention superior work ethics. As for personal integrity, there was scant little on the menu in both their cases. At least in the vending program, we answered to no one but ourselves and the average vendor worked more in one day than these deputy commissioner worms did in a month. I knew that the management people resented me because I saw them for what they were. None of them approached their positions with any passion for helping those whom they were hired to assist. Dave Gavostas was one of the seven and when he was appointed to replace the outgoing Charlie Crawford, they did not even bother to fill his vacated position. That in itself gives some indication as to how little he did in his role as deputy commissioner. They were a nauseating little group, a barren-spirited lot of dispassionate wannabes. There were many occasions that I would walk by an office and glance in to discover that much of their time was spent surfing the internet for personal reasons. On a few occasions I startled one or two while they were sleeping behind their desks. At least a portion of each day was always set aside for just plain stabbing each other in the back. The good, hard-working people who called them their boss deserved the utmost sympathy.

    Most ironic of all, a few of these curs actually resented the fact that I had received some political assistance procuring the position, when they were all political hacks themselves. Not one of them would be in their position if not for a connection to some politician. All of the upper level management people with the exception of Govostas were fully sighted. I often got the distinct impression that they resented the fact that the best they could attain through their political connections was a position at the Commission for the Blind.

    Of all the jobs, the teaching assignments, the judging assignments, of all the countless tasks I had been involved in through my years on this Earth, this experience proved to be the most foul by far. This small group of managers proved to be the absolute antithesis to everything I had found good and decent in all the people I had previously been honored to call my co-workers. It pains me to mention them here in print. It would be the only time in my life I would find myself at odds with my employer.

Therefore, without further adieu, I will end this regrettable tirade. I do not wish to dishonor the hundreds of good people who do put in an honest days work at the Commission, those men and women whom I am thankful to have known and enjoyed working with.

I was content with my decision to resign. I knew that it was either that or go postal on Mike Dziokonski. While that may have brought me some degree of personal satisfaction and made many people happy who worked under him, it was inadvisable and would have led to serious consequences with the law. With all the other carnage occurring around me, the thought of sharing a prison cell with some guy named "Bubba" was something I really did not relish.

I submitted my letter of resignation to the Commissioner in June of 1999. I knew I was walking away from a $50,000 a year state job but my self-respect would not allow me to remain there any longer, and if I had been more familiar with the competency levels of the small group that managed the agency, I never would have taken the assignment in the first place. I was not like the Dziokonskis and Dowlings of the world who apparently had no self-respect and felt no remorse about bilking the taxpayers every time they held their hands out for a paycheck they did not earn. There was one commissioner and six deputy commissioners doing the work that could have been accomplished by two.

I did enjoy a little self-gratification though when I heard from a reliable source that Henry Hoffman, the deputy commissioner in charge of ordering paper clips took a swing at Dziokonski shortly after I left so it was nice to know the upper level management people were continuing to get along so well. Unfortunately, he missed.

It was not long after I gave up my position at Ferguson that a stand became available in the program. I had no choice at the time than to suck it up and go back to pouring coffee as a means to survive. The Chelsea Soldiers

Home was one of the locations that probably should have been closed due to a shrinking work force of somewhere around 100 employees but it was better than nothing. According to Jack Lavelle, there had been a string of vendors who had been through there that did a less than adequate job. The Commandant who oversaw the Soldiers Home operation was considering taking the location away from the Commission. Site-granters had the right to do that, but the Commandant had not yet made the drastic decision and I decided to give it a shot even though I had very low expectations for the place. It was either take the stand or sit at home missing my mom and Julie and die a slow, excruciating death at the hands of that wretched human nemesis known as loneliness.

    Jack met me at the stand in November of 1999 and I got the chance to meet Leo, the vendor who had been running the location for over a year. The kitchen was disgusting and everything was covered with a thick greasy film because Leo was grilling on a hot plate without a grease vent in place. This was against every fire code known to man but people still tried to get away with it and it drove me absolutely berserk. I asked Jack how he could have possibly passed this individual on his twice a year inspections and he just looked the other way. Jack was considering retirement and really did not give a damn at that point in his career. Plus, Dziokonski was his boss and was making his life absolutely intolerable with personal attacks and miscellaneous bullshit. I felt terrible for him and offered to kick his boss's ass but it did not cheer him up much. He was burnt out and just wanted to put an end to his career at the Commission. Jack was not a slack off. He wanted the program to run well and he was genuinely embarrassed every time I criticized him about his lack of efficiency with his inspections, but it was not entirely his fault. He tried to enforce standards but his superiors did not care enough to back him up, so he no longer had the will to fight them.

I got out of there as quickly as I could, cursing the fact that because of this wretched eye condition I had to even consider getting involved again in a shit-hole like that. The reality of my situation was that I was legally blind and approaching fifty years old. My options were becoming more limited with the passing of time.

Kevin Smith called me that afternoon and informed me that the agency wanted to close the Chelsea facility for a week before I took over so that they could put down a new floor in the kitchen area. My level of enthusiasm was so low I really did not care if they blew the place off the map so I said fine and I planned to open the first week of December. I knew there would be little to no usable stock left behind but that was status quo in the program. Outgoing vendors were required to leave two week's worth of usable stock to the incoming vendor but no one ever honored that commitment.

When I showed up the following Monday morning, after the week during which the floor was being done, nothing could have prepared me for the sight that awaited within. I could not even open the door to enter the facility because there was so much trash and debris left behind both by Leo and by the workers who had put down the new floor. It would take me at least a week to clean the place out and get it anywhere near ready to serve customers. The bastards at the Commission had tucked it to me again. This place was the worst dump I had ever seen and I did not know whether I should call BFI and have it hauled away or just put a gun to my head and pull the trigger. I was absolutely incensed and almost called the agency to tell them to take the place and shove it, but I was not about to let them know it bothered me in the slightest. After filling two small dumpsters with trash and calling on my sisters Anne and Laureen to help me clean, we finished the job in five days. The two of them had to spray tables, chairs, and counters 4 to 5 times with industrial strength cleaners before they could even tell what colors they were. They are both saints and I do not know what I would have done without them.

Mike Dziokonski never had the guts to approach me again and kept as much distance between us as he could, which was very wise on his part. But he made Jack Lavelle's life so miserable he collapsed one day on the floor of his cubicle at the commission. Because of his weak heart and the stress after years of dealing with such an obnoxious boss, he decided to retire early from the state work force. I applauded his move and wish him the very best in his retirement.

Richard Leland wanted out and was transferred to the Commission's New Bedford office at his own request. Kevin Smith, who stood in as temporary director, decided to retire shortly thereafter as well. Dziokonski just had that kind of effect on people and the vending program was left completely without a staff for many months to come. The acting commissioner Dave Gavostas just did not see hiring a new staff as a priority and besides, something like that takes effort.

I received a warm welcome from the staff at the Soldiers Home when they first walked in and saw how clean the place was. In all my years in the program, I had always made it a habit to occasionally look around at my facility and ask myself, "would I eat in a place like this if I wasn't the manager?"

I offered a limited menu at first but it was not long before I needed help as business increased so I called upon my brother Steve to come in for a few hours a day and give me a hand. Steve, while spared any catastrophic visual problems, suffered from severe arthritis, which caused him to leave his job at Williams Corporation where he was managing their Boston office. With medication, he was able to perform limited tasks for short periods and I really appreciated his help. Lunch hour really started to pick up and before long, we were actually earning a decent weeks pay.

This was not an easy place to come to work every day, however. Many of the customers were patients of the hospital and veterans dating back to World War II. Some of them were amputees in wheelchairs who often did not have money to pay for coffee so Steve and I would give it to them for free and deliver it to them at their table. I usually maintained very strict rules about extending credit to customers wherever I had worked throughout the program. It was bad business and I strictly forbade it because it could sometimes lead to bad feelings and was just plain unprofessional. I could not walk into a MacDonald's or Dunkin Donuts, ask for a sandwich or coffee, and then say, "Hey, is it OK if I pay you at the end of the week?"

However, when I was looking over the counter at a man who quite possibly lost his legs defending our country and our way of life, who was I to say he could not have a cup of coffee because he did not have the 75 cents to pay for it? My heart went out to these men. One veteran in particular whose name was George could no longer articulate his words and it was extremely difficult at first to understand what he wanted, but Steve and I became more familiar with him and worked out a "pointing" system so that before long we had him down pat. I am not sure if I succeeded all the time, but when I would wait on these individuals, I tried to adhere to an attitude of "how would I want my dad to be treated if he were in their shoes?"

A few months later, Steve and I noticed that George was not coming in any more, then we learned that he had passed on in his sleep one night. That news greatly saddened both of us.

Hanging out all day in an environment with soldiers crippled in war saddened me even further to the point where the depression levels were killing me. I feared that many of those patients just did not have long to live. They were already suffering with serious health issues and many of them were in their 70's and 80's. Coming to work every day after developing friendships with them and worrying about whether or not one of them had gone to their final resting place overnight was not something I was looking forward to doing for very long. Emotionally, I just could not deal with it.

My mom was a nurse and that is probably why I hold the medical profession in such high regard. When I occasionally thought about it, I felt certain that our society has its priorities completely out of whack and it really troubled me at times. It is a wonder how we humans have the audacity to refer to ourselves as civilized. Nurses, doctors, social service workers, they are the true heroes of our culture. They are the caregivers, like the staff at the soldier's home, the people who perform the vital services that are essential to a healthy society. Tending to the sick, addressing the needs of the handicapped and mentally ill, they are the people I put on a pedestal, the true unsung heroes who toil without fanfare day after day. Pop culture chooses instead to idolize the likes of Tiger Woods for something as laughably trivial as hitting a little white ball into a hole in the ground, and Michael Jordan for throwing a ball through a hoop, and spare me the Hollywood ilk for spewing out movies that do little more than insult the intelligence. I keep asking myself, when will we humans just grow up?

Somewhere along the line during all of this turmoil, I found myself not accepting things at face value any more. Was it the wisdom that comes with age, I thought, or was I becoming more and more jaded from the depression?

I was 45 years old and I felt like I had held more jobs in my lifetime than Babe Ruth had round trippers. My diminishing ability to see was the biggest reason but I also was a victim of my own restless spirit. My unwillingness to accept my situation drove me on in a never-ending search for greater fulfillment and personal satisfaction. I did not' care if I ever struck it rich, monetary wealth was not the focus of my quest. I just needed to feel good about what I was doing, and the vending program did not offer such rewards. Despite the fact that I was in a position to help these poor unfortunate broken warriors of yesterday and bring a little sunshine into their lives, I felt like I was dying inside. The depression levels were becoming oppressive and I just could not resign myself to this fate for the rest of my days. I was never really able to accept the fact that I was going to go blind and I still held out hope that all the doctors were wrong. I was still in denial, albeit to a lesser degree, and while it was not healthy to continue to resist accepting the inevitable, emotions often override reason and I was not ready to throw up my hands and surrender unconditionally just yet.

<u>Chapter Seventeen</u>- One last-ditch effort to find redemption

I am not sure if it was a case of my inability to deal with great adversity or whether I simply just could not accept my fate. Then again, perhaps the two are forever intertwined and I am just too intellectually challenged to tell the difference.

As long as I could still walk and breathe, I absolutely refused to accept the possibility that I would be running a vending stand and pouring coffee for the rest of my existence. My self-esteem had sunk so low it was off the charts and my brain was beginning to resemble a caramelized onion with all the negative events swirling around me, but I still had enough strength left for one final act of utter insanity. The crazy notion that I simply had to prove to myself whether I could still function in my previous capacity as an insurance examiner kept dancing around in my head like a zany witch doctor.

I do not imagine that this action, like so many other recent failed attempts to get out of the vending program, was all that dissimilar from a desperate man trying to escape from a life long prison sentence. No matter how many times he is caught and sent back, he will try to escape again and again until his strength gives out and he completely loses his will to resist.

I may have been gasping for air at that point but I had nothing to lose and still possessed the will to attempt one last daring escape. Somewhere deep in the recesses of my mind I remembered that I had not really given myself a legitimate chance when I left my career as an insurance professional. By now, I thought, perhaps the computer software existed that would allow me to give it a shot. While on some level I held onto a slim glimmer of hope, my sub-conscious parrot, which I was trying to suppress, was shouting, "You're a lunatic, you're a lunatic! Hang it up, Hang it up! And while you're at it, give me a friggin' cracker!"

As an interesting segue, I had always admired the Wolverine for his tenacity and absolute refusal to surrender regardless of how hopeless the odds. I kept telling myself, if that scruffy little fur-ball can beat the odds, then so can I. If I did manage to succeed in this unending attempt to escape from the vending program forever, I would have the National Geographic channel to thank for it.

In the event that I needed further motivation, the Millennium had passed safely; all the computers did not implode and the world did not come to an end. That was a major setback to all those religious zealots who insisted we were all doomed. We have all been given a second chance and a new lease on life so make the best of it, I told myself.

I casually perused the yellow pages during a lull at the coffee shop one day and I picked out an occupational specialist, or "head-hunter" as we in the industry called them, who specialized in insurance. I found one in the nearby city of Wakefield and boldly picked up the phone and placed the call.

"Insurance specialists," came a pleasant female voice at the other end.

"Yes, my name is Mike Merrett and I would like to make an appointment to come in and speak with a specialist," I answered.

"Hi Mr. Merrett, my name is Judy. What exactly are you looking for?"

I was anxious as to how I would be received once they discovered that I was legally blind but I was careful not to reveal this up front. Something told me that would be most unwise. When it comes to discrimination issues, no group is more victimized than the handicapped and disabled and I was not about to fall into that trap.

"I am interested in any positions involving automobile or workers compensation claims," I said, adding, "I have 10 years of experience in these two areas."

"Great Mr. Merrett, I think we can do something for you. Can you come in tomorrow at 11?" she asked.

Tomorrow at 11? So soon, I thought to myself. It took every ounce of courage I had just to make this phone call. I had been away from the industry for twelve years. All of a sudden, I felt like I had just fallen into a stream with a very fast moving current. I was not sure if I could prepare myself psychologically for a high-pressure interview in so short a time.

I simply had to do it however. There was no turning back now and in the words of the late great Admiral David Farragut, "Damn the torpedoes, full speed ahead!"

"Sure, 11 o'clock will be fine. Could you tell me where you are located?" I asked with a gulp.

She gave me the directions and I thanked her for her time and hung up. What the Christ was I doing, I thought. My good and evil sides started to bicker incessantly. My brain was throbbing from nervousness and anxiety. "You are legally blind you idiot! You couldn't keep up with the work 12 years ago, what makes you think you can do it now?" screamed the voice in my head.

I despised the work I was currently engaged in though. It was sucking the life out of me to go to the snack bar at the Soldiers Home every day, and I absolutely loathed the idea of being associated with something that even remotely had anything to do with the likes of Mike Dziokonski. I was totally convinced that if we crossed paths again, I could not guarantee I would be able to restrain myself.

A heavy-set man by the name of Mike came up to the counter in one of those blue shirts they wear in hospitals. He was a regular but I was not sure if he was a custodian or a patient. I never really cared enough to ask him but I cringed every time he walked through the door. I just never knew what he was going to say or do next and he was not a very nice person to begin with. Mike represented that one percent of customers that every business has to put up with but would rather not have to if given the choice.

"Hey, can I get a glass of milk?" he asked.

I looked him straight in the eye with the most intimidating gaze I could muster.

"Look, guy," I said, "every day you come up to the counter and ask for a cup of milk and every day I tell you I don't sell it by the glass. There are one-pint bottles and 8-ounce cartons right over there in the refrigerator. Remember?"

"Oh, that's right, I forgot," he answered. His face winced. "Ooooh, my ass is killing me, I don't know what's the matter," he said without the slightest hint of embarrassment.

For a moment, I was speechless. Then I said, "Uh, I really didn't need to know that."

By this time, Rose, the wonderful woman who worked downstairs in the kitchen had walked in and she had overheard Mike's complaint. By an act of God, she came to my rescue.

"Mike, why don't you go sit down and let people order," she said in a commanding tone.

"Ok," he said obediently and sauntered off to one of the twelve tables in the seating area, scratching his ass as he went.

"Thanks Rose," I said with relief. "I never quite know how to take him. What can I get you today? It's on me."

"No, no, that's not necessary," she answered with a warm smile. "Just my usual today."

That meant a veggie burger.

"Coming right up," I said.

I walked back to the food-prep area of the snack bar and asked my brother Steve to whip up a veggie burger with the works. My mind was still tingling with thoughts of my forthcoming insane scheme. Life can be so incredibly strange and unpredictable at times can it not? I never would have guessed that uncertainty would someday become my closest companion.

After Steve fixed Rose's sandwich and delivered it to her table, there was another break in the action so I called the Ride and scheduled a pickup for the following day. Then I turned to Steve to ask if he could cover for me. Graciously, he said yes but I did not want to put him in the position of having to go it alone. His nagging arthritis could be very painful at times. I enlisted the aid of my nephew Michael to be here with him. As luck would have it, He was not working that next day at his full time job.

For the rest of the afternoon I wrestled with my thoughts. I had been going to see Dr. Berson and undergoing that unpleasant battery of tests every few years since 1980, and had nothing to show for it. I had completely given up hope that anyone would find a cure for our condition and I resigned myself to the fact that I would have to learn to live with it, just like millions of others around the world who were struggling with vision loss.

So much had happened over the past year that I began asking myself troubling questions. "Are all of my best years behind me? Is this what I have to look forward to for the rest of my life? Constant turmoil and upheaval? Loved ones dying off one by one?" I could not even remember the last time I felt even the slightest tinge of happiness, and now my mind swooned with thoughts of what the next few weeks would bring. Was my life going to be turned upside down again? I would have given anything for some stability and an end to this constantly changing state of flux with the unceasing stress it brought with it.

The next morning, I waited in the lobby for the Ride van to arrive at my building. I disliked this mode of transportation but I had no other choice. Vanity can be a difficult obstacle to overcome, but the recruiter's office was not accessible by bus or trains so I sucked it up and bit the proverbial bullet.

I arrived 15 minutes early for my appointment, which was a major relief because The Ride could, at times, be about as reliable as New England weather.

The meeting with a recruitment specialist by the name of Irene went well though. My resume looked solid and I impressed her sufficiently enough while answering her questions that before I left, I had an appointment for a bodily injury adjusters' position scheduled with Pilgrim Insurance in South Boston for the following day.

The emotional locomotive I was riding was beginning to pick up steam. I asked Steve to sit in for me one more day and he was nice enough to oblige. Having just been unseated from a professional position as well, he had no love for this kind of work so I appreciated his efforts immensely.

I awoke the next morning after a night of tossing and turning and started my day as I always did with an invigorating hot shower. There simply is no better way to wash away the cobwebs that encroach upon us during our several hours in the hay. I only wish I could have instilled the importance of this daily ritual into the minds of my fellow Blue Line passengers who I was forced to ride with every weekday morning. I have often come very close to turning to the person next to me and saying, "Have you heard of this new thing called soap?"

I donned my finest suit and tried to psyche myself up for the 9 o'clock meeting ahead. It felt strange not to be putting on my dungarees and t-shirt, which had become my standard attire for the major part of the previous twelve years. My brain was totally befuddled and my conscience seemed to be asking, "Where the hell are you taking us today you putz? When are you going to stop this nonsense?"

Traveling to a new destination for the first time had become an increasing challenge over the past decade. I had obtained detailed directions from the Pilgrim Insurance receptionist the previous afternoon but no matter how efficient she had been in directing me, Murphy's Law specifically states that "What ever *can* go wrong, *will* go wrong." I can personally attest from past experiences that Murphy was one smart dude.

  I headed out for the Blue line train, which would deposit me at State Street Station where I would have to transfer to the Orange Line, then I would need to go one stop to Washington Station and pick up the Red Line. This must be how the Rainbow Coalition got its name, I thought to myself. From there it was one stop to South Station. When I arrived in Southie, I remembered how far underground that station was and you really feel like you are down in the bowels of the Earth when you stand on the platform. I am not sure how many feet underground it is but needless to say, in the event of a cave-in, just call 1-800-you don't have a prayer.

  As I ascended the many flights of stairs and escalators that took me up to street level, I ended up just outside the food court. I had to walk through the court to exit the back part of the station and since it was December, they had an absolutely awesome Christmas train set diorama on display right in the middle of the station. It lifted my spirits a bit and I took this as a good omen. It reminded me of my mom and all the unforgettable Christmas's she and my dad had given us.

  I exited the station and took a right down the stairs. Fortunately, the Pilgrim Insurance building was just across the street.

  I entered the building and headed for the elevators to lift me up to the 12th floor and by now, my mind was reeling. I waited for an empty elevator because I hate getting on those things with other people since I cannot see the numbers on the buttons for each floor without bending over and practically kissing them. It is downright embarrassing. Again, I refused to use a cane, so I had nothing to clarify my situation to onlookers.

I wanted so desperately to have my career back and I never quite got over the anger of losing it in the first place. I had never really given myself another chance to prove whether I could function adequately in the position, but anxiety is a truly powerful force and at that moment, it was practically pinning me to the floor. My refusal to resort to using a cane allowed me to pass myself off as a reasonably sighted person. Some may see that as deceptive, but my mind told me that if I revealed the fact that I was legally blind and headed for total darkness eventually, I would never have gotten through the front door.

I got off the elevator and proceeded through a glass door where a pretty, young receptionist greeted me.

"Good morning, can I help you?" she asked politely.

"Yes, I'm here to see William Chen please," I answered as confidently as I could.

"And your name is?" she responded.

"Mike Merrett," I answered reservedly. I really was not sure of myself at all and part of me just wanted to run for the elevator and do a disappearing act. The crazy parrot in my head kept repeating, "This is crazy, this is crazy."

She asked me to wait in the seating area, which I did but I was not there for very long. Bill came out after just a few moments and introduced himself. He was a pleasant looking fellow of 25-30 years old, sharply dressed and quite polished.

"Hi Mike, nice to meet you and thanks for coming in," he said with a warm smile.

I shook his hand with just the right amount of firmness to signify confidence and responded, "Thanks for taking the time to meet Bill. I appreciate it."

"Please come this way," he said leading me through a doorway, then down a small corridor and into a small conference room.

We both sat down and I made myself comfortable. The worst part was over. I had found where I was supposed to be, I was early by ten minutes and I was sitting with the person I was scheduled to meet with. On any given day, there are hundreds of thousands of people residing and working in the city of Boston with hundreds of buildings in which they can hide. Not bad for a legally blind guy so for once, Murphy's Law did not prevail.

"So, your resume looks good," he began. "I understand you have been away from the business for a while though. Can you tell me why?"

I do not like to lie, but the cold hard reality of life is, people with handicaps are at a tremendous disadvantage in the race for good jobs. I was not about to tell him the real reason why I had been prevented from remaining in my career. It is not that I am dishonest; it is just that I am honest only to a point and a firm believer in the adage that little white lies were invented to make life a lot less complicated.

It was time to call upon my greatest skill and sling the BS with the best of them.

"I felt that I was becoming stale in the position I was in, and an opportunity to go into business on my own presented itself so I decided to take a chance. As things turned out, it didn't work out the way I had planned."

"What was the business opportunity?" he asked.

Wonderful, I thought to myself. Now he is going to pry.

"It involved vending locations. I really thought it had a great deal of potential but it turns out I was a bit misinformed by my partners." When in doubt, always blame someone else. It is the American way. In reality, everything I had told him was true and accurate, with a pinch of ambiguity thrown in for flavoring.

"I understand," he replied curtly, even though I sensed he really did not give a crap. He seemed like a nice person but I surmised he was going to leave the heavy lifting to the people he was about to tag off to, which was lucky for him. If he had asked me any more personal questions, I may have been forced to place a call to the planet Zanti.

Bill handed me off as expected and from there, I met with Kirk, the supervisor of the claims department, Bob, the manager of the claims department, John the assistant vice president, and then for the piece de resistance, Richard who was the actual president of Pilgrim Insurance. Pilgrim is by no means a giant in the insurance industry, unlike my two previous employers, Kemper and CNA. Pilgrim was like a family and this was their one office and their only location. I thought this was so cool that I was being introduced to every one right to the top of the food chain. No one had ever introduced me to the President of CNA, the ungrateful heathens.

In every instance, I must have made at least a halfway decent impression. Two hours after I left the building, it was 1 PM and I was sitting at home wondering how it went and feeling fairly positive about my performance when the phone rang. It was Irene from the recruitment office.

"Hi Michael, its Irene from Insurance Specialists," she said.

"Good afternoon Irene," I answered, thinking she had called simply to make sure I had kept the appointment and had not bailed on her.

"So what did you say to these people that inspired them to make you an offer 2 hours after you left the building with several people still waiting in the wings to interview?" she said in a bubbly tone.

"They want to make me an offer?" I said trying not to sound overly surprised. My testosterone levels were having a field day.

"They called me shortly after you left the office. I think they are afraid you will interview with someone else. They are offering $42,000 to start with the full benefits package but I really think you can negotiate for a higher salary. They seem very eager."

I had left CNA in 1989 earning a salary of $34,000. Of course, if I was still with CNA, I would be at somewhere around $60-70,000 but that was now a moot point. I probably could have negotiated for more but I was so caught up in the euphoria of the moment, and so unsure of myself, I said what the heck, $42,000 was fine.

She ended the conversation with a sincere expression of "congratulations," then I hung up the phone and sat there momentarily stunned. It all happened so fast and it went so smoothly, my cynical mentality started to grasp a hold of my mental thought processes, as it so often did of late. The feeling of self-doubt continued to nag at me and I harbored a small degree of fear in regards to what might happen next. I had gone into this with good intentions but with a bit of naivety and self-denial. I was psyching myself up that I could function in my old position without having a clue how Pilgrim's claims office operated. I had been able to make limited visual observations while walking around during my tour of the claims office. I asked the pertinent questions regarding their operating systems and I was certain that my visual aid software was compatible with their computers, but other than that, it was all one great big unknown.

However, I did not care. It was a way out of the vending program. I was living for the moment. I would be back in a work environment where I could actually feel good about myself again and I did not care what it required at that point. I was determined to pull it off.

As soon as I learned that Pilgrim had made me an offer, I contacted Bob Mcgilvary at the Commission for the Blind. Bob is the person I depended on most at the agency and he had never failed me in the past. In twenty years of dealing with anything pertaining to visual aids, Bob had always come through with flying colors. If I had a medal of honor in my possession, I would have given it to him.

I was scheduled to begin my new position the following Monday morning. I asked Bob if he could meet me there bright and early so I could bring in the CCTV as discreetly as possible before everyone else arrived for work. I knew most people in the claims office began arriving between eight and nine so he agreed to meet me at 7:30.

I finished out the week at the Soldiers home and by an act of God, Steve, like a true Saint, agreed to run the operation for a while with help from my nephew Michael until I had the chance to see if I was going to be able to cut it at Pilgrim. As much as I loathed the vending program, it would not have been prudent to give up my vending location and have nothing to fall back on if the situation at Pilgrim began to implode. As they say in the skydiving business, "parachutes are a good thing but if they fail, back-up chutes are even better"

Monday morning arrived and an overwhelming sense of nervousness and anxiety swept over me like a rogue wave. I showered and donned a charcoal gray suit and prepared to head out to catch the train. As I was putting on my shoes, I sat there at my dining room table in my lonely apartment and asked myself repeatedly, "do you know what you are doing?" Something inside me kept telling me I was setting myself up for the biggest fall since the stock market crash of 1929. I had been away from the business world for so long and my vision was getting progressively worse. I was terrified of what I would find once I actually began performing the work. I knew I was acting a bit irresponsibly but desperate men do desperate things. At least if I did fail, no one would be seriously hurt as a result of this insane experiment, with the exception of me of course. To my out of control ego however, I was expendable.

If I did not try, I would simply never know. I had to prove to myself once and for all if functioning as an insurance adjuster was within the abilities of a person with my visual acuity.

Twelve years ago, I had given up without much of a fight. I was forced to leave CNA Insurance because there were no magnification software programs that would work with the computers they brought in. Now, I had the necessary software that would allow me to function. Pilgrim employed Microsoft Windows as their operating system. I had purchased an enlargement software program called Zoomtext and had been using it for the last few years at home. I could install it myself and no one would even have to be involved from the company. Nor would it cost the company any expense to employ me, which was another plus for in my favor. I already had in my possession all the equipment I would need.

I arrived at work at 7:15 and Bob was already waiting for me. I breathed a huge sigh of relief just seeing his face. He had a way about him that whatever you needed done, he was prepared to do it and I never heard a complaint or negative word out of him. I made a mental note to remember him in my will.

"You sure you want to do this," he said humorously. I suspect that he perceived the emotions that were in play here. He knew I was miserable in the vending program. Bob had known me for 20 years and had learned to read me like a book, but it did not stop him from being completely supportive in anything I did. He never made judgments and for that, I was eternally grateful.

"I'm never sure about anything anymore Bob," I answered a bit apprehensively. "But this is something I need to prove to myself and I really appreciate you helping me out here."

"Then into the fray we go," he said optimistically. He grabbed the CCTV he had brought with him and we took the elevator up to the 12th floor.

As we entered the office, it could not have worked out any better. No one was there except the receptionist who buzzed us in. The Pilgrim claims office was a warm and inviting place as claims offices go. It was well lit, nicely furnished with what appeared to be fairly new office furniture, there were plants placed sporadically throughout the office and everyone had their own cubical. The cubical dividers were lined with a cloth material, which helped dampen sound, a very important feature in claims offices. The very nature of claims is adversarial. The last thing you needed was to be on the phone trying to settle a claim and all you can hear is the adjuster sitting next to you who was involved in a hotly contested negotiation session with an irate claimant.

We walked over to where my assigned L-shaped desk was located and Bob set up the CCTV. There was ample room on the desk and a computer, monitor, and keyboard were already in place.

"Thank you immensely my friend, I don't know what I would do without you," I said, shaking Bob's hand.

"Well, good luck," he answered, "call me if you need anything else." He packed up his little CCTV carrier and headed for the door.

I took off my overcoat and sat down in the comfortable chair they had provided. Then I took the CD containing the "Zoomtext" software I had brought with me and placed it in the computer's CD-rom drive. I installed the program without any difficulty and it worked beautifully. I sat back for a moment and glanced around at the spacious office. With no disrespect intended towards my Ferguson friends, I thought to myself that this is what a business office should look like. None of the other employees had arrived yet so I just breathed in the claims office atmosphere. It wasn't heaven but I had always enjoyed that job more than any other I had ever been engaged in.

Another nice aspect of the Pilgrim's claims office was the complimentary coffee set up. Every morning when we arrived, coffee, tea, muffins and bagels were waiting for us free of charge. That was a very nice touch, I thought to myself. I headed over and grabbed coffee and a raisin bagel then I returned to my desk to enjoy my complimentary continental breakfast.

People started arriving at around 8 o'clock and I soon discovered that Kirk, the supervisor I had interviewed with, would not be the person I would answer to. Instead, it would be a woman named Jinni and upon hearing this, I immediately began to perspire slightly. I had a female supervisor only once in my career and it was not pretty, but I was in no position to question such decisions at that juncture. I said a prayer to the Virgin Mary to go easy on me.

Jinni introduced herself to me at 8:10 and she seemed to be a capable woman of 35-40 years of age. She had a bit of a rough exterior and I did notice that the dress code was more relaxed than I was accustomed to. With my pinstriped suit, I was definitely overdressed but I did not mind. I wanted to command some respect and make that all-important positive first impression.

As Jinni escorted me around and introduced me to everyone, I discovered that sitting right next to me in the next cubicles were two female bodily injury adjusters. I learned later that they were both attorneys, and I thought to myself, wait a minute. I will be sitting next to attorneys? One week ago, I was arguing over a glass of milk with a guy who was scratching his ass and here I am in a bodily injury claims unit made up of four people, two of which are attorneys. To top it all off, I am preparing to handle bodily injury cases worth tens of thousands of dollars. I must confess to feeling a tad intimidated.

This was not a case where I was lacking confidence in my abilities. I was a damn good adjuster once, but that was twelve long years ago. It was my failing vision that was causing the anxiety and forcing me to wonder whether I would be able to handle the workflow.

Jinni continued to walk me through the entire claims department and the areas where various functions took place. I met the secretaries, a few of the appraisers, and then we headed for the file room… where I encountered haymaker number one.

The file room looked like something out of grade school. The files were on shelves lying on top of one another like a deck of cards slid across a table and they were color-coded. My imaginary parrot tapped me on the shoulder and said, "Excuse me, but aren't you color blind?" I could see the files OK but trying to find one of the right color and with the correct file number if I needed it would take forever in this mess. If they were willing to give me a day or two, I could have organized that room so it would be far more accessible, but I was not about to suggest such a radical idea my first day on the clock. Finding our own files was part of the job at Pilgrim, unlike Kemper where my secretary would do that for me. My pride would not allow me to ask Pilgrim to make special accommodations for me and create more work for someone else by asking them to fetch files every time I needed one.

My anxiety level increased.

We went back to my cubicle and Jinni left me with a list of 2-digit code numbers that represented all the functions performed on the system at Pilgrim. I thanked her for the tour and logged into the system to familiarize myself with their claims software. It was a bit archaic and appeared to be MS-DOS based but it was manageable. It was simply a case of remembering which 2-digit code brought you to the report you were looking for. 01 was the initial report of accident, 02 the reserves screen, 03 assigning appraisers screen, 04 request a police report and so on and so on. I spent an hour or so familiarizing myself with the codes and then asked Jinni if I could look over a few files. It had been 12 years since I read through a bodily injury case. They are the most complex of any claims that come into the office. Fender – benders, tow claims, windshield claims, are all a piece of cake by comparison. Stolen car investigations may have been more nerve-racking but BI cases were the mother of all claims and usually involved the most money. They involved injuries and as a result, they required the adjuster to have a solid background in liability, medical terminology, and the ability to evaluate the severity of injuries to determine damages. Above all, the adjuster needed to possess strong negotiating skills once the investigation was completed.

The vast majority of our time was spent dealing one on one with claimants attorneys trying to settle claims.

The files were usually the most paper intensive so these suckers were thick, more often than not. Jinni gave me a stack of files, which belonged to the previous occupant of my desk. She had resigned for reasons unknown, leaving behind a backlog of 160 files. When I heard the number, I was tense. When I heard that the following week, they were preparing to dump that entire backlog on me, I began to scope out the exits.

One hundred sixty BI files is a torturous backlog for someone just walking through the door, even if that individual had been handling claims all along and was coming directly from such a position with another company. Under those circumstances, everything would be fresh in their minds and they could jump right in without skipping a beat. I had been engaged in employment that was turning my brain to oatmeal for the past 12 years, had not spoken to an attorney in ages and was not even sure what formulas were still in use when evaluating injuries.

I had much to learn in one week with a great deal of catching up to do, but I was struggling to remain confident that I could do it. I possess what I consider to be, more than adequate communication skills, I was always a capable negotiator, and I was never afraid to take on any claim.

Trying to remain undaunted, I opened up a file and attempted to read the contents. That is when I received haymaker number two, and it was lights out.

A new high-tech device was invented over the past few decades called a fax machine, and it is a scourge to people with visual impairments. In all the years since its introduction into the business world, the copies it produces still leave a great deal to be desired. They are of terrible quality and I soon discovered that unlike Kemper and CNA, the vast majority of the paperwork that came into Pilgrim's claim office came through the fax, not through the standard mail as it did in years past.

Even with the CCTV turned up to maximum magnification, I found myself struggling to read what was on the paper. In all my planning and all my hopes and dreams, there was no way I could have anticipated such a seemingly harmless detail. It was at that precise moment that I realized it was all, in fact, a pipe dream. There were no other devices available to me that would allow me to do the job. I had the very best visual aids right in front of me at my disposal. I could not expect them to tell all their insured's, all their claimants, doctors, attorneys, and other insurance carriers to stop sending faxes. The jig was up. My heart sank, but as I sat there staring at the CCTV screen, I was not as devastated as I thought I would be. Maybe I was just becoming numb to all the setbacks and all the losses, but there was no mistake about this. It was over, and there was simply no denying it.

I spent the rest of the week acting as if I was learning the system when I was really planning my escape. The two women sitting next to me both turned out to be quality individuals. They were very helpful with any questions I had as I continued to play out this bittersweet charade until the week was over. It began to trouble me however, because as I looked around the office, I could tell they really needed some help. They were overwhelmed to the point where one of the two attorneys who's name was Susan, was working until seven every night and coming in on Saturday mornings just to keep up with her backlog. It was further evidence to me that supported the nagging suspicion that I was out of my league. If I had any doubts whatsoever as to the right course of action, all I had to do was look at her and the answer became crystal clear. She was an attorney with far more BI experience than I had, she had 20/20 vision, she was not walking through the door after having been away from the claims office for 12 years and she had all she could do to keep from being buried under with claims and stress. How in God's name did I think I was going to be able to keep up? In this volume based and fast-paced environment, the realization that had tormented me twenty years earlier returned with brutal force. The slower I was, the more the other adjusters would have to do. That was something I simply could not live with then, and I would not live with it now. They needed someone who could function at full capacity and relieve the burden they were under, and I was not that person. So why did I even embark upon this crazy escapade? It was elementary; I simply refused to accept my fate.

 Friday morning came and after I arrived at work and hung up my coat, I went into the men's room to comb my hair. Being legally blind had for years prevented me from seeing my facial features clearly in the mirror. I had grown accustomed to seeing little more than a fuzzy blur staring back at me. I am not overly vain when it comes to my appearance so I really did not pay all that much attention to it. I showered and shaved every morning so I just assumed that I was doing whatever I could that would prevent me from being mistaken for a homeless person. I readily acknowledged the cold hard fact that I had few aesthetically pleasing qualities to begin with. I was not completely delusional and I was comfortable knowing that I would never be mistaken for Robert Redford or Brad Pitt-iful.

 However, something made me look more closely on that occasion. I cannot say what it was but as I leaned closer to the mirror so that I was barely a few inches away, I was momentarily stunned. For the first time in my life, I saw a much older man staring back at me. There were wrinkles on my face that I had never seen before. My hairline that was once a full, lush, dark brown was now severely receding, alarmingly thin and full of grays. I almost did not recognize myself, and more than anything else, the reflection that stared back at me looked terribly sad and weary. Yet another element I had overlooked began to weigh heavily on my mind.

 I returned to my desk feeling broken and shaken. As I looked around the office, I became acutely aware that all the other employees were younger than I was. In many cases much younger. Men at my age were not still working in the trenches. They were supervisors, branch managers or VP's. I would be 50 in 3 years and as I looked around at all the younger people toiling around me, I felt very old and foolish. I started to mentally beat myself up again.

This was not well planned, I scolded myself. A grossly insufficient amount of thought had gone into this action and it was irresponsible and resulted in little more than another monumental effort in futility. After two attempts to escape the vending program, both Ferguson Industries and now Pilgrim turned out to be major-league disasters. It was time to accept the fact that my eyes were just not going to allow me to do the things I wanted to do. I had never been able to accept all the things that were being taken away year after year, but it was time to start accepting it now. More than anything, it was time to stop running from the truth.

When I left Friday afternoon I went home, called Bob McGilvary, and asked him if he could pick up the CCTV early the following Monday morning. My return had lasted just one week. In typical fashion, Bob did not berate me, or act frustrated or put out that he had to come back and pick up the CCTV (and these things had some weight to them and were not easy to cart around). I could hear in his voice that he actually felt bad for me and that was just like Bob. A government worker who actually cared about the people he serviced.

On Monday morning, I arrived at 6:30 and used my ID to let myself in. I then lugged the CCTV down to the first floor so Bob would not have to suffer the indignity of going into the claims office to get it. I left a letter I had typed on Jinni's desk explaining everything and got the hell out of there. I headed home on the train feeling dejected but somewhat relieved. There were no longer any lingering doubts floating around inside my fiendish little mind. This battle was lost; my old career was just that, gone forever. I could go back to my vending stand with a somewhat clearer conscience, knowing that I needed to look to the future with a completely different mindset. I am not really sure what the future will bring but then, who does. Like everyone must do, I will try to make the best of the trials and tribulations life has planned for me and deal with them as best I can.

On Monday afternoon, I received a call from Shirley in Pilgrim's human resources department. I am reasonably sure the letter sent some minor shock waves throughout the office but she was genuinely compassionate and supportive in her tone. Of course, in this new lawsuit fanatical nation of ours, their initial reaction was probably one of; "We've been set up. He's going to sue us!"

"Are you sure there isn't anything we can do or provide you with that would allow you to do the job?" she asked in a caring tone.

"I appreciate it Shirley," I answered, "but I brought every visual aid currently available on the market and I still couldn't read fast enough to justify staying there. It would not be fair to me with the stress it would create nor would it be fair to the other adjusters who would have to pick up the slack due to my slowness. I really thought I might be able to do it but those damned faxes are just impossible to read. We never had those years ago. I am really sorry for any inconvenience I caused your company. I was very impressed with Pilgrim and you have a great group of people there."

I did not mention it in my conversation with her, but I knew deep down in my own heart that I had also lost my edge. That position is a very demanding one and it was ridiculous to think that I could just walk through the door and pick up right where I left off after being away for twelve years. I had been employed for far too long in a menial occupation that was turning my brain into inert material.

She accepted my explanation with genuine understanding, then we said our goodbyes and I hung up the phone. Sitting on my desk in front of me was the box of business cards they had provided me which contained my name, the company's name and my position. There were 100 in the box and after staring at them for a few moments, I took one out to keep as a souvenir and threw the rest in the trash barrel along with any foolish thoughts of attempting something as loony as this again.

    Tuesday morning I went back to the Soldiers Home and schlepping coffee, and wouldn't you know it; Mike was still asking for a glass of milk and scratching his ass.

Chapter Eighteen- Realizations and resolutions

I had not found many answers to the myriad of questions that continued to haunt me in the two decades since that first meeting with Dr. Berson, which left me terribly vexed. I had finally come to some difficult resolutions however. It was time to plant my feet and come face to face with the inescapable truth that I simply cannot avoid the inevitable. I cannot trick fate, and I cannot escape destiny. Many gray hairs had surfaced since I was first given the chilling prognosis that I would be blind by age 40. Here I was approaching 50 and I was still experiencing "functional vision" so I took great solace in knowing that doctors are not always 100% accurate in their assessments. While the timeline they had established may have been off just a bit, the prognosis was indeed proving to be somewhat on the mark. My vision was continuing to deteriorate and there was nothing being offered by the medical community that would slow its' relentless regression. This meant that the day of the cane was coming to be sure in the not too distant future. I was frightfully aware that I could only continue to play my dangerous game of Russian roulette with city traffic for so long before my luck ran out and a passing truck stamped the word "Chevrolet" on my forehead.

It was not going to be easy, but it was about time for me to make peace with my condition, and with myself. I have grown weary and had expended far too much energy in my desperate attempt to stay one-step ahead of my unrelenting enemy. Five of the six sons of Bert and Betty Merrett were losing their sight and there was nothing we, or anyone else, could do about it. It was time to accept it, get over it, and try to move on. The stress of continually being at odds with myself was taking its toll so I forced myself to swallow what little pride I had left and accept my position in life as a member of the handicapped community. It was the biggest pill I would ever be forced to swallow in my entire existence.

By the year 2000, my brothers and I had each been banished from our previous careers and were card-carrying members of the Randolph Sheppard Vending Program. If nothing else, we would share a common bond in our occupational endeavors and would therefore be in a position to assist one another in those efforts.

I have come to realize, with great pain at times, that there are ways to rationalize just about anything in your mind if you really try hard enough. We humans are remarkably resilient creatures and given the opportunity, we can adapt to almost anything. While there are countless psychological elements involved to coping with a disease, in many cases the equation can be reduced to something as simple as mind over matter. I learned over time that by vigorously suppressing one's emotions, (feelings which rarely do anything more than cloud the issue and create confusion), the actual mechanics of getting around with diminishing sight can be managed in most cases by relying on our intellect. That can be quite daunting to someone with my limited capabilities but alas, I must endeavor to persevere.

There were many ways I could adapt by depending upon the millions of sighted individuals who dwelled around me. I began to live vicariously through their eyes in a number of ways and in many cases they were completely unsuspecting. During my morning walk to work and my return home at the end of the day, I merely look for sighted people to "shadow" or follow as they cross the street. I learned to shed any semblance of shyness and learned to become more outgoing. I grew increasingly more comfortable walking up to total strangers and simply asking them to clarify a particular aspect of my surroundings in an effort to get to wherever I happened to be going. I learned to make adaptations elsewhere as well. I make sure that everything I need and use on a daily basis both at work and at home remain in the exact same place each time I go to look for them. To a visually impaired person, establishing an orderly, well-structured environment can lead to peace and tranquility, disorder and chaos can lead to massive amounts of stress and anxiety, which as we all know is not good for the ticker.

    I learned to become comfortable with the realization that I will never engage in many of the activities that once meant so much to me. Driving a car among so many other things were luxuries I could no longer afford. Through the simple process of rationalization however, I remind myself that I will also never have to contend with the high price of gas or deal with excessively high car payments. While such attempts are not always one hundred percent effective in counteracting the depressive nature of my situation, I constantly reassure myself that there is definitely something to be said for looking at the glass as half-full instead of half-empty.

    For additional medicinal purposes, when any situation presents itself in the future, whenever the answer to a dilemma seems impossible to unearth as the mission of finding a tolerable way to live with vision loss has been for me. I intend to do the following. I intend to seek out the nearest CD player and insert a disc containing one of the following two songs, "Don't worry, be happy" by Bobby McFarland or "Always look on the bright side of life" by Monty Python. You may laugh and find this rather trivial but music really can sooth the soul and quiet the savage beast within us. I have spent far too much time and energy stressing over things in my life that I really had little to no control over, but through it all, my love of music has remained a near life-saving companion.

    I suspect that my brothers and I will need to overcome many more obstacles in the days ahead as our vision continues to diminish. I already noticed that my mind was beginning to function less efficiently. Like a car engine that is fed dirty gasoline, the fuzzy blurry signals my retinas were sending to my brain were causing me to take longer to assimilate and comprehend what was happening around me. This probably caused me to appear slow and prodding on many occasions. My reaction times suffered as well. By the time everyone around me witnessed an event, commented on it, joked about it or reacted in some other fashion then moved on, my brain was still struggling to unravel the confused messages my eyes were sending it so I would always be one step behind.

I thanked God that even though my brothers and I were collectively losing the fight against vision loss, (and as a result, we were walking into new and more interesting things every day), one thing was certain. We had at least been blessed with functional vision long enough to enjoy so many of the truly scrumptious items from the awe-inspiring menu of life God has placed before us. We are fortunate indeed compared to those who are tragically born with no vision at all and will never be able to enjoy any facet of the visual beauty the world has to offer. While their road may be a tad easier than ours in the respect that they will never have to suffer the emotional trauma associated with loss as we have encountered, that is a small consolation indeed. Vision is so essential to managing our everyday lives and their path is far more difficult in that they must learn to function and survive with no sight at all from the moment they are born. I am not completely certain if it applies to all those who are born blind but I don't imagine they feel any tremendous sense of loss since you can't lose something you never had to begin with. It was the distressing feeling of cumulative loss over the passage of time that proved most devastating to me. When comparing the basic functional mechanics between the two situations however, it is an open and shut case. I cannot even imagine how unbelievably difficult life must be for those who, by no fault of their own, are doomed to live a life in total darkness. I thank God that although the light in my life is dimming with every passing day, there is still enough there to guide my way to some degree.

Occasionally, my attempts to deal with my situation could be a bit comical and as they say, laughter is the best medicine. As the Retinitis Pigmentosa worsened causing our retinas to become more and more light sensitive, it became increasingly difficult to get around in sunny conditions and the glare became blinding. My brothers and I responded to the problem by wearing baseball caps and darker glasses. This helped considerably and we did not even mind it when people often asked us whenever we were together in a group if the "Blues Brothers" had started a baseball team.

I also noticed the four-power scope glasses I had been using for many years was no longer giving me even limited ability to read certain types of printed material. I have enjoyed a love of books since my youth, but now, the constant eye strain was causing me to become fatigued and I had trouble reading for more than five or ten minutes at a time. It was as if the words were heavy weights that my eyes were straining to lift off the page and I never realized such a simple task could be so tiring. They have a talking books program at the Perkins School for the Blind and while I did sign up and have begun receiving books, listening to a book on tape is like going to a movie or football game and having someone describe the action to you. It just does not compare to the real thing. I bumped up to a six power scope which is heavier on my nose, an inch longer and much more awkward while offering even less of a field of vision, but as my mom was always so fond of saying, when life hands you lemons, make lemonade. Then add some Absolute Vodka. (She did not recommend that last bit. I did, because improvisation has led to every great invention known to man and just where would we be without it?)

I was beginning to become quite adept at problem solving in my newly discovered, less-emotional state of mind. Thanks to modern technology and the internet, I was able to resolve another major developing problem in my life. Trying to shop in a grocery store had become more frustrating than solving a rubiks cube. To my eyes, I felt like I was trapped in a maze, unable to read labels or find what I was looking for. When I heard about an on-line grocery delivery service called "Peapod", I signed up and with the use of computer magnification software, I order my groceries right from the comfort of my own home. It costs a bit more but it sure beats the hell out of dealing with The Ride or having to hail a cab both ways, and then enduring the enormous frustration of searching for what I needed in the grocery aisles.

Some problems are not so easy to solve. I will never find a significant other again unless I can find a way to overcome the nagging stigma of feeling like women in this world will not have anything to do with blind guys. I cannot seem to shake the nagging suspicion that once they learn of the fact that I may be headed for total darkness some day, they are more likely to set land speed records trying to find the nearest exit. I suppose I could always lie and tell them I am really Bill Gates' long lost uncle and that I just dress this way because I reject material wealth. One obstacle at a time, I keep telling myself, for Rome was not built in a day.

As the final act of acceptance, I contacted the Carol Center for the Blind, an absolutely wonderful private institution located In Newton, Massachusetts. I ordered two foldable canes so that I would have them when that dreaded day arrives and it was coming soon my conscience, and bruised limbs, told me. I have made a personal commitment to myself that when that terrifying moment finally comes to pass, I will deal with it in a mature, calm, dignified manner befitting the occasion.

It is far more likely that I will react by falling to the ground, pounding my fists and cursing the day I was born, but then, nobody's perfect.

It never ceases to amaze me that it has been over a quarter of a century since we achieved that incredible feat of landing a man on the moon. Since then, scientists have successfully mapped the genetic code. Research involving Nanotechnology is well underway and the medical community performs kidney, liver, and heart transplants with almost the same degree of ease that I employ changing my socks. We have an International Space Station in permanent orbit and the Hubbell Telescope continues to circle the planet while transmitting truly mind-blowing images of the deepest regions of the universe. Yet, the best we can do for those who are blind is put a plastic stick in their hand so they can walk around aimlessly tapping the ground in front of them in a desperate effort to keep themselves from falling into an open manhole. I would say all of the above provides at least moderate reasons for blind people to be just a tad frustrated.

I was not always going to be able to laugh in the face of adversity. At times, I become introspective and what I find there is not always circus clowns and cotton candy. I find myself asking profound and disturbing questions like "are my happiest days behind me? Is it all downhill from here and do I just switch to cruise control, enjoy a daily dose of Geritol and quietly fade to black?" I still have not fully recovered from receiving my first copy of AARP in the mail, the magazine for America's retired population. It somehow finds its way to our mailboxes no matter how hard we try to hide when we turn 50.

I sadly realized that it was not just vision loss that had finally caught up with me; it was father time as well. With the average life expectancy being somewhere in the mid-seventies, my life was past the half way mark. I was not completely devastated at this realization and I found it very therapeutic to reflect back on all the wonderful things I had been propitious enough to experience. It also felt good to remember all the incredible people I had been fortunate to meet and befriend over the years.

That helped me take stock of all the things I have to be thankful for. I have stood in awe atop the Cliffs of Moore in Ireland and looked West upon the vast Atlantic Ocean, and from the other side of the world I have stared East at the immense Pacific Ocean from the top of Victoria's Peak overlooking Hong Kong Harbor. I have visited so many wonderful places in the United States, Canada and the Caribbean. I could live to be a thousand and never come close to taking in all the splendor that this planet has to offer. I remain determined to continue nurturing my sense of curiosity and my desire to see as much of this world as time and God will allow.

I consider myself blessed in many ways. Even when I think of my brother John, struggling to deal with both vision loss and MS and now confined to a wheelchair while trying to raise 4 young children with the help of his wife Angela, I thank God. He was able to enjoy many years and had many happy experiences before his ailment quite literally knocked him off his feet. We all need to look at our situations this way because if we allow ourselves to just sit around and wallow in self-pity, we would go stark raving mad for sure. I may not be able to completely defeat these attempts to turn us into helpless invalids by diseases as powerful as RP, Macular Degeneration or MS, but I will die before I give in to the sadness and depression that can greet our every waking morn. In that proverbial game of Stratego, I am determined to remain the master.

Like a wayward son, I carry on, constantly reinforcing my commitment to accentuate the positive and continue to embrace the few recreational activities that I can still enjoy. I discovered a wonderful, relatively unknown jazz club called Scullers located in Brighton, Massachusetts in the Doubletree Hotel and together with some of my siblings and friends, we make it a point to take in a show whenever one of our favorite smooth jazz artists comes to town.

I also remain close to my family. After losing our mom and having foolishly walked away from my marriage, my brothers and sisters proved to be an invaluable source of support and encouragement. Dad just turned 85 and though his health is failing, my siblings and I spend as much time with him as we can to help ease his pain. We will survive these hardships just as everyone else dealing with disease and loss needs to do.

My brothers and I made a promise to our dad that every two weeks we would get together, usually on a Saturday or Sunday and play cards with him. He missed my mom terribly and it gave him something to look forward to for a few hours. The games provide some comic relief as well because dad and my brother Stephen are the only two who can see the cards clearly, so they will often assist us in determining what we have. Occasionally, they will try and trip us up in their favor when they find themselves in the midst of an extended losing streak, but it is all in good fun.

Two months after returning to the Soldiers home, a stand went out for bid in Boston and due to the fact that it was another dog, I was the only person in the program who bid on it and was therefore awarded the location. I loved the guys at the Soldiers Home but I was getting tired of food prep and even worse, George had passed on and I just could not hang around and watch them die one by one. They were in the best of hands and the staff at the facility all deserved medals as far as I was concerned.

This new location was a small "closet-sized" room and merely required making coffee and selling prepackaged items. It is a one-man operation on the 12th floor of the JFK building in Boston's Government Center area. I actually welcomed the fact that I would not have to depend on anyone other than myself to operate it successfully. I would not have to impose upon family members as I have always had difficulty asking for help and I really did not mind being completely self-reliant.

The monotony of being at this location however, proved be stifling at times. I often found myself lamenting that it would be nice to have some co-workers again as I did in the Arlington office ions ago. This new stand is just about the size of a jail cell and there are times when I feel as if I am part of a prison release program. I spend all day there pouring coffee, handing out donuts, bagels, and ringing a cash register, then I go home to an empty apartment. The constant drone from the five refrigeration compressors packed into such a small little room makes it impossible to appreciate the quality of music being produced by my CD player. Its inadequate little speakers valiantly strain to rise above the din of the assorted cooling mechanisms. There are times when I am so bored there that I just want to grab a blueberry muffin or powdered donut and ping it off the walls of the more-often-than-not empty corridors just for amusement. Fortunately for the custodial crew, I resist that temptation.

There are no windows and it is terribly confining so I suppose I should consider myself fortunate that I am not claustrophobic. I have resigned myself to the realization that a day in this program is like a day without sunshine. Literally.

So instead, I seek other mindless diversions and turn on the radio where I can listen to the revolting news via WBZ radio in Boston, which unfortunately airs more nauseating, repetitive commercial content than it does actual news. Every few hours that nut case Paul Harvey comes on schlepping some concoction he claims is made from natural herbs and will cure whatever it is that ails you. Few of these products are FDA regulated and one product was of particular interest to me. It claimed to contain a number of highly nutritious ingredients but was more likely a flavorful combination of Wombat saliva and mosquito droppings. The company he was pimping for claimed it could eradicate the symptoms of Macular Degeneration. One day I called the company and asked the representative, "So, can this magical elixir of yours really cure macular degeneration?"

"Well, for your information sir," she began, "in our studies, 1 in 40 test patients actually saw a slight regression in…"

"Ya,ya,ya…" I interrupted, "Look, does it cure it or not? Paul Harvey practically comes right out and says that if I take this swill you call "Ocular Nutrition" my macular degeneration will be cured. Does it work or doesn't it?!"

"It doesn't come with a guarantee sir," she stammered, "but in test studies…"

"Spare me the bullshit!" I shouted. "You tell that two bit scam artist to stop telling people on a nationally syndicated radio broadcast that they can be cured by taking this crap your company is peddling. Nothing pisses me off more than companies like yours exploiting people with diseases by tempting them with phony miracle cures that don't do shit! You sorry sons of bitches wouldn't know an eye disease from irritable bowel syndrome you know that!"

There was dead silence.

"Hello, hello?" I shouted.

She hung up on me. Can you believe that, she hung up on ME!

If there is such a thing as reincarnation, I am coming back as a raging case of herpes and I am going to personally pay a visit to every one of these pathetic, unethical degenerates out there trying to take advantage of people's misfortunes. And while I am at it, I might want to consider anger management classes.

My brothers and I were all grateful to the vending program's founders, and for that matter, all blind people in this country should consider themselves fortunate to have such opportunities, but it was not where any of us chose to be. I give them a great deal of credit for handling losing their respective occupations as well as they did because I am reasonably sure that their careers meant every bit as much to them as mine did to me.

The solitude of working alone at my stand mirrored my home situation also. I know Julie will not be coming back to me because, well, why would she? I am the one who left and after waiting and hoping for me to return for two years, she had wisely moved on with her life and is now living with someone else. Along with all the other emotions I find myself contending with, I have become more acquainted than I care to with isolation and loneliness. It feels very strange too, because I have never had to deal with these party crashers before. Ironically, growing up with 12 brothers and sisters, then going off to march in drum corps where I was constantly surrounded by dozens of close friends conditioned me to constantly need social interaction. I always felt that I was at my best when I was in the company of others. Many of my friends and family have moved away and we all seem to be just drifting further and further apart.

I have a fair amount of customers dropping by every day to keep me company at my coffee shop but it is not the same. They are more business acquaintances than they are close friends. I have always asserted that it is best to maintain a fine line between yourself and your customers and hold fast to a professional relationship. They indirectly help me on one level because they are all government workers and while they are mostly genuinely nice people, some of them seem even more miserable in their jobs than I am.

I conducted some internet research, knowing full well that everything you find on the net is 100% true and factual, right? I discovered that there is a large segment of the blind population in this country living alone and I find that very sad. Living in darkness and solitude might be OK for deep-water sharks but not for socially needy creatures like human beings.

I tried to make some resolutions, and turn negatives into positives. I needed to reconnect with my past, at least on some level, so I learned how to write HTML coding and designed two alumni internet web sites for both the Malden Drum Corps and the Reveries. I purchased a domain name for future use called thefog.com and the sites are located at www.thefog.com/dips and www.thefog.com/reveries. The internet is a great way to get re-connected with old friends and it was not long before scores of people were signing in on the sites. Then in 2001, I organized a 25th reunion at the Reveries old practice hall in Revere and for the first time in a quarter century, over 100 of us got together there to enjoy a night of dining, dancing and priceless memories. It was so good to see my old friends again, even if just for a night because once the evening was over, it was not long before everyone just faded back into the fabric of their post-drum corps lives.

Like most people in my age bracket, my social life has become a mere shell of what it once was. It seems as though everyone has become so preoccupied with the hustle and bustle of every day life that we have lost our connection with family, friends, and neighborhoods that existed and thrived just a few decades ago. I intend to fight to the last breath in my effort to prevent vision loss from encasing me in a cocoon of isolation. I have become more and more resentful of the fact that we all spend more time locked away in our homes in front of our television sets than we do in the company of the people we care about most. I have to confess that I have made a wish on more than one occasion that the next terrorist attack be aimed at all those satellites floating around up there beaming television signals into our living rooms. I for one would not lose any sleep if they just pulled the plug on the media moguls. I would like nothing better than to find a way to force the entertainment industry to release its' hold on all of us and give us our lives back. Think of the pounds we could all lose with our asses no longer glued to our couches. Our kids would no longer be addicted to mindlessly violent video games. There would be no more car commercials, and think of the pure fun of watching all the narcistic nitwits in Hollywood going into therapy and withdrawal because no one was paying any attention to them anymore.

On more than one occasion, I have found myself sitting in front of the boob tube muttering, "I wonder where everybody is?" I think of my friends who were once such a huge part of my life and ask, "I wonder what this one is doing, and what that one is up to?" I curse the fates for denying me the ability to just hop in my car and go visit them. I pledge to continue in my efforts to find a way to overcome my lack of mobility or risk eternal isolation. "No man is an island" as Thomas Mertrand once wrote, but people just do not call each other anymore; instead, we send infernal emails, which are so incredibly impersonal.

I resolved to continue to express myself in prose. Poetry can be a relaxing outlet on occasion so I made a valiant attempt to capture my sentiments and it ended up like this:

The title is "Mid-life Lament" and it is strongly recommended that it be read on an empty stomach.

There once was a time, better days they were then,
When troubles were few, all around stood a friend
There were no heavy burdens, those that you can't see
Our worries were few, there was love, there was glee
Every new waking dawn brought the promise of joy
From a day of adventure, oh, to be but a boy
But manhood did come and with it the pain
The sun seems less frequent, more clouds now and rain
The weight and the anguish from many concerns
Has regretfully caused life to take an ill turn
Dear friends, they are gone now, to where I don't know
I strive to face challenges, the struggles, the woe
And long for those happier days to return
Knowing only too well that to hope and to yearn
Merely heightens the pain, for there's no going back
Our time here is fleeting, always under attack
But perhaps I will see my old comrades again
Before it comes time for that final refrain
And we'll all raise our glasses one last joyful time
And toast days of yore, when life seemed so fine.

I have little doubt that Walt Whitman is rolling over in his grave as I speak.

In an effort to explore new social outlets, I decided to join the Lions Club, which raises money to assist people dealing with blindness. I dragged my two youngest sisters Anne and Laureen along with me assuring them that this would be good for their souls. The three of us, along with my two karaoke-singing buddies Tom Buckley and Chris Langlois, contributed in a major way to a "Talent Show" that proved to be the most successful fund raiser in the history of the city of Everett's Chapter.

305

My brothers and I also reached out to the Foundation Fighting Blindness, which is a national organization that raises money to fund research. Their efforts will hopefully lead to a cure for disorders like RP and ease the plight of hundreds of thousands of people all over the world. Assisting them in their fundraising efforts has had significant emotional rewards because up to that point we had all felt completely ineffective in our efforts to combat the condition.

It is unfortunate that worthy organizations such as FFB and the MS Society just to name a few, have such limited resources to work with. For in truth, how many times is our government going to spend billions of dollars on bombs to blow up Baghdad, only to turn around and spend billions more to build it back up again? But then, who am I to question our political masterminds? Maybe it is a simple case of some genius in Washington being of the unshakable opinion that this beleaguered Middle East city is in need of a good dusting every ten years or so.

I remembered that I have but one dream left, and perhaps this would be a good time to revisit it before my brain turns to coffee grounds completely. The short stint I enjoyed as a small town newspaper columnist had not completely satisfied my life long desire to succeed as a journalist. Only the completion of a novel would achieve that goal. I spent most of my life lacking the confidence to even attempt such a Herculean task, but I have read many books throughout my life and walked away with this lasting impression. There are some truly gifted authors out there in whose company I will never sit. There are also some who seemed to be moderately mediocre and not all that much more capable than I. If they could do it, why not at least give it a try.

And what better topic to cover than becoming a member of the handicapped/disabled community, where I am able to bring a reasonably fresh perspective to the discussion table, having had the unique experience of traveling from the realm of the sighted to that of the visually impaired. I have experienced the best and worst of both worlds and lived to tell about it.

At times, I have felt very much alone and secluded. In all my years of being associated with drum corps and engaging in various occupations, I met thousands of people along the way. Remarkably enough, I am the only person, other than my four brothers, who was dealing with a retinal disorder. I rarely had anyone to talk with regarding the implications. I therefore concluded that we are all destined to experience the full gambit of pleasures and difficulties life has to offer and the possibilities are truly limitless. While one person might be destined to hit the lottery, another is destined to walk into ladders. It is nothing more than the luck of the draw. I try not to let it shake my belief in the Almighty, but I am not convinced that there is any divine intervention at work here. It is just life, plain and simple.

None of us is spared life's miseries and all human beings eventually have obstacles placed in their paths. In many ways, dealing with them is what makes us who we are. Overcoming hardships does build character, of that I am certain. The burdens my brothers and I carry in life are no worse than anyone else's. If life has convinced me of anything, it is this. It is not about what we deserve or what we do not deserve, it is simply a matter of what we get, and whoever the genius was who coined the phrase "shit happens" ranks right up there with Plato and Einstein as far as I am concerned, because he was one righteous dude.

When it comes right down to it, maybe that is what life is all about. We are being tested with one seemingly insurmountable challenge after another. We humans have proven time and time again that we are at our best when times are worst. It is during the periods of great prosperity that we always seem to find a way to muck things up. Maybe somewhere out there across the eighth dimension, someone is judging how we handle these challenges. For what reason I have absolutely no clue, but perhaps when all is said and done and we go to our final resting place, there will at least be an answer to all this madness waiting for us…perhaps with a cup of hot cocoa and some cookies, or is that being too presumptuous? We deserve an explanation as to why things are as they are on this crazy blue ball floating through space.

    I can only speak for myself but rest assured, if I do not get an answer, I will be the first one on the phone to the planet Zanti ordering them to send the misfits, and I mean every last one of them!